PROD

BOOK ONE
OF THE
SEVEN
COVENANT
TRILOGY

by

NATASHA SAPIENZA

Copyright © 2017 Natasha Sapienza

ISBN: 1977513778
ISBN-13: 978-1977513779

My deepest thanks to my Supreme King, Jesus; my Dream Prince, Jonathan; Mama Leah; and Bryan Davis for without the four of you, this book wouldn't be all that it is.

PRODIGY PRINCE

Book one

Nun

"My life constantly hangs in the balance, but I will not stop obeying your instructions. The wicked have set their traps for me, but I will not turn from your commandments. Your laws are my treasure; they are my heart's delight. I am determined to keep your decrees to the very end."-Tehillim 119:109-112

TRIBE GUIDE

Agaponians: Reside in the central kingdom, Agapon, a diverse land of citizens from all five tribes. They deem many aspects of life equal in importance, and share a deep devotion to Supreme King Nifal, who rules from Agapon. Only land with two princes: Prince Tane and Prince Nuelle.

Athdonians: From the kingdom of Athdonia; capital is Necterria; yellow eyed, blonde or pink haired, typically slender with a taller build. They are excellent planters, with a particular love for gardens. In effect, their land is the most abundantly flowered. They are known to esteem wisdom as preeminent. Royal family: King Redmond, Queen Elva, Prince Alden, and Princess Sophana.

Gavrailians: From the kingdom of Gavrail; capital is Mightendom; Gavrailians are red eyed, darker-haired, with a muscular build. Their land is predominantly forested. They exalt combat as the most vital lesson. Royal family: King Lothar, Queen Leora, and Prince Cadmar.

Kaimanas: From the kingdom of Kaimana; capital is Naluso; blue eyed, typically tan-skinned, with an average build. Their land is surrounded by water, in effect, they are usually sea-lovers. They pride themselves in their innate ability to give sound counsel. Royal family: King Bertil (currently missing), widow of Queen Iezabell; and Prince Antikai.

Ideyans: From the kingdom of Ideya; capital is Innovian; teal eyed, usually spectacled, with a smaller build. They are excellent craftsmen whose land boasts of the most man-made structures. They exalt knowledge as the most essential of all achievements. Last royal family: King Vyden, Queen Minda, Prince Ludwig; currently, Ideya is without royal rule.

Sunezians: From the kingdom of Sunezia; capital is Jazerland; purple eyed, with varied complexions and builds. Their land is mountainous and home to many farmers. They exalt faithfulness to their leaders, especially to Supreme King Nifal, as the highest of all virtues. Present royal family: King Eliah, Queen Laelynn, and Prince Maimon.

*For Creature Guide, see page 'a' at the end of the book.

One: Left Behind

"What would you be willing to give us, Prince Nuelle?" A russet-skinned woman stood in front of a blazing cabin, its smoke spiraling upwards into the lavender sky above. Soot shamed the woman's face and covered her arms, cradling a similarly tarnished baby girl. Tear-tracks tainted their cheeks, and a dark hollow consumed their irises, as if the life-orb sealed with Father's breath—the source keeping them alive—had itself fallen victim to the inferno that devoured their home.

As Nuelle approached, his heart weighed heavier with each step. Ash clung to his brown hair and leather tunic; it coated his pants and boots, his face and hands. This devastation exalted itself as hopeless, but that lie would be destroyed. Hope would reign again in this place, and these women would dance upon the ashes.

Nuelle extended empty palms toward the poor woman and her precious child. With the very depths of his core, love's warmth permeated his body, and his hands ignited with blue flames as he answered the woman's question. "My life."

With a blink, the woman's irises glowed green and she cackled. "You would give us your life? You caused this! Your existence has brought this death upon us and we all will die because of you!"

Nuelle's eyes opened to his bedchamber and morning's hazy, golden glow. The warm light reflected off of the sapphire stones embedding his ceiling, like burning coals—or the flames that engulfed his hands in the dream. He raised his palms, his stomach churning. This was now the ninth time he had this nightmare over the last six months, after the wild fire destroyed nearby Middren. But all this time, fire hadn't once emerged from him, and if it did, he'd never use it to harm the citizens in his kingdom. So why then, did this nightmare and the unease that came with it, persist…

He tossed aside his now cotton bedsheets and they landed atop fuzzy-furred Mugro, sleeping with his auburn wings curled around his little body. This pet lay so safe and cozy inside these royal walls while Agaponians suffered outside of them.

But not for long. Nuelle jumped out of bed, his achy back and limbs shouting protest. Lazy Mugro's ears perked, but his eyelids remained shut. The room's door thrust open. Hunched Lady Lovehart and her equally as ancient husband skittered inside, wearing cream, velvet robes. Nickelite's smoky beard hung past his knees, and Lady Lovehart's silvery wisps swirled down to her ankles. Today, she wielded a duster. As she scurried Nuelle's way, he opened his arms to embrace her. She halted before him and swiped the duster across his head, dispersing a cloud of ash. While he coughed she asked, "Young man, when was the last time you bathed?"

"Three days ago." Nuelle smirked as he wrapped his arms around her and squeezed.

Now she coughed as she shimmied her way free. "Dreadful. Have you any time to care for yourself?"

"I'll get to it."

After giving Nick a tight hug that accidentally cracked his back, Nuelle shoved open his wardrobe keeper—full of empty hangers. The rear-wall mirror reflected bloodshot amber eyes and unruly hair half-grayed with ash. A bath would certainly happen—later that evening. At the bottom of the wardrobe keeper lay the leather tunic, pants, and boots he wore yesterday—beside his breastplate and sword-belt.

"Sneaking in through the window again I see." Lady Lovehart pulled aside the terrace curtains across from the bed, allowing brighter golden light to flood the chamber.

Nuelle tossed the tunic over his head. Evading Brother had become easier than arguing with him. He didn't understand that using your hands to help was more important than training your fists to fight. But maybe one day he'd finally agree. Nuelle dropped his boots on the floor. "I have to get exercise in somehow, my lady."

"Aye, don't 'my lady' my lady, your highness." Nickelite ambled to Nuelle's side. "She's too old for you and she's stubbornly in love with this work of art."

Lady Lovehart dusted off the curtains, dispersing ash. "Whoever said he was too young?"

Nickelite raised skinny fists. "Don't make me spar the boy and show you just how young he is."

Nuelle sat on his bed and slipped into his boots. "I'll never spar you again, Nick."

"Ah, come on. My back is healed, and my hip is in its rightful place."

Lady Lovehart peered over her shoulder. "No it's not."

Nickelite shot her a look before peering into the open keeper. "Where are all your garbs?"

"I donated them to the people of Middren."

Mugro growled as his snout and paws twitched—though his eyes remained closed. Nickelite grabbed his beard and waved it. "You should donate this lazy mutt."

Nuelle rose and stood in a battle stance. "Don't make me change my mind."

"You best back down if you still want a wife, Lord Nick." Lady Lovehart opened the terrace doors. A warm, rhythmic breeze flowed into the room, gracing Nuelle's ears as it always did during the Days of Warmth. Gentle chords lulled and then swelled, a vibrating hum carried by a soft drumming. So soothing and tranquil—the wind's calm music shouted for its peace to be shared with all of Agapon's inhabitants—and it would.

Pushing Nuelle's fists down, Nickelite peered with yellow eyes shaded by shrub-like brows that begged for a trim. "Why don't you take your armor and sword with you to Middren? You never know when you'll need to defend yourself against someone as fierce as me."

Nuelle glanced at his breastplate and sword-belt. Dust spotted the hilt of his sheathed weapon, missing its sparring usage out on the courtyard with Brother. He sighed as he grabbed the sword-belt and quickly strapped it on. "I'll be fine, Nick."

Lady Lovehart jabbed the air with her duster. "Better safe than speared, your majesty."

Nuelle frowned at the elderly couple. This was Agapon, not the Obsidian, so why were they advising caution? He raised an eyebrow. "Is there a reason for your wariness of the poor and needy?"

"Not of those citizens, my lord." Nickelite glanced at his wife and she glanced at the door.

Nuelle stepped toward her. "Then who should I be wary of?"

She brushed off the duster and spoke in a low voice. "Just know that not everyone can be trusted." She turned and froze before the cotton bedsheets. "What happened to the silk ones, my lord?"

Nuelle kept his stare on her. Pressing the woman further was tempting. She and Nick trusted everyone—with a little too much information. But the family at Middren needed help. More inquiring had to wait until later. "I donated my other bedsheets to Middren."

"How thoughtful." Lady Lovehart yanked the sheets, jolting Mugro into frantic flight and barking.

Nickelite shook a fist at him. "Quit griping at my bride and go eat your morning meal."

Mugro growled before zooming over to Nuelle and licking his face.

"Not now boy, I have to get back to Middren."

"That you do." Amador's strong voice strutted into the chamber before he did. His open, gold knight helmet revealed more bronze skin than usual, thanks to a clean-shaven face. He wore his customary sword-belt with dagger on his hip, but carried an extra prance to his step—and a large, leather rucksack on his back.

"Uncle Amador." Nuelle strode up to him and after a hearty embrace, smacked his armored bicep. "What happened to the beard?"

"I thought I'd surprise my bride and try something new for our anniversary."

"Very crisp. You look a decade younger." Nuelle leaned over and peered at the rucksack. "What's in the—"

"Don't get the old man going." Ave entered the chamber, wearing his pearly-suede cook attire—minus the apron, but dough still smudged his bronze cheeks. Rather than baring weapons like his father, Ave held a basketful of iris-fruit bread, its warm, sweet aroma taunting cruelly.

Nuelle forced his attention off of the desirable loaves. "I take it you're joining us today?"

"Your father gave me permission," Ave replied. "And I didn't even have to bribe him with frostcake." He slapped Amador's breastplate and continued. "Though I had to bribe Papo here with sweet-stem and vigor-root stew."

Nuelle's stomach rumbled. "Enough—you're making me hungry and I don't have time for morning meal." Nuelle marched out of the chamber and into the jasper hallway. Amador and Ave followed on either side.

"You can have some of the bread I made for the villagers." Ave extended the alluring basket of goods.

"It's all right," Nuelle said. "They need it more than I do."

Amador took on a swift, sing-song tone. "Until you discover your prodigious gifts, you boys are as thin as nestling sticks."

Nuelle unsheathed his sword and raised it. "Though lighter does mean swifter."

"You haven't forgotten my lessons?" Tane swaggered near from the hall ahead in an iron breastplate and leather garbs. Sweat dampened his tousled, brown hair—no doubt from combat training. Sheathing his weapon, Nuelle forced an extra casual tone. "Fair day, Brother."

"It's been ages." Tane smiled, apparently forcing the same casualty, and then scratched Nuelle's chin. "Is that premature stubble I see? Or maybe all this restless service is aging you." His faux-smile dissolved as he sized up Nuelle. "You look like a peasant. Is this what you meant when you told Father you wanted to lead by example?"

Nuelle released a sigh. "I—"

"Don't have time for a bath or much else." Tane dusted off ash from Nuelle's head. "Of course, learning to serve is more important than getting trained to rule."

And this is why I've been avoiding you. Nuelle spoke quickly. "My family at Middren are close—"

"Family?" Tane grimaced. "Did I hear this young prince correctly?"

"You most certainly did." Prince Antikai glided into the hallway and planted himself at Tane's side, who stood a foot taller and miles more fierce-looking. Unlike Brother's messy hair, Antikai's purplish-black strands fell neatly at the sides of his dry, clean-shaven face, as if the wind itself wasn't permitted to ruffle it. Six months at the Supreme Palace and he still refused to lift a sword—for a genuine disdain of violence or to preserve his perfect appearance was yet to be determined.

Tane's tone sharpened. "And what about your true family here in the palace?"

Nuelle's heart stung. "Middren is almost fully functional. When they are, we can continue our training and spar before Father."

Antikai chuckled and applauded. "How bold. You wish to humiliate your elder brother before the Supreme King?"

"Ouch." Ave clasped his belly with his free hand. "I felt that one."

Tane snatched Antikai's wrist and spun him around, twisting his arm behind his back. As he grimaced, Tane smirked and then spoke. "You mean like this?" He released and Antikai staggered, his once perfect hair now disorderly.

Nuelle frowned at the unnecessary display of bravado and addressed his brother. "What a way to lead."

Tane's prominent jawline flexed as though he had a response throwing jabs inside his mouth, trying to break out and deliver their blows. Nuelle held Tane's threatening gaze. Would he strike his younger brother now for holding up an honest mirror? Well, this growing hostility needed challenging. What was causing it and why did he seem more reckless at controlling it than before?

"Pardon me, my lords." Amador gestured ahead. "We need to get going."

Tane stepped close and tapped Nuelle's cheek. "Run along, Nu'. More pressing 'family' matters await you." Tane let his hand fall as he strode past, Antikai following with pin-straight shoulders and a stoic expression.

Swallowing down the acidic anger and its bitter companion, guilt, Nuelle walked onward, beyond the four intersecting ruby halls. As unlikable as Antikai had made himself during this extended stay, the way he was treated by Brother was the opposite of what he'd been expected to exemplify. Supposedly, Antikai needed to learn how to honor others and that's why his father sent him here to be mentored by Tane, but it appeared with each encounter, Tane needed that lesson more…Nuelle reached the triple staircases and rapidly descended the center one.

"Sometimes," Ave said, "I forget which of you is the older one."

"Except when they're sparring." Amador smirked. "Though you did impress that last time."

"Yeah." Nuelle jabbed a thumb toward the rucksack on Amador's back. "Extra supplies for the villagers?"

His Sentry gave a nod before shifting his gaze. Nuelle lifted an eyebrow at Ave as they reached the last stair and stepped into the Grand Foyer, lathered with the aroma of freshly baked bread and other morning delights. Ave shrugged and then took a deep breath. Though the aroma demanded lengthy inhalation, Nuelle eyed Amador. Why was everyone behaving so out of the norm? First Lady Lovehart and Nick, then Brother, and now often too-open-and-unfiltered Amador being secretive? Nuelle's stomach grumbled again as the foyer's delectable scents distracted; minty-sweet mangeen loaves; sugary, melt-on-your-tongue iris fruit bread; savory, rich-cream stew with brye sticks—

"My three heroes!" Lady Purine half-bustled/half-danced their way with a hand-basket. Dough splotched her pearly-suede dress and dark brown hair, pulled back in a delicately braided and netted bun.

Amador pressed a fist to his breastplate and staggered. "Did I die while in battle, because I must certainly be in eternal paradise." He bowed steeply before his bride.

Lady Purine's slanted eyes shimmered and her cheeks reddened with youthful blush as she handed him the basket. "For your journey. You men need to eat as well."

"Oh, my lady, the only thing I need to taste is your sweet lips."

Ave waved an invisible spoon. "Layer it on like frostcream, Papo. I'm taking mental notes for my future Lady Purine."

Nuelle chuckled. Oh yes, it was certainly their anniversary. And though what, their twentieth or so, they'd always transported back in time and acted like youths about to embark on their first romantic outing.

Amador drew Lady Purine in for a kiss. She glided back and scratched his beard-less chin. "Try not to stay out too late tonight. I, too, have a surprise awaiting you."

Nuelle's head bowed. Concern for the Agaponians at Middren had so consumed, it'd become easy to forget Uncle Amador also had a family at the palace missing him...*And so do I.* Nuelle pulled Lady Purine in for a hug. "Thank you for your kindness, my lady. I'll make sure we leave before dusk today so you two can enjoy your anniversary."

When he released, she curtsied. "You're the sweetest prince I know."

Ave pecked Lady Purine's cheek and then she sauntered off, swinging her hips while Amador howled. Nuelle led the way out of the Supreme Palace. The daystar beamed from above, and glowing amber life orbs floated in the air. A chariot sat on the white dirt, its doors open, with ivory vanaphs on either side of them. The creatures' long necks and six wings twitched, ready for flight.

Heronia stood by a third vanaph at the front, tying a saddle. Her wavy purple hair flowed from a knitted hat down to her hips. She sported a lace dress and too-tight leather pants. "My lords." She bowed her head gracefully and then smiled at Ave. "What a pleasant surprise. Welcome aboard, Master Cook."

"Fair day, my lady." He flashed a confident smile, though his eyebrow twitched.

"Prince Nuelle." She extended her hand, palm facing upward.

He hesitated. After thanking her for guiding them last time with a hug, she'd been more...hands on. And now the overly-accentuated apparel? Though she was kind and dependable, courtship hadn't even made the list of things to pursue. Nuelle clasped Heronia's palm and gave a brisk shake. "Fair day, my lady."

Her mouth dipped as he released and then quickly hopped into his chariot.

Whispering, Ave addressed him. "Neither of you told me deluxe ivory cake was your steer-guide."

Nuelle shrugged. "I didn't know you already moved on from Starlene."

Amador chuckled as he and Ave followed Nuelle inside and then closed the doors.

"Son," Amador said, "maybe if you stop comparing women to food, your relationships will last longer than three months."

Ave still spoke in a hushed voice. "Come on, Papo, you know I don't mean it lewdly. There's a food to describe any person—inside and out."

Nuelle reached across to the front-facing window and opened it. "Heronia, would you say you're like a deluxe ivory cake?"

She stroked her vanaph's mane. "Elegant, sweet, with a fair complexion." She smiled prettily. "I guess that's quite accurate."

Ave crossed his arms and grinned smugly.

"Well done, Master Cook." Nuelle patted Ave's shoulder. "He'd like to go on an outing with you this evening, my lady."

Ave's arms uncrossed and squeezed the basket as Heronia fiddled with her cap. Amador stifled a laugh with his gloved fist.

"Um…" Heronia said. "Where would you like to take me?"

"Actually," Ave replied, "I would prefer cooking you a meal."

Nuelle raised a finger. "Just make sure you don't order anything with dragon spice."

Hearty laughter escaped Amador.

Heronia finished tying the saddle. "I shall consider it…"

Ave gave a wry grin, and Nuelle closed the window. Amador pushed Ave's head. "What are royal friends for?"

Eyeing Nuelle, Ave brushed back his now-disheveled bangs. "Thanks, your highness."

Nuelle gestured to the bread basket. "Keep seeing the world through the eyes of a cook-book and maybe one day you'll be a husband."

Shouldering Ave, Amador again spun one of his weak, impromptu rhymes. "And if you gain a few pounds from the food you eat, maybe you'll become a tough Papo like me."

As they all smiled, Heronia hopped onto her vanaph and grasped the reins. "All right, girl. To Middren!"

The three vanaphs' golden hooves kicked off the ground and they soared into the sky. Nuelle peered out of the window as the topaz Supreme Palace, as home, grew farther and farther away.

The weary day's end brought a welcome chill to the small, now fully-functional village. Nuelle sat on one of the unused logs and wiped the sweat from his brow. Though weariness weakened every limb, love for these precious people refreshed the soul. Their abiding hope despite their loss brought such encouragement and strength. And how they worked together so seamlessly, like a perfect harmony among musicians who'd played together for years. This tiny village knew everyone by name, shared food and drink, always kept their doors open. In many ways they reflected the love and unity displayed back at home. Tane's grimacing face punched Nuelle's mind. He tapped his sword's hilt. Well, mostly. But now that Middren was taken care of, the discord with Brother would come to an end—hopefully. He'd been so…defensive lately. He couldn't even be spoken to. And the angry aggression he unleashed on Antikai…Tane always had a temper, but recently, it seemed he had a vendetta against everyone…

"You look like one of us, prince." Little grinning Anya tiptoed near from her and her family's new cabin. Anya's skinny arms hugged four water mugs, and dim life orbs danced around her as if mimicking her girlish glee. She slowly bent toward Heronia, seated on another nearby log with Amador and Ave, whose pearly attire had soiled itself brown. They took a mug each and then Anya sashayed to Nuelle. She curtsied as she handed him the last one. "And you smell like a peasant, too."

"Thank you." He chuckled and wiped mud from her tawny face, though his dirty fingers only made her cheek more russet. "Your village is worth it, Anya."

She batted her purple eyes. "Will you marry me?"

Ave spewed out water, Heronia and Amador laughing with him.

Nuelle smiled at the confident six-year-old. "Can you give me ten years to think about it?"

"Of course. I'll wait for you forever, peasant prince." She kissed his cheek, spun around, and then skipped back into her cabin while her older brothers charged out of it, wearing Nuelle's princely garbs and swatting at each other with sticks. Nuelle's heart ached as he grasped his real sword, tucked uselessly in its sheath. Training with Tane could finally continue the next morning. Brother had waited patiently—for the most part—and would be thrilled at returning to their routine. The last few times they sparred, he was tougher than usual, more passionate than ever to bring his younger brother to a higher level of skill. Actually, bitter or not, everything Brother did had more passion lately…

Amador gazed up at the lavender sky, spattered with slowly darkening clouds. "Forgive me, my lord, but you did make a promise to my bride." He gestured to the rucksack on his back—the one he refused to set down all day. "And I still have an errand to run."

Nuelle rose. "An errand?"

"One King Nifal tasked me with." Amador stood and looked up again. "I have to deliver the sack not too far from here and it's close to the meeting time."

"Then we'd better get moving." Ave walked over with Heronia. "Maybe we'll make it back in time for evening meal. I can eat enough food for this whole village."

Nuelle surveyed his Sentry. The 'sack' he'd referred it to, still evading sharing what lay stashed within. But he'd unveil the big secret eventually. Wouldn't he…? Nuelle waved to big Miss Menalee and her seven sisters, huddled around a cauldron perched over blue flames. As always, they blew kisses and told him to pray about pursuing their daughters. And as always, he answered with, "Whatever is willed for me will be mine, my ladies."

Heronia meandered ahead with Ave, whispering something to him, while Amador strode at Nuelle's side. Nuelle eyed the mysterious rucksack. "So what's really in there?"

"I ask that you wait until we are inside of the chariot, my lord."

Nuelle's heart-rate spiked and his palms moistened. "I'll grant your request."

As Heronia mounted the guiding vanaph, she tossed her purple hair over her shoulder and smiled briefly at Nuelle before facing forward and grabbing the reins. He frowned as Ave opened the chariot door for him and Amador. When the door closed, Ave's eyes narrowed, and he donned a fake grin. "Just when I start to get my hopes up, deluxe ivory cake exposes her real motives for being all buttery with me." His voice imitated a feminine pitch. "'I was wondering if Prince Nuelle ever talks about me, and if you know what attracts him most in a woman?'"

"Good question," Nuelle said and then turned to Amador. "But I have a more pressing one that's supposed to be answered now."

The vanaphs ascended. Once the village disappeared beneath the clouds, Amador finally faced Nuelle. "This sack holds a very dangerous weapon that is no longer safe in the palace."

Nuelle tensed, Ave also stiffening.

"What weapon?" Nuelle asked. "And why wouldn't it be safe at home?"

"I'm afraid that is all I can tell you, my lord." Amador leaned over and stuck his head out of the window. As he gave Heronia directions, cold sweat coated Nuelle's already moist neck. There wasn't a place in all Zephoris safer than the Supreme Palace, where the Supreme King—Father himself—dwelled. Many palace servants and Elite Knights faithfully served for decades, centuries even. So what—or who—caused Father's concern?

Fifteen silent minutes dragged by until the chariot descended in the midst of a dense forest on the outskirts of Onipur, the next town north of Middren. When it landed, Amador spoke firmly. "King Nifal commanded that you both are to stay in the chariot."

"But"—Nuelle closed his mouth. If Father gave the command, he needed to heed it.

"I won't be long." Amador climbed over Ave, opened the door, and leapt out of the chariot.

When the door closed, Ave ran his hand through his hair. "So maybe we'll make it home for dessert. Mother said she was gonna bake puffle cakes and—"

"Shh." Nuelle crouched to the parallel bench and peered out the window. Amador stood under the shadows of vast orange leaves, one hand on the rucksack's shoulder-strap, the other gripping his sword's hilt. Someone cloaked in an emerald robe emerged from the trees in front of him. He slid the rucksack off and held it out. Green Robe just stood there like a statue, hesitant. Amador shoved the rucksack in Green Robe's arms before unsheathing his sword and waving the person away. Green Robe backtracked and stumbled. The emerald hood fell, revealing long purplish-black hair and wide, blue eyes.

Nuelle and Ave jumped. "King Bertil!"

"Why would King Nifal want Antikai's father to have the dangerous weapon?" Ave asked.

Nuelle shushed him again. King Bertil ran and disappeared into the forest ahead. As Amador looked around, three shadowy figures rose from the magenta grass behind him. Pale, human skin rapidly formed on the shadows. Amador spun around. Masculine limbs elongated from the surprise visitors, and soon, three beastly men with torn, ebony garbs faced him. Scarlet wisps dangled from the head of the center man. One side of his face sagged as if overstretched, while the other half accentuated every bone and vein. A baggy vest draped him, and crimson fur covered one of his arms, leading to a clawed-paw. Teal tufts topped the thinnest man, standing to the left. Though his head and legs faced forward, his torso twisted to the right. And beside him, purplish gray bangs shaded an eye of a shirtless, nearly eight-foot man whose shoulder blades protruded from his back like broken wings.

Heronia scrambled off her vanaph and ran into the chariot. "Prince Nuelle, what's going on?"

His heart-rate climbed as he addressed her and Ave. "Stay here." He pushed the door open and crept out of the chariot. Crouching under the tree's covering, he stalked closer to the gathering.

"Amador, you look well kept," Crimson Claw purred.

Amador squinted, his hand on his hilt. "Zagan?"

Nuelle squeezed his own sword's hilt. *Antikai's Sentry. But what in Zephoris happened to him?*

The too-tight side of Zagan's face smirked as he gestured to Twisted-Teal. "And you remember your good friend, Jilt."

Amador gaped while Jilt winked. Zagan pointed his clawed-paw at Bone-Wings. "And Brone."

Amador's face contorted as he pointed his sword. "What welcome curse has befallen you savages?"

"This is no curse," Zagan said. "This is the Obsidian's blessing, old friend." His head tilted to the side, his droopy cheek dangling. "Where's the rucksack?"

"I'm afraid I have to cut this reunion short." Amador swiped his sword at Zagan. He vanished while broken-wings Brone swung his massive fist. Amador dodged it and lashed his blade. Brone slapped Amador's forearm and he staggered.

"Papo!" Ave shouted from the chariot.

Unsheathing his sword, Nuelle raced toward the battle. As he neared, the ground quaked and a cloud of steam burst from the grass beneath Brone. A gushing fountain surged from the ground, raising him with it. Zagan vanished as Jilt appeared several yards behind Amador. Glowing-green energy streams extended from Jilt's hands like whips. He snapped them at Amador's ankles. The whip-like energy wrapped around them, and Jilt tugged, yanking Amador backwards and causing him to drop his sword. The vibrant whips dragged Amador toward Jilt while Zagan appeared outside of the chariot. Nuelle hollered and sprinted that way with sword raised. Zagan faced him and grinned as he neared. Nuelle swung his blade. Zagan's claws smashed into it. Blue sparks burst and the sword flew out of Nuelle's grasp. He raised his fists and punched Zagan's tight cheek.

Something cracked. Zagan's blue eyes glinted as the bones on his face shifted. His crimson-furred arm raised and swiped down. His claws slashed across Nuelle's jawbone and thrust him onto the grass. Nuelle writhed as blood spilled and pain seared through his face.

Amador closed in and jammed his sword into Zagan's shoulder. Zagan roared as he veered around, yanking out the sword and chucking it aside. His clawed-hand swung. Amador blocked with an armored forearm and kicked Zagan's chest. He crashed against the chariot door, bending it inward. Heronia screamed while Ave cheered. Amador unsheathed his dagger and lunged forward. Zagan reached his human-hand beneath his vest and removed an iron, sawtoothed dagger. He rammed it into Amador's stomach, stopping him.

"No!" Ave shoved open the other chariot door as Nuelle fumbled to his feet, his stomach churning as blood seeped from his Sentry's mouth.

Amador groaned. "Go."

Zagan drove the dagger in deeper. More blood spilled from Amador's mouth. Lightheaded and body searing with rage, Nuelle raised his fists and lunged at Zagan. Amador stomped as his eyes rolled back. A steamy spout burst beneath him and Zagan, whisking them both hundreds of feet upwards and blasting Nuelle back. The hot water of Amador's prodigious gift rained on Nuelle and the chariot. His head reeled. *King Nifal commanded that you both are to stay in the chariot.* Amador's firm warning echoed in Nuelle's mind, but his heart screamed for him to stay, to fight, to help his Sentry and bring him home to his wife.

"Papo!" Ave appeared beside Nuelle. Tears welling in his eyes, Nuelle pushed himself to his feet and grabbed Ave's arm.

"We have to go." Nuelle cringed, the words sour on his tongue and foul like he'd uttered a curse. His tears escaped and with the same fists that begged to battle, Nuelle pulled Ave back toward the chariot. Heronia scrambled out of it and ran to the guiding vanaph.

Ave stared up at the bursting water, his hair soaked. "We can't leave him!"

Go. Amador's command thundered in Nuelle's reeling brain. The vanaphs stamped their hooves and hovered above the ground.

"Hurry!" Heronia tugged the reins, the three vanaphs growing more and more frantic.

I'm so sorry. Nuelle used both arms to hold Ave, fighting with all his strength, and dragged him back into the chariot. He yelled as Nuelle slammed the door. The vanaphs shot into the dark expanse, leaving the forest and Amador behind.

Two: Sent Away

Even the walls are trembling at Brother's rage. Nuelle paced outside the Throne Room, his own body still quivering from everything that just happened. Amador, the man who was more like an uncle than a Sentry; the man who faithfully protected his life from the moment of birth; his daily companion and the father of his best friend, fell in battle, slain by what once was a man, a fellow Sentry, but was now nothing but a savage beast.

Weak-kneed, Nuelle leaned against a wall as the image of Lady Purine falling on all fours and wailing at the news of her husband taunted. *I'll make sure we leave before dusk today so you two can enjoy your anniversary.* That's the word he'd failed to keep. If they only left earlier, right when dusk first made its appearance, Amador might still be alive. A sharp pang dug into Nuelle's chest. With his back still against the wall, he sank to his bottom. His failure cost the life of his closest friend apart from Ave. *How can I forgive myself? And now this news of Antikai?* Nuelle ran his fingers through his wet hair. *This morning I dreamed of hope, but now I'm living a nightmare.*

The wall-torches' bluish flames crackled as if riled by the argument happening inside the Throne Room.

"He tried to slay you, and his Sentry killed Amador!" Tane roared, once again causing the hallway to quake. "He must be destroyed!"

"He is no longer a threat to me, son," Father said, his own rumbling voice somehow as calm as the evening sky.

"Just like the citizens of Agapon are no longer a threat, and the rest of Zephoris?"

Nuelle peered through one of the windows on his left, overlooking the homes of Agapon, of their people. The stars' faint glow shined upon the gem structures as they rested in darkness. Agaponians lived, moved, and breathed faithfulness. They walked as peacefully as the wind's melodies. One of the beasts who attacked—he shuddered—and killed Amador came from afar off Kaimana—the tribe who ignited the Great Kin War of Old. And Brone was definitely a Gavrailian. So then why did Tane deem his fellow Agaponians dangerous?

"Why do you live with fear?" Father asked, as if hearing Nuelle's thoughts.

"Because an uprising has already begun. And you sit here on your throne, refusing to act." With each sentence, Tane's voice grew louder, bolder. "The citizens will deem us weak, and soon they will demand your dethroning, as they have with Vyden!"

Nuelle's empty stomach knotted. Ideya disposed of their king?

"A just king will not rule by force, Tane."

Brother sneered. "A just king will do what is necessary to maintain peace."

"To maintain peace, or power?"

The churning in Nuelle's gut worsened. If only Father hadn't commanded him to wait outside the Throne Room. He could read Tane's facial expression and body language; try to discern what roamed his mind and finally tamed his tongue.

"You belong by my side, son." Father severed the silence. "We can restore peace together."

The *zing* of a sword rapidly leaving its sheath sounded. "The start of restoring peace will begin with Antikai's death."

Brother's response cut down Father's offer like his double-edged weapon.

"Your words speak of victory," Father said, "but your heart has already been defeated."

Swift clatters of boot heels drew close to the door. Nuelle rose. The Throne Room door swung open, and Nuelle staggered back. Like a glacier overshadows the frost beneath it, Tane stood in the doorway with an icy stare, and chest high. The torches' fire shined off his breastplate and bronze eyes, but fury darkened his features. He strode past.

"Brother, wait!" Nuelle followed beside him. "You're journeying to the Obsidian?"

Tane marched through the hall and hurried down the far-right staircase, his boots slapping the marble. He reached the bottom and treaded to the entryway where only one wall-torch shed dim light. Two Elite Knights stood guard on either side of the doors. The knights' golden armor appeared black in the darkness. They opened the doors for Brother and Nuelle, and the two scampered outside.

A few stars flickered in the sky above, and a vanaph waited on the white dirt below, its long neck and six wings erect. Tane sheathed his sword and hopped onto the creature. He nudged its side with his boot, and it hovered above the ground. "I must go, Nu."

Nuelle stopped beside him. "Why? That traitor has already been eternally banished. But Zagan is still out there with those savages."

Brother gripped his sword's hilt with his right hand—his signet-ring missing from his ring-finger. "You are too young to understand now."

Nuelle frowned at the usual excuse. "Where's your Sentry?"

"He's a coward."

Nuelle reached for the vanaph. "Then I'll go with you."

Brother pulled on the reins, and the creature ascended higher. "You must stay here, Nu, for Father."

"Father doesn't need me."

"And I do not need you in order to defeat Antikai." His words stung like a cut from a blade.

Heat swelled in Nuelle's blood. "It won't just be Antikai. His Sentry and the other—"

"I can handle those men."

Nuelle spoke swifter. "They're not just men anymore, Tane. You'll need help—"

"Enough, Nu!"

Nuelle's temperature cooled. Convincing his stubborn brother would be impossible. Wrath controlled him and made him harder than the courtyard stone they used to spar on each morning. He'd changed over the last few months. And now he was going to forsake his family to fulfill a blood mission. Yet, despite the bitter truth, a twinge of hope urged Nuelle to speak once more. "Please stay. You're needed here."

Tane slowly inhaled the night air, and his coppery eyes moistened. "No matter what happens, I will always be your brother." He booted his vanaph's side and soared into the sky. The blackness rapidly swallowed him, and within seconds, he disappeared in the night. Tears streamed down Nuelle's cheeks. *I pray I see you again, my brother.*

"My son." Father's voice, like thunder warning the skies of a coming storm, resounded from behind.

Nuelle's stare lingered on the place where the darkness last consumed Tane before turning to Father. His diamond crown gleamed like Agapon's life orbs in the day. And his eyes, how they blazed like an amber fire, powerful and frightening, yet gentle and kind. He clasped a leather tunic. "Gather a satchel and enough food to last a week. You are going to Knight's Elect Academy."

Nuelle gripped the garb. "The academy?"

Father stepped closer and removed something from the pocket of his robe. "This place is no longer safe for the new Supreme Prince."

Nuelle winced, his similar exchange with Amador just hours ago rang in his mind. *"What's really in the rucksack?" "A very dangerous weapon that is no longer safe in the palace."* Nuelle's tears instantly dried as Father's fist unraveled. In his large palm lay Tane's golden signet-ring with the fiery sword emblem. Nuelle stiffened. How could he take Brother's ring...Brother's place? Slowly, Nuelle extended his free hand, the gesture shouting betrayal. It suddenly seemed like choosing sides...

Father set the ring in Nuelle's grasp. "You will know the right time to put it on."

As he placed it into his pant-pocket, Nuelle's mind raced. This nightmarish day only grew worse. Amador's death, Antikai's attack on Father, Brother leaving without warning, this news about the academy and becoming Supreme Prince. Was Tane's one act of defiance truly enough to cost him his position as the succeeding heir? He was years ahead in experience and ability—nor had he finished training his younger brother to lead the people. And with the timing, being a faithful Supreme Prince seemed all the more out of reach.

"You will leave immediately following Amador's funeral," Father said. "And if Ave so chooses, he may join you."

Nuelle's sinking heart lifted an inch as Father continued.

"When you arrive at the academy, be sure to find the Acumen."

"I have a copy."

"Not the original." He rested his warm hand upon Nuelle's marred cheek. Father's palm glowed orange, and the powerful warmth melted into Nuelle's face and then surged through it like smoldering waves. Tingles gradually traced his jawline before fading away. As Father lowered his hand, Nuelle raised his. His fingertips met smooth, intact skin. He blinked at Father who smiled faintly before speaking again. "There are many lessons you will learn, not all of which will be easily comprehensible at first, and within the Acumen's pages, there is specific instructions for you, instructions regarding your destiny."

Nuelle's heart jumped as if jolted by lightning. Insight into his purpose. Being the *second* son born to a king, his existence remained a nagging mystery. No one understood why King Nifal made him. Not even he did. Nuelle looked at the leather tunic he clutched, the knight academy beginners' attire. "But why all of this now?"

Father released Nuelle's shoulder. "Because it has begun."

Three: First Day

If someone besides Father would've called this place safer than the palace, a laugh would've been the immediate response. Nuelle slung his satchel over his shoulder and slipped off his vanaph. Crumbling steps led to the lodge's entryway, surrounded by a railless porch. Green mildew decorated the wood, and cobwebs drooped from the porch's ceiling. A splintery water barrel sat a few paces from the topaz-centered door, with a soup-ladle attached to it by a chain. Ave, bronze and slumped like a waterless branch, hesitantly dismounted his vanaph, satchel in hand. Tragedy had aged him inside—had aged them both. The vanaphs soared away as he joined Nuelle. Tear-tracks descended from Ave's blue eyes down to his chin. Nuelle winced. Seven days wasn't enough time to grieve all that they'd both lost.

Nuelle cleared his throat. "You didn't have to come with me."

"Hogwash." Ave swiped a palm. "Though seeing this place in person does have me second-guessing my decision. The Supreme Palace offered silk sheets, royal garbs, pretty steer-guides—"

"No mold."

"Rich, decadent, savor-for-your-life regular meals."

Nuelle grasped his stomach. "Stop before you make me doubt my decision, too."

Ave straightened some. "But your father sent you. I thought you didn't have a choice."

"I could've chosen not to listen to him." He let his hand fall and lay itself against his pant-pocket where Brother's signet-ring hid. "Like Tane."

Ave lifted his chin toward the lodge's entrance. "So what do we tell the Overseer?"

"The truth. That my father sent me here to get the Acumen and to train." Nuelle jogged up the steps and stood before the door, his face across from the large topaz stone in its center. "Prince Nuelle."

He tapped his foot as he waited for the stone to swell with light and unlock the door, but it remained unlit. All the prodigies invited and accepted into the academy were already within. He hadn't been on that list so apparently, his voice commands wouldn't unlock Father's sonar-lumina gateway. Nuelle knocked forcefully. A minute passed, and he stepped back and studied the surroundings of his new home. A breeze swirled through the orange forest and magenta grass encircling this lodge for first-year prodigies. As Ave trudged to the water barrel beside the door, Nuelle's head bowed. Ave's father had trained here.

Nuelle slowly approached, unable to keep postponing the inevitable question that taunted their entire journey. "Did... Amador ever mention Jilt and Brone to you?"

Ave grasped the water barrel's sides and peered into the pink water. It reflected his scowling face. "All I know is those beasts were prodigies when Papo was here."

Nuelle gave a nod. Although twisted and evil, they did have prodigious gifts and Zagan must have graduated amongst the highest in the academy to be accepted as a royal Sentry. How he managed to fake nobility was a talent in itself, unless he actually was honorable at one point in his life.

Ave lifted the soup-ladle attached to the barrel. "Any ideas on how to get inside?"

Nuelle strode to the left of the porch and peered out and up. About twelve feet above, a large open window invited easy access into the Servants' Lodge.

Ave spewed a stream of pink water and dropped the ladle. "This tastes like foul feet!"

"Foul feet?"

Ave wiped his face. "Old Lady Flemm stepped on a tooth pick in the kitchen once. When I pulled it out, her flaking fungi-foot rammed straight into my mouth."

Nuelle laughed as he jogged to the barrel. "I'm going to miss her."

"I'm not."

"But you'll miss her granddaughter I'm sure."

"Ah, Starlene. The girl who lit up my world and set me on high."

Nuelle gripped the barrel's soggy sides. "And whose tongue you set on fire."

Ave cringed. "I haven't used dragon-fire seasoning since."

"One day you'll find a girl who can handle absurdly spicy, but for now, let's dump this out."

"Gladly."

They tossed the water, and Nuelle rolled the barrel across the porch and shoved it off. He leapt down beside it and then rolled it to the lodge's wall. As he flipped the container over and positioned it beneath the window, Ave spoke.

"We're breaking in, aren't we?"

Nuelle mounted the barrel. "Climbing in."

"Lady Lovehart would have a heart failure."

"I don't think that woman is killable." He jumped and grabbed hold of the windowsill. A noisy chattering poured from inside the window, and a trumpet bellowed. Nuelle pulled himself up and leapt into a large chamber with walls of quivers, wooden shields, and bows. Youths stood at attention before a huge rock of a man wearing silver armor—a three-foot sword strapped to his hip. Sir Dangian. So Amador's tales of the Gavrailian combat trainer's legendary stature weren't exaggerated.

The man's stare landed on Nuelle. "An intruder!" He unsheathed his sword and bounded toward him like a boulder rolling down a hill. Nuelle snatched a shield off the wall and raised it in defense as the man neared.

"It's Prince Nuelle!" a prodigy cried.

Sir Dangian halted, his sword frozen above Nuelle's shield. Every eye fixed on him. No warm smiles, no bows of respect, only shocked gawking. Nuelle lowered his armor. *This is awkward.*

"Smash meh head on limestone and strike meh gut," Sir Dangian said as he bowed, the prodigies continuing to gawp.

"A little help here." Ave panted from outside.

Nuelle leaned out the window and pulled him into the room. As Nuelle faced Sir Dangian again, the giant straightened. "What brings you and this bag o' bones to the academy, Prince?"

While some of their peers laughed, Ave's cheeks flushed and he opened his mouth, but Nuelle spoke first. "We were sent by my father."

"A prince training to be a knight." Sir Dangian grinned as he sheathed his sword beside a dagger. "You sure your father sent you?"

Ave nodded. "He even sent my bony self along with him. Hard to imagine, huh?"

The Gavrailian sized up Ave and smirked. "Bony and mouthy. Why didn't you two come in through the door?"

"No one answered my knock," Nuelle replied, "and our attending wasn't planned."

Sir Dangian raised a bushy eyebrow. Nuelle leaned close and spoke in a hushed voice. "I need to know where the Acumen is—the original one."

The trainer's eyes widened just slightly and then he cocked his giant head. "It's not in here, but if you came to be trained, mch suggest you get in line, Your Highness." He turned and stomped to the stiff youths.

Nuelle returned the shield to the wall, and he and Ave joined the others standing at attention. Gossiping whispers reached Nuelle's ears: "What is Prince Nuelle doing here?" "Was he banished from the palace?" "He's wearing the Servant's tunic so maybe King Nifal did send him." "But why?"

Nuelle averted his gaze from the gossips. The prodigies weren't ready to know about Tane's defiance and removal from his high position. Picturing the golden signet ring in his pocket, Nuelle clenched his jaw. *Not even I was prepared for it. And I'm still not.*

Sir Dangian marched across from a blackboard marked with battle formations. On the left, a portrait from floor-to-ceiling displayed Father standing in gold armor, clutching a translucent sword, one side of the blade trimmed gold, the other, black iron. Crystal? Why would anyone—especially Father—choose to wield a sword wrought from such fragile material?

As if lifted by an invisible hand, Nuelle raised his chin and stared at Father's face. Nuelle's heart instantly warmed—like it always did when they locked eyes. The sensation eased the painful ache that weighed on his heart since his brother left and Amador fell in battle. Father's hair, although white and longer, grazed his cheeks the same way as Nuelle's, his similar amber eyes smoldering as they peered back. Why wouldn't Father place the Acumen under the protection of the daunting Gavrailian? He did nearly slay two youths who seemed to be invading his room. Did the trainer lie, fearing that a few prodigies overheard the inquiry regarding the book's whereabouts? Or did he tell the truth?

Sir Dangian halted. "You must always be prepared for battle. You never know when your enemy will strike." As he continued walking, he drew his huge head just inches from the prodigies' faces. "Meh name's Sir Dangian, your combat trainer." He slowly stroked the hilt of his sword like a greedy man caressing a pearl. "Meh don't know if it was your old pappy, or your sweet mammy, but one o' 'em has a prodigious gift that makes you a prodigy, so here you are." He slammed his boot on the ground in front of a blonde girl, strikingly beautiful and hard-faced like a diamond. She alone wore leather gloves and a long-sleeved tunic.

Nuelle lifted an eyebrow. Why would anyone wear long sleeves during the Days of Warmth? Her modesty seemed a bit much for the hottest season in the land.

"Some o' you rich kin"—Sir Dangian glanced at Nuelle —"won't be able to stand living an entire year like a peasant, and others o' you, after training, will want to throw on one o' this little princess's dresses."

The blonde girl clenched her fists. "I'm not a princess."

Sir Dangian huffed. "Meh guarantee you'll wish you were after today's lesson."

Some prodigies laughed, but Nuelle and Ave kept their mouths shut.

"You first-years get the fitting title o' Servant." He unsheathed his dagger and dug its point between a gap in his teeth while he continued marching down the line. "Throughout your time here in the Servants' Lodge, you'll need to survive three levels o' training. You'll start at Fundamental Combat, then, if by a miracle you make it through to the second trimester you'll move onto Central Combat, and in your final trimester, Vital Combat." He sheathed his dagger. "These three hours o' training are going to become your favorite, or most dreaded time o' the day, so soak 'em up, servies, because starting now, your lessons on servant-hood begin." He stopped pacing. "Everyone grab a shield from the wall."

Nuelle, Ave, and the blonde girl strode to the shields.

"Move it! Battle isn't something that waits for you."

As the prodigies bustled toward the wall of armor, pushing and shoving, Sir Dangian rolled his eyes.

A girl with red, white-tipped hair snatched a shield beside Nuelle and curtsied. "Most noble and handsome Prince Nuelle, did you come to the academy to find a future queen?"

Nuelle grabbed two shields. "I, um—"

"What's wrong? You look nervous."

"Forgive me. Girls at the palace aren't as frightening—I mean forward."

She gaped. "Are you saying I'm ugly?"

Ave grabbed one of Nuelle's shields. "Uh, we're kind of in the middle of a combat lesson, not a class on courtship, so if you don't mind…"

The girl turned, flipping her white-tipped hair. Frost spurted from her ends, splattering onto his forehead and eyes and sliding down his nose. He quickly wiped it off as she walked away. "I think frightening was the right word."

"Thanks," Nuelle said as he scanned the perimeter.

"My pleasure. Do you think the Acumen's here?"

Nuelle spoke low. "Sir Dangian did seem extra alert, but it could just be a warrior's instinct. The combat trainer might also be too obvious of a choice."

"You're probably right." As Ave's eyes flitted to the blonde girl who weighed her armor, his eyebrow twitched.

"Unfortunately, we have to put the search on hold for now and just focus on training."

"All right, servies," Sir Dangian said, "turn around."

As they faced the rear of the room, many prodigies gasped. Three stout, ebony-furred creatures with slanted nostrils and eyes stood before the open window. A leather strap lined their puffy chests, leading to a quiver of arrows on their backs. The creatures' arms reached the floor, and clawed hands clenched a longbow.

Nuelle locked stares with one of the creatures as he and his peers inched toward the back of the room. Its head tilted downward in acknowledgment. Nuelle furrowed his brow. Did his seemingly barbaric opponent just pay him a nod of respect?

Sir Dangian lifted his shield. "Hold your armor high enough to guard your upper body and make sure it's covering your face." He demonstrated with his own shield before lowering it. "Go on, try it."

Nuelle raised his with ease as some of the other prodigies —including Ave—struggled.

"O toe-biting weemutts," Sir Dangian said, "meh great grandmammy can do better than that. Rebellion is starting in the kingdoms, and you toddlers are supposed to be the next batch o' knights to protect the people?" He addressed the black creatures. "Eebons, attack!"

With two flicks of the hand, the eebons set arrow to string. Their long arms stretched the elastic back much farther than any mortal could. The prodigies quickly lifted their shields again. The creatures fired.

Nuelle gripped his armor. *Clunk, clunk, clunk!* The pelting arrows rang in his ears. As the merciless barbs pounded Ave's shield, his cheeks reddened. "Safer than the palace."

An arrow penetrated Nuelle's shield, right by his eye. He looked around at his peers, many trembling as arrows pelted their shields. Indeed, Father's words hadn't made sense—yet.

"Halt!" Sir Dangian cried, and the eebons stopped their assault. "Would you look at that, you tawters are stronger already." He marched to the wall of quivers, snatched three, and tossed them to the eebons.

Nuelle steadied Ave's shield.

"I'm fine." He squinted at the combat trainer. "He's more brutish than the eebons."

Nuelle met eyes with the one who nodded at him. Unlike the prodigies, for some reason this creature had offered its respect, and honoring a person was certainly not brutish.

"Put your shields back on the wall and grab a bow and quiver." Sir Dangian pointed at the rear wall as the eebons leapt out of the window with their quivers. "We're going to the archery grounds." He treaded to the room's door.

As Nuelle exchanged their shields for a bow and quiver, Ave grimaced. "Red-eyed barbarian. Why does your father let those savages teach here?"

"Not all of them are as reckless," Nuelle replied as they followed their trainer and the others out of the room. "And if anyone knows about combat, they do."

"And it seems he's taken a few good hits to the head."

The blonde girl sauntered beside Ave as he and Nuelle walked through the hallway. She glimpsed at him before striding past, her yellow eyes reminiscent of someone.

Ave wiped his sweaty forehead, his eyebrow twitching. "She's interesting."

Nuelle slanted his eyes. "Just interesting, Ave?"

"All right, let's get the evident out of the way. She's beautiful, but I am more intrigued by her extra modest apparel in the Days of Warmth."

Nuelle nodded as they reached the end of the corridor. "So am I."

Sir Dangian and the others stood across from square stone-platforms that ascended and descended in midair through rectangular openings in the ceilings.

Their trainer marched onto a platform, and a group of prodigies followed. "First floor." At his command, the stone slab dropped. Nuelle and Ave mounted one and imitated Sir Dangian's lead. The platform swiftly descended. In seconds, it landed on the first floor beside a cobblestone fireplace in a commons reeking of dirty socks. Wash barrels and badly-patched couches crowded the space.

"This way." Sir Dangian gestured the prodigies to follow him across the commons. They proceeded past terrace doors and to an archway that led into a dark, floor-less tunnel. "A life-saving combat lesson: never fear." He strode onward and stepped down into the void. A stone stair appeared under his foot. With each step, another stair materialized. "Don't lag behind," he said without looking back.

Nuelle swiftly descended the rocky steps, Ave close behind. When they reached the bottom, the ceiling ignited into blue flames, and the ground glided forward. The fire's bold hue mirrored Ave's eyes, though his irises had lost the spark they had just last week.

Nuelle adjusted his gaze. What words could be said to comfort someone who just lost his father? Would the right words ever come, or was there simply nothing to say to soften so great a blow? Death was new to them both. Nickelite and Lady Lovehart were among the oldest in the palace, three-hundred-years young they'd often say. But Amador, only thirty-eight...the first of Elite Knights in Nuelle and Ave's day to fall in battle and the closest to them both...Nuelle forced his tears back.

Straight ahead, a golden light grew. The ground stopped gliding, and he walked with Ave and the prodigies into the brightness. Nuelle's boots met the lush pasture of a hill that sloped downward into a valley. A breeze gently brushed back his hair as if it sought to console him. In the distance, a pink lagoon glimmered by its lonesome, and yellow dust flowers adorned the grass.

"Targets!" Sir Dangian cried into the hills. Wooden target dummies sprang forth from the ground, and the delicate flowers dispersed. "Who wants to go first?"

Nuelle and a number of boys raised their hands. The blonde girl did as well.

Sir Dangian smirked before spitting on the ground. "Let's let the little lady go first, boys."

She marched to his side, clutching her bow.

"All right, blondie—"

"My name is Fiona."

"Yeah, yeah." He pointed at the ground. "Now you wanna make sure your feet are planted—"

She drew back the bowstring and released. Her arrow darted forward, striking the dummy farthest away right between the eyes. Ave's jaw dropped. Nuelle managed to smile. She'd been invited to the academy for a reason, and apparently, that was one of them.

Sir Dangian blinked a few times. "All right then. Who's next?" He sifted the prodigies with his glare while Fiona rejoined them.

As she walked past Nuelle, she kept her yellow eyes ahead, as if purposefully avoiding contact with his. He had seen that face before, but where? His heart skipped. Princess Sophana! What in Zephoris was she doing at the academy? No princess —no one of royalty before today—had ever trained to be a knight. What Father had him do was unheard of, but a princess—a disguised one—training at Knight's Elect Academy was even more unusual.

"Prince Nuelle." The trainer beckoned.

Whispers had spread among the prodigies after Princess Sophana's bull's-eye, but now a hush descended on the highland like a burial ground. Nuelle took his stance beside Sir Dangian.

"Focus," the trainer spoke into his ear. "Meh want you to hit that target." He pointed to a dummy off to the far left about a hundred yards away.

Nuelle carefully positioned the bow, trying to utilize the silence to strengthen his concentration, but thoughts bombarded his mind. Why did Princess Sophana flee Athdonia? Or was she sent here? Had an uprising come to her land as well? And why did she hide her identity?

Something black appeared in his peripherals. He looked to the right. A dark figure disappeared behind the hills. Nuelle released the string. His arrow missed the target by a foot. New whispers circulated amongst his peers.

"It's all right, Prince," Sir Dangian said. "Some are built for the battlefield, while others are meant for the palace." He slapped Nuelle's back and almost made him lose footing.

"Something's down there," Nuelle said as he regained balance.

"I saw it, too." A lanky boy pointed at the hill. "Something dark."

Sir Dangian squinted at the area. "Probably an eebon."

"I think it might've been someone wearing a cloak," Nuelle replied.

Dangian gripped his sword's hilt. "I'll give it a look. You servies stay put." Unsheathing his weapon, he marched downhill.

As Nuelle rejoined the tense group, his heart raced faster than his steps.

"You think there's a threat?" Ave asked.

"Not sure." Nuelle peered at Princess Sophana while she studied the barb of an arrow. "But I am sure the Acumen isn't the only mystery hidden here."

Clink. Nuelle cocked his head toward the sound. A bronze knight cloaked in black and wearing an elaborate utility belt on his waist and around his thigh limped their way, gripping a long-barreled device. Nuelle blinked at the bizarre sight. What was the ex-prince of Ideya's Sentry, Icabod, doing at the academy?

A netted ball fired from Icabod's long-barreled device. The ball unraveled midair into a large net and then landed atop half of the prodigies where Sophana stood. As she and the group collapsed, Icabod fired another net at the rest of them. Nuelle tossed his bow forward and dove into a roll, evading the net that now trapped Ave and his peers.

Clasping his bow, Nuelle set an arrow to string and released. The barb pierced the knight's bicep. He grunted and staggered. As he tore out the arrow, Nuelle charged. Icabod whipped out a shooter from behind his back. Nuelle knocked Icabod's hand as he pulled the trigger. *Zing, zing, zing!* Three blades darted past Nuelle's ear. He swiped his leg under the knight's and then kicked his shin. Icabod stumbled, dropping the blade-shooter. He snatched another shooter from his thigh and pulled the trigger. A blast of energy slammed into Nuelle. He tumbled back. His face smashed against the ground. Spitting out grass and blood, he looked to his left. The hills swirled as his head pounded and his ears rang.

"Let me go!" Sophana shouted.

Warmth crept into Nuelle's ears. The ringing eased, and his vision steadied. He looked right. With back turned, Icabod dragged Sophana from under the net and bound her wrists with shackles.

"Release her, you ignoble coward!" Ave clawed at the net entangling him and the prodigies.

Nuelle slowly rose and stalked toward Icabod as he reached into a square compartment on his utility belt. Nuelle's wobbly gait quickened as the knight removed a fang-spiked choker and began forcing it over Sophana's head. "I said let me go!" She kicked her calve behind her, right between Ichabod's legs. As he grunted and staggered, Nuelle body-slammed him. They plummeted to the ground. The knight unsheathed his shooter again and aimed it at Nuelle's head.

"Arrrrgggghhhh!" Sir Dangian charged, his three-foot sword raised and glaring, as if set on fire by the daystar. Icabod aimed his shooter at the trainer. A blast exploded from it. Dangian breezed through the energy wave like an unstoppable avalanche. In a flash, he swung his sword. It rammed into Icabod's side, and he toppled off Nuelle.

As Sir Dangian towered over the limp knight, Nuelle rose and rushed to help the others—starting with Princess Sophana. Removing her shackles, he whispered, "Great disguise, Sophana."

Her yellow eyes widened, but then she smirked. "Clearly, I didn't have much time to come up with something elaborate."

Nuelle glanced at the rest of the prodigies as Sir Dangian pulled off their nets, and then continued to speak low. "Why was Ludwig's Sentry after you?"

Something twitched beneath her sleeves. "Please don't reveal my identity, or something worse will come for me."

Nuelle frowned. "But—"

"Are you okay?" Ave strode to Sophana, his eyebrow twitching.

She sneered as she hopped to her feet, her yellow eyes on the fallen knight. "For now."

Four: The Acumen

There were knights half the Overseer's age and still not as fast-footed. Nuelle and Ave hastened their steps to maintain pace with the silvery-haired man as he led the way to his office. His black, knitted robe flapped behind him, trying to keep up. The corridor drummed with his skittering steps, and his jutting chin seemed to turn corners before he did.

After traveling through two more hallways, they stopped before a pair of double-doors.

"Overseer Enri." At his voice, an orange stained-glass circle in the doors' center glowed, and the entry opened. Nuelle and Ave followed him into the room. As they passed walls of bookshelves, a sweet-mint aroma intensified. The Overseer strode beneath a floating chandelier. Its light shined upon a central table holding a plaque inscribed: *Enri Neitman, Faithful Overseer of the Servants for a Century.* He hurried behind an immaculate desk—besides a half-eaten blue mangeen fruit—and sat in a chair. "Please sit." He waved at two chairs across from him. As they did, Overseer Enri's lavender eyes locked onto Nuelle's and the man spoke as quickly as he walked. "Forgive my nerves, my lord. On top of the eventful morning, I was not expecting your presence at the academy."

"My father believes the palace is no longer safe for me." Nuelle gestured to Ave. "He sent my"—his throat stung —"Sentry's son to accompany me."

Ave kept his face slack, but he sank a little in his chair.

"Has an uprising begun in Agapon?" the Overseer asked.

"Not that I'm aware of."

"And is the Supreme Prince safe?"

A pang rattled Nuelle's chest. He gripped the sides of his chair before answering. "My brother went on a voyage."

Overseer Enri's pointy chin twitched. "And Ludwig's Sentry, do you think he came to the academy for you?"

Princess Sophana's words echoed in Nuelle's thoughts: *Please don't reveal my identity, or something worse will come for me.*

Nuelle shook his head. "I don't see why he would have any reason to capture me."

Ave sat up. "But he did try and capture—"

"He cast a net on all of the prodigies," Nuelle said quickly.

Ave eyed him.

"He did?" Overseer Enri removed a white handkerchief from a desk drawer and dabbed his sweaty forehead.

"I engaged him in battle until Sir Dangian returned and killed him," Nuelle said.

"Nothing like this has ever happened in the history of Knight's Elect Academy. It is all very bizarre and troubling." His face whitened like the linen he held. "I will sit with Sir Dangian and every witness today to try and sort this all out, and I will make arrangements for you and your companion —"

"Ave Purine," Ave said.

"Ave, to lodge in the Tower of Advocacy on the seventh floor, and will add your name to the list of enrolled Servants so you may have access to all the rooms in the academy."

"Thank you, sir." Nuelle laid his hand on his pant pocket, where his brother's ring still wrongly sat… "My father wanted me to train, and he told me to acquire the Acumen."

Overseer Enri dropped his handkerchief. The trumpet indicating the start of third lesson bellowed. Enri grabbed his handkerchief and returned it to the drawer. "I will summon the Wisdom Preceptor. The Book is in his care."

"The Wisdom Preceptor?" Nuelle rose, his heart pounding. "We'll go to him now."

The Overseer stood and bowed steeply. "And I will ensure your first day ends on an exceedingly worthier note."

"Thank you, but that won't be necessary."

"I insist, my lord. It is the least I can do."

Nuelle nodded. "Fair day, Overseer Enri." He hurried out of the room.

Ave trailed. Once he closed the door behind them, he whispered, "Why didn't you tell him that Ludwig's Sentry was trying to capture Fiona?"

"I can't say now." Nuelle dashed into the commons. "Besides, you're better off moving on."

"Moving on? Who said I liked her?"

"Come on, Ave. You've had your share of flash-love for servants at the palace. When you look at or talk to a girl you like, you do this strange eyebrow twitching thing."

Ave covered his eyebrow. "What are you talking—"

Nuelle halted.

"You're acting so str—" Ave bumped into him. Above the fireplace and beside the stone platforms, burned into the wooden wall, fresh smoke rose from the words: *Disappear like your brother, Supreme Prince.*

Dizziness clouded Nuelle's head, and weakness crept into his knees. Who wrote this message, this threat? And how did the person know about Tane leaving? And about Father delivering the ring into his youngest's hands? Overseer Enri had just learned half of that information moments ago. Only one other at the lodge knew about Tane's voyage to the Obsidian, but not about the ring...

His lightheadedness cleared. He spun around and faced Ave. "Did you tell anyone?"

Ave's brow furrowed. "How could I? I've been with you the whole time."

Nuelle stared into Ave's eyes. Traces of pink from mourning for his father still tinted the white areas. Nuelle inhaled a steady breath that calmed his trembling. Of course he hadn't told anyone. Ave had a big mouth, but not when it came to sharing secrets. "We have to figure out who did this and how the person knew about Tane."

Ave swiped a bang from his face and then stiffened. "You think a preceptor wrote it?"

"Not sure, but maybe the Acumen has answers." Nuelle strode onto a platform. "Third floor." It shot upward. The moment it stopped, he and Ave ran through the narrow corridor and stopped at the entrance to Basic Wisdom. "Prince Nuelle." The sapphire stone in the door's center illuminated and the door opened. He and Ave stepped inside.

Prodigies occupied desks, and bookshelves covered three of the four walls like a coliseum of information, and a vast window spanned the back wall. On its sill sat an array of colorful flowers. Toward the room's front, a pole on wheels stood behind a wooden table with a vase of translucent limpid flowers, famous for their ability to help with concentration. To its left, glowing orange light encircled a strange corkscrew-shaped table where a huge golden-covered book rested.

Nuelle's heart jumped to his throat. *The Acumen!*

With hurried steps and racing thoughts, his anger extinguished like water dousing flames. Finally, he would grasp the book that held answers to his destiny! Unprotected copies of the Acumen remained available to all interested in its writings, but Father made only one original—guarded by a territory sphere—for his second son.

Dust particles floated around the orange beam. The Acumen must have slept for a long time, waiting to be awakened. With each step closer, an invisible force, powerful and magnetic, drew Nuelle to the book. His heart thumped. Every beat pulsated with rising warmth. A round, golden medallion with rays like the daystar protruded from the Acumen's center like a shield, or a lock; Father's emblem, the insignia he always used in his letters and written decrees. This book was written firsthand by the Supreme King himself, the only original copy...Nuelle reached his hand toward the radiant cover—

"Prince Nuelle." A tall, slender man in a russet robe glided toward him and Ave from the back of the room. The man's yellow-eyed gaze riveted on Nuelle as if he were a rare artifact of great wonder just discovered by an archeologist. The apparent preceptor halted before him and for a long, very awkward moment, the preceptor just stared as a thin-lipped smile slowly formed on his face. Ave cleared his throat and the man blinked rapidly as if awoken from a dream, and then bowed.

Nuelle coerced himself to turn from the Acumen. "I need to—" he glanced at his similarly awestruck peers. They didn't even blink. With more forced and now painful effort, he turned from the Acumen. Maybe waiting to acquire it until the prodigies left was best. They'd all be questioning why he took it, and someone at the academy was an enemy who didn't need to know his reasons for coming.

The man smiled at him and Ave. "I am glad the rumors were true." He gestured to two empty seats, one in the fourth row, another in the back. "Please join us."

Ave's eyes squinted at Nuelle, clearly wondering why he hadn't grabbed the Acumen. Nuelle looked away and took the farthest of the seats. He could explain later.

"I am Preceptor Sage," the yellow-eyed man said, "and this is where you will learn Basic Wisdom." He stood to the left of the desk. His body blocked the golden book, whose strong, magnetic pull had barely weakened. "In this course, you will learn the foundational principles of wisdom and how to apply them to servanthood. To start, tell the person next to you the best advice you know."

Prodigies glanced around as if the counsel they sought flitted about the room. Nuelle turned to his right and faced a boy. His bright red-and-blue eyes contrasted his sickly pale skin. Yet the fire in his gaze made him look far from sick, far from weak…

Nuelle spoke first. "If you're not willing to give your life for a friend, then you're not a true companion."

The boy's lips curled. "There are worse enemies than fear." He spoke just loud enough for Nuelle to hear, and then tapped his fingers on his desk, his stare not leaving Nuelle's. On the boy's right hand, he wore a metallic ring with an onyx stone. A red spark like a trace of lightning ignited at the tip of the boy's index finger. His grin widened as he looked away.

Nuelle's heart skipped. Was he the one who burned that threat into the walls of the commons, desecrating this place created by Father and threatening his second son?

The class quieted, and Preceptor Sage approached spark-boy. "What is your name?"

He raised his chin. "Colden Ackerbus."

"Colden, was the advice you gave the result of experience, or was it passed on to you by another person?"

"Both."

The hair on Nuelle's neck rose. Who would give Colden that kind of advice? And what did he encounter that was worse than fear itself?

The preceptor gave an approving nod. "How wise it is when one speaks from knowledge rather than assumption." He focused on the class. "Wisdom, like everything else, has a beginning. All wisdom comes from a source."

"Who was the original source?" a prodigy asked.

"History tells us King Nifal is the longest living being in Zephoris and its founder."

A green-haired girl seated on the other side of Nuelle raised her hand. "My mother told me he's the one who brought life to Zephoris."

"He was. From a drop of his own blood he formed all the first beings of Zephoris. From his blood came the five tribes." Preceptor Sage grabbed the rod's top and spun it. As it twirled, tiny three-dimensional images of five couples appeared: thin, yellow-eyed Athdonians; muscular, red-eyed Gavrailians; bronze-skinned, blue-eyed Kaimanas; short, purple-eyed Sunezians; and youthful, teal-eyed Ideyans. "In the beginning, these couples walked with King Nifal and began to populate Zephoris." As he spoke, children and adults rapidly appeared. "But after sixty years of peaceful cohabitation, the two elders of the Kaimana tribe began to look upon their neighbors with envy and greed."

As a few prodigies looked at their Kaimana peers, Ave included, he shifted in his seat and kept his stare on the preceptor. Nuelle did the same.

"Being gifted planters, the Athdonians' land had an abundance of trees, flowers, and other plant-life, while the Kaimanas had settled on a shadeless island daily exposed to the daystar's heat. They conspired with their offspring to attack the Athdonian tribe and seize a portion of their land. This caused a chaotic war." The images turned violent, attacking one another with their fists, spears, and fire. "Ideyans banded with the Kaimanas, while Sunezians sided with the Athdonians, and the Gavrailians chose to attack everyone. Yet, a remnant still desired peace, so they fled their lands and gathered to Agapon, King Nifal's territory."

Nuelle and Ave smiled at each other, but Nuelle's smile quickly dipped to a frown, and Father's words shook his thoughts: *This place is no longer safe for the new Supreme Prince.*

"After the Great Kin War of Old," Preceptor Sage said, "battles continued to arise."

Father materialized in the midst of the violence and everyone froze. Many prodigies fixated on Nuelle. He set his attention on the preceptor as he spoke. "Angered and hurt by their perpetual, selfish betrayals, King Nifal cursed their lands with what would later be called, 'The Great Terrestrial Curse.' Peaceful beasts turned violent, attacking the tribes, and enemies arose from the grounds and seas. Now focused on protecting themselves, the tribes' violence was directed elsewhere. But soon, the threats became too great, and the tribes were fast dwindling to extinction." He paced, his long legs taking slow strides. "Too ashamed to visit him themselves, each tribe sent a servant to King Nifal, asking for forgiveness and weapons. Instead, our gracious Supreme King breathed upon each servant and gifted their bodies with a special power to use against their differing adversaries. The servants returned to their lands as warriors and warded off their foes."

Someone in the back of the room snored. A greasy-haired boy's head lay on his desk, his mouth open and drooling. Preceptor Sage aimed one of his hands at the limpid flowers on his desk. The vase rapidly slid off the table and zoomed into the preceptor's grasp. Removing a handful of the flowers, he threw them at the sleeping prodigy. He jolted awake, his eyelids abnormally wide.

"Concentrate." Preceptor Sage set the vase down while prodigies laughed and then he continued pacing. "After rescuing their tribes, the servants were exalted as kings. These five kings formed a covenant of peace known as the Five Covenant, in which they promised to never use their gifts against one another. Then together, they revisited King Nifal.

Full of gratitude, they pledged allegiance to him and elected him as their Supreme King."

Ave lifted his head. "And in turn, he also breathed on five faithful Agaponians, giving them prodigious gifts and designating each to be a king's Sentry." He lowered his head again. Nuelle's shoulders sagged. Yet another reminder of faithful Amador…

"And from then onward"—Preceptor Sage motioned to the class—"the descendants of those five kings and Sentries would have prodigious gifts as well." He stopped pacing and studied the image, now displaying the five kings bowing before Father. "Six-hundred and forty years of peace followed the Five Covenant, but history tends to repeat itself, doesn't it?"

As a deafening silence smothered the room, Nuelle watched Father, smiling down on the kneeling kings. Yes, Antikai was a Kaimana once again stirring rebellion, but his was even worse. He didn't just envy his neighbors and covet what they had, he envied Father, his position, his power and authority. So rather than attacking other lands, Antikai attempted to slay Father and take his place. Ideya also rebelled, and who knew which land would follow next?

"Is Prince Nuelle the only one with amber eyes like King Nifal's?" the green-haired girl inquired.

Everyone's head turned in Nuelle's direction.

Preceptor Sage clutched the rod. It stopped spinning and the images disappeared. "Yes he is, but we need not discuss —"

"Why? It's not like he's King Nifal's only son." A confrontational tone colored the voice of a scraggly-haired blond boy seated in the back. His beady eyes challenged Preceptor Sage.

Light gleamed off the preceptor's irises like an agitated flame. "We will not discuss this matter at the present." He walked to his desk. "For the remainder of our time I want you to write down a few ways you can use wisdom to serve another. You have ten minutes, and then we will hear some of your thoughts."

As Preceptor Sage sat, Nuelle looked at the orange beam circling the Acumen. The dangerous ray grew brighter, as if sensing a threat. Father's visible territory sphere shouted a warning that if anyone dared touch the ancient book, there would be painful consequences. But was it just the information within that needed to be protected? Nuelle forced himself to remove a parchment and quill from his satchel. *I'm so close to finally grasping the Acumen myself and making some sense of all this confusion and disarray bombarding my life. But, I have to wait. So far, this place hasn't proved to be very safe.*

The minutes dragged by, and Preceptor Sage finally arose from behind his desk. He strolled to the front of the room and stood beside the stand carrying the Acumen. "Young man in the back, since you are so outspoken, why don't you be the first to share what you concluded?"

The blond boy grinned. "My name is Darcy Pennit, and I couldn't come up with ways wisdom would benefit others, but I came up with a couple of ways it could benefit me."

A few prodigies laughed. Nuelle's eyes narrowed. This prodigy spoke so arrogantly toward his elder. What was happening to this generation? Rarely did a youth speak this way to authority back at ho—the Supreme Palace.

"How unfortunate." The preceptor shook his head. "If you continue with that kind of attitude, you will never become a knight."

Darcy's grin faded as Preceptor Sage addressed the class. "The very essence of knighthood is sacrificial service. If you will not defend your people to the death, you will never become a knight."

The trumpet resounded, and the Servants swiftly gathered their satchels.

"Before you leave," the preceptor said, "collect a book from the left wall, fourth shelf up. Be prepared to discuss the first fifteen pages next class."

Darcy sauntered past him. As the prodigy neared the exit, Colden left his desk and approached. He whispered something to Darcy, and the two walked out together. Nuelle grabbed a book from the shelf and then strode to the spiral table. One of Lady Lovehart's lessons: trouble draws more trouble.

"Something isn't right about those two." Ave appeared at Nuelle's side.

"Whatever is wrong will come to light eventually," Nuelle answered. "We'll stay guarded."

Several prodigies observed the Acumen before leaving. The greasy-haired boy who had been sleeping during the preceptor's lesson glided to the other side of Nuelle. "Prince Nuelle! You're like, the prince of everyone right?"

"Yes…"

"Far off, sir royal-sir."

Nuelle glanced at Ave as the boy rambled on.

"So since you're like, super prince, you can do anything, like say the academy's out for a week—"

Nuelle smiled. "Or pardon a prodigy from home-study for a year."

"Yeah, exactly!" Greasy-hair slapped Ave's chest. "That's what I'm talking about!"

Nuelle spoke again. "And then banish him for being lazy."

"Hey, hey." He raised his palms and slowly backed away. "Wrath of the prince, sirs. No harm done." He turned and ran from the room.

The last remaining prodigy, a freckly girl, poked her finger toward the Acumen's orange beam. Preceptor Sage grasped her wrist. "I wouldn't do that if I were you."

She quickly retracted her hand and shuffled out the door. When only the preceptor, Ave and Nuelle remained, Nuelle looked at the Acumen, then up at Sage. "May I?"

"Of course you may." He stepped aside. "It has been waiting for you."

The book's magnetizing pull strengthened with zeal, its invisible pulses penetrating Nuelle's heart with a rush of warmth and adrenaline. He reached his hand in the orange light. The beam got brighter for a moment then disappeared completely. Nuelle lifted the heavy book, warm in his hands, as if alive. *Finally.* He traced his fingers around Father's protruding daystar-like insignia and then opened the mysterious book.

The Acumen

The principles of Supreme King Nifal, written for the obtaining of wisdom and guidance.

My son, may the light of truth guide your mind and lead your heart.

He smiled as he turned the page.

The Beginning

An age shall return when voices rage and fists strike against all authority. Restless souls shall stir unrest, and quivering kingdoms will collapse. Only in One does Zephoris' hope reside. But the Banished shall send Savage Shifters to hunt the One's life, and if Six do not rise to protect Him, all will be destroyed.

Sweat dampened Nuelle's palms. *The Banished? Savage Shifters? All will be destroyed?* He read on…

The Seven Covenant

My son, if I have sent you to retrieve this book, then know for certain the kingdom is in great danger. Enemies shall come for you, for they know you can become greater than all, and that you shall lead the Faithful to the land of the Incandescia. But if you are to succeed, you must choose a prodigy from each tribe who is willing to lay down his or her life, and when the time is right, a Sixth shall be added to you. Together, you will be called the Seven Sentinels.

The adrenaline coursing through his blood amplified, his heart now hammering in his chest. *If I'm to succeed I need to find five youths who are willing to die for me—technically six?* He glanced at Ave and closed the Acumen with trembling hands.

Preceptor Sage frowned. "Are you well, my lord? Your face has gone pale."

"I need to go. Fair day, Preceptor." Nuelle stuffed the Acumen into his satchel as he hustled to the door, Ave trailing.

"My lord!" Preceptor Sage glanced at Nuelle's satchel. "Make sure you keep it safe. And if you need me, I will be staying here for a few hours to study."

Nuelle gripped the shoulder-strap of his bag and nodded before walking into the barren corridor. He was destined to become greater than all? What about Tane? He was the first-born son. None of this made any sense.

"What did it say?" Ave asked.

"We'll talk about it in the tower." Nuelle rushed to the commons and up to the seventh floor. Being the second son born to a king, his position in life was never clear. Only one son is born to kings to become heir, and then his sole son would reign, and the royal lineage continued accordingly, ever since the beginning. So why did Father choose to create him and give him the potential to be greater than all instead of Tane? Did it have to do with his temper? Apart from that, he was a mighty warrior, well experienced with all his many travels to the various kingdoms. He was the most driven and assertive person in Agapon. What did he lack?

Nuelle hurried to the Tower of Advocacy and faced the large door with arched-top. To its right, a compartment along the wall carried a scroll. Nuelle snatched it and spoke to a hefty topaz stone in the door's center. "Prince Nuelle," he panted. The stone lit up, and the door opened. He and Ave strode into a large common room. Three giant, floating wood chandeliers alighted several worn couches near a grand, twisting fireplace. Sitting on a leather couch with Ave, Nuelle opened the scroll and read fancy cursive letters.

Prince Nuelle,

You are cordially invited to the celebration being held in your honor tonight at the seventh hour in the banquet hall. We will also be honoring Ave Purine, the son of Amador Purine, your great Sentry. May you both be pleased with the garbs left in your chamber, and Knight's Elect Academy looks forward to seeing you this evening.

Graciously,

Overseer Enri

Nuelle handed the parchment to Ave. That must've been what Enri meant by ending the day on "an exceedingly worthier note." But a celebration in the midst of everything that happened would only be an elaborate distraction. Besides, dance was taught to the Supreme King's sons, but neither of them ever mastered it.

Ave finished the scroll and then looked up with a twisted face. "A celebration?"

"That was my reaction," Nuelle said. He glanced around the empty commons. "Everyone is probably at the banquet hall for midday meal, but let's continue this conversation in one of our bedchambers."

"Over a quick meal. I'm starved." Ave jogged to the left and into a tiny kitchen with a miniature stone oven. Rapidly, he opened drawers, snatched seasonings, pounded and flavored dough and then tossed it in to bake. Nuelle smiled. All the years of cooking palace fare with Lady Purine had made his best friend an expert cook. Taking a moment to enjoy one of his dishes was worthwhile, especially after skipping morning meal so they could arrive at the academy sooner.

The bread finished and they carried it with them up a creaky, spiraling staircase. When they reached the landing, Ave and Nuelle scurried through a corridor lit by more hanging wood-chandeliers. Orange, glowing names inscribed closed chamber-doors: *Archin Appleton, Marketh Bindle, Ragne Dinks, Riff Hardy.*

Nuelle stared ahead. How could he ask anyone to risk his or her life? Even if he did bring himself to do it, apart from Ave, not many prodigies displayed their respect or support, but rather the opposite. His presence at Father's school was unannounced and scandalous, already shrouded with rumors of banishment and now the threat marring the main commons' walls. No wonder none desired to befriend him.

The last door in the hall maintained the inscription: *Ave Purine* and *Prince Nuelle.* Nuelle strode inside their chamber and shut the door. Ave closed a circular window to the left of a copper wardrobe keeper. Sitting on one of two thin beds, Nuelle opened his satchel and removed the Acumen.

Ave tore the bread in half and slowly sat beside him. The gold cover reflected off Ave's glassy eyes. "So…what did it say?"

With a tight grip on the smooth exterior, Nuelle opened it. "I'm destined to lead the Faithful to the land of the Incandescia, but I have to find five prodigies that are willing to die for me, and then a sixth will come. But if I don't find them, I'll perish at the hands of Savage Shifters."

Ave stared at the scarlet letters penned by Father, gulped, and then handed Nuelle a piece of bread.

"You don't have to be one of the five," Nuelle said as he took it.

"Hokum. You're my best friend."

"But if you died, your mother would be alone."

He took a deep, unsteady breath and then managed a half-smile. "Maybe I was destined to take my father's place."

That heavy, dull pain cloaked Nuelle's heart. If Amador was still alive, would he have wanted his only child to leave his mother, like he often had in order to keep guard over a prince's life? And then someday die in battle, too?...Nuelle frowned. "Would Amador have wanted this?"

Ave narrowed his eyes. "You're not going to talk me out of it, so I advise you stop trying."

Though his heart still hurt, Nuelle smiled. "I guess that means I only have to find four prodigies now."

Ave nodded, his gaze on the pages. "I've never heard of the land of the Incandescia."

Nuelle's eyes locked onto the mysterious word. "Me either."

"Then how can you lead people there?"

"Maybe my father reveals its location later on in the book."

"Maybe…" Ave's brow scrunched. "Has it said anything about Tane yet?"

"No." Nuelle tried to ignore the extra weight now laying itself on his already heavy chest. "Let's just focus on recruiting Sentinels. For now"—his stomach hollowed—"I just need to survive."

Ave exhaled as he brushed the crumbs from his mouth. "Good idea. We'll start at tonight's celebration." He strode to the wardrobe keeper and opened it, revealing a burgundy velvet-robe with silver trimming. An ebony tunic and pants hung beside it. He cracked open the window. Deep purple began darkening the sky. "We better don our esteem-ness. Close your eyes."

Nuelle chuckled as Ave grabbed the tunic, and then Nuelle closed the Acumen. Its warmth graced his fingers with a touch of mercy, almost as if it understood his grief…He returned it to his satchel. Day one at this new dwelling, thousands of miles from home, and so far, threats continued springing up like the Archery Ground's target dummies. Almost getting beheaded by Sir Dangian, then nearly exploded by Ichabod; the threat burned in the commons' wall, and now a warning about blood-thirsty Savage Shifters? Father had incredible foresight and wisdom, but why did his words seem to contradict themselves? So far, the Supreme Palace hadn't been an inkling as dangerous as the academy— apart from Antikai. But he'd been banished, and even Father said he was no longer a threat. If that held true, why in Zephoris would Father send his youngest son somewhere on the opposite side of the land? What worse threat could possibly dwell in the royal compound than the ones experienced thus far at the knight academy—and the ones to come? Could Father have somehow been wrong…or outwitted? But that was impossible—unless there lived someone greater…

Miraculously losing his appetite for Ave's bread, Nuelle slid the satchel onto his shoulder and approached the keeper. While Ave strutted about in his new garbs, somewhat parading his lighthearted, prior-to-mourning self, Nuelle donned his robe, hiding his satchel beneath it. Like a trumpet's distant cry of warning, Preceptor Sage's words resonated in his mind: *Make sure you keep it safe.*

Besides the crackling of wall-torches, the bottom of Nuelle's robe dragging across the wooden planks, and Ave's shuffling, a heavy silence quelled the commons. Silver light from the night star speared through the terrace doors on the left. Everyone must have already been at the celebration.

"We're making a bad habit of being late," Ave said.

Nuelle lifted the sides of his robe. "I wasn't the one who spent extra time on my hair."

Ave patted his smoothed-to-the-side bangs. "I wanted to look presentable."

"Forget about your hair, you need to control that eyebrow."

"One fresh-cooked meal from me, and it won't matter how much my eyebrow twitches." He snapped the collar of his ebony tunic.

Nuelle chuckled. "Yes—if you don't let your nerves cause you to mistakenly put in dragon-fire seasoning rather than dearling spice."

Ave winced. "Stop bringing that up."

Nuelle shook his head. "Poor Starlene couldn't talk for two months."

"One could say I gave her the opportunity to learn sign language."

"That's not what her mother said."

Weeping filled the commons. A pretty red-haired girl in Servant's attire scuttled toward the stone platforms, her thick curls covering half of her face.

"Hey, are you all right?" Nuelle strode after her.

"Sixth floor," she said, and the platform jolted upwards.

"Wait!" Nuelle ran onto a platform.

Ave trailed him. "Maybe she just wants to be left alone."

"Maybe she was injured. Sixth floor." At his command, the platform jerked into ascension. It halted at the sixth level of the Servants' Lodge.

The girl jogged to the end of the corridor and turned into another one. Nuelle raced through the hall, Ave at his side. They followed her into a short hallway. At its end, a large round door layered with dust stood cracked open, the girl's weeping flowing from within. Nuelle and Ave stalked forward.

"What's happened?" Nuelle said as they crept into the dark room. The door thudded closed behind them.

Ave flinched, but Nuelle took another step into the darkness. A chandelier in the center ignited a sickly blue glow, scarcely illuminating a chamber. Numerous scrolls overflowed barrels, and several ancient books occupied grimy shelves and lay in stacks across the floor. The girl's crying stopped.

"What happened to you?" Nuelle asked as he searched the room for her with his gaze. He stepped forward, knocking over a barrel of scrolls. Emerald seals kept the tattered parchments bound. As he picked them up, one of them unraveled. Faded cursive smeared in certain spots marked the scroll.

Great King,

I cannot shake these feelings of darkness around me. They are getting worse with each day that passes. I cannot escape the nightmare. It haunts me, even when I am awake. I am starting to believe it will come true, that I could become just as evil as…Him.

I have little confidence that I am fit to keep this task you have entrusted me with. If I fail, the cost will be too great, and I would not be able to go on, knowing my failure caused the prophecies to be unfulfilled.

Nuelle rose. The face of the cackling woman with glowing green eyes from his own persistent nightmare burned in his mind, along with her words: *You would give us your life? You caused this! Your existence has brought this death upon us and we all will die because of you!* Stomach churning, Nuelle held out the scroll to Ave. As he approached, the lights flickered, and a cool draft enveloped the room. The girl peered out from behind a pile of books stacked on a barrel. Her red hair ignited into flames, casting light on a purple eye. Somehow, the flames didn't burn her. She grinned as she tossed her flaming hair back, revealing a half-burned face. With her head still facing forward, her torso twisted to the side. The hairs on Nuelle's skin rose. The girl disappeared.

Something moved on the floor to his left near a pile of books—a shadow. He stepped back, dropping the scroll and clenching his satchel, hidden beneath his robe, as another shadow glided across the dusty planks, drawing closer.

"Savage Shifters," Ave breathed. A gust sent parchments swirling around them.

"Run!" Nuelle raced to the door as a pile of books collapsed from behind.

"Nuelle!" Ave shouted.

He turned. A shadow rose off the floor, shaped like a man —identical to the shadowy figures that morphed into Zagan and the men who attacked Amador. The shadow-man clasped Ave's wrist. Nuelle dashed toward them, but the other shadow shot up from the ground and blocked his path. It wrapped its legs around his body like a coil, binding him.

"Nu—" Ave's cry got smothered by the hand of a Savage Shifter. Nuelle opened his mouth, but his adversary's black palm gagged him. Two shining, ebony eyes watched his— hollow and cold, like its form. Tilting its head to the side, it lifted its free hand. The shadow's long fingers stretched toward Nuelle's heart. They expanded, their tips closing in on his chest.

"Master Antikai says hello," the Savage Shifter whispered with icy breath. Its fingers penetrated the skin over Nuelle's chest. He shuddered at the piercing cold.

The door burst open. Preceptor Sage charged at the shadow restraining Nuelle. The preceptor lifted his palm, and the Savage Shifter's arm jerked away from Nuelle and into the preceptor's grasp. Nuelle staggered aside while Preceptor Sage raised his free hand, the shadow's other arm zooming into his grip as if magnetized to it. As he twisted the Savage Shifter and hurled it onto its back, the second shadow thrust Ave aside and vanished. Nuelle scanned the area. Both had disappeared.

Preceptor Sage faced him. "Are you all right, my—" The shadows leapt out of book piles. One latched onto the preceptor from behind, while the second struck him in the face.

Nuelle front-kicked the attacker's back while Ave slammed a book into the other's head. It released Preceptor Sage and stumbled over barrels. The one still standing spun toward Nuelle. As he raised his fists, a warm wind stirred within them. He frowned at the strange sensation in his hands, and the shadow lunged. The preceptor magnetized its neck into his hand and then knocked the savage into a stack of books. Preceptor Sage looked at Nuelle. "Go, my lord—" A shadow appeared behind him and thrust an iron, sawtoothed dagger through his back—the same one Zagan killed Amador with!

"Preceptor!" Nuelle opened his fists, and wind surged from his palms, blasting the preceptor and Savage Shifters across the room and into a wall. As he and Ave darted to Preceptor Sage's side, the shadows disappeared, and the lights steadied. Blood seeped through the preceptor's tunic near his abdomen. "Help me carry him!" Nuelle grabbed his arm as Ave held the other, and they mounted him onto his feet. Resting each of his arms over their shoulders, they walked him out of the room. His head bowed as they rushed through the hallway, and blood spilled onto the floor.

"You're going to be okay," Nuelle said, his body trembling and mind flashing with images of Amador as he slowly died in the Onipur forest beside that beast Zagan. "You're going to be okay."

Five: The Challenge

I *should be dead right now. I should be the one lying in that room fighting for my life.* Gripping his satchel, Nuelle leaned against the rough wood of the Medic's waiting area. Death had stalked their lives and almost seized them. The prophecies were beginning to pass, and he and Ave barely made it out alive against only two of these Savage Shifters—the same ones Amador couldn't defeat. And Antikai sent them. Nuelle squeezed his fists as he remembered the last time they crossed paths—at home in the hallway. *The traitor must have somehow discovered what Amador carried in his rucksack and sent the Savage Shifters to follow us. Antikai apparently wanted whatever weapon Father gave to King Bertil, along with the Acumen. But why? And how can me and Ave stand against more of these savages if the Seven Sentinels have yet to be assembled? Could the prophecies be broken like the writer of the emerald-bound scroll believed?* His heart-rate hastened. *Wait. If Antikai sent these beasts, then he's alive… That means Tane hasn't killed him yet.*

Weakness struck Nuelle's knees. *If that traitor is still breathing, does that mean Tane is…No. He couldn't, he wouldn't…he was the strongest warrior in Zephoris. Wasn't he?* Nuelle clenched his fists and shoved the morbid thoughts away. Ave slumped into one of the wooden chairs lining the wall, his head in his hands, still in shock.

The door on the left burst open, and Overseer Enri skittered into the lobby and began pacing. "In my one hundred years as Overseer, nothing like this has ever happened." He turned his head toward Nuelle. "Please explain everything, my lord."

As Ave looked up, Nuelle pushed himself away from the wall. "On our way to the celebration, we followed what appeared to be a fellow Servant into an upper room. Then, after her hair alighted into flames she—"

Overseer Enri tripped. His eyes darted briefly as he continued to pace.

Ave's hands slowly lowered to his thighs as Nuelle scrutinized the Overseer. "Do you know the prodigy I'm speaking of?"

"In my time here, I do not recall any prodigy with flaming red hair."

Exchanging a quick glance with Ave, Nuelle took a stride closer. "I never said she had red hair."

Overseer Enri spoke as fluidly as his steps. "I must have misheard you. Do continue with the story of what happened."

"Then"—Ave rose from his seat—"the girl said you weren't a good Overseer."

Nuelle held his tongue as Ave continued his tale.

"She told us you were hiding something."

The Overseer suddenly froze. As his arms trembled, the color leaked from his face like rainfall washing away dirt. He sank into a chair and with remarkably slow words he said, "Her name was Edrei."

Ave watched Nuelle as he neared. Tears rolled down Overseer Enri's face. "Her ghost is haunting me because of my failure to protect her."

"From what?" Nuelle asked.

Overseer Enri drew in a lengthy breath, but his trembling only worsened. "Approximately twenty-two years ago, my daughter was a Servant at this academy. Her prodigious gift of flaming curls was the most powerful among her peers."

Ave and Nuelle exchanged another glance as the Overseer went on.

"Quickly, Edrei became the strongest in her combat class —much to the dismay of two particular prodigies." He sniffled. "One day, a pair of her male counterparts made lewd comments at her during combat. You can say she taught them a lesson that morning." He managed to smirk. "She used her locks as a whip and singed their pants, exposing their undergarments to all of their peers. A fight commenced, but both of the young men were quickly and shamefully subdued." His purple eyes peered up at Nuelle. "Jilt and Brone's hatred toward my daughter only grew as she continued to defeat them in training, and their peers continued to scorn. Until finally, on the evening she was proposed to by..." Now his gaze shifted to Ave. "Your father —"

Ave slowly sat down again, beside him.

"—Jilt and Brone snuck into her dormitory while she slept and..."

"We understand." Nuelle's voice quivered from anger.

Overseer Enri turned to Ave. "Amador fought so valiantly, the cowards fled and were never seen again."

As the Overseer attempted to calm himself with slow, deep breaths, and Ave slumped in evermore shock at the new information that included his father, Nuelle's anger only gradually intensified. Boldly and foolishly dishonoring a woman had been vile enough, but these men—no, these beasts—had somehow mustered such lavish evil that they were able to end a fellow prodigy—a fellow human's—life. They'd been savages long before their warped bodies displayed them so. And as if finishing a decades-old feud, they killed Edrei's once betrothed who scared them off the academy grounds. Nuelle's heart seared. *Amador Purine, that valiant and fiercely loyal man who would later become my Sentry, become family, and then die protecting me...*

"Those savages were seen again," Nuelle said. "After coming forth from their new abode, the Obsidian."

Overseer Enri swiftly straightened. "That accursed land?"

Ave nodded and then cleared his throat. "Edrei isn't haunting you. I made that part up." He frowned. "I'm sorry, sir."

The Overseer yanked his handkerchief from inside of his knitted robe and wiped his tears away. "But then how did you know about my daughter's gift and what she looked like?"

Nuelle sat on the other side of him. "Jilt and Brone are Savage Shifters."

Overseer Enri, with miraculous slowness, returned the handkerchief to his robe.

"I heard them say the Obsidian 'blessed them'," Nuelle continued, "and I think it has something to do with why they can warp their bodies."

Ave addressed the Overseer. "What I want to know is how they were able to get in here. Doesn't King Nifal have unseen territory spheres protecting the academy?"

"Yes, from certain dangers, mostly environmental. Storms, quakes and the like, but I presume not from such enemies as we are experiencing." Enri scratched his jutting chin. "Perhaps it is because all of these adversaries, including Icabod, were formerly Servants they are able to get past, but I cannot say for certain."

As he and Ave stewed, Nuelle recalled some of Father's final words of warning at the palace the night Tane left: *There are many lessons you will learn, not all of which will be easily comprehensible at first.* Why couldn't Father just destroy these savages himself? Why let them come for his son and harm others in the process? Certainly, it didn't make sense. More of Father's words trickled in, this time, from a conversation they'd had years prior...

Nuelle was only a boy of eleven years. He'd been sitting at one of the stone tables in the palace's Grand Library alongside Father, beneath the slowly revolving chandelier.

Blue and silver light surrounded on every side, for evening's stars shone through the windowed dome-ceiling, and many lanterns floated about, illuminating the three-floors-high of books encircling them. Before Nuelle lay an open history book on that first and last great, ancient war...

"After the Kin War of Old," Nuelle said, "when all of Zephoris had turned on itself and evil reigned, the people were almost destroyed, but you rescued them. If everyone was so bad, why not just start over?"

"Not all had forsaken love. There remained a remnant of those faithful to my laws. And had there been but one, I would've spared the land."

"But the tribes...they felt remorse after you made the terrestrial curses. What if they hadn't?"

"Then Zephoris would have been destroyed."

"And what would've happened to the remaining Faithful?"

"They would have another place to rest, where destruction and evil have no dominion."

Nuelle peered up at the second floor, where spectacled and gray Miss Salen, the library keeper, returned loaned books to their places on the shelves. "Father, if you built this land and these people, couldn't you just destroy all those practicing evil and keep Zephoris and the Faithful safe?"

"I'm afraid evil must run its course and drain itself, until it drinks its final dregs."

"But why let it get that far again?"

"For love is patient, and who knows until the last hour who might turn back from evil and return to love again."

As the old memory dissolved, Nuelle focused on Overseer Enri. "Tonight, Jilt and Antikai's Sentry came for me because of what I may become."

The Overseer's trembling returned. "Are you saying you are the...Young Prince?"

The Medic walked into the room from the left door. Crimson stained her pocketed dress, and her dark bun had fallen into a ponytail.

"How is he, Miss Alesia?" Nuelle rose to his feet, Ave and the Overseer also hurrying to theirs.

She wiped her sweaty forehead with the back of her hand. "He is stable, but still critical."

Ave approached, wincing. "Is he…going to live?"

Nuelle's heart hung heavy. What torment Ave must've been going through after again seeing that vile weapon, after seeing the beast, who killed his father two weeks ago.

Miss Alesia's blue irises, mirroring his, glistened. "At this point, I cannot say."

As Overseer Enri rubbed his temples, Nuelle's head bowed. An innocent life might die because of him, and who knows who else would suffer the same fate? He looked at Ave. His closest friend was his only Sentinel, and had it not been for the preceptor, both of them would be dead. "Can we see him?"

"He is asleep, but you may." She led them into the hallway on the left. They followed her through a wide corridor to a door midway in. Nuelle walked inside.

A dim, vital-monitoring orb floated above Preceptor Sage as he lay on a bed. The orb pulsed slowly; a reflection of his frail heart-rate. Splotches of blood stained the white sheets covering him.

Nuelle clenched his satchel, warm from the Acumen. He needed his other Sentinels—and fast. "Please keep us updated on Preceptor Sage's status," he said to Miss Alesia.

"Certainly, my lord." She bowed as he faced Overseer Enri.

"Regarding your previous question, sir, yes. I am the Young Prince."

The Medic gasped as Nuelle removed the Acumen from his satchel. "And according to my father's instructions, I need six prodigies willing to defend me to the death if I'm going to survive and eventually lead the Faithful to the place he's assigned." He put the book back in his bag and gestured to Ave. "I already have one."

Overseer Enri lifted an eyebrow at him before focusing on the Medic. "May you please excuse us, Miss Alesia?"

"Of course, sir." She scurried out. Once her pattering steps faded, the Overseer spoke in a low voice.

"I will ensure this academy is heavily guarded, my lord, that you may be able to accomplish what King Nifal has instructed you to do. And I will move you and Ave out of the Tower of Advocacy into a dwelling at the Staff Tower, telling no one of your new lodging."

"The move may help," Nuelle said, "but besides half of her face looking like an elderly woman's, one savage was able to imitate a prodigy, and both could turn into shadows so I don't know how much setting up a guard will do."

"You're right," Ave said. "We have to recruit the other Sentinels before they return."

"How about a challenge?" the Overseer asked. "I would imagine you want both willing and capable prodigies so I can send messengers to all the Servants' staff tonight, including the Squires' and Warriors' staff, and have all willing prodigies enter a challenge where you will be able to see their skills and choose accordingly."

"That should work." Nuelle's mind raced. The Squires and Warriors had to be much farther along in their gifts than the Servants were. And of all six-hundred prodigies in Knights' Elect Academy, he was bound to find four willing to be his Sentinels—four willing to die…

"We should do three games." Ave paced across the small room. "One should test skill, the other wit, and another strength."

"The games should also reveal their character," Nuelle said.

"I think I know where each should be held." Overseer Enri bowed and then swiftly straightened. His gaze latched onto Nuelle. "King Nifal suggested I take a leave of absence to mourn the loss of my daughter, but I refused. I made a vow to myself that never again would a prodigy perish under my watch. Tomorrow, you will have your Sentinels!" He scuttled out of the room. When the door closed behind him, Nuelle flinched as if slapped by the irony in the Overseer's words. He had no idea what he was aiding in…

Ave spoke quietly. "So the same men who…" He inhaled before continuing. "…Were at the Onipur forest show up here. They obviously want the weapon your father entrusted to King Bertil and now they want the Acumen."

"Maybe the Acumen has answers for something they're in the dark about."

"Or it's somehow a weapon of its own."

Nuelle slipped his hand into his satchel. It met the Acumen's sleek, warm cover. The item he carried was certainly no ordinary book. The territory sphere guarding it, the tangible power that emanated from it…Somehow, the Acumen was more. But what? Its heat intensified and sent gentle waves through his palm, like Father's touch…Comfort trickled into Nuelle's heart, but guilt warred against it. *Tomorrow, I have to choose four youths who might die for me someday.*

Hope dueled guilt in these vast woods. Dawning light rose over the orange forest, its leaves rustling with the wind. Nuelle gripped his satchel. Each step further into the dense woodland was a step closer to recruiting four Sentinels, enhancing his and Ave's chances of survival—and increasing someone else's chances of death.

About thirty prodigies with satchels, bow and quiver— most Squires in bronze mesh and Warriors wearing silver breastplates—communed in a clearing ahead, encircled by massive, twisting and intertwining trees. Nuelle frowned as he neared. Of 600 prodigies, not even a quarter of them desired to protect him? What had happened to the offspring of the brave generation past? Were there truly so few fearless and selfless in the land—or did that many deem him unworthy of protection?

As he, Ave, and the Overseer strode in their direction, some peered back and quickly bowed. The rest followed while Nuelle and the others stopped in front of the courageous group. One of them, a giant Gavrailian Squire, towered in the center, the sleeves of his tunic ripped off. Unlike his peers, he wore his satchel on his back, and apparently didn't bring a shield.

Nuelle gazed at the prospects, love's warmth already kindling in his heart, though guilt's icy fingertips clawed at it. He dug his boots deeper into the magenta grass beneath them as if doing so would squash the poisonous emotion. "As you can see, not many have answered the call. The cost of sacrifice is too high for most, but not for those of you who stand before me. Already, your courage blows stronger than this rising wind." He pressed a fist against his chest. "I am moved by your willingness to surrender all for the faithful in the land, to surrender all for me. Your trust in my father's words strengthens my hope that not all in our generation have bowed to pride and forsaken love. You standing here is evidence that love is still alive in Zephoris." The warmth strengthened, consuming his upper body and spreading to the rest. "No matter what comes, we will ensure that faith, hope, and love remain—even if we have to lay down our lives to do so."

The wind slowed to a still. The big Gavrailian Squire bowed a knee. Prodigies followed his homage. As though stirred by their respect, the breeze picked up again. Nuelle lowered his fist, the heat within simmering like boiled water ready to overflow. Yes, his Sentinels stood among these thirty, and before the day's end, he would have his four.

When the group straightened, Overseer Enri spoke. "As informed in the letter, your first test will be to determine your level of skill." He pointed ahead at several iris-fruit trees beyond dense shrubbery. The trunks spanned at least ten feet wide and a hundred feet high, and fuchsia fruits dangled from their thick vines. "The fastest to return with five fruits will make the best impression."

Squires and Warriors chuckled as they lifted their shields.

"Sounds easy enough," the big Gavrailian boy said.

The Overseer smiled. "Prince Nuelle, if you will do the honors."

"All right everyone, on my count." Nuelle raised his voice. "One."

They stooped into running position.

"Two." He, Ave, and Overseer Enri stepped aside. "Three!"

The crowd plunged ahead, some using their shields to smash through the thick patches of undergrowth. A blonde girl in long-sleeves effortlessly leapt over bushes and surface roots like a young graether. The wind hissed in Nuelle's ears. *Princess Sophana!* She veered to the right and dove over a small boulder while several prodigies latched onto tree-trunks and climbed over one another.

A tousle-haired girl holding an open umbrella emerged from behind an iris tree on the left. A belt lined her waist, over her tunic. After stuffing the umbrella into her belt, she slowly began climbing the daunting wood. As leaves rained on her umbrella, some nearby, rapid-climbing squires laughed.

Nuelle frowned. Having an open umbrella despite no sign of coming rain and ample shade from the trees was definitely odd, and why she didn't close it to make for a much easier ascent was all the stranger.

Arrows *zinged* through the shrubbery and slammed into numerous trunks. Some tree-climbers jumped off and crouched behind their shields while others hid on branches. Packs of eebons fired barbs from each angle—four of the creatures appearing alongside Nuelle, Ave, and the Overseer.

A set of feathered arrows whizzed by in rapid-fire, each hitting a different vine on the iris tree. The plump fruits collapsed on the ground in a pile. Nuelle looked toward where the arrows had launched from. Princess Sophana, crouched behind the small boulder, swiftly fired another shaft with her leather-gloved hands. Two more fruits fell atop the others.

"Whoa," Ave breathed. "She's smart and lethal."

As Sophana raced to the fruits, the giant Gavrailian boy, more than halfway up a trunk, reached a hand into the satchel on his back and removed a large stone. It turned into round, orange energy that he consumed in one bite. Arrows slammed into his back and then bounced off as if hitting a concrete wall. He smirked as he reached for a long vine and yanked. It tore off and he slung it over a shoulder. Then, gripping the trunk, he slid down, thumping to the ground near Sophana who rapidly gathered the fruits she'd shot down and then stuffed them into her satchel. After collecting the last of five, she sprinted in Nuelle and Ave's direction. Sophana halted before them and extended the bag to Nuelle. As he grasped it, Overseer Enri applauded, and Ave blinked, dazed by either her graether-like agility and skill or her undeniable beauty. Or both.

The Gavrailian boy dashed to Nuelle with his vine of iris fruits, but six eebons leapt in front of him, their arrows outstretched—aimed at his heart. In a sudden burst of speed, he swung the vine at the creatures like a whip, causing several fruits to fall off. The vine went through the eebons as if they were three-dimensional images. A giggling girl with blue hair and a colorful gem headpiece emerged from the shrubbery and rapidly collected the fallen fruit. While the boy poked at the mirage of eebons, the girl ran toward Nuelle.

"Hey!" the Gavrailian yelled.

The girl squealed, and the eebons in front of the huge youth disappeared. The boy bounded after her. They stopped in front of Nuelle. The glaring giant tossed the vine on the ground as the girl curtsied before dropping her fruits.

She threw wavy hair over her shoulder and adjusted her spectacles. "Don't glower, you had plenty."

Nuelle crossed his arms. "Collecting your own would have been more impressive."

She blushed as she looked down and Nuelle continued, only half-hiding a smirk. "But you are clever."

She quickly peered up, a smile spreading. The giant shrugged. "Slice me up with jagged rocks or put needles in my socks if I let her slight me again—which I won't."

The girl huffed. "You will be painfully proven otherwise."

"Painfully?" He grinned. "You part Gavrailian?"

"Not a drop." She turned on her heel and marched several paces away as the Overseer grabbed one of the fruits from the grass and the rest of the prodigies finally returned, scathed and breathless. "Shall we move on to the next round?"

"Wait," a soft voice panted from behind the group.

As they moved aside, the tousle-haired girl walked forward, umbrella still open and cheeks bright pink. With her free hand, she held a lumpy satchel. As several contenders laughed, she dropped her satchel atop the pile of others. A lean, greasy-faced boy poked at her umbrella. "If you're afraid of the rain, what makes you think you're brave enough to be a Sentinel?"

More Sentinels laughed. Nuelle stepped toward the fat-tongued boy. "Bravado and true bravery are two very different things. I see you've yet to learn that."

Silence captured his peers as he focused on the girl. "What's your name?"

"Elisena."

He smiled. "I'm glad you're here."

She peered at him with soft yet piercing purple eyes. Gaze remaining on him, she bowed, moving her umbrella aside. A warm sensation prodded Nuelle's chest, as if some invisible force attempted to melt the surface…and create an entrance. She realigned the umbrella and straightened.

The blue-haired girl grabbed Elisena's hand and gave a rapid shake. "Surta Ragnild. We have Courtship together."

"Yes…you're the one who somehow made Clindon look like a hideous beast after mocking me and Maylin."

Surta tapped her temple. "Merely an illusion presenting him as how he likely appears on the inside."

Elisena—and Nuelle—smiled. Yes, this girl was clever, and apparently a natural defender.

"So"—Ave glanced at Princess Sophana before addressing the Overseer—"where's round two?"

As Overseer Enri led the competitors out of the forest, Nuelle watched as Surta showered mysterious Elisena with bubbly chatter. She wasn't the strongest of the group, but to come here proved she had heart. She also emanated a sincerity about her that couldn't be ignored. And though her frame appeared fragile, deep inside there stirred a hidden strength that was almost tangible. What prodigious gift did Father grace her with?

Nuelle shifted his gaze to Princess Sophana as she strode on the outskirts of the throng. Her strength and courage were unquestionable, but if he did choose her, she'd have to explain her incognito presence at the academy and why Ludwig's Sentry tried to capture her.

As they neared a foggy river, the magenta grass morphed into mud. Red-and-yellow four-eyed swamp-leapers expanded their stretchy limbs and latched onto tree-trunks, while other creatures hissed and croaked from the shadows. Nuelle and the others reached the water's edge. The cool mist thickened, raising the hair on his arms. A purple creature covered with needle-like spikes paddled toward them, a twig stretched between two long top and bottom teeth. The stench of fish and moldy wood preceded it.

The Overseer stopped walking and faced the crowd. "The test of wit is next on the list. The first to crack three of the kastora's riddles and retrieve the item it needs wins."

The kastora wobbled out of the river, exposing webbed-feet and clawed-hands carrying a large rock. Its beady eyes darted to-and-fro at the prodigies as it held the stone closer to its belly.

Overseer Enri's palms shot up so fast the kastora and many of the prodigies jumped. He spoke just as rapidly. "We are not here to hurt you."

The creature scrutinized him. He motioned to the competitors. "They are challenging one another in wit. If you give us riddles, the first person to crack three will retrieve an item you cannot so you may continue building your home."

"Why didn't you say so sooner?" the creature replied in a scratchy voice as it dropped the rock. It stroked its long teeth, and then with a wide grin, stopped stroking and peered over the prodigies. "It does not run, yet its speed cannot be outdone. Mean it is, and mean it'll be. If you cross it while it's hungry, you'll soon see."

Surta jumped. "A graether!"

Brow furrowing, the kastora clacked its teeth. Elisena continued holding her open umbrella as she clapped. A few of the others followed her lead—including the big Gavrailian boy.

The purple creature hopped onto its rock. "Only two can look like these leaves, and when cut down, they too grow again like the trees."

Nuelle looked around while the prodigies stewed. Look like these leaves? What creatures in Zephoris had orange fur, or some orange attribute to them? And there's only two…but what two beings in Zephoris were able to "grow again" after being "cut down"?

"Prince Nuelle and King Nifal," Elisena said.

The kastora jumped off the rock while the competitors stared at Nuelle. Slowly, the creature scanned the swamp as though searching for another riddle hidden in the trees.

Nuelle's heart-rate climbed. Yes, he was called to the daunting task of being the Hope of the Faithful, but could he really be indestructible as well? And if he was invincible, why did the Acumen say in order to survive he needed six Sentinels? Death stalked close in the form of shadowy men who had nearly seized his and Ave's lives. Nuelle rubbed his heart. The Savage Shifter's icy hand almost made it stop beating. And what would have happened if it did? Would he have…rose from the dead?

The spiked creature continued giving riddles. Only a dozen or so prodigies had guessed at least one, and even fewer answered two—Surta and Elisena being among them.

Ave crossed his arms. "Such wise little creatures. I wonder if they can cook, too."

"I wouldn't be surprised." Nuelle stared at the kastora. Its riddles had only grown more and more complex and seemingly paradoxical. Surta impressively figured out a bizarre one about flying glowfish and winged skies, and even cheered for her competitors when they answered rightly, showing a supportive, team-like spirit. Sophana on the other hand, nearly punched a boy after teasing her the third time for being wrong. Surely, he could've used the busted lip, but it also displayed a lack of self-control and a concern for what others thought on her part. For someone who seemed so confident, and a princess at that, why did she care what a foolish Warrior said to her? And the giant Gavrailian youth unfortunately answered none, but stood cross-armed and dumb-founded the whole time. Though much to Overseer Enri's annoyance, the boy did shove the Warrior teasing Sophana into the water—and a Squire who kept flicking Elisena's umbrella. He wasn't the smartest, but he didn't stand for disrespecting women.

As it came to its twenty-second riddle, the kastora grinned, its three-inch teeth gleaming. "Like water, it brings forth both raging and peaceful waves, cold tides, and hot springs."

Nuelle rubbed his chin. Yet another paradox. What in Zephoris would cause such powerful yet contrary forces?

Elisena stepped forward. "The heart."

The contenders grumbled as the kastora plucked a spike from its rear and peered up at her. "Get me a massadon fang."

Many prodigies gasped. Ave looked at Nuelle.

The small creature pointed the spike beyond the river. "There is one asleep in a cave not far north from here." It handed Elisena its purple spike. "Use this for protection."

Nuelle turned to Overseer Enri. "I don't think the prodigies should go into a massadon cave."

"Me either." A barefooted boy in Servant's attire jumped down from a tree. The Gavrailian and a few others raised their fists as the boy approached. Orange leaves dotted his hair and clothes, and two fluffy white tawters clung to his shoulders, their bulging eyes darting. Did this wild boy belong to the academy or the forest? He approached Elisena, and a putrid odor like…tawter feces choked the air. Nuelle covered his nose while prodigies coughed.

Elisena's irises lightened. "Javin, what are you—"

"You are not going to do this, Elly," the reeking boy said. A thin scar lined his eyebrow and ran along the side of his purple eyes—identical to Elisena's. He stared at Nuelle. "No one is worth giving your life for."

Some competitors glanced at one another, others kept their gazes riveted on Nuelle.

"You are wrong, Brother." Elisena turned. A small, bronze, open clamp protruded from the belt on her back.

"I am not going to let you do this." Her apparent twin reached for her arm with a dirty-nailed hand. The two tawters dove off his shoulders and scurried behind the trees. The giant Gavrailian grabbed Javin's wrist, stopping him.

"Let her do what she wants," the Gavrailian said.

With his free hand, Javin punched the giant's stomach and then recoiled. "Let me go!"

"Sure." He tossed Javin, sending him tumbling across the ground until he slammed into a tree-trunk.

"Again, Riff Hardy!" Overseer Enri glowered at the huge boy.

"What? He's being a toothpick in the toe."

Elisena raced to the water, shutting her umbrella. She placed it on her back, into the open clamp jutting from her waist-belt. The clamp snapped shut around her umbrella, and she dove inside.

Nuelle clasped his satchel and sprinted after her as she paddled across. Ave and the Overseer called after him. He lunged into the warm river. Elisena reached land and dashed onward through the woods. Heart pounding, Nuelle swam to the end of the river and darted out of the water.

He bolted through the forest. Thorny bushes clawed at his garments as if purposing to slow him. He tore away, ignoring the bleeding cuts dripping down his arms. "Elisena, wait!" He stumbled over a fallen branch and then quickly scrambled to his feet. Thick gashes marred trunks, and torn branches the size of Sir Dangian dangled from surrounding trees.

Straight ahead, Elisena disappeared into the blackness of a large cave. Nuelle ran to the entrance. A breeze swept past, reeking of carcasses. Wind currents filled his palms as he stepped inside. A faint red glow pulsed on the walls, illuminating only a few yards in. Lightsquirms clung to the stone. Instead of squirming around, the small creatures remained still, as though too frightened to move.

"Elisena?" Nuelle skulked forward. If the beast was awake, it would have pounced by now.

"Over here," she whispered from the darkness.

His blood rushed. "We need to get out of here." He took another step. Something cracked beneath his boot. He cringed before squinting in the dim light. A thin bone lay snapped in two on the ground. Loud growling rumbled throughout the cave.

Nuelle raised his palms, hoping his wind power would work as effectively as it did against the Savage Shifters. Elisena backed into the light toward him, clutching the kastora spike and a large black fang. The beast that lurked in the shadows gave a few rapid sniffs. Nuelle glanced at the blood on his forearms. His wounds had closed...they were... healed? But the blood had yet to dry, making him smell delectable to the likes of strict carnivores. The sniffing stopped. He held his breath. The unseen creature grunted. Wind poured from Nuelle's palms, creating a hissing that reverberated off the walls. Only silence followed the grunt.

He slowly inhaled. "Let's go—"

Roaring boomed throughout the cave and a powerful gust blew against Nuelle and Elisena. They stumbled to the ground. An enormous gray beast stepped into the light, dried-blood staining thick fur on its face and neck. Black fangs like pillars protruded from the beast's mouth. Elisena and Nuelle's reflection consumed its huge three-pupil eyes. Nuelle jumped to his feet and pulled Elisena to hers. She still carried the fang.

The massadon stomped its front paws. Bones layering the ground clanked against one another. The beast sprang forward. Nuelle darted to the side and aimed his wind at Elisena, pushing her out of the massadon's path. Nuelle circled behind the creature. It spun around and charged. Nuelle rolled aside, and the massadon crashed into the cave's back wall. The ground quaked, knocking Nuelle onto his back. His head collided with the stone floor.

"Prince Nuelle!" Elisena cried.

Warm liquid seeped into his hair as the walls spun. His temples throbbed with pain. The massadon shook its head and jerked it in Nuelle's direction. It growled and then bounded toward him. The beast sprang into the air. Nuelle released a gust from his palms. It slammed against the massadon and it hovered over him, carried by the wind. Its gigantic head loomed above as it snarled, exposing a few feathery heads and a furry arm wedged between its back teeth.

Nuelle's stomach churned as warmth seeped into his aching brain. The massadon's blood-stained face drew close. Its mouth stretched open wide. Arms trembling, Nuelle forced more wind from his hands. The beast grunted and its large eyes crossed. Nuelle rolled out of the way as it collapsed. A purple spike protruded from its back, Elisena shaking behind it, still carrying the black fang.

Nuelle's headache vanished. He touched the back of his head as he rose to his feet. Blood covered his hand, but the pain had dissipated.

Elisena frowned. "You should see the Medic."

"I think I'm...okay."

She blinked at him while handing over the fang.

Nuelle smiled as he took it. "I knew you were strong."

Elisena blushed. "Sometimes."

"And humble, I see." He bowed before her.

"No need to bow, my lord." She touched his arm with a shaky palm. "I should be the one bowing to you. You didn't have to come after me."

He straightened. "How could I not?"

Her head lowered. "Your life matters more than mine."

"Pardon me?" He lifted her chin and peered at her. "Elisena, all life is invaluable. Especially one with a heart like yours."

That same stare which captivated earlier locked onto him. Her deep purple irises lightened to lavender, and a subtle pulse tapped the surface of his chest. He held onto her gaze. Why did it cause these strange, new sensations? They triggered an alerting reaction, but somehow, they felt... trustworthy. Even though it almost seemed as if some secret, hidden force attempted to enter his heart and—Elisena's irises quickly darkened, and the sensation dissolved.

"Elly?" Javin's voice echoed through the cave.

Elisena reached behind her back and pulled out her umbrella. "We're safe. The massadon is unconscious."

Javin ran toward them, and a powerful stench clouded the cave, overpowering even the carcass odors. Ave, Overseer Enri, the kastora, and only fifteen competitors trailed, all holding their noses. As Elisena opened her umbrella, Javin halted. His stare moved from the sleeping massadon to his sister. "Did you ..."

"Your sister is quite impressive." Nuelle gagged as he answered. "She won the challenge—and saved my life." He handed the kastora the fang while the remaining prodigies cheered—and most coughed. "And the others?" Nuelle asked Overseer Enri.

"They no longer desired to compete, my lord."

Nuelle frowned, though at least not all gave up. "Lead us to the final challenge."

Javin wrapped his arm around Elisena, but she wriggled out of his embrace. "Can you stop smelling like dung?"

"Don't despise the pleasant stench, sis'," he said. "It's saved you before."

The eye-watering odor vanished. Nuelle gawped. How in Zephoris could that wretched smell just dissipate? And what in the daystar did it have to do with saving Elisena in the past?

As Overseer Enri led them from the cave, Riff slapped Javin's back, making him stagger. "You've got one brave sister. You sure you two don't have Gavrailian blood in you?"

Javin grabbed Elisena's hand and sped away to the front of the crowd. While Overseer Enri skittered from the swamp, the trees thinned until only hills remained. Darkness bled into the sky, forcing the daystar's golden light to pale. Overseer Enri marched beyond the archery grounds and finally stopped in a broad valley. Spurting water shot fifty-feet upwards at random from a steamy lake ahead, spraying the group. As the hot water slid down Nuelle's face, images of Amador's prodigious gift raining on him and Ave in the forest stabbed at him. He winced them away. A few dozen vanaphs waited by the lake, their six, large wings expanded, and long necks erect. Bronze lances and body armor rested by the creatures' golden hooves.

Overseer Enri strode to a vanaph. "For your test of strength, you all will be jousting over the water." He glanced at the lake. "The last flying contender wins."

As prodigies shoved into armor, Riff mounted a vanaph and removed one of his rocks from his back-satchel. Again, the stone transformed into amber energy before he consumed it. He winked at Surta as she climbed onto a vanaph. She grimaced and tossed her blue hair over her shoulder. Princess Sophana kicked a lance up into the air and caught it before hopping onto a vanaph.

Javin grasped Elisena's hand as she held her umbrella and mounted a creature. "Please, Elly," he said. "Don't do this."

She pulled away and gripped the bronze reins with one hand. Nuelle rubbed his creased forehead. Why in Zephoris did she carry an open-umbrella so frequently—especially in times where she really needed both hands?

"Okay everyone," the Overseer said, "get ready to take flight."

Prodigies clutched the metal bridles.

"And…joust!"

They booted their creatures' side. The vanaphs soared above the spouting lake, several warriors already knocking Servants into the water. Riff took out a group of the older prodigies who had mobbed him, while Sophana bent backward and dodged the lances of two Squires while simultaneously dodging giant spouts. Surta rode beside Elisena. The pair extended their lances and knocked prodigies into the water. Three male Warriors charged from ahead of them, zig-zagging between multiple spouts. Six replicas of Surta and Elisena on their vanaphs appeared, flitting about the three Warriors, confusing the competitors.

A muscular Squire with a brown ponytail charged in their direction. Riff zoomed after him. The Squire closed in on Surta, his lance raised. He swung. Riff flew overhead, spun his lance, and knocked the Squire's helmet. He flung off his vanaph and into the steaming lake. Surta and Elisena smiled as Riff soared away with his lance extended, thrusting more prodigies from their vanaphs.

"Sovereign of all!" Ave pointed at Princess Sophana. She dangled upside-down above the water, her boot caught in the vanaph's reins. A spurt burst from the lake and splashed into her face. As she coughed, the vanaph flew higher, dragging her upward, away from the water and over solid ground. Ave jumped onto one of the creatures nearby and soared after her.

Within seconds, he swooped beneath the princess. He extended his hand. She peered over her shoulder at one of her vanaph's six flapping wings. Two of them whacked her, and she swung violently. Ave booted his creature's side and it rose. His fingertips stretched inches from Sophana's. Her foot slipped from the reins and she dropped. Ave clasped her hand as she hung from the side of his vanaph and then pulled her up and onto its back. Nuelle applauded and chuckled as his best friend and the princess descended. Surely, Ave's courageous rescue had to impress her more than his parted hair or even one of his epic recipes. Nuelle's stomach grumbled. Well, maybe not.

Only three competitors remained: Riff, Surta, and Elisena. The giant Gavrailian tossed his lance into the water and lifted his hands in surrender. The girls swapped looks before doing the same. Ave and Princess Sophana landed alongside Nuelle and the Overseer. Sophana quickly dismounted as the last of the fallen competitors swam out of the water.

"Well," Ave, flushing, said to Nuelle as Riff, Surta, and Elisena descended beside them on the grass. "I think you know who your sen—"

An enormous red dragon emerged from the lake, splashing hot water on the group. Gigantic spikes protruded from the beast's flapping wings and swinging tail. As prodigies screamed and dispersed, the dragon craned its head and bellowed fire from its snout, creating a circle of blue flames around them, closing them in. Wind consumed Nuelle's palms as he motioned the others to get behind him. Maybe he could blow this thing back while everyone ran away. The dragon swooped down in their midst, blocking out the daystar with its enormous head. Okay, maybe he could direct an airstream at its eyes to blind it for a few seconds instead. Javin walked by, a smoky odor of rust and fish surrounded. He stepped toward the dragon, his palms raised.

"What is he doing?" Ave asked Elisena.

She squeezed her umbrella with both hands, her lavender eyes rapt on her brother. As he neared the beast, its scaly brow furrowed. Its giant head lowered, and it observed the brave Sunezian. The dragon's nostrils expanded, while its scarlet irises thickened and thinned.

Javin glanced at Overseer Enri. "He says there's a princess around—that he can smell her royal blood."

Nuelle gawked as the prodigies exchanged anxious looks. Javin could communicate with creatures? His strange odors must have had something to do with it.

Princess Sophana paled. A strange, light blue tinted the skin on Ave's hands and forearms. "A princess?" He whispered as he looked at her.

The dragon roared. Prodigies shrank back. Javin wiped the water from his forehead. "He said if she doesn't come forward, he'll scorch us all."

The dragon tossed its head back and fire surged from its snout into the skies. Prodigies shrieked and ducked. The beast's tail whipped the ground. It quaked, and many prodigies collapsed. The dragon snapped its snout.

"Wait!" Nuelle ran in front of it, his warm wind whistling.

"Nuelle!" Ave yelled, the skin on his forearms and hands even bluer and somewhat … spongey. His attention briefly shifted to his changing body parts.

The dragon glared as Nuelle spoke. "You desire gold?"

Its avid gaze flitted to Javin. "He says your blood smells just as royal," Javin said. "In fact…even more so."

Nuelle's wind strengthened. "I'm Supreme Prince Nuelle, second only to my father, King Nifal, the Supreme Ruler of all Zephoris."

The dragon flapped its wings.

"My ransom will be"—Nuelle raised his palms, and a powerful gust burst into the dragon's face. The beast staggered, but then quickly regained balance. Nuelle swallowed. *That didn't work out as planned.* The dragon's clawed hand snatched him. He writhed and pushed against its tight, scaly squeeze.

"No!" Ave ran forward, his skin sponge-like and as blue as the waters of his home kingdom. He grabbed a lance off the grass. Green and blue coral spread onto the weapon.

Riff sprinted to one of the beast's wings and latched on. The dragon's head jerked in his direction as he scaled its limb and mounted its neck, punching its head. Standing upright, the beast flailed while Ave thrashed at one of its hind legs with the lance. Fire gushed from the dragon's mouth. It released Nuelle and spun. He smashed into a mound as Riff flew off the dragon and crashed behind a hill in the distance.

Ave darted backwards, and the raging beast stomped its feet. Its gaze locked onto Nuelle as he rose, his back aching. The dragon bounded toward him, snout opening wide. Surta darted Nuelle's way and grabbed his arm. Ten replicas of them appeared, each running in different directions. The beast's head swiveled back-and-forth in confusion. With another roar of fire, it spun in a circle, its tail swinging. The armored limb smashed into Surta and Nuelle's backs. Nuelle coughed out whatever oxygen he had as he and Surta dove face-forward, her headpiece soaring. Her illusions disappeared. Nuelle groaned, sharp pain spearing down his legs. The beast treaded toward them, and the ground trembled beneath its weight. Blue Ave leapt in front of it with his coral-covered lance raised. He chucked it aside.

"What are you doing?" Nuelle stumbled to his feet and scooped up unconscious Surta and her headpiece.

The dragon's snout stretched a few paces from Ave. He lunged forward, his spongey-blue arms extending ahead of him. Ave thrust them into the beast's nostrils. Coral sprouted rapidly, clogging the dragon's nose. Its head drew back, taking Ave up with it.

Nuelle propped Surta over his shoulder as the dragon lifted Ave a hundred feet from the ground. It shook its head, swinging him around. Wind encompassed Nuelle's hand. The dragon snorted, sending Ave flying backwards. Nuelle raised his palm toward him. Air streamed forth. It blew beneath Ave, preventing him from slamming into the grass. Nuelle stopped the airstream, and Ave landed on his feet. He grinned, his arms flimsy and stretching to the ground. His grin disappeared as the dragon's tail swiped around.

"Look out!" Nuelle yelled, just as the scaly limb smashed into Ave, knocking him fifteen yards away. With Surta propped over his shoulder, Nuelle ran toward Ave. The beast plucked the back of Nuelle's tunic with its fangs, ripping through his satchel's strap. The carrier fell onto the grass. *The Acumen!* Nuelle released Surta and her headpiece. The dragon lifted Nuelle off the ground. The beast's head swung back, flinging Nuelle into the air. His stomach lurched. The dragon's snout opened. Nuelle plummeted into its mouth and slid down its hot throat, blackness engulfing him.

"No!" Ave staggered to his feet, every inch of him sore from the tail-whip, and his arms still coral-like and over-stretched. *Nuelle can't be—he couldn't—it was just—he was just.* Ave's lungs tightened, and his mind spun.

Peering at the prodigies, the dragon sniffed rapidly. Fiona stood frozen with Javin and Elisena, their eyes glazed over in shock. The dragon exhaled against them. Their hair blew back, and a blonde wig flew off Fiona's head. Pink tresses flowed to her hips. Ave's heart skipped. *Princess Sophana!*

She tore off her long sleeves, revealing pointed, pinkish-gold leaves protruding from her arms. They glistened in the daystar's light as if wrought from metal. Sophana plucked one from her bicep and launched it at the dragon's face. The sharp leaf impaled one of its crimson irises. The beast screeched as its eye closed. Its tail whipped out parts of the fiery wall encircling the prodigies. As Javin pulled Elisena through an opening, the Overseer followed with the others. Riff limped to a dazed Surta. He grabbed Nuelle's satchel and lifted Surta off the grass. Blurred mirages of her and Nuelle running surrounded. They blended with images of him getting swallowed by the wretched creature. The projected thought stabbed Ave's heart. A wave of nausea churned within. *It did happen. Nuelle died.*

Surta pointed to her fallen headpiece. Riff handed her Nuelle's satchel and then grabbed the accessory. When she put it on, her mind-projections vanished. The evil dragon hovered above the ground, its wounded eye twitching.

Princess Sophana dashed to Ave and clasped one of his spongey blue arms. "Let's go!" As the princess pulled him, he stared at the beast that killed his best friend. He didn't even get to say goodbye, just like he was never able to bid his father farewell.

"He's gone, Ave." Sophana tugged. "We need to leave."

"Wait." Ave shrugged out of her grasp. The beast suddenly stopped flailing. Its scaly brow twitched. The dragon gave a long belch. It stopped belching and frowned. After another moment, it continued rising. Its wounded eye fixed onto Ave, and the beast zoomed his way. His body trembled with rage, hot blood pouring into his temples. He released a bellowing yell that stung his throat. The ruthless beast halted. With eyes now bulging, the dragon's abdomen inflated. Its cheeks rapidly swelled as its body grew into a gigantic ball.

Elisena, Javin, Riff, and a now fully-conscious Surta ran to Ave's side as purple blood oozed from the dragon's ripping scales. It released a smoky wail and then exploded. A thousand chunks of scaly flesh showered them. Ave wiped the thick blood from his eyes, vomit instantly surging from his stomach. He stooped over and released the bile. Now light-headed, he coughed as he straightened. Princess Sophana stood close, grimacing at him. He quickly rubbed his mouth and looked away.

Laying on the magenta grass a few yards ahead, one of the dragon's dismembered wings wiggled from underneath. Ave swallowed sour saliva and crept toward the limb. Princess Sophana and the others did the same. The wing stopped squirming. Ave held his breath. *No, it couldn't be*—the wing twitched again and then sprang backwards. Ave and the rest recoiled.

Nuelle stood before them, drenched in purple blood.

Somewhat dizzy, Nuelle peered at his bloody hands and smiled. It worked! The wind gift had been powerful enough to blow up the greedy beast! Thinking while in that gut-oven about all that would be lost if he died—remembering Father, Ave, Surta, Elisena and the other prodigies competing to be his Sentinels—love's warmth blazed within and somehow made the dragon's heat bearable, soothing even. Though breathing was another issue, the drive to live and fulfill his purpose overtook every physical need in that moment and strengthened the concentration needed to increase his wind. If foretold that the dragon would swallow him whole, imprisoning him in its rancid gut, rather than grind him to shreds, he could've gotten eaten sooner.

Beaming, he pulled in Ave for a hug and then proceeded to squeeze the rest of his new friends; Princess Sophana, Javin, Elisena, Riff, and Surta—carrying his satchel. None of them returned the sentiment; they just stood rock stiff, blinking at him.

Nuelle's heart skipped. "Did the others get away safely?"

"You're..." Ave gawped, his arms still spongey-blue and stretching to the grass. "Alive."

"Yes, thank Sovereignty. But the others, are they safe?"

Javin gave a half nod. Surta slowly handed Nuelle the satchel. He sighed as he grasped it, still heavy from the Acumen within. "You're amazing, Surta."

She pinched his cheek.

"Ow." He rubbed it.

"So this isn't my imagination." She slapped her thigh. "You are even more fascinating than the 378 books I read about you described."

Riff snapped out of his daze. "Smitten much?"

She whipped her blue hair back, tossing a scaly chunk onto his cheek. "I find many people with a decent amount of wisdom and worthwhile achievement fascinating."

Riff grabbed the scaled flesh and chucked it over his shoulder. "Well, this wouldn't be the first dragon I helped slay."

"For which I can't thank you all enough." Nuelle plucked a gooey slab of dragon-insides off his forehead. His best friend and the others—also covered in purple blood—had survived. But what if they hadn't? He looked at the mostly still-stunned-but-no-less-brave group before him. *But if you are to succeed, you must choose a prodigy from each tribe who is willing to lay down their life...* These prodigies had clearly done just that. They were the last contenders standing—with a dead dragon a few paces away. Even though he'd gotten swallowed several minutes ago, they apparently fought on and together, kept each other alive...

He smiled at the diverse and rancid-smelling group before him. "Seems like you fighters make a good team."

Six: The Setup

*F*avor *is surrounding us like a shield—mostly. Four Sentinels in a single day and it would have been all five if Javin hadn't flown away.* Nuelle held his satchel close. Apart from their looks, Elisena and her twin didn't share the same personality or view. After again pleading with her not to become a Sentinel, and after she again ardently refused—and Riff threatened to knock his mouth into his skull—Javin hopped on a vanaph and departed, leaving her behind. Nuelle touched his soggy pant-pocket where Brother's signet-ring still haunted. *Like Tane left me.*

He nodded at two silver knights standing guard outside Overseer Enri's office before following him and the new Sentinels inside. Ave's blue, spongey arms had at least shrunk back enough to stop dragging across the ground. An... interesting gift, but it proved useful. Nuelle exhaled as he closed the door behind them. He had more help now, but his enemies began waging a fierce war. Clever and stealthy, only two had attacked, and the damage one alone inflicted was devastating. What if there were more Savage Shifters out there? How many of them could Seven Sentinels—six at the moment—stand against if merely two had been that dangerous?

Overseer Enri sat behind his desk. Still stained with dragon blood, Nuelle, Ave, Riff, Surta, Elisena with open umbrella, and Sophana sat across from him and set their satchels on the floor.

"I am so very pleased you have found your Sentinels," the Overseer said. The back wall's spherical window revealed a dark evening with only a faint, silver glow from the stars, as if also wearied from the eventful day.

"I wanted to first thank all of you for believing my father's writings." Nuelle peered at his new guardians, his next words heavy in his throat. "I'm going to need you in order to keep the Hope of the Faithful alive, and to lead them to the place my father has chosen."

Beyond the purple stains streaked across their faces, determination and intensity shined through their fixed gazes.

"Your gifts and courage made a great impression, but"— he glanced at Princess Sophana—"we will need to train together so we are prepared for all future attacks."

"About training…" Overseer Enri folded his hands and gazed at the princess. "I was quite astonished by the revelation of your presence here at Knight's Elect Academy, your highness."

She plucked a glob of dragon eyeball off one of the sharp leaves on her arms as he continued.

"I received no messenger from King Redmond concerning your arrival, and it is my understanding that you somehow slipped into this academy unawares under a false identity, and this rather concerns me."

Nuelle looked at Athdonia's only princess, everyone following his stare. "Can you please explain why you're here?"

She kept her eyes down and pressed her lips together. Ave fiddled with his now only pale-blue hands. "We just want to make sure we can trust you."

"I did the challenges didn't I?" She glared. "What else do I need to prove?"

"That you aren't hiding something," Nuelle replied.

"I risked my life out there for you, Prince Nuelle. And you"—she addressed Ave—"I could have left you alone with that dragon as you stood there gawping at it, but I didn't."

Surta and Riff swapped stares.

With umbrella tilted and gaze locked onto Princess Sophana, Elisena brushed a frizzy strand of hair behind her ear. "Maybe she isn't ready to tell us why she's here." She straightened her umbrella.

Sophana frowned as she looked at her chest and rubbed it. The office door shoved open. King Redmond strode inside. His blond, silver-rooted hair hung the same length as Sophana's, and his fierce yellow eyes also mirrored hers.

She stood. "Father—"

"Sit down, Sophana."

She dropped back into her chair.

Nuelle and the others rose and bowed.

"Prince Nuelle." King Redmond lowered his head as the Sentinels took their seats. "What are you doing here?"

Nuelle pressed his palm against his satchel, warm from the Acumen. "My father sent me."

The king looked at Sophana. "I wish my daughter could say the same."

All eyes fixed on her. She lowered her gaze again.

"Of all the places in Zephoris ..." He stood at Sophana's side. "Have you no consideration for your mother? You worried her ill with your unannounced departure." His voice rose. "You disappeared for almost two weeks, Sophana. We began to believe you had been killed!"

A small frown twisted her rosy lips. "But I only wanted to —"

"I do not care what you desired to accomplish through your disobedience."

"But Father—"

"Silence, Sophana." King Redmond faced the Overseer. "My daughter shall be returning to the palace where she will continue her duties as Princess of Athdonia."

A tear rolled down her cheek as the King continued.

"Let us be going."

Nuelle spoke. "With all due respect for you as King of Athdonia and as Sophana's father, may I say a word?"

His wrinkly forehead wrinkled more. "You may ..."

"I don't know how familiar you are with my father's prophecies."

King Redmond raised his chin, his eyes squinting. "I am somewhat familiar."

"Well, I am the Young Prince, and I was instructed by my father to recruit Sentinels for my protection—"

"You are the Young Prince?"

Nuelle nodded, the others doing the same.

King Redmond raised an eyebrow at Overseer Enri as if to confirm the truth. The Overseer gave a nod. King Redmond refocused on Nuelle. "Go on ..."

"Today we conducted a challenge to determine who I'd choose, and I was taken aback by Princess Sophana's agility and precision—"

"If you are asking that my daughter become one of your 'Sentinels', the answer is a resounding no."

"But you don't understand—"

"Do not tell me what I do and do not understand, Prince Nuelle." His yellow eyes flashed with anger. "My daughter is a princess, not a knight. In fact, she would be married by now had not the people of Ideya lost their senses."

A few of the leaves on Sophana's arms quivered. "Because that is my purpose, right, Father? To be an accessory to a man!"

His mouth fell open as she continued.

"What I wish to do with my life is of no importance to you, or to mother, or to anyone for that matter."

"Sophana—"

"I would rather be unwed my entire life and use my gifts for something far greater than an arranged marriage."

"Not another word, or you will become a bride by tomorrow morning!" He turned to leave.

Sophana's words rang in Nuelle's thoughts: *Please don't reveal my identity, or something worse will come for me.* This must've been what she meant. An overbearing and overprotective father who wouldn't even let her speak. Nuelle stepped in front of the king, his heart-rate climbing. "Has my father not been a faithful friend to you? And did he not show you his foresight when he joined you on your search in the Aurora Forest?"

King Redmond's hard brow softened as Nuelle spoke.

"What my father has written—uprisings, kingdoms falling, wicked people coming for me—it's all being fulfilled, and if I don't have six Sentinels, I'll die, and the Hope of the Faithful will perish with them."

Silence overtook the room. Ave, Sophana and the others seemed to hold their breath as they watched King Redmond. He looked at his daughter. "What's happened to you?"

Sophana's lips pursed tightly.

The king's gaze lingered on her before finally shifting to Nuelle. His yellow eyes scrutinized as if searching beyond the surface. "How can I know my daughter will be safe?"

Nuelle peered back into this king, this father's face which shown full of concern. The answer sat in Nuelle's throat. If he released it, would the chains of fear bind them all, damaging their confidence, rather than strengthening it? He glimpsed over his Sentinels. Their stares latched onto him. Yet, fear was a force everyone had to face at one point or another. And that inner war needed to be won before they encountered their enemies again. "Everyone standing here today has risked their lives to save me. Beyond a doubt, their courage is one of the reasons my father invited them to this academy." His heart warmed with each word. "They are also uniquely gifted and dedicated to overcoming every challenge they face. We will train diligently to perfect our gifts, and if I'm kept alive long enough, Antikai and his savages will not be able to defeat me."

As the Season of Life melts away the Days of Frost, traces of anger dissolved from King Redmond's stiff frame. His tense shoulders remaining, he lowered his chin. He gazed at Sophana who still watched expectantly. After a long inhale, his stare returned to Nuelle. "For your sake, I pray your father was right about you." He turned to Sophana. "You think you are ready to lead your own life, so be it." He leaned over and kissed her forehead before striding out of the office.

As Sophana stared at the door her father exited from, a tear grazed her cheek, but a smile curled her lips.

"Well then." The Overseer removed a blue mangeen and knife from one of his drawers. "Would anyone like a slice of ___"

Riff snatched the mangeen and swiftly tore it in pieces. "My mammy's mangeen tree kept us nomads alive for a year until we got thrown out."

"Pardon me?" Surta said.

"Me and Mammy could take on ten men. But we couldn't take on eleven and a half." As he gobbled a chunk, he held out the rest.

"Thank you." Nuelle took a piece and then distributed the remainders. "Let's walk the girls to their dormitory."

"Escort the girls." Ave's eyes met Sophana's. He quickly looked away, his cheeks reddening. "Of course."

"Thank you for all your help, Overseer." Nuelle gave him a squeeze farewell and then walked into the hall.

Surta followed at his side. "You're rather…affectionate for a prince."

"To Nuelle," Ave said, "once you're a friend, you're family."

"I don't hug family members often." She frowned. "Perhaps I see them more as enemies than friends."

"Likewise." Sophana sauntered to Nuelle's other side. "I don't know how you managed to convince my father to let me stay, but thank you."

Glancing at Ave, Nuelle hesitated before answering. "We're glad to have you, although I do expect more answers from you soon."

She smiled as Riff set his bulky arm around Surta. Nuelle shook his head in disapproval at the touchy Gavrailian. Familial affection was fine, but after the wink he gave her earlier, the Sentinels needed to focus, not flirt. And when it came to young women, it was usually best to practice caution. After many of the palace maidservants started clinging to Nuelle after hugs and expressing romantic interest, he'd decided to rarely share embraces with girls around his age.

Riff quickly removed his arm. "I forgive you for stealing my iris fruits earlier. I'm not used to losing to girls—unless I'm playing dodge the boulder with my mammy."

Surta tapped her temple. "A wise person can conquer the kingdom of the mighty and tear down the stronghold in which they trust."

Riff huffed as he slapped his bulging chest. "Strength always wins battles. Gavrailians show best."

"And pride comes before a fall," Elisena said as they entered the commons.

"I've never fallen to anyone!" He marched into one of the worn couches. As it slid back, screeching against the wooden floor, he staggered.

While Ave and the others laughed, Nuelle mounted a stone platform. "Our enemies aren't just anyone."

His Sentinels quieted as they joined him. The green-haired girl from Wisdom walked into the commons. She halted. Her yellow eyes landed on Sophana, and then her face paled. She strode to a platform and hopped on. "Fifth floor." She glared at Sophana as it rose. Elisena shivered and reached back for her umbrella as if instinctively. She grasped the handle, but then released it.

Nuelle looked at the princess. She shrugged as Surta commanded their platform to travel to the fourth floor. Elisena watched the floor as Nuelle watched her. Eventually, she'd need to open up about why she always hid beneath that umbrella. When alone with her, he'd ask.

As Nuelle removed the Acumen from his satchel, every eye riveted onto the shiny gold book with Father's protruding center-insignia. "My father says Zephoris is in great danger. The Faithful in the land will need to be taken to a place called the Incandescia, and I'm the one prophesied to lead them there."

"The Incandescia?" Riff scratched the top of his head. "What's that, Prince Nuelle?"

"I'm not sure."

"Do you know where it is?" Sophana asked as the platform stopped.

Nuelle dismounted first. "Not at the moment."

Surta walked beside him, her big teal eyes even bigger behind her spectacles. "I've read 213 books on geography and never has my mind had the privilege of imagining such a place. Why do you suppose it isn't mentioned anywhere else?"

"I'm not even a quarter-way through this book yet, but I'm sure it will answer all of our questions." He slipped the Acumen back into his satchel.

Surta led them into a hall with garments of silk and rich purple pinned on the uncomely walls. "Now your father, what an amazing being. I've read 332 books about him and—"

"How old are you?" Riff scanned her from head to toe.

"How old do I look?"

"You can't be younger than sixteen."

"I will be seventeen in forty-one days."

"How do you find so much time to read?" He grimaced. "Being inside sitting for hours would be torture for my muscles."

"Who needs muscles when you have knowledge?"

"Knowing tons of facts won't help against someone stronger than you."

She snapped her shoulders back. "A wise man is strong, indeed, a man of knowledge increases strength, for by wise guidance you can wage your own war, and in a multitude of counselors there is victory."

He huffed. "Who told you that lie?"

Nuelle rubbed his chin. "I believe it was my father."

Riff's shoulders slumped. "I guess it isn't a lie then."

Surta tapped her temple again. "I believe your brain muscles can use the exercise."

As the group laughed, Nuelle nodded. "Surta's right. We need to focus on both reading and training. Our mornings will be dedicated to combat and strengthening our prodigious gifts, and our evenings we'll devote to reading the Acumen."

As she applauded and bounced, Nuelle gestured to Ave. "We've experienced what these Savage Shifters can do, and we must all be prepared to face them."

Riff cracked his thick neck. "When do we start training?"

"Tomorrow at dawn, on the mountain where the vanaphs dwell."

Surta and the girls stopped before a wooden door with a lavender stone in its center. "Surta Ragnild."

The door opened.

"See you then!" Surta bowed, Elisena doing the same.

Sophana's pointed arm-leaves curled inward and she hugged Nuelle. "Thank you again." She glimpsed at Ave before following Surta and Elisena inside.

Nuelle's face burned as he, Riff, and Ave walked back to the platforms.

"So Prince Nuelle," Riff said, "since I'm one of your Sentinels now, shouldn't I room with you?"

"That's a great idea, but tell no one of our lodging."

Ave stared at the floor as they mounted the platform, his bottom lip pouting slightly. As they descended, Nuelle whispered to him. "I don't believe she likes me."

"How do you know?"

"What's most important now is focusing all our efforts on sharpening our gifts. The less distractions we have, the better."

Ave gave a small nod—not a very convincing gesture of agreement. The platform jolted to a stop in the commons and they strode off, Nuelle leading the way. Already, both of his male Sentinels liked a girl Sentinel, and it was hard to blame them. Pretty faces captured the attention of most men, but these girls were even more than that, they were extraordinary. Thankfully, Surta didn't seem to share Riff's interest, but Sophana looked at Ave as if he were a watch and she couldn't stop checking the time. But for the group to operate at its highest potential, self-control was a must. Romance wasn't evil, but at the wrong time and in the wrong way, it could be devastating. Nuelle pushed open the terrace door and walked into the starry night.

Riff cleared his throat. "So, uh, I was just wondering, do you two think Surta likes me?"

Nuelle halted. The stars' light twinkled off Riff's eyes, making him look years more innocent than his rugged appearance suggested. Nuelle's gaze shifted between his Sentinels as he spoke. "A pure courtship is a noble thing, but do you really believe now is the best time for it?"

They both shook their heads. Nuelle smiled. "I appreciate your devotion. My father would be pleased."

"But to answer your question"—Ave smirked at Riff—"I know a woman who wants to stay single when I meet one so I'd give up now if you don't wanna get your not-so-stony-heart hurt."

"Thanks, hillock." Riff looked at Nuelle. "And I take it you don't plan on marrying anytime soon."

"It's honestly not something I spend much time thinking about."

Ave clasped his tunic by his chest. "Much to the dismay of every young single maiden in Zephoris—except Surta."

"And I'm sure there's plenty of young women who likewise desire to remain unwed, like Sophana expressed." As Nuelle continued leading them to the six-floor Staff Tower, fashioned from gray pebbles, Ave frowned. When they reached the huge entry door with a jasper center-stone, Nuelle stood before it. "Prince Nuelle." The reddish stone glowed. Slowly, the door creaked open, and he marched inside. His Sentinels followed him through the granite hall with vaulted ceilings sparsely lit by wooden chandeliers. Staying alert needed to become as second-nature to them as breathing. Though the Savages apparently couldn't imitate faces perfectly, they could shift into shadows, and there was no better time for shadows to manifest than at night.

He reached the end of the hallway where four knights stood guard by the giant stone platform. They bowed to Nuelle as he and his Sentinels mounted the elevation device. "Second floor," Nuelle said quietly, and the stone square rose, slower and smoother than the ones in the Servants' Lodge. The platform stopped, and Nuelle led them through the lengthy corridor. A wall-torch at the end flickered its blue light upon the ground, casting a jittery shadow. Wind consumed his hands as he and his Sentinels halted. Riff gulped one of his orange energy stones. Ave stepped closer to Nuelle. The shadow continued its fidgety motions, mirroring the pace of the crackling flames.

Nuelle's wind ceased. The shadows seemed genuine. He walked to the only door in the hall and stood before the great ruby stone in its center. "Prince Nuelle."

Light swelled inside the gem, painting their faces and upper body with its crimson hue. A lock clicked, and the door opened.

"This is pretty grand," Riff said as he followed Nuelle and Ave into the dormitory.

Ave closed the door and sealed it shut with two hefty wooden blocks. "Remember not to tell anyone where we're staying."

Riff kicked his boots off. "Shut my lips or bust my hips."

"Let me guess, a golden nugget from your mammy?"

"You know it."

Ave rubbed his hips. "That's quite brutal."

"That's why I love her." Riff slapped his cheek. "So where's this mountain sleeping?"

Nuelle gestured to one of two mid-sized beds against the left wall. "You can take one of those. I'll sleep in the cot."

"Are you sure, Prince Nuelle?"

"You're much bigger. I'll make do." He strode to the woven cotton and wood corner cot beside the stone fireplace. Through the only window on the back wall, a pool of silvery light illuminated the floor, jarred by restless shadows from the trees blowing outside in the wind.

"Who wants to keep first watch?" Ave said as he and Riff sat on their beds.

"I will." Nuelle removed the Acumen from his satchel and sat on the floor beside his cot.

"I'll do the second." Riff sprawled out on the mattress, his calves and feet hanging over the footboard. He didn't bother to take the rock-filled satchel off his back.

"All right," Nuelle said. "It'll be two hours each. And remember, starting tomorrow, our evenings are dedicated to reading this book."

"Can't wait." Riff closed his eyes.

As Nuelle opened the Acumen, Ave laid on his side and yawned. "Let me know what it says tomorrow."

"I will." Nuelle flipped the pages to where he last left off as his Sentinels fell asleep.

Darkness is like a disease. It infects slowly, often times unbeknownst to the infected. From evil thoughts it spreads to the heart, where wickedness and every lawlessness is birthed. Those under its gloom are blind; they walk and are unaware of what makes them stumble. Though they believe they are free, shackles bind their hands and feet. Though they think they are liberated, truly, they are slaves to whatever—or whoever—controls them.

With whispers of sweet poison, those who love darkness lure their victims, young and old alike. Using the lust of the eyes, the lust of the flesh, and the pride of life, they convince the unwise to follow their lead. The path they travel is the road to destruction. In the end, they all that practice darkness shall be burned, but the Faithful will be embraced by inextinguishable light.

Nuelle peered up at the silver rays shining on the floor, divided by the blackness of the tree-shadows. *That must be the Incandescia, a place completely void of darkness, a perfect place...like Zephoris used to be.* He smiled as he looked up at the dark-spotted ceiling above. The countless times Lady Lovehart had barged into his room without knocking, making him and

Mugro jump out of bed with racing hearts, and then scold them for not being up yet rather than apologize for waking them. Lady Purine never failing to amaze everyone with ever-better desserts on birthdays, which, having over four-hundred residents at the palace, happened often. The melodious clanking of busy chefs in the Grand Kitchen and the mouthwatering aromas that daily filled the entire first floor because of them. But the best things about home were the sparring sessions with Tane; watching him wield a sword as if painting with the blade, his fluid movements, swift, strong, and painstakingly precise. Learning from him, becoming more and more like him in combat; sharing the joy of mutual passion for training, for growing...

And then there were the many conversations with Father in the royal gardens. The poetic wisdom he'd share, sometimes orating at length, other times speaking less and listening more, asking questions as if he'd not only read your mind, but saw deeper into your heart than you yourself ever could. Nuelle closed his eyes and envisioned his seventeenth birthday when he and Father sat beneath the awning of twisting purple vines and red florets in the Plethora Garden. Fading amber life orbs floated around them, and in the distance, dusk's golden beams sank slowly behind the forest's massive trees.

"You are growing into the son I'd always hoped for," Father said.

Nuelle frowned. *What about Tane? He carries his responsibility as Supreme Prince with bold confidence and innate skill. Surely, he too is a son to be proud of. Isn't he...?*

Keeping his gaze on the woods ahead, Father continued. "What do you suppose pleases me most in my children?"

Nuelle lifted his eyes to the darkening sky. "Strength, integrity, courage, honor."

"Those are admirable virtues, indeed. But what is the greatest virtue?"

"Love."

Father smiled. "How you are willfully caring for the needy in Middren, even to the point of bodily neglect—that is what ignites my heart."

Nuelle chuckled. "Do I really smell that bad?"

"Your stench has preceded you lately. And Lady Lovehart complains of the 'ashen filth' you've been tracking the floors —and windowsills—with."

Nuelle's face burned. *So he knows about my avoidance of Brother. Hopefully Tane hasn't figured it out as well.*

The glowing amber orbs around Father blazed like his irises as they shifted to Nuelle. "A person can slay an army of ten thousand single-handedly, delivering the oppressed, and even offer his body to be burned for the sake of another, but without love, he is merely a polished tomb."

"But if someone does those things, how could they not have love?"

"It is easier to do the right things for the wrong reasons."

"But isn't the essence of love sacrifice?"

"Certainly, but what motivates the sacrifice?" Father asked. "The desire for accolades? A lust for exaltation?"

As the last of dusk's rays melted away and evening's purple darkness overcame, Nuelle nodded. "So ultimately, the sacrifice is for yourself, not for others."

Father rested his hand on Nuelle's back. "I trust that even when it seems nothing is worth fighting for, you will remember to love despite how you feel."

Nuelle opened his eyes to the Acumen in his grasp. He read on, taking his time with each scarlet-lettered page, each prophecy. So far, his survival had yet to be promised, though his enemies coming for him and his Sentinels was. Like fog in the morning, it seemed his life and theirs could vanish in a moment. The only glimmer of light had been the potential to grow in power. If his Sentinels kept him alive long enough, his strength would become difficult—and eventually impossible—to defeat. But that was the foundation upon which everything depended: not falling to the Savage Shifters before fulfilling these prophecies. His survival carried the fragile hope of many. His fate meant their safety, or their destruction.

He closed the Acumen and awoke Riff for the second watch. After returning to his cot, Nuelle clung to Father's book. Soon, the chamber blurred and faded. Blackness overcame...

Roaring thunder quaked outside. The floor quivered. Nuelle batted his eyes open. The Acumen rested beside him and his satchel. Outside the window, the mauve night had fled. Dark gray dominated the skies. Red lightning burst over a mountain in the distance—the mountain where the vanaphs dwell—the mountain where the girls were supposed to meet them! Nuelle shoved the Acumen into his satchel and scrambled to his feet. "Wake up!"

Ave jumped out of bed as Riff grumbled something and turned on his side.

"Wake up now! We must go to the vanaphs' mountain." As Nuelle dashed to the entryway, Ave and Riff hurried into their boots and then trailed him out of the chamber. They raced through the hallway and mounted a stone platform to the first floor. Nuelle sprinted to the Staff Tower entryway, he and the others' boots clattering against the stone floors. He lifted his palms and launched a gust at the doors. They flung open, and he and his Sentinels darted outside into the chilly morning. Darcy—the defiant blond from Wisdom—mounted a vanaph near the woods, the four knights who kept evening guard stood frozen like statues behind him. A sack lay over his shoulder. His gaze locked onto Nuelle, his eyes lilac and ... apologetic. He kicked the vanaph's side and flew away from the lodge. Another crimson bolt crackled in the skies— like the red spark from Colden's index finger after he'd said,

"There are worse enemies than fear." Nuelle ran through the moist grass toward the Archery Grounds' rolling hills.

"Who was that prodigy?" Riff asked.

"Darcy Pennit," Nuelle replied. "We'll find out why he fled after we get the girls."

About twenty yards away, two vanaphs ate from the magenta pasture at the edge of the highland. He rushed toward one of the creatures. The violent weather proved Colden had bad intentions.

Two Savage Shifters rose from the grass in front of the vanaphs. Nuelle and the others halted as pale flesh materialized on the shadows' limbs, mortal legs also forming rapidly. Loose, black bottoms ripped-off at the knees draped the men's thighs as similarly shabby garbs covered their torso and arms. On their right hands, they wore a metallic signet-ring with an onyx stone.

Nuelle's skin crawled. The exact same ring Colden wore on his right hand. Teal tufts sprouted on one of the Savage Shifters' head, while flat, crimson wisps grew on the other. Nuelle's knees weakened. *Jilt and Zagan.* Ave froze beside Nuelle as Zagan's cloudy blue eyes and half-sagging-half-tight face formed.

"We're sick of waiting, Prince," Zagan said. "We need the book."

Nuelle squeezed his satchel. Colden must have been assisting these savages.

Jilt smirked. "Allow me, Zagan." He vanished and then reappeared a pace from Nuelle.

Nuelle lifted his palm and released a gust of wind, thrusting Jilt backwards into Zagan. Riff grabbed a rock from his satchel. It transformed into the orange energy. He consumed it and charged, but both men disappeared.

"Where'd they go?" Ave looked around.

Jilt materialized behind Ave and locked him in a choke-hold before both vanished. They reemerged several yards across from Nuelle and Riff. Zagan appeared beside Jilt who shoved Ave at him. He grabbed Ave and unsheathed the sawtoothed dagger.

"Wasn't this one with you at the Onipur forest." Zagan raised his dagger and pressed it to Ave's throat. "Give me the book, or your friend dies."

Nuelle's hands seared as he gripped his satchel. He couldn't let these savages have the Acumen. Wind stirred in his palms. "No."

Ave's eyes widened. His forehead veins bulged and his nostrils flared. Nuelle's temples throbbed. He couldn't hand over Father's book, but allowing his best friend to die at the same hands who killed his father wasn't an option either.

A piercing squawk stabbed the air to Riff's left. Jilt stalked toward them, a metallic beak now protruding where his mouth was, and jagged talons replaced his fingers.

"Give us the book, or your friend dies now." Crimson fur grew on Zagan's face, and silver fangs protruded from his upper gums. Ave's own skin rapidly morphed to blue.

"Your coral!" Nuelle yelled.

Zagan looked at Ave as his body turned sponge-like. His hands expanded and he smothered Zagan's face. The savage stumbled back. Ave ran to Nuelle's side while Jilt leapt into the air. Ebony wings sprouted from his back, flapping as they swiftly enlarged. Hot wind whistled from Nuelle's palms. *Great, they have the advantage of aerial attacks now. They need to be separated.* "You two distract the foecry-thing," Nuelle whispered.

Zagan growled and sheathed his dagger, both of his arms now massive and beastly. He dropped onto all fours, scarlet fur replacing his skin, and dagger-like claws ripping from his left hand, matching the right. He pounced.

Riff side-stepped the attack and kicked the beast's neck as Jilt completely transformed into an overgrown foecry. Nuelle blew a gust at Zagan while Ave's arms stretched upwards and pulled on one of the foecry's wings, Riff racing toward it with fists raised. Nuelle opened his satchel and partially removed the Acumen. He grinned at Zagan—now entirely a scarlet graether-beast-thing. Nuelle dropped the Acumen back in the bag and dashed to the highland's edge. Thunder bellowed. Red lightning bolts circled the mountain peak like a barricade. A herd of vanaphs flew away from the mount.

"Look out!" Ave shouted from behind.

Nuelle peered over his shoulder. The scarlet beast gained on him while Riff uppercutted the foecry's beak. Nuelle looked ahead. His foot stepped over the end of the highland. Zagan crashed into his back, knocking him forward. He tumbled downhill. His shoulders smashed into the hard terrain with every roll. Graether-Zagan toppled downward beside Nuelle. He collided face-first with level ground. The beast landed a few paces to the right. Spitting out grass and blood, Nuelle staggered to his feet, his vision spinning, and body numb. Beastly Zagan shook his head and then jerked it in Nuelle's direction. He bolted to the forest, zig-zagging as he tried to maintain focus. He blinked away his dizziness and leapt onto a tree trunk standing as tall as the Servants' Lodge. Rapidly, he scaled it, his vision steadying. Warmth eased his body aches. Was he…healing again? He'd forgotten all about his cuts closing in the massadon cave!

Zagan howled—now at the tree's base. His claws dug into the bark, and he ascended the trunk. He jumped onto a branch. The tree trembled at his weight. Nuelle grasped a thick stem and mounted it as Zagan-beast leapt from branch to branch, swiftly rising. Nuelle reached for a higher stem. The Savage Shifter grabbed his ankle. With a tug, the beast yanked Nuelle down and slammed him onto a branch.

Savage-Zagan towered above. His snout opened, and his silver fangs lengthened.

Cold breath hit Nuelle's face as heavy paws pressed against his shoulders. He winced at the crushing weight. The beast cocked his head back, ready to sink his metal fangs into Nuelle's flesh. Zagan's jagged teeth clamped onto Nuelle's collarbone. He hollered as searing pain poured into his shoulder. The Savage Shifter's lips curled. Nuelle's blood dripped off Zagan's fangs. Scorching heat rushed through Nuelle's arms, surging into his hands. He clenched Zagan's brawny limbs. His fur melted, and he roared as smoke rose.

This is new. Nuelle tightened his grip. The heat boiled inside, bringing sweat to his brow. Orange fire ignited on the Savage Shifter's arms. Zagan stood and wailed as the flames spread to the rest of his warped body. The fire descended to his abdomen, engulfing the iron dagger sheathed at his hip.

Nuelle scrambled to his feet. Amador's murderer wobbled on the branch. Nuelle front-kicked Zagan's chest. He fell off the tree and plummeted to the ground in flames. Nuelle heaved. A blast of thunder boomed, and cold rain poured from the clouds. Thick water drops seared his gaping wound. Weak from blood loss, Nuelle clumsily descended the tree. Hopefully, Ave and Riff made it out alive, and the girls were still okay. And hopefully, his healing power would kick in soon.

As Nuelle reached the bottom, his foot slipped on a branch. He dropped forward and fell ten feet onto his shoulder. Fresh pain wracked his broken collarbone. Only a faint, slow pulse of healing warmth crawled through, as if weakened from the multiple injuries. He willed himself to stand. *I pray my Sentinels are in better condition.* His heart accelerated. *I pray they're still alive.* A few paces away, a metallic and onyx signet-ring sat atop a large heap of wet, green ash —Zagan's remains. He snatched the ring and a handful of ashes and hobbled out of the forest. A peal of thunder shook the ground. With his healing power still gradual, Nuelle could barely keep his balance. He'd never make it to the mountain on time at this rate. The girls could've already lost their lives.

Ave and Riff flew down on vanaphs. Nuelle beamed as they landed next to him. "Thank Sovereignty." His warmth quickened and strength returned to his legs. He hopped onto Ave's vanaph and took the reins.

"Are you sure you're fit to steer?" Ave asked. "You're covered in blood."

"I'm healing." He kicked the creature's side as Ave gawped. It jumped into the air and soared above the trees.

"Healing?" Ave asked.

"A new power I forgot I had."

"Interesting," Ave yelled above the rushing wind and pouring rain. His voice took on a weaker, nervous tone. "And what happened to…the beast who killed my father?"

Nuelle glanced back at his best friend. "He's dead." Unable to focus on Ave's reaction, Nuelle steered the vanaph toward the mountain. "What about Jilt?"

Riff followed beside them. "After I tore off one of his wings, he fled."

"Good." Nuelle leaned forward as the vanaph zoomed toward the mountain. It would've been better if the foecry savage had likewise fallen, but at least he was wounded enough to flee. Red lightning still barricaded the top of the mount. "Faster, boy!" As the creature quickened its pace, the chilly rain stabbed Nuelle's skin like shards of glass.

A lightning bolt crashed into the mountain peak. It crumbled as yet more bolts struck various magenta ridges. Massive boulders tumbled to the ground below, mud seeping off the mountain-top. Nuelle veered the vanaph upward. Surta, Sophana, and Elisena clung to clefts, their hands deep inside the sliding mud. He jerked the reins, and his vanaph swerved sideways, flying between two lightning bolts, Riff on his and Ave's tails. Nuelle tugged the reins, and the creature maneuvered upright again. It hovered over the girls.

"Everyone," Nuelle called, "grab a wing!"

They slowly wobbled onto their feet. A bolt crashed behind the girls. Rushing mud surged their way and knocked them onto their backs. Sliding muck rapidly dragged them toward the decaying cliff. Nuelle reeled his vanaph around just as the girls reached the edge. He and Riff bolted their way, swiftly gaining on them.

"Almost there!" Ave shouted.

Another bolt struck the cliff, and the girls tumbled over the edge.

"No!" Nuelle reached for them as they plummeted to the ground. Wind burst through his palm and blew after them, but the storm's gales diverted it. Ave's arm jutted and expanded toward the girls as they neared the bottom—twenty yards, fifteen yards, ten yards. With a shout, Ave's palm rapidly expanded. Sophana and Surta grabbed it. Elisena grasped Surta's legs. Ave groaned. The girls clung to his spongey hand, Elisena's toes an inch from the ground.

"Fangs of a furscrabber!" Riff shook his fists at Ave as he and Nuelle's vanaph descended onto the ground. The girls now stood upon it, still clinging to Ave's hand.

As Nuelle and Riff dismounted their vanaphs, Ave winced. "I think you ladies will be fine if you let go now."

Sophana released his flimsy blue limb first, chuckling as he sighed and rubbed his bicep. His arm shrank to normal much swifter than it had after facing the dragon. Nuelle smiled at him before addressing the girls. "Are you okay?"

Surta patted her headpiece. "I managed to trick Colden into thinking we'd fallen off the cliff so he fled."

"I see that accessory is more for just decoration."

She adjusted it. "My thoughts tend to cascade from my mind. This device keeps them in place." Her gaze lowered to his chest. "Thankfully, we are sound, but *you* certainly need medical attention."

Nuelle lifted his blood-stained tunic and peered at his collarbone. It appeared connected and the gash had almost finished closing. "Actually, I don't."

She thumbed mud off her spectacles. "But your tunic is soaked in blood."

"I can ... heal myself."

Everyone besides Ave traded wary glances. Something massive plummeted from above. Nuelle looked up. A boulder zoomed their way. Nuelle lifted his hands. The boulder bore down on them. A gust burst from his palms. Darkness engulfed. A crushing weight pressed on Nuelle's arms. They quaked with strain. He grew dizzy. Light appeared.

Nuelle's wind held up the rock, and so did Riff's hands. "We'll toss it on three," he said. "One, two, three!"

Nuelle exerted another gust while Riff shoved his palms. The boulder flew five yards away. Nuelle doubled over, while Riff merely panted. The cold rain pelting his back suddenly calmed to a drizzle.

A hand grasped Nuelle's shoulder. He slowly raised himself and peered at Ave, standing in front of him. Water soaked his brown hair and bronze skin. The memory of his similar appearance as his father's steaming spouts drenched them in the Onipur forest slashed Nuelle's heart. Tears rose in Ave's eyes, but they weren't sad ones. A smile formed on his face. Nuelle smiled back and then pulled him in for a hug. Though bittersweet, maybe Ave was right after all. Maybe he was destined to take Amador's place. And perhaps he wouldn't die doing so.

After Nuelle released Ave, Surta and Riff gave each other a bewildered look. But Elisena smiled faintly. "Thank you for rescuing us." Her smile faded. "But Colden still needs to be captured."

Seven: Prisoner

Clink. Clink. Clink. Metal boot-heels slapped the wooden planks dominating the Master Hall. Silver knights from the Squires and Warriors staff patrolled the Servants' Lodge. Nuelle peered behind at his Sentinels as he neared the entryway to the Medic's office. Overseer Enri had increased the guard and ordered Colden to be hunted and captured. The Overseer also alerted preceptors and knights to be watchful for any prodigies wearing metallic signet-rings. But there was no telling who lurked around a corner or in the shadows, awaiting their opportunity to pounce. The Sentinels needed not only to remain alert, but to stay together. When their enemies returned, they'd have a stronger force to face.

His gaze lingered on Elisena and the girls. Warmth pumped into his chest, enveloping his heart. How close they were to losing their lives—extremely close. Maybe having girls as Sentinels was a bad idea. Men falling in combat somehow didn't sting like when women did. There was a code—though voiced less often in the current state of Zephoris: the first to die defending the land would always be men, ensuring that the children and elderly still had the gentle hands and hearts of women to support them. Sophana, Surta, and Elisena displayed much courage and gifting, but having their lives just moments away from death brought a nagging prickle. If the light of their womanly beauty and nurturing essence was snuffed out in battle, it would leave behind an almost unbearable darkness.

Nuelle stopped before the Medic's office door and faced the three girls who had almost lost their lives. "Do you really think it's best if—"

"Oh no." Elisena touched her waist belt—her umbrella missing. Her body trembled as she closed her eyes and leaned against the wall.

Nuelle clasped her shoulder. "What's wrong?"

Surta and Sophana stood on either side of her, each grasping a bicep.

"Elly!" Javin, barefooted again, weaved around the marching knights and ran toward Elisena. A baby eebon holding a bow clung to his back, its long arms wrapped across Javin's shoulders where a leather quiver dangled. As he neared, a musty and milky odor swelled. Elisena sank onto her bottom, squeezing her thighs.

"Elly!" Javin dropped to his knees. "Where's your umbrella?"

Her trembling worsened.

Javin attempted to scoop her into his arms, but she pushed his hands away. He spoke more firmly. "Elly, you need to get out of here."

"No," she said through gritted teeth.

Javin shoved himself upward and stood, his fierce stare on Nuelle while the baby eebon hissed. "My little sister almost died this morning." He took a step closer, his neck reddening. "And now she lost her umbrella. She shouldn't be here!"

His truthful words tossed acid onto Nuelle's already stinging heart. "You're right."

Elisena's eyes opened and she frowned at him. He peered into her kind, tender eyes, shifting to lilac. "You shouldn't continue as my Sentinel." He turned to Sophana and Surta. "And neither should you two."

"Am I really hearing this right now?" Sophana chuckled bitterly. "After you convinced my father to let me stay? You knew what we were setting ourselves up against, and now after choosing us you want to throw us away?"

"It's not that—"

"It's because we are girls, and you presume we're incapable, isn't it?" Surta straightened, making herself a few inches taller. "You think we are too weak for this."

"No, not at all. You girls are extraordinary. But I want you to be safe."

Javin reached for Elisena's hand, but she recoiled. Still shaking, she slowly rose. Ave and Riff reached for her, but she raised her hands. Her penetrating stare bore into Nuelle, causing his chest to burn with the growing love he had for her, for all of them. "Since I can remember I have been ridiculed and outcast by almost everyone except my father and brother."

Javin bowed his head, and the baby eebon on his back whimpered as Elisena continued.

"But for the first time I was accepted, I was chosen, and not just by anyone, but by the second son of the Supreme King." Tears swelled in her eyes like a slow-rising tide. "You say you are the Hope of the Faithful. Well up until now you have given me hope, hope that I was actually born for a purpose. You gave me something to live for."

Though Nuelle's heart ached, Elisena's confident faithfulness somehow lifted it.

"I know I might die trying to protect you," she said, "but at least every second I breathe will have meaning."

Surta nodded rapidly, maintaining her erect posture, and Sophana held her chin high. Ave and Riff both stood with wrinkled foreheads, and stares fixated on Nuelle.

Javin peered up at Elisena, his irises glistening with the same lavender hue. "You can still train to be a knight, Elly. You can still make a difference for the citizens in our world."

"Maybe. Maybe not." Her tears escaped, cutting through the dried mud on her cheeks. "But if I stand by Nuelle, I won't just be making a difference for the people, I'll be helping to save them."

Javin sucked his teeth. "According to an ancient book his crazed father wrote?"

Nuelle's arms seethed. "Have you read his writings? Everything he's prophesied would happen so far has come to pass."

The baby eebon snapped at Nuelle as Javin replied, "Just because he's right about some things doesn't mean he's right about everything."

"I know my father well enough to know he can always be trusted."

"Well I don't!" Javin grabbed Elisena's arm. She squirmed and tugged to free herself. Riff shoved Javin. He collapsed onto his bottom. The eebon snatched the quiver from his shoulder and set an arrow to its bow and aimed at Riff. Nuelle and Ave stepped in front of Elisena as Surta and Sophana stood at her side.

Javin hustled to his feet, nostrils flaring like the enraged dragon they faced yesterday. The eebon growled as Javin glared at his sister. "I guess you're ready to die."

The Medic's door opened. "Prince Nuelle." Miss Alesia's stare passed over everyone before she quickly bowed.

Javin turned and stomped away, the baby eebon hobbling after him as he stomped past the patrolling knights. Surta pulled a damp handkerchief from her pocket and handed it to Elisena.

"Thank you." She smiled weakly as she grasped it and patted her tears dry.

Nuelle's palms cooled, and the smoke rising from them disintegrated. His heart ached worse as he faced Miss Alesia and gestured to Ave's expanded blue-green arm. "I've come to see Preceptor Sage. Is he well enough to speak?'"

"He is, my lord." As she turned and scurried ahead, Nuelle's stare passed over Elisena, Sophana, and Surta.

"We will continue this conversation after our visit." He strode into the Medic's office and followed Miss Alesia through a white doorframe into a corridor. Floating wooden orbs carrying flames illuminated the wide hall.

The Medic stopped at a door in the middle and stepped aside. "He might be asleep."

Nuelle nodded, and walked into the small room with his Sentinels, Miss Alesia beside Ave. She examined his expanded arm while Nuelle and the others approached Preceptor Sage. A bright vital-monitoring orb floated above him as he lay on a bed, reading a book. A mug of water sat untouched on a night table to his right. The orb's white glow pulsed at a steady pace; a reflection of his apparently normal heart-rate. His yellow eyes looked up and then widened as Nuelle and the others approached.

"It's good to see you are still alive," the preceptor said as he lowered the book. Father's daystar-like emblem decorated the cover; a copy of the Acumen.

Nuelle smiled while warmth permeated his heart. He leaned over and gave the preceptor a hug. He grunted.

Nuelle quickly pulled away. "Sorry."

"No apologies needed, my lord." Preceptor Sage glanced at Nuelle's satchel. "Is the book safe?"

"Yes." He knelt beside him. "But not without much effort."

Ave leaned against the night table. "The Savage Shifters attacked again—and a prodigy helped them."

Miss Alesia snatched the mug of water off the table and poured it onto Ave's overstretched arm. His sponge-like skin soaked it in and began shrinking. He gaped as she released his limb. "I suggest carrying around canisters of water." She scurried from the room.

Preceptor Sage slowly sat up. The ivory sheets covering him slipped off, revealing a bloody bandage wrapped around his abdomen. Nuelle winced, recalling how that heartless savage had thrust a dagger through the brave preceptor. "One of them is Antikai's Sentry. The other two, Jilt and Brone, used to attend the academy, and apparently, there's a fourth."

"Yes," Preceptor Sage answered. "All three were my prodigies. And I remember Zagan as having no human companions apart from his older sister. Poor girl was just as friendless as he was."

A rush of blood spiked Nuelle's heartbeat. "Was her name Raysha?"

He lowered the book to his lap. "Yes, it was."

"What do you know about her?"

"She was teased because she wore a veil, concealing scars that lined either of her cheeks. Their mother was vilely abusive." He frowned. "She and her brother often secluded themselves and traversed the woods, befriending creatures and beasts alike."

Nuelle snuck a glance at Elisena—the others also sneaking side-looks while the Preceptor proceeded.

"This book says these individuals' darkened hearts led them to live in the accursed land of darkness. After pledging allegiance to another master, they lost their identities, yet they obtained dark powers to transmute and teleport."

Ave rubbed his arm, now back to its bronze hue. "It seems they can only transform into warped versions of the true things."

The preceptor set the book down beside him. "I read today that the unnatural and continuous contorting of their bodies disfigures them, and that they are unable to perfectly imitate anything in this world. When they shift, it is always a warped version, like their hearts." His irises shined in the orb's light as he picked up the copied Acumen and read an underlined paragraph. "In the beginning of the Reign of Darkness, safety will flee the land. The Fallen Prince shall send Savage Shifters for the Young Prince before His power has fully matured. During this time, if six prodigies do not rise to defend Him, all hope will be lost." The monitoring orb's pulsing hastened, and Preceptor Sage's hands trembled. "Those who desire the Young Prince's life will discover that the Book and the Young Prince are one, and thus, in order to defeat him, they must destroy it."

Cold sweat slid down Nuelle's neck, his five Sentinels sharing nervous glances. Hush invaded the room as though death itself had entered it.

Surta wiped mud off her spectacles. "How can Prince Nuelle be one with a book?"

"I do not know." Preceptor Sage peered at him. As Nuelle removed the Acumen from his satchel, everyone watched. He traced the engraved cover with his fingertips, and the book emanated its warmth. That was why the Savage Shifters had been searching for it, and why it felt the way it did and pulsed with a powerful energy; it reflected that of his own. It was literally...alive.

The preceptor glanced at the door, his temples sweaty. "I assume these are your Sentinels?" he asked Nuelle.

"Yes."

"Where is your sixth?"

Nuelle slipped the Acumen back into his satchel. "He—or she—hasn't arrived yet."

The preceptor wiped the sweat from his face. "The Savage Shifters will not relent. They will be back for the Acumen."

Elisena rubbed her muddy palms against her pants. "Maybe by then Prince Nuelle will have his sixth Sentinel."

"Let us hope, for the fate of the Faithful depends on it." Preceptor Sage eyed each of them. "You all must protect Prince Nuelle and prepare. Train every day and let nothing distract you. And if you ever need me—once I am no longer in the Medic—I dwell on the fifth floor of the Staff Tower."

Nuelle's stomach churned. For his sake, yet another faithful citizen willingly risked his life.

The preceptor glanced at the door. "Be on the alert, for Antikai's followers are lurking around this academy, waiting for opportune moments." He clasped Nuelle's shoulder with surprising strength. "Don't give them any."

"We won't." Nuelle gripped his satchel. The Acumen's warmth brought a subtle yet strong peace. *I'm not going to leave my Sentinels unprepared and without a fighting chance. I'll do everything in my power to keep them alive.* He clenched his fists, heat rising within. *Everything.* He turned to Elisena and glanced at Surta and Sophana. "Let's finish our talk outside."

The door opened and the Assistant Overseer, Lady Bridie, bustled into the room. Her ebony braided hair stood on end, and her tunic's sleeves were torn and smoking. "My lord, we have apprehended Colden Ackerbus."

Frigid darkness had made itself more and more familiar, like a worsening disease or a growing blindness. Nuelle released a subtle airstream, lest anyone decided to attack as he and his Sentinels followed the Overseer through the tunnel. Their footsteps echoed off the stone walls, surely alerting the traitorous prisoner of their arrival.

A torch sputtered in the underground chill, across from a door with a barred-window and a silver-armored knight standing on either side. Overseer Enri removed a key from his pocket and unlocked the door. Nuelle and the others trailed him inside the large dungeon. Two more knights stood against the back wall. In the center, Colden lay shackled in a tub of pink water, his red-and-blue eyes narrowed. His dark, wet hair made his face appear paler than usual and though still not weak, he did seem more...lifeless. His head lifted. "How thoughtful of you to have the Supreme Prince come and visit me."

Riff spat on the ground. The corrupt prodigy smirked.

"Mr. Ackerbus." Overseer Enri folded his hands behind his back. "It is my understanding that you were the artist behind that vile display in the commons, and now you were involved in attempting to slay three prodigies—one of whom being the Princess of Athdonia."

As Colden chuckled, Sophana placed a hand over one of the pink-gold leaf-blades on her arm.

"So observant," Colden said. "Is this why Nifal made you Overseer to the Servants?"

Wind whistled from Nuelle's palms. "Have you no care for your life? You can be slain for what you've done."

Colden sneered. "There are worse things than death."

"Like the Savage Shifters?" As Nuelle approached, the water inside the tub stirred. "Or Prince Antikai?"

Silence overcame the treacherous prodigy.

"Redeem a shred of your honor and tell us what you know."

Colden shook his shackles, causing the water to ripple. "But I'm really enjoying this long bath in solitude. I can reflect on how ignoble I am and how much I or anyone else can care less about honor."

Nuelle's wind slowed to a hum. "You truly believe your lack of morality disappoints no one? You were invited to this academy by the Supreme King. Surely, he saw some value and honor in you."

Colden watched the water tremble above his palms. "Old age has made him blind."

Sophana tore off two leaf-blades and strode to the side of the tub. "Tell us what you know or I'll start using you for target practice."

Nuelle gently grasped her hand. "There are better ways to get answers, Sophana."

Riff punched his palm. "I'm sure I can make him talk."

"As much as he deserves it, one blow from you and he won't be able to say a word for days." Ave walked to Nuelle as he released Sophana's hand.

"He's afraid." Elisena left Surta's side, her gaze boring onto Colden. As she slowly approached, her trembling returned, worse than before. "Very, very afraid."

He glared at her, his eyes shining. "Get out of my head, fat girl."

She froze.

"Don't listen to him." Surta scurried to Elisena. "He is simply bitter because he knows his time is short."

Colden smiled. "Because Ideyans know everything, right? You people of great knowledge and little class." He concentrated on Nuelle. "How do you know you can trust her? Or any of these fools?"

Nuelle knelt beside the tub and removed from his pocket the handful of Zagan's green ashes. He held his open palm before Colden's face. The metallic and onyx signet-ring shined atop the remains. "How did you conclude you can trust a Savage Shifter?"

Colden swallowed. Nuelle looked through the tub's pink water where Colden's pale, chained hands rested on his lap. He still wore his signet-ring.

"Did they gift you that after you decided to align yourself with Prince Antikai?" Nuelle asked.

The water reflected off Colden's red-and-blue eyes. "What do you think?"

"I think it's a sad and vile display of your corruption."

Colden coughed out a laugh, his breath frigid.

Nuelle gripped Zagan's ashes and ring. "Why did Darcy flee?"

"Because he's a coward."

Sophana crossed her arms. "I only see one coward in this dungeon—and he's bound inside a bathtub."

Colden tilted his head to the side as he observed her. "You're rather rough for a princess. Somebody scrape up your tender heart?"

She lunged at him with one of her leaf-blades outstretched. Nuelle wrapped his arms around her and then groaned, her sharp leaves piercing his skin. Colden erupted into shrill laughter as Nuelle recoiled. Blood spilled from his limbs. Sophana dropped her leafy weapons and stepped back, her eyes wide.

"I knew they couldn't be trusted," Colden said between cackles.

Nuelle bit his lip, flickers of his healing warmth nursing his wounds. He addressed the princess. "Wait for us outside."

Sophana touched her arm where she'd plucked the leaf-blades and then strode out.

Nuelle exhaled and then faced Colden again. "Are the Savage Shifters recruiting more prodigies?"

"I don't know, but it looks like you're the one in need of more recruiting."

"He's lying," Elisena said. "He does know."

Colden growled. "I told you, get out of my head."

"I'm not in your head." She peered at his chest, and he frowned.

Despite his bleeding wounds, Nuelle managed a smile. So that explained the gentle, prodding chest sensations every time Elisena scrutinized: she attempted to read his heart. That was her gift. And her umbrella must have had a connection to it, which would also explain Javin's anger over it being missing. But for now, discovering what else headed their way took precedence.

Looking at Colden, Nuelle slowly twisted Zagan's ring. "This Shifter was named Zagan. We already know about Jilt and Brone. How many more are there?"

"There's one more." Colden shifted in the tub. "Raysha."

Surta gasped, her magnified eyes on him. She quickly shifted her stare to Nuelle. "I apologize. Please continue."

Nuelle's gaze lingered on her before shifting to Colden. "Who are they recruiting?"

"I don't know who's next on their list, but they recruit prodigies who show defiance or disdain toward authority— and you."

"When are they returning?"

"They don't tell us, they just show up."

Nuelle looked at Elisena.

Her irises lightened. "He's telling the truth."

Nuelle dropped Zagan's ring into the tub. "When you are tried before the king of your land, I will intercede for your life and request banishment instead."

"If Antikai allows me to last that long," Colden said in a low voice.

The Overseer gestured to the entryway. "Though you do not deserve it, there are more knights keeping watch right outside that door. They will remain there until you are taken to face trial."

"That's real comforting. Thank you, great Overseer."

Rolling his eyes, Overseer Enri turned and walked out of the dungeon. Ave and the others shook their heads as they followed him, but Nuelle kept his stare fixed on the twisted prodigy. How could Colden dread Prince Antikai and a group of Savage Shifters more than the Supreme King, the very one who brought life to Zephoris and built it from the ground up? Yes, the savages proved to be highly dangerous, but their power was not even close to Father's. The primary reasoning then for Colden's alliance had to have been his own corruption; a desire to rebel and assume power over others by fear and dominance, rather than by service and love. Nuelle turned away from the fallen prodigy who chose his own self-destructive fate, and strode out of the dungeon.

Surta scurried to Nuelle's side. "Remember that gasp I couldn't refrain as you interrogated that horrid boy?"

"Yes." He trailed the others up the underground stairwell.

"As I watched him, something ghastly appeared in my mind. A massive green beast with eight legs and a three-pointed tail like a giant fork."

"That's strange," Nuelle said as they walked outside to the edge of the forest. "Do you think it was your own imagination, or a memory you somehow saw in his mind?"

She frowned as they strode back into the Servants' Lodge. "I admit, my imagination is rather creative and sometimes nightmarish, so I'm unsure."

"Just tell me if it happens again." As the lodge's entry door closed behind them, Nuelle stopped walking and spoke to the Overseer. "Can I have a word with my Sentinels?"

"Of course, my lord." He bowed and scuttled off.

Nuelle looked at Sophana. "Self-control is the foundation of strength. If you lack it, you will be easily defeated."

She peered at his closing wounds. "I understand."

Then, he addressed all three girls. "And you understand our enemies are growing in number now that prodigies are working with the Savage Shifters?"

Surta glanced at Elisena and Sophana before speaking. "All the more reason to stay with you during this crucial time."

"And you also understand your lives are not promised you?"

"We understand," Sophana answered. "And I don't think that's going to change any of our resolves."

Nuelle held her determined stare. With her pin-straight posture and the jagged metal-leaves protruding from her arms, she appeared strong and confident, like an unwavering warrior. Surta tried to look the same, but with her magnified teal eyes and without the weapons, she couldn't pull it off as well. And Elisena. She didn't try to portray ferocity. Her lavender eyes were softer. They pleaded with his, begged that he would let her stay.

He opened his mouth, but Elisena spoke first. "We all understand what this costs, and none of us would have entered the competition if we didn't. I know how much this means to all three of our hearts, and giving us this most honorable position just to take it away is beyond devastating. And I understand you are concerned for our lives, but you should feel no guilt if we were to die, for this is our choice as much as it is yours so please, Prince Nuelle, let us choose for ourselves."

Though concern still pressed upon Nuelle's heart, the majority of it eased. Elisena was right. He wasn't alone in this decision of who would be his Sentinels. These girls had chosen to take on this role, were old enough to comprehend the sacrifice it entailed, and apparently, counted the cost worthy. They believed in him—they wouldn't have offered up their very lives if they hadn't. And now he had to choose to believe in them.

"Okay." He smiled at the three precious and courageous girls. "You can remain my Sentinels."

They beamed and bowed before him. Surta quickly straightened, her face glowing. "You won't regret it, Prince Nuelle! I'm ninety-eight point three percent certain of it!"

"What about the other one point seven percent?" he said as she strode ahead with Sophana.

She glanced back. "You must always leave room for doubt. It keeps you prepared for unfavorable outcomes."

Elisena walked at Nuelle's side as he stared at the back of Surta's blue-haired head. Her interesting answer reminded him of how Tane viewed things...

He turned to Elisena. "So you can read hearts."

Her face reddened. "Unfortunately."

"Why is it unfortunate? It proved useful when questioning Colden."

"Yes, but it was terrible feeling his heart and then hearing the thoughts that began to fester in my mind..." She rubbed her temples. "And not just his, but everyone's in the room."

Nuelle frowned. "You can't block out people's hearts?"

. "Not without my umbrella."

As they walked onto a platform with the others, Nuelle commanded the platform upward. "How does your umbrella work?"

"After one very bad experience at the marketplace back home, my father worked on it for months, trying to figure out how to make a forcefield I could carry with me wherever I went. I wish I knew how he did it."

Riff coughed as the platform stopped and rubbed his chest. "Do you know what I'm feeling right now?"

Elisena bowed her head. "Unfortunately."

Ave and Surta snuck glances while Sophana strode off the platform. "Well, I personally would like some privacy. I don't need someone nosing their way into my heart."

Nuelle stopped, the others following. "She can't help it. That's why we need to find her umbrella."

Ave scratched the back of his neck. "But Nuelle, we all just had a really long night. Shouldn't we eat something and then rest?"

Nuelle lifted Elisena's chin and peered into her knowing eyes. "I will speak to the Overseer and ensure he sends out a search party. We will find your umbrella."

"I sure hope so." Sophana marched onward.

As the rest followed, Nuelle sighed. The princess didn't understand that although she could try and hide whatever lay in her heart, eventually, a person's words and actions expose what is within. Her time for delaying secrets was coming to an end. In due time, whatever she hid would be revealed.

Eight: The Sixth Sentinel

I might die in approximately a minute or so. Ave lay on his back, quivering as Nuelle and Riff gripped his bluing arms. Sophana and Surta clasped his ankles, and Elisena stood nearby, carrying a pitcher of water. The daystar hid behind the clouds above the forest clearing where they trained, as if it too feared what would happen next. A chilly wind swept through the trees, worsening Ave's quivers. If only he could have one more puffle cake before he died; soft, moist, melt-in-your mouth, bursting with sweetness, pure goodness—

"Ave, are you thinking about food?" Nuelle observed the bluish forearm flesh around where he gripped. "Your coral-morphing will probably happen quicker if you try to focus and relax."

"My arms and legs might get torn off! I'd say that's a valid reason for daydreaming about puffle cakes and being a bit tense."

Nuelle's amber eyes pierced like a sword dividing skin and soul. "Do you trust me?"

Ave squinted at his best friend. He was so good at making people forget he was royalty, making them feel like family, like they were on his level rather than beneath it. But sometimes, even though it was rare, he'd say things and look at you with those bizarre amber eyes as if he held some unknown, ancient power over you. Ave pushed the supernatural thoughts away and spoke steadily. "Of course I trust you."

Nuelle smiled. "Good."

"I am tempted to see what would happen if we did tear off your limbs," Sophana said. "But I know Prince Nuelle wouldn't let us find out." The feisty princess's hair flickered and shined in the breeze like pink silk hung out to dry.

Ave tilted his head at her. "I'm not sure if you're more beautiful or scary."

"Focus," Nuelle said while the others laughed.

"Right." His trembling instantly eased as Sophana fixed her gaze on the trees ahead. Ave willed himself to concentrate. *Strange, blue, coral thing, take over. Uh, overtake me? Please? Now! Um...Waters of Kaimana, make me spongey. Oh, come on, Ave Purine. What would Papo say?* As if his father's spirit heard the question, Papo's strong voice spoke within. *Your gifts aren't just for you, son. They're for others. Use them for King Nifal first, the people of Zephoris second, and yourself last.*

As if responding to Papo's advice, his pores opened. Moistness covered his body, and his muscles loosened and became less dense. "All right." He forced a confident tone. "Ready when you all are."

"We've been ready," Riff quipped.

Nuelle spoke. "In battle, patience can also be the difference between victory and defeat." His words echoed a lesson his brother often taught.

Ave flinched at the reminder of Tane. The night he voyaged to the Obsidian was the same night Papo fell in battle.

"All right everyone, start pulling." Nuelle and the girls gently tugged on Ave's limbs, but Riff jerked, causing a painful tearing sensation in Ave's underarm and shoulder.

He yelped. "Not so fast, you brute!"

Riff's nose curled. "Kaimanas are so weak."

"Weak? I can wrap my arm around your bulky head and easily silence your mockery!"

The red in Riff the giant's irises leaked into his whites. Ave's face burned. Thankfully, he was currently blue, otherwise, his fear would be blaring from reddened cheeks.

"I wonder how easy it would be for me to pluck this spongey arm from your bony body and use it as a back-scratcher," Riff said.

Nuelle's amber eyes flickered like a kindled fire. "Are you Savages or Sentinels?"

As Elisena poured water from the pitcher over Ave's shoulder, his face seared all the more. "I'm a Sentinel."

Riff's grasp loosened. "I am, too."

"And that's why I allowed you to join me," Nuelle replied. "But your attitudes need to change soon. Our enemies have clearly mastered their dark powers. We must master our gifts —and unity—if we're going to survive."

Ave's coral-like skin grew back, closing the tear on his shoulder. "Okay. Keep pulling."

Nuelle, Riff, Surta, and Sophana once again tugged on Ave's limbs. His muscles and skin loosened and stretched. Surprisingly, no pain struck just yet. Nuelle and the others gradually stepped farther away. Ave's stomach knotted. Now, they stood five yards from him, on the edges of the clearing. A tingling pricked his expanded arms and legs. They chafed and stiffened, growing heavy.

"What's happening?" Sophana asked, she and Surta bending their knees to bear the increased weight.

"Good question." Ave locked his gaze onto Nuelle. "This is getting extremely uncomfortable."

"Okay everyone," Nuelle called, "carefully set him down."

They complied, and Ave attempted to raise his arms. He strained, the weight more than anything he'd carried in his life. His limbs lifted only two inches from the grass.

"Intriguing." Surta paced, observing his hard body. "You appear to be having the same reaction a coral would when out of the water. The drier your skin, the firmer it becomes." She stopped beside Elisena and reached for the pitcher of water. "May I?"

Elisena handed over the jug, and Surta paced again, pouring water along Ave's left arm. His skin instantly softened and lightened.

"Magnificent!" She emptied the pitcher and then scurried to Ave. Nuelle and the others joined her.

"So you're going to need to carry water with you at all times," Nuelle said.

Ave frowned at his right arm, still rigid. "Apparently."

"I can make you a water carrier!" Surta dropped the pitcher, kneeled and then stretched her arm from Ave's left shoulder to his right hip.

He flinched. "What are you doing?"

"Measuring you." She drew back and chuckled. "Your troublesome limb rigidity will no longer be a trouble."

Ave rose his torso to a slump. "Thank you. But"—he grasped his hard right arm—"I'll need more water so I can continue training with you all."

Nuelle removed a canister from his satchel. "Let's give Ave our drinking water, and we can refill them after the next training session."

"No need." Sophana removed three canisters from her satchel. "I brought extra in case he'd need it." As she opened the canisters and poured them along Ave's arm, nerves tickled his insides. Sophana actually thought of him when they weren't even together? And willingly carried extra weight in her satchel for his benefit. Could this frigid princess be warming up to him?

A strange sensation descended over Ave's chest, as if it peeled back, exposing itself...Ave glared at Elisena. Sure enough, her lavender eyes watched. He set his hand over his heart. "What do you think you're doing?"

Pink tinted her round cheeks. "Nothing."

"Except worming your way into my heart!"

"I'm not worming my way into anything. I can't help—"

"But be nosy." Sophana clutched her hips.

"Ugh." Surta placed her arm over Elisena's shoulder. "And apparently you cannot help being vicious, and I'm finding it more and more painstaking to believe you're royalty."

Sophana's leaves turned. "You want to see vicious?"

"Enough!" A powerful gust exploded from Nuelle, causing everyone to stagger. His eyes swept over them. "What did I just say about your attitudes?"

Sophana spoke again. "But—"

"I've heard enough from you!"

Her head bowed as Nuelle continued. "What are the most important laws in the land?"

Riff shrugged his bulky shoulders. Ave cleared his throat. The first time he'd heard the two laws above all laws was from the mouth of Papo. "Love the Supreme King with all your heart, mind, and strength, and love others as yourself."

Nuelle's amber stare bore onto them, one by one. He was doing it again, that eerie, presence-of-an-ancient-power thing. Was one of his gifts random intimidation? And was he even aware of it? "Choosing to defend me, even to die for my sake means nothing to me or my father if you don't love each other."

Sophana's yellow eyes gleamed in the daystar's glow. "How can we love if we've never been loved?"

Ave clenched his teeth to prevent his jaw from dropping. As beautiful and gifted and strong as the princess was, how could she have never been loved before? He glimpsed at the shining leaf-blades adorning her arms. Right, she was lethal and scary, and a bit temperamental.

Nuelle faced her. "You exist because you are loved, and if you can't understand that, I pray in time you will."

As she looked away from him, Sophana's leafy weapons drooped just slightly, as did her mouth. Ave hid a smile. Once again Nuelle pricked someone with his father's knowledge. There wasn't another youth who spent as much time with or enjoyed listening to their father more. It was strange, but nice, and more often than not, proved helpful.

"Prince Nuelle!" Overseer Enri sped across the forest clearing toward them, his long legs moving as swift as a foeery's wings. He held Elisena's umbrella. "We have found the lady's umbrella, my good lord!"

"Excellent!" As Nuelle and the others spoke with the Overseer, Ave inched closer to Sophana.

"Are all princes and princesses as paradoxical as you and Nuelle?"

She snorted. "No. Some are quite typical. Pampered, entitled, obsessed with themselves."

"Well-mannered, orderly, actually wanting to be heirs of a kingdom."

"I know, so boring right?"

"Well…I'm still trying to decide if I prefer predictable or lethal. And scary."

She chuckled. "Scary, that's a first."

Ave fake-gasped. "You mean everyone just sums you up as a beautiful princess?"

"Is turning into a fish your only gift, or can you see into peoples' pasts as well?"

"I think if I look deep enough, I might be able to."

Sophana bit her lip. "Then you'd better stop looking."

Ave ignored the hair-raising her comment induced. "What is it that you're—"

"Well! I mustn't take up any more of your time." Overseer Enri bowed. "Fair day, Sentinels!" He spun on his heel and skittered from the clearing and beyond the trees. Elisena stood under her umbrella. Ave forced his mind off of figuring Sophana out as Nuelle and the others approached.

"We still have some time before first lesson," Nuelle said. "Let's work on combat."

Time had been graceful this morning. The daystar finally began brightening over the clearing, giving them ample time to train. Nuelle gulped down the rest of his canister while the others finished theirs. After a few more backbites between Riff and Ave, Riff and Surta, and Surta and Sophana, the group also finally managed to maintain civility for an hour. Surta even accomplished making Sophana laugh after spooking Riff with a mind-projection of himself who kept appearing at random and tapping him on the shoulder. And Ave, "muscled a mound of respect," from Riff after coiling his extra-long sponge-limbs around him for an entire minute before breaking free. But Elisena's training hurt the most. While everyone thought of memories or people that angered or scared them, she had to practice enduring the toxicity without her umbrella. She collapsed the first four times, but eventually mustered the fortitude to stand for an entire minute, to which everyone applauded.

Nuelle slipped his now empty canister into his bag. "There's still time for two more rounds of combat training."

"With pleasure." Riff lifted a fallen branch from the ground—thicker than both of his burly arms combined—and broke it in half. "You need to build strength and stamina." He pointed a branch at a massive stone about twelve yards away.

"I want all of you to run to that boulder, climb it, run back and then punch my palms—one punch with each arm—ten times in a row." He tossed the chunks of wood aside. "Starting ... now!"

Nuelle and Ave plunged ahead. They scaled the boulder in seconds and ran to Riff again, throwing swift punches in his palms before returning to the giant rock.

"Nice job, Ave!" Riff called after him. "You hit harder than I thought you would!"

Nuelle looked over his shoulder. Sophana and Surta ran close behind, but with her open umbrella, Elisena lagged. Facing the stony obstacle, Nuelle gripped the rock and climbed. He reached the top and dismounted quicker than his first time. In seconds, he sprinted toward Riff, passing Elisena on his way. Sweat dampened her hair-line, and her cheeks splotched red, but she pushed onward, staring at the boulder. Nuelle smiled as he faced ahead. Her quiet determination was inspiring—and remarkable after all the emotional toil and draining she endured earlier. She'd been a prize pick for a Sentinel. They all were...Nuelle stood before Riff and struck his palms.

"Nice, your highness. That actually stung a little."

As Nuelle dashed to the boulder, Elisena trudged toward Riff. Nuelle smiled at the strong-minded girl. "You can do it. I believe in you."

Her mouth lifted. She hurried to Riff with a boost of energy. When Nuelle reached the rock, he ascended with ease, his grip stronger since his palms had calloused. He jumped off and rolled when he landed, then leapt onto his feet and continued to Riff, Ave trailing. Nuelle came to his final round. Somehow, his heart-rate remained at a steady pace, even as he threw his last punches into Riff's palms. Whether because of his healing ability or Tane's arduous training wasn't clear...Ave finished next, then Sophana and Surta. Elisena completed her final climb and plodded to Riff.

"You're doing great, Elisena," Nuelle called. "Don't give up."

She wheezed as she stood before the big Gavrailian. Taking a deep breath, she tapped his palms. As she rejoined the others, Nuelle asked, "Are you okay?"

She nodded, her irises light.

"You sure?"

Elisena smiled weakly. "I'll be fine."

"All right"—Riff faced the group—"let's do some leg-work now." He assigned partners to practice kicking and dodging blows. After everyone completed eight sets, the trumpet for first lesson bellowed.

Nuelle clasped his satchel as his Sentinels gathered theirs. "You all did great today. Remember who is walking who to first lesson, and we'll meet after third—" The branches above shook. As leaves fell onto his shoulders, he looked up, everyone following his stare. Several pairs of thirsty silver eyes watched. He and his Sentinels froze. Low growls emerged through the leaves.

Elisena whispered, "Graethers."

Nuelle glanced at the others. "Everyone, stay still—"

"Run!" Surta shouted, bolting through the forest. Riff, Sophana, and Elisena followed, shutting her umbrella.

"This was not part of the plan!" Nuelle sprinted after them, Ave at his side, and then peered back. Flashes of large silver-furred bodies with knife-like claws leapt from tree to tree. He and the others raced through the undergrowth. Everything blurred around him. He jumped over surface roots. Thorns scratched his face. While he dashed ahead, a rushing sound like cascading waters grew. *Oh no.* Nuelle dug his heels into moist dirt, stopping behind Ave, Sophana, and Surta. Ahead of the group, Riff extended his arms, preventing them all from following a waterfall off a cliff.

"Where's Elisena?" Nuelle asked.

Surta gasped. "Right behind you!"

He looked back. Elisena darted his way, six graethers leaping into the trees—right on her tail. She crashed into him. Riff lost his footing. All of them toppled over the cliff as the graethers halted at the edge.

Nuelle and the others fell through the rushing water. His stomach lurched. He plummeted into the river below. He twirled beneath violent, crushing waves. His head spun as he thrashed his arms to escape. He swam under the pounding water and to the surface. Breaking through, he coughed out liquid and blinked away dizziness.

The graethers glared down at them from the plateau. With a deafening howl from their long snouts, they dug their claws into the cliff and began descending alongside the waterfall. Riff busted above the surface, Surta, and Elisena in each arm. Ave appeared on his left, Sophana beside him. A cave lay beyond the waterfall.

"Everyone, get underwater and swim into the cave!" Nuelle dunked and swam through the cascading water. His knees quickly scraped solid ground. Planting his feet, he rose above the surface and rushed into the small cave, his Sentinels trailing. He signaled everyone to go against the back wall. As the howling neared, his heart pounded. If they all just remained still and didn't make a noise, they could possibly get out alive.

The howls stopped. Nuelle glanced over his trembling Sentinels and held his finger to his lips, signaling silence. His beating heart now banged in his eardrums. Their scents had probably been washed away by the river so if they waited quietly, the graethers should eventually move on—six graethers leapt through the waterfall and landed two yards across from them with loud thuds. A graether in the center, larger than the rest, growled.

Nuelle and his friends pressed themselves more into the rear wall. The carnivorous beast curled its lips back, flaunting bloody silver fangs as the other graethers shook water off their thick coats. The giant pack-leader crept forward. As it and the rest advanced, their large gray shoulders rose and fell, and their wet paws smacked the ground. A few of their long, black tongues lapped at the sides of their snouts, anxious for a taste of blood. Nuelle stood in front of his Sentinels. The graethers snarled in unison like a violent song. Their fangs grew longer, preparing for the hearty meal. Wind filled Nuelle's palms. The creatures' snouts opened. He slowly raised his hands.

The beasts' heads veered back. The graether in the center ducked. Six kastora spikes pierced through the waterfall and stabbed five of the graethers, but the sixth flew over the giant in the middle. The spike sped toward Nuelle's face. Riff reached his hand in front of Nuelle's head. The spike bounced of his palm as if hitting a rock wall.

"Thanks," Nuelle said as the five struck-graethers swayed and then collapsed unconscious.

A stench of moldy wood and fish permeated the cave. Javin walked through the cascading water, a kastora on either side of him. Elisena gasped. Javin's gaze locked onto the last graether standing. Its throat rumbled, taunting him.

"Javin, move!" Nuelle released a gust at the graether as Javin jumped aside. The blast of air slammed into the beast, knocking it onto its belly, a few paces from the cave's entrance. A kastora plucked off a spike and handed it to Javin. He jabbed the spike in the graether's snout. It stiffened and paralyzed. Nuelle sent another squall. The beast tumbled through the waterfall, and the river's current carried it away. Nuelle and the others walked over the rest of the paralyzed graethers and approached Javin.

Elisena stood before him. "How did you get to us?"

"I was watching you all train"—he glanced at Nuelle —"and when the graethers started chasing you, I followed, knowing I'd be able to communicate with them and possibly change their minds. But then, when all of you fell over the cliff, I had to think fast because they were going after you. I took the dive"—he gestured to the kastoras—"and saw these two in the river. Turned out this is the same one you gave the massadon fang to so when I asked for help he agreed and got his mate to join him."

Nuelle bowed his head at the creatures. "Thank you."

The male kastora wiggled his bottom, showing a pink bald spot. "Hurts a bunch, but for friends like you, I'll pluck the best spikes from my rumps." He and his mate chattered their three-inch teeth and hobbled out of the cave.

Nuelle smiled at Javin as his moldy fish stench evaporated. "That was very brave of you."

He stepped over a graether and faced Nuelle. "I knew all of your lives were in danger." He looked at Elisena. "I had to help."

"Thank you, Javin," Nuelle said.

He nodded and then glanced at the others. "Where's your sixth Sentinel?"

Nuelle gripped his soggy satchel. "I don't have one yet."

"Then I offer my services."

Elisena touched her chest with a trembling hand, her eyes watery. Riff slapped Javin's back, accidentally knocking him to his bottom. Then the dangerous youth-giant yanked Javin to his feet and while Riff proceeded to ask about family bloodlines, thoughts swarmed Nuelle's mind. *But if you are to succeed, you must choose a prodigy from each tribe who is willing to lay down their life, and when the time is right, a Sixth shall be added to you. Together, you will be called the Seven Sentinels.* It had already been a week since their first day, and no one else asked about becoming a Sentinel. Slaying a dragon from within its gut caused many to fear, and word of Colden the Savage Shifters only added to that dread. Could Javin truly be the last prodigy destined to be the sixth? But he hadn't originally desired to be a Sentinel, and he showed how ardently he didn't want Elisena to be one either. *"She and her brother often secluded themselves and traversed the woods, befriending creatures and beasts alike."* Preceptor Sage's tale of the savage siblings, Raysha and Zagan, taunted—or warned. But although shy, Elisena did seem amiable. Her twin however…

Nuelle crossed his arms and scrutinized Javin. "Why now?"

"I wanted to know everything my little sister was getting herself into so I borrowed a copy of the Acumen from the library." His irises lighted to the lilac hue Elisena's often faded to. "You were right. Everything King Nifal wrote would happen in the beginning, has happened. I wish I knew sooner and didn't act like such a constipated eebon suckling." He bowed his head and knelt before Nuelle. "So if you would have me, I will also protect you as best I can, Hope of the Faithful."

Nuelle's heart blazed with joy and relief. He pulled Javin to his feet and embraced him. "Welcome to the Seven Sentinels."

When he released, Javin took a few awkward steps back. "Human hugs are weird." He walked to Elisena. She stumbled toward him with open arms. Javin frowned as he held out his. Her knees wobbled and then gave way. Javin caught her. "Elisena!" He held her as her eyes closed. "What's wrong with her?"

Surta scurried to his side. "She's fainting."

"We have to take her to the Medic." Nuelle gestured to Riff. "Let him carry her."

Javin reluctantly released Elisena, and Riff scooped her into his arms.

"Let's hurry!" Nuelle jumped over the unconscious graethers and ran out of the cave with the others.

This is all my fault. Nuelle tapped his soggy boot as he and his friends sat in the small Medic commons. Pushing Elisena so hard during training was foolish. She had a rough training and struggled to keep up and even began to wheeze. But instead of insisting she take a rest, he allowed her to continue training. He lowered his head and covered his face with his hands. *I'm so sorry, Elisena. Please stand fast.*

Miss Alesia stepped into the room. "She's awake now. You may follow me."

Nuelle and Javin stood first. The Medic led them through three sets of white double-doors and finally stopped in front of one at the end of a long hallway. Nuelle turned the squeaky knob and opened the door. Elisena lay on a high bed, her face almost as white as the sheets covering her. Her umbrella sat closed on the night table beside the bed. A vital-monitoring orb floated above. The round and vivid light scanned her from head-to-toe. Its faint pulsing mirrored her weak heartbeat. They walked inside, and Miss Alesia closed the door behind them. As Nuelle and the others approached, Elisena turned her face toward him. Her tired eyes watched his with hurt and...regret?

Javin strode to her side and grabbed her hand. "How are you feeling?"

"Okay," she said quietly.

"Did the Medic find out what was wrong?"

Her rich purple irises faded.

He frowned. "What is it, Elly?"

She glanced at Nuelle. "Can I have a moment with the Supreme Prince?"

"You can't talk in front of me?"

"Please, Javin."

He hesitated before releasing her hand. "Fine, but I'll be right outside the door." He glimpsed at Nuelle before walking out with the others.

"This is my fault." Nuelle knelt at the bedside. "I pushed you too hard—"

"It's not your fault."

"But you were wheezing, and instead of having you rest, I encouraged you to keep going."

"I didn't faint because of the running." Elisena's eyes glistened. "I fainted because my heart is weak."

Nuelle glanced at the vital monitoring orb, still pulsing dimly. "Because you didn't have your umbrella for a time?"

"That was certainly difficult, but no." She looked away.

"I don't understand," he said. "Do you have a condition?"

She took a deep inhale and then exhaled slowly before answering, as if relieving herself of a heavy burden she'd carried for years. "I haven't been eating."

Nuelle sank as thoughts stormed his mind. Not eating? How could she do that to herself? Her life was so precious. Did she not know that? A soft prodding pressed into Nuelle's heart. He peered up at Elisena. Tears rolled down her cheeks.

"I don't understand," Nuelle said.

She watched the orb. Its pulsing shined off her lilac eyes. "I was sick of the taunts. Ever since I was a little girl I've heard the same thing, even from my own mother before she abandoned us. And add to the fact that everyone thinks I'm crazed because I always have to carry around this cursed umbrella. I thought maybe if I lost the weight, I'd be at least somewhat more accepted."

"Unless they're perfect, their opinions shouldn't rule your life." He rose and took a seat on the bed. Using his thumb, he wiped her tears. "You have a purpose that goes far beyond what you look like. Besides"—he removed his hand—"you are pretty."

A subtle redness tinted her cheeks.

"But your loyalty far surpasses the outer beauty of any girl I've ever met."

Elisena smiled, radiating a joy she had not shown before.

"I chose you as a Sentinel for a reason. But you can't fulfill this calling if you're hurting yourself…"

She nodded. "I know."

Nuelle took a slow breath in, praying his words came forth gently. "For whom did you become a Sentinel?"

Elisena watched the light hovering above. "For myself, so I can have meaning in my life, something worth living for. And for you. After seeing that wretched threat Colden made on the walls of the commons, I felt like I had to do something. Then I received the invitation to the challenge and knew that was my chance at fighting whoever would threaten the Supreme King's son."

"And when you were born, were you alone?"

Her stare left the vital monitoring orb and studied him. "Well, no. Javin was obviously there, and our mother, and her midwife, and Papa."

"And as time went on, were you alone?"

"I mean, there were times I felt alone, but I guess I wasn't ever alone in the sense of absolutely no one being around, unless I needed privacy of course."

"And right now, are you alone?"

She shook her head, confusion wrinkling her brow.

"You see, Elisena, we are put in this world with others. No matter where we go, eventually, there will always be someone who crosses our path. And that's because we weren't meant to live for just ourselves." He rested his hand on his satchel, where the Acumen's faithful warmth emanated from within. "I know you accepted this position because you're trying to live for something more than yourself. As long as you keep focusing on that, on others, on the grander purpose and who this is really for, it should help when thoughts creep in and try to distract you from the truth."

Rich purple poured into her irises. "Thank you, Prince Nuelle."

He smiled at her and stood as someone knocked. "You can come in."

Javin and the others scuttled inside.

"Everything okay?" Javin stooped next to Elisena.

She chuckled. "Yes, Javin."

He glanced at Nuelle. "So what did you talk about?"

"If you desire to know, you can ask your sister in private later."

Javin put his palms up. "Look, I know you're the prince of everyone, and I respect that, but, as a fellow man, if you'd like to court my sister—"

"Javin!" Elisena sat up.

"All I'm saying is that I'd like to know before anything becomes official."

Nuelle smirked at Elisena's protective brother. "No need to worry about that. Courtship isn't even on my things to accomplish before I die list."

Surta shook her wet, blue tresses. "It isn't on mine either."

Riff crossed his arms. "That's just because you haven't been looking for the right Mountain to rest on."

She gasped. Nuelle glared at him. He uncrossed his arms. "That's not what I meant!"

"Let's hope not." Nuelle sat on the floor by Elisena's bedside. "We'll stay here with you for the night."

Riff wrung out water from the bottom of his tunic. "Where are we supposed to sleep?"

"The floor." Nuelle sat on the cold ground and patted it. "You'll sleep right beside me."

Elisena brushed a strand behind her ear. "But aren't boys and girls not permitted to sleep in the same room?"

"I already spoke to Miss Alesia," Nuelle said. "We're not leaving you alone."

"All right, move over then." Riff dropped next to him and kicked off his boots. A sweaty, fungi odor intoxicated the room.

Ave held his nose and looked at Javin. "Must you always stink?"

Javin shrugged. "It isn't me."

Riff laid back. "That, pebbles, is the smell of a stone-hearted, rock-headed, boulder-bodied Gavrailian warrior!"

Nuelle laughed with the others. "More like the smell of someone who needs to bathe for two weeks straight."

Riff lifted Nuelle's hand and whiffed his underarm. "You smell as dainty as a puffle cake."

Ave clenched his stomach. "Ah, I'd love to whip up some puffle cakes right now."

Riff dropped Nuelle's arm and grimaced at Ave. "You cook?"

"Not very manly to you Gavrailian rock-heads, but I bet you wouldn't last five minutes in the Grand Kitchen with Old Lady Flemm."

Now Javin grimaced. "Old Lady Flemm? Sounds like something a weemutt would hurl after a sour meal."

"Please don't get him started," Nuelle said. "Too many traumatic memories."

"Oh, I've got to hear this." Sophana sat with her back against the night table.

"All right, you asked for it." Ave stood. "Once I was in the kitchen, de-furring a furscrabber with a butcher knife practically the size of a sword, and you know those things have fur for ages so you really have to saw through them—"

"Revolting, please skip the details." Surta touched her gemstone headpiece. "If you haven't realized yet, I have a very vivid imagination."

"Right. Well, I sliced off some skin from my thumb to my wrist and was bleeding like a broken fountain—"

"What did I just say!" Surta snatched her satchel and removed a sizable book from it. "I'm tuning out now and will be joyously imagining baby tawters cavorting through dust flowers."

Ave clasped his hand and moved frantically, picking up where he left off. "Blood was spraying everywhere, on the floor, on the walls, in the pots, on the food. And so Old Lady Flemm charges at me with a huge wooden spoon and starts beating me over the head with it. And I'm trying to block her with my other hand like, 'What in the blazes are you doing, woman!' And she cries out, 'Trying to knock you cold so you'll stop panicking and let me help you!'"

Sophana, Javin, and Riff burst into laughter while Elisena gawped.

Nuelle smiled. "I think she knew what she was talking about."

"You're always taking her side." Ave sat down beside book-reading Surta.

"Someone has to."

Sophana chuckled. "Reminds me of Old Man Twigley, my personal preceptor since I was three. He was always scolding me for using my leaves as darts and to impale things like books."

Surta gasped as she hugged her massive book to her chest like an endangered infant. "Criminal!"

Sophana chuckled again. "Don't worry, I eventually learned to only stab and slice things I don't like."

Surta sighed in relief and caressed her book's pages while Riff leaned close to Sophana. He lifted a hand toward a leaf-blade on her bicep. "Can I have one?"

She slapped his hand away. "Don't make me cut you."

He grinned. "It'll take a lot more than cuts to scare this fortress."

Surta raised her book. "How about a two hour lecture on the importance of literature?"

He shivered. "Now that's scary."

She narrowed one of her magnified eyes. "Have you even attempted to read a book?"

"Not once."

"Ah." She slapped her open book. "I will find a novel you will enjoy. One with plenty of brutal violence."

Riff slapped the floor. "Challenge accepted."

Javin licked his thumb and raised his fists. "I'll tell you what. I'd face Old Lady Flemm if it meant I got to live in the Supreme Palace."

Elisena huffed. "You mean live outside of it."

"Same thing." He lowered his fists. "I wouldn't mind sleeping inside sometimes. Prince Nuelle, you have a pet fursoar, right?"

Nuelle laid on his back. "Mugro. The most faithful—"

"And lazy of them," Ave said.

Javin sat at the foot of the bed. "I've always wanted to speak with one."

"Speak with?" Elisena asked. "Or stink with?"

He smirked. "Both."

Surta peered up from her bulky book. "It is a rather… unique way to communicate with creatures. When did you first discover your stench could speak?"

His smirk dipped into a scowl. "When the woman who birthed us ran off with another man."

As Surta lowered her book onto her lap, silence congested the small space. Moving his gaze from scowling Javin, Nuelle surveyed Elisena. Sitting with her knees against her chest, playing with a piece of lint on her covers, she suddenly appeared...younger, as if the reminder of her mother's betrayal had literally brought her back in time to whatever age she'd been when it happened. Maybe that was the real or the greatest reason why she harmed herself with not eating. Back at the palace one afternoon, a young servant girl, Livianne, had confessed to loathing herself after her father had likewise left her and her mother for another woman. Livi blamed herself, thinking if she was smarter or had a prodigious gift, he would've stayed. *It was your father's own selfishness that sent him away,* Nuelle had told her. *And if a man can't choose to love and be there for his family, they're better off with him gone.* Nuelle shifted his gaze between the twins. "The path you two have chosen"—he looked at the others—"that all of you have chosen, to sacrifice yourselves for the greater good of Zephoris's Faithful, is true and selfless love. And it's what my father has once told me was the most impressive virtue in his sight. So again, on my behalf and his, I say thank you. And know this, one day, all of you will celebrate eternal victory and peace in the Supreme King's presence."

Sophana smiled as she lay her head atop her satchel. "No more fighting. Sounds nice."

Riff slapped his muscles. "Even these hills need their rest."

"All right, mountain man," Nuelle said, "let's all get some sleep now. We have even longer days ahead of us." Nuelle laid on the hard wood. Although someday they'd enter into that resting place, and it was great Javin joined them, fulfilling the Sixth Sentinel prophecy, more prophecies remained unfulfilled—and not all of them were good. Evil never slept, and with Darcy gone and Colden captured, it was only a matter of time before the Savage Shifters made new recruits.

Nuelle scowled. Why would anyone turn against the innocent, turn against Father, after all he'd done for the citizens of Zephoris? Knowing you'd been invited by the Supreme King himself to his prestigious academy, one of the highest honors in the land, and yet have the gall to threaten his son and attack fellow prodigies was just…deranged. But then, evil didn't make sense, for the one under its sway drank of its deception; that to live for oneself was the ultimate prize and epitome of satisfaction. It failed to grasp that judgement awaited the wicked, that inevitably, all lawlessness would be accounted for. Father was patient, but he always delivered justice in due time. For now, until one's dying breath, the door to his grace remained open, but in that final day, the gates of forgiveness will be shut forever.

Looking at his new friends, his new family, Nuelle balled his fists. *I'll do my best to lead you all there. Even if I must die to do so.*

After volunteering to take the first watch, Nuelle removed the Acumen from his satchel and continued reading from where he left off. The scarlet letters that often brought comfort, now delivered evermore urgent warning…

Brutality is not always violence from a hand or sword. The vilest of adversaries knows a strong soul is not easily defeated by force alone. If his defenses are great, a noble warrior must be weakened by other means. With patience, the enemy of his soul will strike his most vulnerable area until he is broken: the heart.

Nine: Revenge

Nuelle's sword smashed into Tane's. Blue sparks showered them both, and orange life orbs burst around them as they sparred in the palace courtyard. Tane swiped with his blade, cutting through more of the floating amber specs. Nuelle countered, but his brother's force thrust him back, and he collapsed onto the courtyard's searing stone.

"Get up!" The daystar beamed behind Tane, veiling his face in a silhouette. Ave, his father Amador, and Tane's sentry spectated near the courtyard's entry door a few yards away.

Nuelle scrambled to his feet as Tane brought his sword down. Nuelle raised his. Tane's blade clashed into it. More sparks scattered, burning Nuelle's exposed forearms as he dropped to his knee.

"You forgot to roll, Nu." Tane pressed his blade down further.

Nuelle's arms trembled against the weight. *Not the same mistake again! Now how to get out of this trap?*

"Fight, Nuelle!" Ave shouted.

Nuelle glanced around. Light gleamed off the silver mesh on Tane's thighs. Attempting to trip him would be a wasted effort. His powerful legs were too sturdy. Tane's blade slowly pushed Nuelle's lower. If he tried rolling out of the way, the blade would surely pierce him. Only one option remained. Fight. He propelled upward, warring against his brother's power. The heavy opposition gradually drained the strength from his shoulders and biceps. Body trembling, Nuelle's arms fought to prevail. The pressure weighed down on his chest now, his abdomen tightening.

"Do not give up, Nu," Tane said.

Nuelle closed his eyes, weakness prevailing. He couldn't win. Tane was too str—*You heard what your brother said.* Father's voice filtered through the agony. *Do not give up, son.*

He opened his eyes. A flicker of warmth ignited in his heart. It pulsed, sending rifts of warmness across his chest. The warmth surged through his arms, drowning the pain until it no longer existed. The comforting heat receded and flowed into his lungs. Nuelle swallowed a breath. His quivering stopped. He thrust Tane's sword back.

Tane staggered and then swiftly steadied himself. His brow furrowed as he sheathed his weapon. "Well done, brother. You've grown stronger."

The courtyard door opened, and Prince Antikai strolled toward them, passing Ave and the others. As he approached, the orange life orbs scattered as if repulsed by his presence. Antikai's blue eyes glinted in the brightness as he approached. "Careful, Tane, it appears your younger brother has some strength. You do not want him to take your place as Supreme Prince, do you?" He smiled at Nuelle as a chilly breeze swept past.

Tane clasped Nuelle's arm and pulled him in for a side-hug. "He still has much to learn before that happens." Tane steered Nuelle around. "Walk with me, brother." He raised a hand to Amador and Ave, and then walked out of the courtyard and toward the highland upholding the Twirl Blossom Garden. Nuelle followed him up the stony steps to the top. Tall, curled and twined blossoms of every color lined either side of them as they walked to the ivory bench at the hill's edge. Together they sat, overlooking the sea of Agapon's gemstone homes stretching below. The orange life orbs swirled above them in the warm, melodic wind.

Tane's bronze eyes surveyed the structures. "You know why I'm so hard on you, Nu?"

Nuelle followed brother's stare. "Because you want me at my best."

"That's just one reason." He gestured to the palace. "Our world is much larger than this place. This is like one life orb in the expanse of Zephoris. Outside of these gates, not everyone fears you and there will come a day when you must face them."

Nuelle frowned. "Everyone here is faithful. Our land has been peaceful for centuries."

"This is exactly what I'm talking about. Don't be so naive, Nu. You haven't been out there."

"Does this have to do with your visit to Innovian? Surely the rumors about a coming rebellion are just that—rumors"

Tane's steely gaze met Nuelle's. Brother breathed in slowly, carefully. "Do you trust me, Brother?"

"Of course."

"Then listen to me." His heavy hand gripped Nuelle's shoulder. "Not everyone can be trusted. You must always keep your guard up. Understood?"

Nuelle's throat dried as the life orbs shined off of brother's eyes. "Understood."

Thunder roared, causing the hard ground to tremble. Nuelle shot upright to a seated position. Tane? Antikai?

His Sentinels slept soundly around him, Elisena still on the Medic's bed. He sighed. It was only a dream. Thunder shook the floor. The window on the back wall revealed a clash of red lightning tearing through the sky. *Colden!* Nuelle scrambled to his feet. "Wake up!"

Ave and the others awakened, blinking away sleepiness. "What's happened?"

"We have to go to the dungeon, now!"

Everyone rose. Elisena slipped out of bed and bustled into her boots. Nuelle hesitated before running to the doorway. She probably still needed to rest, but leaving her alone would be even more dangerous. He and his Sentinels raced out of the Medic's office and into the storm outside. Cold rain pelted his face and arms as he and the Sentinels sprinted toward the underground dungeon's entrance near the forest. The stone door stood open.

Nuelle jogged down the steps into the damp tunnel. The two silver knights who had kept guard lay with backs against the wall by the open dungeon door, their helmets tossed aside —revealing brown, shriveled faces with eyes deeply sunken in. Surta and Elisena covered their mouths.

Sophana ripped off two leaf-blades from her arms. "Thorkkis."

"Wait here," Nuelle told Elisena before dashing into the room, wind gushing from his palms. With stony hands, Lady Bridie blocked a red bolt from Colden who now wore a second metallic ring—Zagan's. Sir Dangian swung his sword at the green-haired girl from Wisdom who had glared at Sophana in the commons. A vine protruded from the girl's mouth, and several vines wriggled where her arms were supposed to be. Overseer Enri lay on the ground in water beside the fallen-over tub. His body had browned and it gradually shriveled.

Sophana threw a leaf-blade. It struck one of the girl's vines. She shrieked like a hurt weed as Nuelle thrust a hot gale at Colden, slamming him into a wall. Lady Bridie charged at the wicked prodigy.

Nuelle darted to the Overseer. His mouth hung open, exposing a shrunken tongue and throat. "Javin," Nuelle called, "summon a vanaph!"

As Javin nodded, Riff leapt to Nuelle's side. One of the green-haired girl's vines slammed into Riff's chest and bounced backwards. Colden fired a thin bolt at Lady Bridie's shoulder that catapulted her into Sir Dangian. As they collapsed, Sophana launched another leaf-blade, but a vine whipped it off course. She tore off another and jabbed at the plants.

The thorkkis girl laughed as she evaded the blows. "Your father thought his knights killed the last of us, didn't he?" She raised her arm, and the vines knocked the leaf-blade from Sophana's grasp. "Old age has made him a fool." She lifted a vine. Thorns jutted from it as she pointed at Sophana's face. Thorkkis-girl whipped the thorny stem back, ready to launch.

Ave stretched his blue sponge-arm and wrapped it around her legs. He yanked, sweeping her off her feet. She collided with the wall near Colden. A shadow-man emerged from the stone and clasped Colden and the girl's shoulders. The three vanished. Elisena ran into the chamber. Lady Bridie, Sir Dangian, and the others gathered around Nuelle as he gently raised Overseer Enri, now the size of a small child.

A tear fell from one of the Overseer's eyes. His chapped lips quivered, and his tiny fingers gripped Nuelle's. "St—" he gasped and choked.

Nuelle's vision blurred as a vanaph trotted through the entryway toward him and Overseer Enri.

"Stay," he strained to whisper, "alive." His lavender eyes slowly closed, and his grip loosened.

Javin held Elisena as she gaped, Surta and Riff doing the same. Sophana clenched her fists. Sir Dangian dropped to a knee, and Lady Bridie bowed her head. Ave rested a hand on Nuelle's back. Grief mingled with wrath coated his heart as he laid his palm over Enri's withered chest and whispered, "Faithful soul, we will meet again." He turned away from the corpse and faced Lady Bridie and Sir Dangian. "How did this happen?"

Sir Dangian spoke swiftly. "That trickster girl, Thrine, came to the dungeon saying she knew who the Savages were going to recruit next. Then she all disfigures into what you just saw and attacks meh and Lady Bridie!"

Lady Bridie's voice trembled. "But we were able to gather some information from Colden before she came, my lord." She winced, touching her smoking shoulder. "He said Prince Antikai sent the savages, and that he was the one who caused the uprising in Innovian. He said a great rebellion was coming, and that he was promised if he joined Antikai, he'd become a prince in the new kingdom."

"New kingdom?" Javin asked, Elisena pulling away from him.

Sir Dangian gripped the hilt of his sword. He peered at Nuelle, red seeping into the whites of his eyes. "Prince Antikai is bent on killing off you and your family, so he can make a new kingdom—one without peace, or honor, one without hope, or love."

Heat burned within Nuelle, and smoke rose from his arms. That traitor already tried to kill Father after he kindly allowed him to live at the Supreme Palace as a favor to King Bertil. The rebellious prince kept disobeying his father, Bertil, who hoped Antikai would learn respect from Tane, but evidently, Antikai was too reprobate to change.

Colden's message in the commons invaded Nuelle's mind. *Disappear like your brother, Supreme Prince.* His heart dropped to his stomach. As he looked at Lady Bridie, his voice shook. "Did you gather any information regarding my brother?"

Her gaze rested on Sir Dangian before focusing on Nuelle, and then she spoke slowly. "Yes, your highness. Antikai has... killed him."

A wave of dizziness washed over Nuelle. His gut twisted. He staggered. Ave grabbed Nuelle's arm and steadied him. Colden's message in the commons about Tane made sense now—the corrupt prodigy knew Tane was dead!

Elisena trembled, no doubt feeling the crushing weight of his grief. The others lowered their heads as Nuelle shook his, tears falling. He hadn't even been able to hug his brother goodbye when he left for the Obsidian. That slaughter in Bertil's kingdom provoked by Antikai's attempt at murdering Father caused Ave to lose his father. Because of Antikai, the Overseer was killed. And now to add to his evil, the heartless savage ended Tane's life!

"I'm sorry, Supreme Prince," Lady Bridie said quietly.

Nuelle wiped his eyes. "You and Sir Dangian protect the prodigies as best you can." He turned to his Sentinels. "As for us, after burying the Overseer, we leave for Agapon."

Ten: The Riot

*T*he princess was almost mine to kill! Thrine and the others emerged from black dust layering the floor of a cold, dark chamber. *But now that I have the Savages' help, her life will be mine to take.*

Jilt still squeezed Thrine's and Colden's shoulders. Dead-tawter stench soaked the icy air, worsening the queasiness caused by the Savage Shifter's surprise teleport of the three of them. A flame flickered on a useless mantel against the back wall, fighting with all its might to ward off the chill. It sputtered desperately, yet the shadows it caused remained motionless.

"Leave us." Master Antikai's voice caused Thrine and Colden to shudder. Jilt transformed into a shadow and seeped into the floor as the flame on the mantel brightened. The fire illuminated a pond of black water with a frozen strip across the center, leading to Master's scaly feet. He sat in an over-sized onyx throne with a fuzzy white tawter-head at the end of an armrest. Thorns bulged from the chair's top rail, making Master's scaled-flesh and glowing green eyes appear all the more beastly. He caressed the tawter-head. "Is the prince still alive?"

Colden trembled as he removed Zagan's signet-ring from his finger. "Yes, my lord."

His eyes glowed brighter as he beckoned Colden closer. He slowly crossed the frozen strip and stood before Master.

"And I imagine you do not have the book either," he said as he took the ring from Colden.

"No, my lord, but Overseer Enri is dead."

Master set the ring down upon an armrest while tapping the tawter-head on the other. "And the prince's followers?"

Colden lowered his eyes. "There's six of them now."

Master Antikai sprang off his throne and clasped Colden's throat. "How is this possible?"

"We tried to kill them"—he gasped for air—"but that weakling, Darcy, abandoned us—"

"Do not blame others for your stupidity, you useless fool." Fog from Master's icy breath blew against Colden's face.

"I'm sorry—"

"Apologies are pleas from the weak who deserve nothing less than a slow, agonizing death"—he dug his green nails into Colden's neck. Blood spilled from fresh cuts. "Which I am all the willing to inflict upon you, you pathetic excuse of a life."

Thrine's heart punched the walls of her chest as Master grinned, his pointed teeth gray against black gums. "O, how pleasing it is to watch the life you do not deserve fleeing your body, to see the light of your eyes dim." His grin vanished.

The frozen strip of ice began to crack under their feet. Master released his hold and glided backwards as the ice shattered. Colden plunged into the black water. As he flailed, Master sat on his throne and bent over, reaching his fingertip —the one wearing the metallic and onyx signet-ring—into the liquid. The pond started freezing rapidly. Thrine's knees quaked as the water froze around Colden's neck, his head the only part of his body above the surface. Purple tinted his lips as he peered at her. "Help me."

Master removed his finger from the pond and laid his back against the ebony throne. "If you even attempt to, you will suffer a worse fate."

Thrine looked away from Colden.

"Brone, Jilt," Master said as he clasped Zagan's ring.

The shadows on the back wall grew. They separated from it and glided onto the floor, creeping toward them. The shadows stopped before Master Antikai. They rose from the black dust and morphed into bodies. A giant Gavrailian with painfully-protruding shoulder blades bowed a knee, his silvery-purple hair sweeping over his crimson eyes as Jilt did the same, his purple irises shining.

Master's gaze scanned the room. "And where is my Raysha?"

A huge, green beast emerged from the dust. Eight legs protruded from its sides, and a long tail with three sharp points like an enormous fork bulged at its rear.

"Ah"—Master smiled—"there you are."

It scurried toward him as Brone and Jilt stood. The beast's round eight-eyed head shrank, and ruby curls emerged from its top. The eight legs and fork-tail condensed and, a feminine and curvy body now in their place. Pale flesh formed on the now human head. A pair of abnormally beady, blue eyes watched Master, and plump, womanly lips grew, marred by thick, green, crawler-like fangs that protruded from her cheeks. A leather weapon-belt with a sheathed dagger hugged her hips.

Raysha strolled to his side. "How may I serve you, master?"

"I have an assignment for you." He handed her Zagan's ring.

Her irises glistened. Her fist closed around the ring, and her other hand gripped the dagger's hilt at her hip. Her green cheek-fangs jutted. "To avenge my brother?"

"Not yet." He scratched one of the dead tawter's black eyes. "Now that the six are assembled, the prince's heart is getting confident. We must show him the people of this land are not worth saving."

Raysha's fangs curved inward again and she kissed the ring.

Master caressed her repulsive cheek with the back of his flaking hand before letting it fall. "You know which kingdom to begin with." His gaze scanned Thrine from foot to head. "You will be able to morph into a shadow now. Use this power to discover who at the academy the prince is particularly fond of."

She swallowed, her throat extra dry in the chill. "Yes, my lord."

His glowing eyes lowered to her right hand. "You won't need to hide it anymore."

Thrine hurriedly removed the signet-ring from her pant-pocket and slid it around her middle finger.

"Soon enough, you will learn how to teleport without assistance. But until then"—he nodded at his Savage Shifters.

Jilt grabbed Thrine's shoulders. They transformed into shadows, Raysha and Brone doing the same, and then disappeared.

The enormous purple mountains of Jazerland, Sunezia's capital, materialized ahead, dimly visible in the evening skies. But the lavender palace atop Maimon Mount gleamed in the distance and defied the darkness. Only a hundred miles left till they reached Agapon.

As he neared the peaks, Nuelle jerked the reins of his vanaph, his Sentinels following close behind. His last visit to this faithful land three years ago was full of welcome hospitality. The people celebrated his and Father's arrival with a grand feast that stretched four villages wide and lasted a week. Night and day they grilled meals over hefty stone fire pits and sang joyous songs to hand-drums and tin pipes. For all the vastness, there lived no room for sorrow and enmity, only love and unity as tightly knit as their wooden basket-homes.

Nuelle ascended over a mountain. Down below, hundreds of people crammed the commercial square, cheering before a tall man standing on a crate, half of his face shrouded by wiry brown hair. "The people of Ideya are doing exceedingly well!" the man spoke through a silver cylindrical amplifying tube. "It is time we follow their lead!"

The crowd hollered in agreement. Nuelle tugged on the reins of his vanaph. It stopped in place, hovering over the mountain peak. Ave and the others halted at his side.

"This gathering reminds me of home." Surta's spectacles shined in the faint, evening light. Elisena unclipped her umbrella from her waist-belt and opened it. Nuelle grasped his satchel where the Acumen hid, and kicked his vanaph's side. It slowly descended, Ave and the others reluctantly following.

"Though King Eliah may not agree, we are fully capable of ruling ourselves!" The man on the crate continued as Nuelle and his Sentinels neared the ground toward the back of the gathering. Royal guards in silver helmets stood at every corner of the boisterous plaza, armed with sword and shield.

"My people"—the wiry-haired man extended his arms to them—"if you are ready to obtain your freedom, let the mountains hear your voices!"

The citizens shouted in one accord, their cry echoing in the highlands. Nuelle slid off his vanaph. Ave trembled as he dismounted, while Sophana slowly reached for a leaf-blade. Sweat drenched Javin and Elisena's foreheads as they got off their vanaphs, Riff and Surta doing the same. Surrounding citizens pointed and gasped. The commotion stopped, every eye in the square—buyers, sellers, and guards alike—fixed on Nuelle. The majority of their demeanors seemed to be saying the same thing: Why are you here? You are not welcome.

Nuelle and his Sentinels' vanaphs flew away. He gripped his satchel and whispered, "Javin, summon them back quickly."

"Working on it."

"Look who has come to our land!" The man on the crate glared as he pointed at them. "The Supreme Prince!"

Grunts and whispers circulated amongst the crowd.

"He has come to silence our petitioning!"

Nuelle stood in front of his Sentinels while the citizens roared, their shouts like angered beasts. How did this man know he was the Supreme Prince? Had word of Tane's departure and displacement already spread to the kingdoms? The man grinned as a breeze brushed his hair back. Deep wrinkles covered half of his face. Wind filled Nuelle's palms as the citizens inched closer. *A Savage Shifter.*

Darcy pushed through the horde toward Nuelle and the others. "Follow me!" He turned and ran.

Grabbing Ave's arm, Nuelle raced after Darcy, the Sentinels following.

"Stop them!" The Savage on the crate vanished as the mob chased Nuelle and the others.

Darcy leapt over a shopping stand, knocking down boxes of round fruits. Nuelle and his Sentinels trailed. A few of the citizens stumbled on the fallen food.

"This way!" Darcy led them out of the square and down a rocky mountain path, his steps swift. As they descended, a nauseating odor like creature feces raided. He reached the bottom and hid behind a huge pile of tan mush.

Nuelle held his breath as he and his Sentinels crouched beside him, Elisena closing her umbrella. The mob stampeded by, running on a gravel road to the left. Ave squeezed his eyes shut as his body quaked. Undoubtedly, the wrathful throng must've reminded him of the angry citizens who killed Amador...Nuelle spoke into his ear. "Do you trust my father?"

"Yes."

"Then release this spirit of fear and embrace the spirit he has given you. One of power, love, and self-control."

Ave opened his eyes. His quaking eased, though some trembling remained. The last of the rowdy citizens disappeared down the road.

Darcy peered at Nuelle. "Why did you come here?"

"Why did you leave the academy?" Nuelle replied.

Looking at the others, Darcy's irises lightened. "Follow me." He crept into the open and then scampered to the right along a dirt path.

Nuelle glanced at where the rioters had run. Darcy couldn't be trusted yet, but clearly, he knew his way around this part of Sunezia. And the rioters would probably trek back their way soon. Nuelle gripped Ave's shoulder. "We have to keep moving."

Ave shakily rose and they all scurried after Darcy. The path broadened, and they entered a small village with nest-like homes burrowed in crags on the mountains. Besides the few open windows, the village appeared to have been abandoned for decades, and although early evening, darkness reigned inside the homes—as if the lodgers were afraid to expose their whereabouts.

As they passed a cobblestone tavern, Nuelle's skin prickled. Four men sat on the porch and drank. A burn-faced man lowered his mug. His purple eyes trailed Nuelle.

Elisena shivered as she reopened her umbrella. "That man's heart is scheming. We need to move fast."

Darcy quickened his pace. The men watched them until they turned a corner. Nuelle stared ahead, holding his satchel close. They'd get whatever information they could from Darcy and then leave immediately. After another quarter-mile, Darcy veered toward the last twig-home on the mountain's edge. A walkway enclosed by leafless undergrowth led to a dilapidated porch with cobwebs on either end. Like the other homes, no lights flickered from inside.

Darcy jogged through the undergrowth, Nuelle and his friends trailing. They ascended three steps and walked onto the porch. Darcy removed a key from his pocket and unlocked the circular door. When it opened, a skinny woman with scraggly blonde hair rose from a cushion-less couch in a living area. A dim table-lantern shed light to her wide eyes as she strode toward him, observing Nuelle and his Sentinels.

Darcy closed and locked the door before facing her. "Where's Genya and Adira?"

"In their bedchambers."

"Good." He embraced her. As she pulled away, she looked at Nuelle again. Darcy clasped her hands. "Ma, do you mind going to your bedchamber so I can talk to Prince Nuelle and his friends?"

She nodded and then scurried out the room. Darcy walked to a window and peeked through tattered curtains. "Are the Savage Shifters still after you?"

"Yes," Nuelle answered as Riff and Javin stood beside him, and the girls sat on the couch, Sophana clinging tightly to her leaf-blade. "That's part of the reason we're going to my father. The academy isn't safe." His throat tightened. "They killed Overseer Enri."

Darcy winced and shook his head.

"I need to know any information you have about Antikai's plans that Colden may not have known."

Elisena closed her umbrella and watched Darcy. He turned away from the window and faced Nuelle. "All I know is that they wanted you dead, Prince Antikai is trying to set up his own kingdom, and"—his irises faded like Elisena's would.

"I know." Nuelle's chest ached and his heart thumped slowly at the reminder of his deceased brother. As his other friends watched the floor, he looked at Elisena. She nodded, confirming that Darcy spoke the truth. Nuelle focused on him again and he continued.

"I have a pet roto that can fly you all to Agapon." Darcy frowned. "I'd offer food, but we ran out of our last jar of sweet stems this morning."

"That's kind of you." Nuelle opened his satchel and removed the remainder of iris-fruit bread Lady Bridie gave him for the journey. "Take this. We're not too far from the Supreme Palace."

Darcy's eyes gleamed as he took the bread. "Thank you, Prince Nuelle."

"We have company!" Elisena opened her umbrella.

"He's in here!" a man shouted from the front-yard.

Darcy strode to the window as the girls jolted off the couch, Sophana tearing off another leaf-blade. Darcy peered out. "That's not good."

A clash like that of shattering glass sounded outside the door. Blue flames engulfed the entrance. Nuelle and the others backed away. Darcy's mother and two small, bony, blonde girls bustled into the room as the flames spread, and thick smoke shrouded the space.

"Let's go out through the back." Darcy led everyone through a kitchen and then to a door.

"Call for two rotos, Javin," Nuelle said as they trailed Darcy and his family outside.

He held Elisena's hand. "Already did."

"Great. How long till they get here?" Nuelle asked Darcy.

"If she isn't giving birth, only a minute."

"Giving birth?" Surta gawped.

Ave's arms rapidly turned blue. "I don't think it will take more than a minute for them to realize we're not inside anymore."

"Over here, boys!" The burn-faced man from the tavern strode from the side of the house, about thirty men behind him. He grasped a glass bottle stuffed with a dirty handkerchief. "Can you believe it?" he asked his entourage. "We have Supreme Prince Nuelle—Supreme King Nifal's special second son—here in our kingdom." He removed a match from behind his ear and scraped his scarred cheek with it. A spark ignited, and he lit the handkerchief. "I think this call's for a festivity, don't you agree?" He threw the bottle at Nuelle.

Wind poured from his palms as he aimed them toward the man and glanced at Ave—stiff beside Sophana. The bottle collided into Nuelle's gust and burst into flames. Burn-face pulled two large daggers from behind his back as multiple replicas of Nuelle and the others running in every direction appeared. Nuelle and his Sentinels mimicked Surta's illusions as the mob wagged their heads back-and-forth, jabbing knives and throwing fists at the images.

Riff charged, knocking a row of men onto dead grass, while Sophana's leaf-blades took out others. Nuelle launched a sweltering gust at burn-face and those near him, while Darcy raised his palm, freezing a group of them in their tracks. Javin punched some of the frozen men, and Elisena closed her umbrella and whacked others. Ave rolled his shoulders and expanded his hands. He balled his now giant fists and plowed them into a handful of the ruffians, sending them flying.

Burn-face hollered, boils sprouting on his face and arms. He dropped his daggers and bounded off. Darcy lowered his palms and the men unfroze. Their heads twisted back from Javin and Elisena's blows. The throng ran after the burn-faced man. Nuelle's wind calmed and he smiled at Ave. "Power, love, and self-control."

Someone applauded from behind. Nuelle peered over his shoulder as his Sentinels encircled him. A petite woman cloaked in black glided in their direction. Scarlet locks flowed from underneath her hood, lining a bizarre, crawler-like face —two irregularly beady blue eyes, and human lips bordered by large, green fangs bulging from her cheeks. Jilt and a towering Gavrailian with jutting shoulder blades appeared next to her. *Brone.* Nuelle pressed his satchel against his side.

The woman stopped. A smile stretched across her blood-red lips, but her lifeless eyes bore into his with a hatred that could be felt. "Isn't it ironic that the so-called, 'Land of the Faithful' has become so riotous, so violent?" She glanced at his satchel. "The citizens of Sunezia have grown weary of their Supreme King, as the rest of Zephoris has."

"Not all of them." Elisena trembled as she glowered at her. "And you know it."

The woman rubbed her chest and chuckled. "Maybe you haven't grown weary of your king, but you have grown weary of the way he's made you." She flicked her fingers toward Elisena's umbrella as she tensed. "Unveil your true self. You know you desire the liberation I have, the confidence I now possess—"

"My sister doesn't wanna be anything like you!" Javin growled.

Raysha's head tilted to the side. "You get a thrill from the presence of incredible beasts." Her cheek-fangs lifted. "Imagine becoming one."

Nuelle's body simmered. "They're already discovering who they were made to be, not trying to warp themselves into something they're not. Their trust is in someone greater than Antikai."

"These souls appear to be for you now, Prince, but what happens when their loved ones begin to turn on you? How will their loyalty fare then?"

Nuelle's eyes narrowed at the beastly woman. "They're willing to die for me, just like Zagan was willing to die for Antikai."

The woman's smile vanished. She and the other Savage Shifters disappeared. She reemerged behind Nuelle, ripping the satchel off his shoulder before vanishing again. Brone appeared and restrained Riff, while Jilt punched Ave, thrusting him into Sophana and Surta. As they collapsed, Surta's headpiece fell off. A swarm of images—the chase from the rioters, the faces of the men from the mob, the hooded woman and the other Savages—blended together and surrounded. Surta brought her knees to her chest and dug her head into them. The projected memories and thoughts seized Jilt and Brone's attention, but the woman materialized twenty yards away. She knelt, removing the Acumen from the satchel.

"Stop her!" Nuelle shouted as he blew a steamy gust at Jilt. Riff broke away from Brone.

Sophana scrambled to her feet as the female Shifter dropped the Acumen and unsheathed a dagger from her belt—Zagan's iron, sawtoothed one. She raised it. Sophana launched a leaf-blade. It sliced the woman's cheekbone, above her fang, shearing one of her curls. She recoiled and fired a green orb from her palm. Sophana dove aside, and it crashed into Darcy's flaming home.

Nuelle ran to the woman, sending a gale in her path. She snatched the Acumen and disappeared before the gust could reach her. Nuelle looked around. Something scorching hot crashed into his back, propelling him face-forward and onto his stomach. He groaned as his skin seared and blood seeped through his tunic. The crimson-haired woman reappeared on his right. She released a green orb. It smashed into Nuelle's side, thrusting him onto his searing back. His rib smoked from the sphere of hot energy. Blood spilled from the burns, his back now soaked.

The soulless woman laughed as she glided toward him. "You aren't that strong yet, are you, Young Prince?" She opened the Acumen and thumbed the pages. "The Hope of the Faithful will now be a lost hope." She snapped it closed. Another green orb grew in her palm. Beyond Surta's surrounding images, two large balls of red feathers rolled down a mountain, grabbing the wicked woman's attention. As the feathery spheres neared the bottom of the slope, they picked up speed. They unraveled three paces from the rocky path. Massive wings stretched eight-yards long and a large black beak pierced the air—rotos. Javin and Elisena peeked out of a pouch on either of the creatures' stomachs. The winged-beasts glided above the ground, zooming the woman's way. "Jilt!" she shouted.

He appeared at her side and released a blast of green wind. It protruded from his palms like a rope and spiraled around the rotos. He thrust his hands upward, launching the creatures into the air, and then brought his palms down, slamming the rotos into the ground.

Warmth spread across Nuelle's back and rib. Surta's uncontrolled mind projections vanished. Gripping Zagan's dagger, the evil woman kicked Nuelle's ribcage. As he writhed in agony, she dropped the Acumen at his side and stooped. She raised the dagger. "You stole my brother's life, and now I will take yours!" She thrust the weapon into Father's protruding insignia. The blade bounced off the metal and flung from her grasp. The savage woman looked at Nuelle, her eyes consumed with wrath. She blinked and they duplicated into six more. Her head rapidly enlarged.

Jilt grabbed the Acumen and glided to the side while the woman's cloak shrank until it disappeared. Short, dark-green hair sprouted on her pale skin. Eight long legs protruded from her expanding torso, and a fork-like tail jutted from her bottom. In seconds, a gigantic crawler towered over Nuelle. The beast glared at him as its jaw dropped open. Green fangs bulged from the sides of its mouth. Its head and tail cocked back, ready for the venomous kill.

"Raysha!"

The beast jerked its head in the direction of the call. A man garbed in ebony with purplish-black hair covering only half of his flaking scalp stood a few yards behind her. Green scales distorted his face, his eyes glowing an unnatural jade, yet, he looked familiar.

Nuelle's heart skipped. *Prince Antikai.*

Jilt glided toward Antikai with the Acumen. "Master, I have the book!"

"Wonderful. Toss it here."

Jilt complied, and the book landed at Antikai's feet.

"How did you bypass Nifal's territory sphere?" Jilt asked.

"I have my ways." He looked at the crawler. "Raysha, do not kill the pathetic boy just yet."

The crawler peered at Nuelle, tears welling in its eight eyes.

"Return to the Obsidian while I handle the Young Prince."

Jilt approached. "But—"

"Do not question me, fool!" Antikai's green eyes glowed brighter.

Jilt halted and then disappeared. The crawler's head and fork-tail drew close to Nuelle's face. His countenance reflected off its blue irises as the three-pointed tail neared his neck. The beast hissed, then turned into a shadow and vanished. Antikai faded away.

"Prince Nuelle!" Surta ran toward him, her headpiece back on, and Sophana at her side. She grabbed the Acumen.

Warmness seeped into Nuelle's wounds and eased the pain as he sat up. Surta and Sophana helped him to his feet and then handed him the Acumen.

"That was the beast that appeared in my mind while you were interrogating Colden!" Surta said.

He exhaled as he pressed Father's book against his chest. "Words cannot express how grateful I am for you right now."

She smiled. "And Sophana. If she didn't put my headpiece back on, I wouldn't have been able to help."

"Thank you both." Nuelle did a quick scan. Riff— bloody-faced—and Ave limped toward them. The rotos wobbled onto their feet, the twins still in their pouches. Elisena had a cut on her head; Javin a busted and swollen lip. For the most part, no one looked severely hurt. Near Darcy's burning home, Darcy knelt beside one of his sisters, his mother on her hands and knees weeping while his other sister stood still, crying silently.

No. Nuelle raced to Darcy's side, the Sentinels following. Dirt and tear-tracks stained his cheeks as he gripped his smaller sister against his chest. A gaping wound marred her little forehead, and her body lay limp in his arms.

Nuelle's stomach churned as Darcy's mother whispered repeatedly, "Adira, wake up."

Ave and the others encircled them, Surta and Elisena holding hands. Nuelle squeezed the Acumen as fire seared within. Another innocent life—this time a child—seized from this world by those abominable and accursed beings. They had to be stopped before someone else perished at their ruthless hands.

"Prince Nuelle," Surta said in a low voice. "That wasn't really Antikai, so I suggest we leave soon before they return."

Javin peered at the two rotos, and they shuffled over.

Nuelle gently grasped Darcy's shoulder. "We have to leave now."

He nodded and lifted Adira's body as Elisena and Sophana supported his mother and Genya. As Riff and the others helped the family into one of the roto's pouches, Ave followed Nuelle inside the other. "We're taking them to the Supreme Palace?"

Nuelle slipped into the creature's feathered-sack and looked toward Maimon Mount. "Not my father's palace."

Eleven: The King's Hope

Darkness could not prevail against this light. Ivory glowfish teemed in the moat beneath the drawbridge of the lavender fortress, making the water glimmer with a supernatural sheen, like white fire. It reflected off the granite walls and expelled the evening void—though it could not expel the voids within.

Nuelle, his Sentinels, Darcy, and his remaining family, walked across the drawbridge. Dirt stained Darcy's palms from the grave he dug for his sister in the burial ground outside the kingdom's capital. His mother gripped little Genya's hand. None of them had said a word since they left the village. And what was there to say? The death of loved ones always rendered speechless those most unprepared for it.

Five silver-armored knights stood guard at the entryway. As Nuelle and the others approached, the knights bowed in unison. The two in the center opened the gloss-wood doors. Thousands of glowing purple strands dangled from the Master Hall's ceiling, dazzling the marble floors below and the sapphires embedding the walls. The indigo lights amplified the splendor of the welcoming palace. Surta sauntered closer to a sapphire wall and observed it.

Nuelle walked alongside her. "How did you create an illusion of Antikai in his new, twisted form?"

Her teal eyes locked onto his. "As I drew closer to you and that Raysha woman after she transformed into a crawler, I saw an image flash in her mind, like I had with Colden's. It was of her saying, 'To avenge my brother,' as she stood before

Antikai. He sat on this revolting onyx throne and told her, 'Not yet.' So I envisioned him and created the illusion that he had teleported here."

Nuelle smiled. "So your gift has grown."

"It has."

He guided everyone around a corner. Hopefully, all of their gifts would grow stronger sooner than later—his as well. Those savages had almost killed him.

Elisena smiled, her hands dangling loosely at her sides. "The hearts here are refreshing." Her smile dimmed. "Unlike our adversaries."

They passed an aquarium-wall full of blue and purple glowfish. As they swam peacefully, indigo light glided across Elisena's face.

"What did you see in them?" Nuelle asked.

"Greed, bitterness, a lust for power. And Raysha, had a vicious hatred for you particularly and a lust for revenge that was as terrifying as her appearance."

Nuelle sighed. "Apparently, Zagan was her brother."

Elisena gave a nod. "That explains a lot."

"Prince Nuelle?" a voice called from the end of the corridor, and the glowfish in the aquatic wall brightened. "Is that you?"

Nuelle quickened his steps. "It is, with my Sentinels and a few guests."

Prince Maimon scurried through the hallway, his long curls and the bottom of his mauve robe flowing behind him. He stopped before them, and they bowed. "Why didn't you send messengers? We would have deployed fifteen knights to deliver you here safely."

Nuelle looked at Darcy, and a pang struck his already wounded heart. "It wasn't a planned visit."

Prince Maimon gazed at Darcy and his despondent family. The prince's purple eyes faded to lavender.

"This is Darcy Pennit and his family," Nuelle said. "Their home was destroyed and they are in mourning for his sister. Can they lodge here until another home is built for them?"

"Of course they may. Gillean!"

A shriveled man scuffled from the hall on the left. "My lord?"

"Please take this young man and his family to the guest quarters and ensure they receive an abundance of provisions."

"Yes, my lord." Gillean led Darcy and his family through the corridor he entered from.

"Let us go to my father." With swift steps, Prince Maimon led Nuelle and his Sentinels out of the Master Hall and into a marble commons. As he strode to a staircase, Surta and Elisena gawked at hovering diamond flame-holders that brightened whenever he passed. He jogged up the stairs and then glided into a silver and ivory throne hall lined by knights on either side.

Javin drew close to Nuelle. "Is every throne hall this guarded?"

"No." He locked his stare onto Prince Maimon. Just like all the extra security stationed at the square, the increase of defense only meant one thing—rising rebellion.

As they neared two knights standing before a pair of platinum doors, Prince Maimon slowed his gait. The knights stepped aside.

"Father," Prince Maimon called, "Prince Nuelle has arrived."

"Please, come in," King Eliah spoke from inside, his voice higher than usual, strained with worry. The knights opened the doors, and Prince Maimon led the way. King Eliah's lilac eyes matched his silk robe and the stone molding his throne.

He strode toward them, more wrinkles lining his forehead than the last time he visited the Supreme Palace, and his once thick silver beard now appeared thin. "What a pleasure it is to see you, my boy." He embraced Nuelle. "I sent the last of my knights to deliver you from the commercial square, but they knew not of your whereabouts." He pulled away and surveyed the blood-stains on Nuelle, and the wounds of his Sentinels. King Eliah frowned. "My sovereignty. What has become of my people?"

"This wasn't done by your people," Nuelle said.

As more wrinkles creased his forehead, he turned to his son. "Can you please have a meal with healing fruits prepared for our guests, and fresh garbs as well?"

"Right away, Father." He hurried out the room, and Nuelle recounted the events that befell them while at Darcy's home.

As he neared the end, a wave of heat surged in his palms. "We fought off the mob from the tavern, but then three Savage Shifters arrived who were sent by Prince Antikai to destroy me"—he removed the Acumen from his satchel—"or this."

King Eliah's mouth fell open. As he gazed upon the lustrous golden cover, his eyes glistened. "Thank Sovereignty they were not able to."

The heat in Nuelle's arms intensified. "One of them tried to impale it with a dagger, but it didn't leave a scratch."

The King rested his palm on Father's golden insignia, protruding from the Acumen's center. "They will need something much stronger in order to destroy this book."

"What can destroy it?" Ave asked.

"That, I know not." He peered over everyone. "And let us hope Prince Antikai does not either."

Nuelle slipped the Acumen back into his satchel, and King Eliah trudged to the throne. His robe dragged on the floor behind him as if it too could feel the weight of his grief. He slumped into the chair. "I am afraid things are getting worse."

"Worse?" Nuelle approached.

"Riots began a week ago. At first they were just petitioning, but then the people started fires to shops and in the villages. I had to deploy more guards to patrol the main square and set a curfew." He rubbed his forehead. "There are even rumors spreading of schemes to attack the palace. Soon, they will demand I step down from my kingship." King Eliah held his face in his palms. "The poison of darkness is ravaging our land and it is rapidly infecting the people."

Elisena peered at him with lavender irises. "I don't understand how the citizens of Sunezia—our people—can turn against the will of the Supreme King."

He gazed at her and rested trembling palms upon his armrests. "Oh, my dear girl, although our people were fashioned with the characteristic of faithfulness, we were also created with free will."

"But what reason have they for disposing you of your kingship? When have you ever led us astray, or taken advantage of your rule?"

He sighed. "When the hearts of men are enticed to do evil and they entertain the voice of darkness, it is but a matter of time before their pride is fed and they become blinded—hardened to the truth of the Supreme King…as they did long ago."

As Nuelle's mind reeled, his temples hammered beneath his skin. Hadn't the people learned from their past failures? The Great Kin War of Old nearly destroyed them all; their own greed and jealousy rapidly devoured one another until Father's rage could no longer be tamed and the Terrestrial Curses were unleashed. They'd been so humbled by that near annihilation, retracing old paths seemed impossible. Love had won...or so it seemed.

Tane's words of warning on Nuelle's fifteenth birthday infused his thoughts: *The presumption of human goodness is man's greatest plight.* In the eyes of a younger brother, thirteen years shorter and often within the secure gates of home, Brother appeared to be wrong. They'd basically lived in a compound of faithful residents who, though not blood, were no less like family and acted as such. How Tane could believe the opposite when the obvious surrounded on every side is what was deemed presumptuous. But then there was Colden, Zagan, Jilt, Brone, Raysha, and Antikai; the men from the tavern who'd just attacked them for no reason; the people of Ideya and now the once faithful Sunezians. They'd all proved brother's belief. But if true, then did unbreakable goodness even exist at all?

King Eliah rose to his feet as Elisena and the others stood with taut faces. He planted himself before Nuelle and rested shaky palms on his shoulders. "Supreme Prince, you have your Sentinels now, but you must be fervent in training, understanding your enemies never tire of doing evil so you must never tire of doing good." Deep purple poured into his irises—determined, convinced. "Young Prince, you must stay alive until the prophecies come to pass. You are our only hope."

Twelve: The Supreme Palace

The wall of rushing water that bordered Agapon burst fifteen yards ahead. Nuelle clutched the reins of his vanaph and looked at his Sentinels, riding alongside him with the four knights King Eliah sent as extra guards for their journey.

"Line up behind me!" Nuelle tugged the bronze reins, and his vanaph picked up pace. "Supreme Prince Nuelle!" At his shout, a large hole formed in the liquid wall, and he and the others soared into the wide, watery tunnel.

"This is too grand!" Riff yelled.

Nuelle smiled as they zoomed through it and emerged into Agapon. Millions of tiny orange lights filled the warm sky. The mini life-orbs bounced gently off his body.

Surta poked at them. "This is all immensely whimsical."

"Wait until you see the palace." Ave held an arm out, and the orbs dispersed around it.

The subtle, airy melodies sung by Agapon's wind kissed Nuelle's ears as he and the others flew over multi-stone homes on the lowlands. He patted his vanaph's neck. "We're almost there, boy."

Elisena gasped and pointed ahead. Evening's silver light glowed above the palace, its rays glistening on the topaz exterior. Though not as evident as in daytime, the banner of colors that swirled around it like a ribbon sparkled. Nuelle loosened his grip on the reins. Finally, he would be in the presence of Father and all of his old family again, the servants and cooks, seamstresses and medics, at a place that actually welcomed and embraced...at home.

A thousand citizens gathered on the white dirt in front of the palace entrance. Their shouts drowned out the wind's soft melodies. Chants joined together: "Freedom isn't silent! Speak now or we will become violent!"

Nuelle veered his vanaph to the side, his palms moistening. This couldn't be happening. Agaponians threatening Father? They'd just left one riotous kingdom to enter into yet another, here, in the central kingdom, in the supposedly most faithful place in all of the land? Would this nightmare ever end? Nuelle led the others to the courtyard. "Down, boy." His vanaph descended onto the gray stone where he had so often sparred Tane. Hurrying off. And gripping his satchel, Nuelle addressed the knights King Eliah sent to escort them. "Tell the King thank you again."

As they bowed and soared away, Nuelle turned to his Sentinels. "Follow me."

Elisena clung to her open umbrella while she and the others trailed Nuelle to the courtyard entrance where two Elite Knights stood. Their golden armor shined in the evening daystar's luminance.

"Supreme Prince," a familiar voice said as the knights bowed. Sir Umbus lifted his visor as he and the other knight straightened. He quickly opened the door, the knight beside him quiet. One yellow eye peered at Nuelle through the golden helmet. Sir Prototis—Tane's Sentry. A prickling sensation ran up Nuelle's arms. Strange. He had felt the same sensation with the men from the tavern in Sunezia. Sir Prototis looked away, and Nuelle strode into the palace, his Sentinels close behind.

Golden flame-holder orbs floated a few feet below the hallway's barrel-vault ceiling, offering faint evening light. Oddly, no knights patrolled. Nuelle's Sentinels whispered behind him as they traveled through the amethyst-stone corridor. Besides the angry cries of those petitioning outside, an abnormal silence smothered the palace.

Ave scurried to his side. "Something isn't right."

"I agree." Nuelle engulfed his palms with hot wind. "Stay alert."

Elisena closed her umbrella. His friends stopped whispering. Sophana readied a leaf-blade while Riff transformed a rock into energy and consumed it. Nuelle walked swifter, but maintained quietness. He turned into the Great Room and hurried to the center staircase. More golden flame-holders hovered above the railings, and the large crystal chandelier carried low, smoldering flames as if they feared shining brighter and being noticed. The last time everything seemed so still within these walls was after Sir Amador died...

"Wait." Elisena stopped walking. She looked around, sweat glistening on her forehead. "Someone is coming, but there's some sort of barrier over his or her heart that I can't get past."

The chandelier's flames grew, flickering violently. As Ave's arms shifted to blue and stretched, everyone circled Nuelle. He gripped his satchel with one hand while lifting the other, his wind now whistling. Surta gasped. A figure stood at the top of the staircase, moving slowly, stealthily. Nuelle pressed his satchel close as smoke billowed from his arms. The person glided down the staircase. Nuelle's hands dropped to his sides. *Father!*

Diamonds and sapphires gleamed on his gold crown. The velvet robe he wore graced the steps behind him, and his amber eyes blazed brighter than the flames he passed. As he reached the bottom, he opened his arms. Ave and the others trembled and bowed—Javin shaking the most—as Nuelle hurried into Father's embrace. The warmth that entered every time he healed swelled in his heart and saturated his mind. In Father's strong yet gentle arms, concern, dread, uncertainty, it all seemed to crumble beneath the refuge of perfect love. Nuelle held on tighter. This was home; safe in Father's presence.

"I see you have brought friends," Father said as he released. "And that you visited King Eliah."

Nuelle turned to his Sentinels, sweating in the garbs King Eliah provided—Riff pulling on Prince Maimon's small tunic, attempting to cover his half-exposed stomach.

"The academy is no longer safe for us," Nuelle said.

Father's eyes swept over the commons and he spoke in a low voice. "Nowhere is."

The Sentinels and Nuelle, looking specifically at Riff, frowned. *Then we're all nomads now, like he and his mother were…*

"Follow me." With swift and silent steps, Father led them into the emerald kitchen-corridor. He descended steps leading to the kitchen's entrance and strode inside. Several evening cooks swept and scrubbed the stuffy room. Two giant-rollers protruded from a silvery head—Old Lady Flemm. She hunched over one of the six iron ovens, viciously scrubbing its top with a toothbrush—probably her own. Ave's mother mopped swiftly and precisely nearby, her brown hair netted as usual, but now a gray strand hung down her face. She looked up and stiffened. The mop slipped from her grasp and clattered against the glossy floor. Her slanted eyes widened. Those nearby stopped cleaning and followed her stare.

Old Lady Flemm's roller-head craned in Ave's direction and she pointed the toothbrush at him. "Am I having a nightmare?"

He crossed his arms. "Or maybe you died and didn't make it to paradise."

"Retire to your bedchambers." Father's voice managed to reverberate in the crowded space. Everyone but Old Lady Flemm dropped their wash-articles and scurried from the kitchen. After sticking the toothbrush in her mouth, Old Lady Flemm slapped Ave's cheek with it. As he cringed, Lady Purine sniveled and gave his other cheek a quick kiss before bustling out, closing the door behind her. Nuelle gazed at Ave, wiping his cheek and frowning. His countenance made plain the worry he had for his mother. Lady Purine already lost her husband. And that blow aged her, like it had Ave. How would she handle knowing the danger her son was in? What would it do to her already broken heart?

"I know why you have left the academy," Father spoke in a hushed voice, "but you must return."

Sophana gawped. "But your highness, there was even a half-blooded thorkkis there, and she killed the Overseer."

Fire ignited in the ovens. "I know what Emmer has done. But she is not a thorkkis."

"Emmer?"

"Her real name."

Sophana clasped her forehead. "But then how come she looked like a thorkkis, and even identified as one?"

Riff raised a palm. "Pardon me, your highnesses, but what is a thorkkis?"

The oven's flames reflected off Father's irises, making them blaze more fervently. "After I cursed the lands nearly six-hundred years ago, weeds and thorns sprang from the ground and twisted together, rising up into beasts that would plague Athdonia for all its days."

Nuelle stared at the fire, though he could feel his Sentinels watching—and sense their fear. Yes, Father's rage was dreadful for the one beneath its glare, but that was only one element of him, and his patience often seemed even greater.

"Being able to have limbs morph to vines is Emmer's gift. Like the leaves that grow on your arms." Father looked at Sophana, then at Ave. "And the coral that you can shift into." He sighed. "But Emmer grew to hate her gift and eventually, herself. She managed to attract the thorkkis with her similar abilities, and began to befriend them. I thought at the academy she would make new friends and learn to accept how she was made, discover how she could be used for the good of Zephoris. But I see now she is still lost, having yet to understand my purposes for her."

Javin shook his head. "I've been there."

Father surveyed him. "And don't return."

As the Sentinels' attention shifted to Javin, Nuelle watched Father. Did he think Javin would go back to not trusting him or his son? Indeed, Elisena's brother had rough edges that pricked if brushed against, but he remained with them till this day. But did his loyalty rely on his sister's?

Father glanced at the entryway. "I regret to say the number of trustworthy knights here is steadily dwindling."

Nuelle's heart sank, never believing he'd ever have to utter his next words. "Have they attempted an attack?"

"Not yet. But it won't be long before they do."

"How can your knights turn against you?" Ave said.

A subtle anger layered Father's rumbling voice. "It is only the beginning."

Elisena stared at him with lilac eyes. "The beginning of what, your majesty?"

He gazed at everyone. "The Perilous Eve."

The Sentinels traded apprehensive glances. A heaviness unlike any other pressed down on Nuelle's chest. The Acumen mentioned the Perilous Eve; nights of unrest that usher in the greatest rebellion Zephoris has ever seen—one where many fall, souls are lost, and chaos begins to reign while unbeknownst to the people, a new king sits on the throne...

Ave looked toward the kitchen's entry. "What must we do, my King, and what about my mother?"

"I will look after her." Father's smoldering eyes scanned him and the others. "The hour is already late. Stay here for the night, and tomorrow make your leave before the daystar rises." He focused on Nuelle. A pulsing warmth prodded his head, as if it gently searched every thought within. "You have had a long day," Father said, turning to the Sentinels. "Take your rest, for who knows what dawn will bring."

The hairs on Nuelle's skin attested to the wrongness suffocating the burgundy hallway outside Father's bedchamber. A silver ray snuck in through a window on the left wall. Brightening and dimming, the weak light struggled to illuminate the corridor. Overpowering darkness warped its color and painted the walls black. Nuelle approached the ivory door, appearing to be a deathly gray in the lack of lighting. It creaked open. His stomach churned. Father's door never stayed open at night…

He stepped inside. An unnatural coldness saturated the air. Nuelle glanced at the fireplace. The wood lay unlit. Evening light poured into the chamber through the terrace doors on the left. Someone stood beside Father's bed, peering down at him as he slept. Nuelle raced toward them. Father stared at the ceiling, the usual blaze in his eyes extinguished. Crimson liquid seeped through the velvet sheets around his chest.

"Father!" Nuelle looked at the person standing at the bedside, and his heart skipped. An exact replica of himself smiled. In one hand, he carried the Acumen, and in the other, the crystal sword Father held in the portrait from Sir Dangian's lesson room. Nuelle lunged at the imposter. He vanished. Nuelle spun around. Father no longer lay in bed, and the now folded sheets stretched clean of blood. Nuelle surveyed the bedchamber. Where had they gone?

"Prince Nuelle!"

The terrace doors burst open. He inched away from the bed and walked onto the terrace. The gemstone homes of Agapon rested. Only the wind stirred the sleeping capital.

"Prince Nuelle!" The cry came from somewhere far beyond the central kingdom...

The ground below his feet cracked. Lavender grass sprouted up, rapidly covering the floors. Walls peeled back. Glowing trees of multiple hues replaced them. Warmth engulfed, shunning the dreadful cold. A lush forest with sparkling leaves encircled, and green trees surrounded a clearing ahead. An emerald robed man stood in the center. Wet strands of purplish-black hair stuck to his forehead, and fear darkened his blue eyes. "Prince Nuelle, please find me beyond the blue trees. There are secrets that can no longer be hidden."

Nuelle jolted awake. Sweat doused his head. The man's eyes clouded his mind as he studied his dark bedchamber. Besides Mugro, sleeping on his back with his auburn wings sprawled, the room remained empty of human company and still intact.

Slowly, Nuelle lay back down, his sleep taken captive by his pounding heart and racing thoughts. Was it all merely a dream, a nightmare? Could Father die—and by someone who looked just like his second son? Or was it a Savage Shifter? And did King Bertil, Antikai's father, who ran off in the woods at Onipur while Amador stayed behind, hide in the Aurora Forest? There remained only one way to discover the truth...

Thirteen: Treachery

Please be alive, please be alive. Slithers of golden rays crept through the window outside Father's bedchamber, illuminating the rich burgundy walls and bright ivory door. The corridor's blend of royal colors welcomed, rather than intimidated—as the nightmare falsely depicted. But then again, depending on which side you stood with Father, joy or dread could be a reasonable response.

Sentinels following with their belongings, and Ave, wearing the leather, crisscross-strapped water carrier Surta made him, Nuelle gripped his own satchel and sack. Only once in his life had he witnessed Father's rage firsthand. Lumen, who'd been a palace Medic, began practicing strange chants and methods of healing on servants who'd been seeing him. After one such encounter caused Seamstress Poema to excessively vomit before passing out, her husband told Father. An order was made to search Lumen's bedchamber and a number of books on the power of darkness were discovered. Wanting to obtain gifts he hadn't been given by Father, rather than asking for them, Lumen chose another route to gain what he desired—even though those powers were far lesser and eventually proved harmful. With a single shout that cursed Lumen with boils and caused the entire corridor his bedchamber was in to quake, destroying everything he owned, Father had Lumen expelled from the palace. No one had ever been caught delving into darker knowledge since.

Stopping before Father's bedchamber door, Nuelle turned to his Sentinels. "Keep watch. I shouldn't be long." He faced the entry and knocked with a clammy hand. "Father?" A bead of sweat slid down his temple as he awaited Father's powerful voice. Surely—at least the dream's beginning—was no more than a nightmare. Nothing and no one could ever kill Father. It simply wasn't possible. Or was it? He knocked again, firmer and more rapidly. "Father? Are you awake?"

"Enter, my son."

A torrent of relief washed over as he opened the door and strode inside. The usual inviting warmth coated the air, the fireplace's flames crackling.

"Come." Father sat at the edge of his bed, robed in white silk. The fire shined off the smooth material and made him glow.

Nuelle glanced around the chamber as he approached. Perhaps the imposter lurked in the shadows.

Father patted the space beside him. "It feels like ages since you've sat at my side."

Nuelle's chin dipped as he set his rucksack down and took a seat. He'd spent almost two weeks in Middren before departing to the academy. It had been nearly three months too long since he enjoyed Father's company.

His flickering irises watched. "You are wearing guilt."

Nuelle averted his gaze. "I just feel bad for giving all my time to Middren and neglecting you and Tane. It's time I'll never get back."

"Ah, my son. Love compelled you to spend yourself for the stricken in their greatest time of need. Certainly, you were missed, but both Tane and I did not need you as they did."

Nuelle's stare reconnected with Father's. "Maybe if I was here, Tane wouldn't have gone to the Obsidian. Or maybe he would've been able to witness my improvement in combat and trust me to go with him. Maybe he'd still be alive."

Father inhaled slowly, carefully… "Why are you carrying the burden of life and death?"

"Several lives stalk the gates of death because of me."

"But Tane chose to voyage to the Obsidian, against both my will, and yours."

Nuelle rubbed his thumbs together. Father's words were true, but the sense of responsibility still nagged.

Father looked at his bedchamber door. "With free will, your Sentinels have also chosen their paths."

"But I accepted them."

"Why?"

"Because I believed I had no other choice."

"That was your only reason?"

Nuelle touched his rucksack, where the Acumen rested. "No. They also displayed their gifts with courage and offered them in sacrifice."

Father placed his warm hand over Nuelle's. "And those are the kinds of people you need at your side. Not just for your sake, but for others' as well."

Father's warmth seeped from his palm and melted into Nuelle, rolling over him in gentle waves. Indeed, duty hadn't been the only reason for choosing the six. Just like it wasn't the sole reason he woke up early each morning and went to bed late every evening for those two weeks of service in Middren. Yes, it was love that compelled him. And love shouldn't be motivated or hindered by fear. Nor did it force submission, but it invited, and hoped for the best. Just as he invited any willing prodigies to the Sentinel challenge. And it was of course his hope that none of them would perish. Besides, it wasn't about just him and his Sentinels, but about the Faithful who needed them to fulfill their purpose.

Father's hand slipped back into his lap. "You have come to ask about the dream and the nightmare."

The peace Father brought strived to stay in Nuelle, but the unpleasant reminder threatened it. "Yes, my king."

"What do you think of them?"

Nuelle's empty stomach twisted. "I'm not entirely certain."

Father smoothed out a crease in the velvet bed covering. "Dreams can be confusing things. They can be merely our subconscious thoughts, they can be messages—or something more menacing."

The fireplace's flames brightened.

Nuelle swallowed. "Was mine a message and … something else?"

Father peered at him. "I think you know the answer to that question." The fire returned to a gentle smolder.

"The sword in my nightmare," Nuelle said, "it was the same one you carried in the portrait in Sir Dangian's lesson room."

Father's knowing gaze stirred Nuelle's heart with warmth.

"When the time is at hand, your destiny will lead you to the sword." Father leaned in and spoke with a subtle urgency. "Do not fear the troubles ahead, my son, but concentrate on the tasks at hand."

"Yes, Father."

A small smile lifted his mouth, and he rested his hand on Nuelle's again. "I am proud of you, Supreme Prince."

Nuelle's chest ached as he touched his pant's pocket where Tane's signet-ring hid. Though brother was gone, it still didn't feel right wearing it yet. Maybe it never would.

Someone crashed into the door from outside and grunted.

"Ave!" Sophana shouted.

Nuelle and Father jolted off the bed. Hot wind gushed from Nuelle's palms as he raced to the door and threw it open. Sophana and the girls stooped beside Ave, lying near the entryway. Blood leaked from his abdomen and onto the floors. Nuelle dropped to his knees and grasped Ave's cold hand. His face had paled, and his eyelids hung heavy. With bare hands, Riff sparred two knights. Another knight lay on the ground while Javin wielded a sword against a fourth knight whose blade dripped with blood. The knight's one yellow eye glanced at Nuelle. Sir Prototis! He dodged a blow from Javin and then bolted out the corridor shouting, "Attack! Attack!"

Nuelle squeezed his best friend's cold palm, fiery heat consuming his chest and arms. More Elite Knights sprinted into the corridor. Father yelled. His voice echoed through the hallway, causing the walls to tremble. The knights collapsed.

Tears hazed Nuelle's vision as he pulled Ave into his arms and rose. "Hold on, Ave."

Sophana wept as Father strode to Nuelle's side. "We must hurry." Father swept through the corridor. As they turned the corner, two knights sprang at them, bringing their swords down. Father pressed his palms against the knights' breastplates. Dropping their weapons, they writhed in agony and sank onto the floor.

Nuelle and the others swiftly descended the staircase, several more Elite Knights attacking and then falling by Father's touch or command. Three knights ran into the commons as Father and the rest reached the bottom. Blood spattered the knights' swords and gold armor.

"Your highness!" Sir Umbus and the knights bowed. "Sir Prototis has lowered the drawbridge. The citizens are forcing their way inside!"

"Get Lady Purine and the other servants, and ride vanaphs to the Twirl Blossom Garden. I will be there shortly."

"Right away, your highness." He and the others darted off as Father hurried to the courtyard door. A trail of blood oozed from Ave's mouth.

Tremors rippled across Nuelle's chest as he gripped his best friend's cold body. "Stay with me, Ave."

Father and the group rushed into the courtyard. The daystar's golden light bathed the stony ground. The floating life orbs reflected the star's luminance. When Father passed, the orbs around him brightened, as if energized by his presence. Seven vanaphs flew from the forest and landed before them.

Father patted one of the six-winged creatures. "Quickly now."

Riff, Surta, and the twins mounted one. Sophana continued to cry as she watched Ave. Approaching him, Father lifted a palm, and a clutter of life orbs stuck to it. He gently pressed it against Ave's stomach. Sophana stepped closer. An orange glow filled Father's palm, and the life orbs disintegrated. Tears still streamed from Sophana's yellow eyes as she observed. Father exhaled and removed his hand.

Ave's eyes slowly opened. He frowned as he blinked at Nuelle. "Why are you carrying me?"

A rush of warmth swelled in Nuelle's heart as he set Ave down. Sophana beamed and embraced him. He blushed as she pulled away.

Nuelle smiled at Father. "Thank you."

"Stop them!" Sir Prototis shouted from the courtyard's entrance, and a horde of his traitorous knights stampeded toward Nuelle and the others.

"Make haste," Father said.

Nuelle, Ave, and Sophana each hurried onto the last three vanaphs. Nuelle grabbed the reins. "What about you?"

"I am not ready to depart just yet." Father tapped the long neck of Nuelle's vanaph, and it kicked off the ground. "After you find the King, return at once to the academy. They need you." His eyes gleamed with tears. "And when the first battle is over, do not come back here."

Nuelle and the Sentinels' vanaphs zoomed into the sky as Father dashed up the highland of the Twirl Blossom Garden, fifty of the treacherous knights trailing him with swords raised.

Fourteen: The Aurora Forest

Father, please stay safe. The increasingly warm wind brushed Nuelle's tears away. The time with Father had been painfully cut short—literally. Bearing swords given to them to protect, Elite Knights instead wielded their weapons in rebellious attacks against their Supreme King and those who sided with him. Father's words engrained Nuelle's mind and bled into his heart ever since the moment he and his Sentinels departed from the palace. *And when the first battle is over, do not come back here.* If returning home wasn't an option, where else was there to go when the third trimester finished? Where would Father and Lady Purine, Sir Umbus, and the other remaining palace faithful go? And had they even made it out alive? It appeared anyone who chose to stay the course and remain aligned with Father would be killed or forced to live as nomads.

Nuelle's vanaph panted heavily from the three-day journey. He stroked its white fur. They had only rested once, and for a short time. All the attacks, all the fighting and now running. Would real rest ever come? *...You shall lead the Faithful to the land of the Incandescia.* Father's written words seeped through the doubt. Yes, that mysterious place reserved for the Faithful, a place of inextinguishable light, the only place left apparently unmarred by darkness, rebellion, and hate. Could that be where Father headed to now...

Down below, the Aurora Forest's glowing leaves trembled in the wind like bleeding rainbows. The colors blended together, their luminance rising to the nighttime sky. At the woods' end, forbidden blackness stretched for what seemed like eternity. The Obsidian upheld a reputation of terror—a haunt for beasts and a land plagued by Father's wrath—but from the sky's point of view, the dreaded territory appeared to cower from the Aurora Forest's light.

"We're here now, boy." Nuelle pulled his vanaph's reins and peered over his shoulder as the creature veered to the shimmering grass beneath. His friends remained close, their vanaphs also descending. As they landed, the temperature in the wind increased to a draining heat. Nuelle clenched his satchel and slipped off the vanaph. Without much effort, his exposed arms quickly moistened with sweat. Javin untied his rucksack, the trademark sweet, grassy scent of a vanaph flowing from him. He patted his creature's head. It grunted as if responding and then leapt into the air.

"I told him I'll summon him when needed," Javin said.

"Thank you," Nuelle replied.

Ave and the others grabbed their satchels and rucksacks as the rest of the creatures soared away.

"Wow." Elisena unclipped her umbrella from her back, opened it, and gazed up at the radiant trees. "The pictures I've seen in books aren't nearly as beautiful."

Surta plucked a handful of glowing lavender pasture and examined it. "Depictions are never as good as the real thing."

"Yours are." Riff smirked at her and she rolled her eyes, though she did smile as well.

"Let's find a place to rest." Nuelle led the six underneath an expanse of glimmering purple-and-red leaves. They needed to find King Bertil quickly so they could return to the academy as Father instructed. And in all the land, no forest stretched as vastly as this one.

Ave spoke quietly, the tree's light revealing his moist eyes. "I didn't get to thank King Nifal for saving my life."

Nuelle's chest ached as he stopped under a purple tree surrounded by a thick patch of grass. "You'll be able to one day."

Ave nodded and then stared at the woods ahead. "You think my mother is safe?"

"My father said he would look after her. You know he keeps his word."

Ave smiled weakly and then rummaged through his rucksack and sat with the others. He removed sweet stems, other vegetables, and a few vials of seasoning before walking a few paces off. As he built a fire and began cooking, Nuelle joined the rest of his Sentinels on the warm grass, more pain pressing into his heart. What would Ave do when they found the man he witnessed his father die to protect; the man who fled while Amador fought off Antikai's savages? What would this man, this king, have to say for himself, and could the secrets he held help their journey, or hinder it…

As Ave returned with handfuls of speared sweet stems carrying other vegetables, Nuelle's heart skipped. Did Bertil write the letter they found in the cluttered room the Savage Shifters had attacked them in? An intense sensation probed his heart. He peered at Elisena. She watched intently, her umbrella tilted.

As Ave handed out the stems, Sophana looked at Nuelle. "What's wrong?"

He scanned the perimeter.

"I've been checking," Elisena said. "We're the only ones in this area—for now."

"Thank you for staying alert." Nuelle addressed Ave. "Remember that scroll from the room the Savage Shifters attacked us in?"

"What about it?"

"I believe it was a scroll to my father. It was bound with an emerald seal the same color as the robe King Bertil wore back in"—he swallowed hard—"the Onipur forest, and the one in the dream."

Ave's eyes widened as he handed a sweet stem to Javin.

Nuelle continued. "The writer wasn't sure if he was fit for a task he'd been entrusted with. He was afraid that he would fail and the prophecies wouldn't be fulfilled."

"What do you think the task was?" Riff asked as he took a stem from Ave.

"I think we're going to find out soon enough."

Riff spat out a mouthful of the green and blue food. "Graether waste?"

Ave bit off the end of a sweet stem. "Vegetables…"

"Where's the meat?"

"You can't just carry around meat in your bag for three days."

"What do you mean?" Riff snatched his satchel and pulled out a large foecry sandwich. "I do it all the time."

Javin choked on a stem. "Was that once a living foecry?"

Riff chomped into a leg. "I hope so."

"You do know they're incredibly intelligent creatures with semi-complex feelings."

"Actually, I didn't know that."

Javin straightened. "And now that you do?"

Riff spoke with his mouth full. "I'll take a minute longer to appreciate their complexity before I hunt them."

Javin glowered. "You're heartless."

"Us Mights' need meat, a little bread, and more meat!"

Surta removed a book and a handkerchief from her satchel and daintily set them over her lap. "You need more manners, too."

He shook his sandwich, a greasy wing hanging from it. "Manners don't fill stomachs!"

Sophana addressed Ave. "Well, I think this was both creature-friendly and creative, using sweet stems to carry the rest of the vegetables—delicious, too."

He choked on a bite, and she smiled before speaking again. "Why do you cook so well?"

Ave cleared his throat. "My father was Nuelle's Sentry, but my mother served as the head cook. Ever since I could walk, she'd bring me into the kitchen and have me help out."

Nuelle smiled. "He cooked his first meal when he was four."

Sophana licked her lips. "Impressive."

Ave pulled his shoulders back. "And I learned how to handle a knife when I was three."

"Hmm," Sophana said, the leaf-blades on her shoulders curving. "I learned how to wield these when I was three. My mother stopped giving me dolls because I kept using them for target practice."

"Yes, she really is lethal, Ave." As Nuelle took a bite of the soft stems, smokey and salty, tangy and sweet, Ave fidgeted with a piece of vegetable. He cooked almost as good as Lady Purine and was usually just as confident. But not with Sophana...

A purple glowflitter flew atop Javin's shoulder. He smiled as he finished the last of his meal.

"And how long have you been using your gift, Javin?" Nuelle asked.

He and Elisena looked at each other. He slowly wiped his mouth with the back of his hand before answering. "Since the night our mother left." He set his palms on the ground and leaned back some. "She'd taken the mother roto of our two flocklings. I couldn't sleep that night so I went outside to their nest. Apparently, they couldn't sleep either. So I climbed inside and sat between them while they cried. I cried with them and told them I was sorry that our mothers left us."

Elisena kept her eyes down as he continued.

"And then I heard these strange, high-pitched voices in my mind, asking where she'd gone and when would she return. It took me a few minutes to realize it was the baby rotos."

Surta closed her book. "Incredible."

Javin sighed. "It was." He raised his index-finger, and the purple glowflitter floated atop it. "It still is."

Riff swallowed the rest of his sandwich and also sighed. "I miss my mammy."

"You'll see her again," Ave said.

"In eight months," Sophana replied. "And if we survive."

Everyone stared at her. She shrugged. "What, it's true."

Nuelle focused on Surta as she folded her handkerchief. "And you? When did you learn about your gift?"

"A week after starting children's school. O Sovereignty, it was dreadful!" She tapped her colorful, gem headpiece. "Before I made this, I couldn't control my mind projections. I'd be in class, bored to sleep by my preceptors since I usually already knew what they were teaching, and I'd awake to my peers screaming at my dreams that had invaded the room." She raised her hands and wiggled her fingers. "And then, if I was able to stay awake, I'd begin imagining things, like dragon offspring bursting through the windows and attacking the preceptor and children."

Everyone laughed as she concluded.

"It didn't take but another week of chaos and panic before I was banned from community schooling."

Elisena twirled her umbrella. "Sounds familiar."

Surta's head perked. "You were also forbidden from attending community schools?"

"I wasn't banned, but all the mocking I received for always carrying around this umbrella caused my father to forbid me from community schools. After my first year, I was removed and schooled from home."

Riff pulled a stone from his satchel. "I was never schooled with books and all that."

Sophana mock-gasped. "I'm shocked."

Ave chuckled as he rested his back against a trunk. "And how'd you learn about your…interesting gift, Riff?"

He tossed the stone and caught it. "I just chewed on a rock one day."

As Surta and the others laughed, Nuelle looked closely at the tough youth. "After the challenge, when we all were in Overseer Enri's office, you mentioned you and your mother were nomads. Why did you live that way?"

Riff brought his big knees in and rested his elbows on them. Gradually, the red in his irises leaked into the whites. "My pappy's a drunkard. The tavern was his first home and our crack in the cave was his inn. Almost every night he'd come and beat on my mammy. She's strong, could almost hold her own against him, but he always won." He squeezed the rock. "For a long time I was just a boy, bigger than most my age, but not nearly as big as Pappy. So I'd have to just watch and wait, watch and wait, until one day, I became a young man." His crimson stare locked onto Nuelle whose blood temperature rose by the minute. "In my land, men are the head of their tribes, and the stronger you are, the more you're respected. Never mind if you beat your wife and children. If you're the mightiest warrior for miles, no one challenges you. But after I bit on that rock and found out what I could do, I faced Pappy—with my fists."

Javin put his arm around Elisena. "I don't blame you."

"Ha. You do have Gavrailian blood in you."

Elisena scooted away from her brother. "Not in our blood, but maybe in his heart. But please continue."

Riff's rock glowed orange. "I won."

Nuelle gave a nod, his back and neck hot with anger. All injustice was loathsome, but the abuse of women made his stomach reel. Like that brief time in Rickles, that congested city at the heart of Innovian. He'd joined Father on a visit to the then-king of Ideya. Hearing of an upgraded water-system that malfunctioned, causing a massive flood to one neighborhood in particular, he dedicated the rest of his time helping with clean up and restoration. One morning, screams were heard from a first-floor room in a nearby communal tower. Racing to the cries led to a man beating his wife with a broken pipe while their three little girls watched in terror from the kitchen. Nuelle balled his fists. They'd been used to both knock out and drag that man to the nearest dungeon.

Surta slowly raised her hand like a timid student. "But then why did you have to become nomads if you were now the greatest warrior in your village?"

"King Lothar is a mighty warrior, but also a mighty hypocrite. It's legal to attack when it's self-defense, unless you're defending yourself or someone else against a man who served in the elite ranks of Lothar's army." His gaze returned to Nuelle, the white returning, and now Riff's eyes pleaded. "I couldn't go to the dungeons because Mammy wouldn't have made it without me. Divorced, widowed, or son-less women in Gavrail get forced into harlotry. We had to go on the run."

Nuelle spoke firmly. "Riff, if my father invited you to his academy, clearly, your past doesn't matter to him, so it doesn't matter to me either."

His bottom lip trembled. "Thank you."

Nuelle gave a nod. Father always believed the best in people, until they proved otherwise. Just as he did with Antikai…

As a warm breeze stirred the glowing lavender leaves, Elisena peered at Nuelle. "I wanted to ask, my lord, how do you know you can trust King Bertil?"

"I don't." As Nuelle finished his meal, everyone swapped looks. After swallowing his last bite, he answered their silent concern. "But I know if I didn't come, I'd always wonder what it was he wanted to tell me, and if it would have helped us on this journey."

Riff belched. "Well if King Bertil is as evil as his son, he's completely outnumbered."

"I don't think it's going to come to that," Nuelle said as the huge youth laid back and put his hands behind his head.

"I'll still sleep with one eye open." He closed an eyelid. "Wake me up when you're ready to move on."

"We'll move on in a few hours." Nuelle addressed Javin as he rolled his satchel to make a pillow. "Can you be the second to stay up an hour for watch?"

"Sure."

"Thanks. I'll do the first." Nuelle stood as dim golden light crept into the sky. "In four hours, the search for King Bertil begins."

Fiery embers burned Nuelle's face and arms. Waves of heat pressed against his skin, suffocating his sleep. The afternoon daystar smoldered above. Its light united with the encompassing trees. Sweat soaked Nuelle's sleeveless tunic. He jumped to his feet. "We have to start moving."

Ave slowly sat up. He rubbed his eyes before they widened. Sophana's head leaned against his chest. "Uh … fair day," he said.

Her eyes opened. She jerked away and snatched a leaf-blade before scrambling to her feet. She extended it to Ave's throat, its sharp point touching his skin. "How dare you!"

He quickly raised his palms. "I didn't try anything!"

Nuelle slowly approached Sophana. "I know my best friend. However you got there, I'm sure it was an accident."

Javin laughed as he and the others stood. "I actually know how it happened."

Sophana directed the leaf-blade to him and threw it. It barely missed his cheek.

He jumped. "Composure, woman!"

"Speak before I add another scar to your face."

"Listen, princess—"

She tore off another and chucked it again. It whizzed past Javin's ear. Nuelle lifted his palm toward Sophana and released a controlled gust of wind. She stumbled, but quickly caught herself. "Tell me what happened, Javin!"

He smirked. "It's simple. I was on watch and saw you roll over. Your head touched Ave's chest, and I guess it felt comfortable, and since you were asleep, you probably dreamed it was a pillow or something so you stayed there."

She stared at Ave, doubt in her eyes.

"I told you ..." he said slowly, "I didn't try anything."

Elisena peered at him, her umbrella closed. His brow furrowed as he rubbed his chest. Elisena approached Sophana. "He's telling the truth."

Sophana continued to survey Ave, her eyes shimmering with rage.

"Trust me," Elisena said.

Finally, Sophana turned from him and then marched to a tree a few yards away.

Surta pulled a handkerchief from her satchel and wiped the outside of her spectacles. "She is rather unpredictable, isn't she?"

Riff took off his shirt. "Isn't every girl?"

Javin covered Elisena's eyes, but she slapped them away and fixed her stare on the glowing leaves above. Surta masked her spectacled eyes with her handkerchief.

Riff grinned as he rested the tunic on his shoulder. "Like the mountain view?"

She spoke from behind the linen. "Young men like you are the reason I avoid courtship and never imagine anything romantic."

He pouted. "My strength doesn't impress?"

Nuelle blew a gust at Riff's clothing and engulfed it in a mini cyclone. "Stop pouting and stay covered."

Surta lowered her handkerchief and curtsied before Nuelle. "Maybe if the haughty hill behaved more like you, I wouldn't be so prude."

His cheeks burned. "I prefer prude Sentinels."

She giggled. "Not to fear, your highness. I plan on being single for a very long time—if not forever."

"Likewise." Sophana approached.

Ave grabbed her rucksack as she returned and held it out. She hesitated before taking it.

Nuelle locked his gaze onto her. "Work harder at self-control, and before the day's end, I want more answers."

Pink highlighted her cheeks.

"Do you know which direction to go, Prince Nuelle?" Javin chugged from his canister before putting it away.

Nuelle studied the foliage in the surrounding trees faintly pulsing with light. On his left, a purple-and-red tree flickered in straight lines toward the northeast. "This way." He grabbed his satchel and marched forward, checking his canister as the others trailed. Only a quarter of water remained. They had to find a stream soon. The rising temperature threatened to be potentially fatal, and their search could take hours, if not days.

He surveyed the leaves every few minutes, following a specific pattern he hoped would lead them to the King. Sophana, Ave, and Elisena stayed quiet, but Surta, often commented on the structure of the glowing trees and plants—or made standoffish remarks at Riff, which rather than shut him down, caused him to tease her all the more. And Javin spoke a lot…to creatures. A pair of tawters rode his shoulders for a while; a baby nestler had slept atop his head and used his messy hair as a blanket, and then a slime-choker coiled itself around his neck, though he reassured everyone that it wasn't hurting, but rather "hugging" him.

Hours painfully passed. Dizziness clouded Nuelle's brain, muddling his vision. His parched throat begged for water. He checked his canister. Not a drop of liquid remained. The heat must have evaporated what little he had left. He peered over his shoulder. His companions dragged their feet, their clothes and hairlines drenched in sweat. Even Riff panted and walked with slumped shoulders. Nuelle's heart ached. They needed to find water, quickly.

"Prince. Nuelle," Elisena huffed under her umbrella, red splotching her neck and cheeks. "Do you think. We're getting. Clos—" She staggered.

"Elly!" Javin and Nuelle ran to her side.

Surta hunched over. "She needs water."

Ave poked one of the leather containers strapped across his chest. "All my water is dried up."

"We have to find a stream." Nuelle strode forward, his Sentinels trudging behind. An hour passed in search of a water source, but none came.

Ave sank to his knees next to Sophana, his face bright pink. "Why'd you bring us out here, Nuelle? To find a possible enemy, or to have us die of thirst?"

"Ave's right!" Tears filled Javin's lilac eyes. "We're going to die! And for what, Prince Nuelle? A crazed king you had a dream about?"

Surta slowly straightened. "Javin—"

"No, Surta." Riff approached Nuelle. "I'm with Javin and Ave. Prince Nuelle's the one who had us come here." He shoved him. "This was your idea!"

As his Sentinels turned on him, anger invaded Nuelle's heart. "And you agreed to come."

Javin's voice rose to a shout. "Being around you is like a death sentence just waiting to happen!"

"If that's how you feel, then leave." Nuelle faced the others. "I never forced any of you to be my Sentinels. It was your choice."

"I didn't have a choice." Sophana gripped a leaf-blade. "It was become your Sentinel, or go back to Athdonia and be a slave to my father's will."

Ave feebly rose. "Now we're all slaves to your will." His voice grew loud. "And here we are dying of heat, searching for the man responsible for my father's death!" He turned and stormed off.

An invisible dagger impaled Nuelle's heart. His vision blurred, worsening the cloudiness. Brother's words whispered in his thoughts: *Not everyone can be trusted. You must always keep your guard up.*

"Please." Elisena's umbrella hung at her side. "Stop. Fighting." She released the umbrella and collapsed.

"Elly!" Javin dropped beside her. "She's not breathing!"

Tears tickled Nuelle's cheeks as he peered at Elisena. She lay limp in Javin's arms with her mouth hung open. Nuelle bent down and clasped her hand, warm and sticky with sweat. "Elisena?"

She remained motionless.

Nuelle's grip on her hand tightened. Sorrow and disappointment washed away his wrath. His Sentinels were right. His very existence proved life-threatening to each of them. He brought them to the Aurora Forest unprepared and with no evidence that King Bertil could be trusted. Brother was right, but beyond not trusting others, Nuelle couldn't even trust himself. From now on, he needed to keep his guard up, for everyone's sake.

Javin wiped wet strands of hair off Elisena's forehead. Nuelle's shoulders drooped forward. *And Father…how could he call me the Hope of the Faithful when all I bring to those I care about is pain and death?* Tears dropped from his eyes and onto Elisena's cheeks. They swiftly evaporated in the dense heat, leaving only marks of their touch.

As Javin wept, Nuelle squeezed Elisena's hand. The passionate words she declared after leaving Colden's dungeon streamed into Nuelle's mind like a somber melody: *"You say you are the Hope of the Faithful. Well up until now you have given me hope, hope that I was actually born for a purpose. You gave me something to live for…"* Nuelle groaned within as her kind voice echoed in his thoughts.

"I know I might die trying to protect you, but at least every second I breathe will have meaning… If I stand by Nuelle, I won't just be making a difference for the people, I'll be helping to save them."

Another of his tears fell, landing in her mouth. She knew she could die, and now here she was, fulfilling that possibility. Elisena's eyes suddenly opened. Javin recoiled.

"Elisena!" Nuelle scooped his arm beneath her, and Javin helped lift her upright. The blotchiness rapidly left her cheeks and neck. Javin's weeping morphed into laughter. He embraced her as she blinked and peered at Nuelle.

"What happened?" she asked.

He smiled, though his words grieved him. "You almost died."

"I did?"

"Oh, Elly. I thought I lost you." Javin slowly pulled back from Elisena and then frowned. "Wait a minute. How did you become conscious? You had stopped breathing."

"I'm not certain if this is why," Nuelle said, "...but one of my tears fell into her mouth and then her eyes opened."

Javin's brow scrunched as he looked at the others.

Riff gestured to Sophana and Surta. "We all saw it, she woke up right after."

With glassy eyes, Javin helped Elisena stand as he handed her the umbrella, and then turned to Nuelle. Javin bowed, and as he realigned, his irises lightened. "But how do we know your tears did it?"

Surta stumbled. Riff grabbed her as she looked at Nuelle with heavy eyelids. He glimpsed at Riff's large bicep—flexed as he gripped Surta's arm. Nuelle's heart raced as he gazed up at the strong Gavrailian. "Hit me."

Riff cocked his head. "Pardon me, Prince Nuelle?"

"You heard me." He patted his abdomen. "Right in my stomach."

Elisena frowned. "Supreme Prince, I don't think that's the best idea."

"Don't worry, I'll heal." He peered at Riff. "Hurry before I change my mind."

"Okay ..." The giant youth gently helped Surta sit and then planted himself in front of Nuelle. Riff drew his massive fist back, his crimson eyes fierce.

Nuelle bent his knees as he awaited the painful blow. *But what if Riff strikes too hard? What if he accidentally kills me? He did hurt Ave when training, and he even confessed to killing his own father.*

A searing warmth prodded his chest. Elisena watched, but then quickly looked away.

Nuelle looked at Riff. "Come on. My tears might help."

Riff lowered his chin. "Sorry beforehand." He thrust his fist forward. It smashed into Nuelle's abdomen. Piercing pain shot through his stomach and into his spine. His legs gave out and he collapsed onto his knees. Tears instantly fell from his eyes while he coughed.

Surta grimaced as she held her canister beneath his chin, catching his tears. "I am appalled at myself, Prince Nuelle."

"It's"—more stabbing pangs pierced his abdomen and back—"okay."

"I'll get extra for the others so Riff doesn't have to do this again."

"Thank. You." Nuelle inhaled, trying with difficulty not to heave or vomit so Surta could continue capturing his tears. Riff's gift was definitely his incredible strength.

After another moment, Surta smiled. "This should suffice."

Riff lifted Nuelle onto his feet. "King Nifal isn't gonna come after me for this, right?"

Nuelle chuckled as warmth crept into his stomach, easing the pain. "You should be fine."

Surta tilted the canister and dipped her finger inside. She hesitantly licked it. Like Elisena, her redness instantly disappeared. "Incredible!" She held out the canister to Nuelle. "Try it!"

The warmness seeped into his back. "Let the others have some first."

"Okay." Surta extended it to Sophana. "Your highness."

She tossed her pink hair over her shoulder and grabbed the canister. She sniffed it before also dabbing her finger in and tasting a tear. Her eyes widened as she passed the canister to Riff. "That's just eerie."

He and Javin did the same. Javin trembled as he gave the canister to Nuelle. He poked at the tiny puddle of tears and licked his finger. Strangely, the tears tasted sugary-sweet, as if meant to be consumed. The tiny swallow saturated his dry throat, and a rush of water surged through him. It replenished his dehydrated muscles and cleared his fogged vision.

"I'm so sorry, Supreme Prince," Javin said. "You really are the Hope of the Faithful."

Nuelle closed his canister. Javin said that now, but what if Elisena got hurt again? Would he really still believe that? Nuelle looked toward the path of yellow and turquoise trees his best friend had stormed off down. "We have to find Ave." He trotted ahead.

Ave's tracks imprinted the turquoise grass, crushed by his hot-headed stomping. His anger was understandable. He always yielded to the will of others if he thought it was best, even when he didn't want to. He also faced many painful reminders of his father while not yet healed from that great loss. As Nuelle quickened his pace, Sophana gasped. Ave lay still in the distance, face-down on the ground. Nuelle raced toward him while the others trailed. He stooped beside Ave and turned him over. A bump protruded from the bridge of his nose, and fresh blood oozed from his nostrils, staining his upper lip. Nuelle grabbed Ave's chin and forced his mouth open before pouring a tear-drop inside.

His eyelids batted open, and then with bulging eyes, he peered up at Nuelle. "What did you do to me?"

Surta smiled as Ave sat up. "He gave you his tears to drink."

He spat and wiped his tongue off.

"You'll be fine." Sophana extended him a hand. "We all drank some."

Ave grasped it and stood. He released her palm and patted the dirt off his pants.

She frowned. "You should probably wipe your face as well."

Ave rubbed his nose. "Ah!" He recoiled and looked at the blood smeared on his hand. "Dragon! I think I broke my nose!"

"Let me see." Nuelle's palm pulsed with warmth as he reached it toward Ave's face and gently touched his nose. Agonizing pain struck Nuelle's own nose. He yelled. Elisena and Surta gasped.

Riff swiftly raised his fists. "What just happened?"

The bridge of Nuelle's nose throbbed with pain, but the warmth in his hand strengthened.

Javin grimaced. "Maybe you should let go of Ave's face."

Nuelle closed his eyes. The memory of Father healing Ave's abdomen consumed his mind. His arms tingled, and his heart-rate climbed. He opened his eyes. His hand gradually glowed orange. Soothing warmth permeated his nose.

Surta tilted her head. "Incredible…"

The orange light brightened, and the bump on Ave's nose shrank until it disappeared.

Riff lowered his fists and leaned in. "Break my ankle in a kick-stone game and give me two black eyes."

Nuelle's hand stopped glowing. The pain in his nose eased. He removed his palm from Ave's face, revealing a once-again straight nose. Ave touched his bump-free bridge, and his eyes widened. Tears welled as he looked at Nuelle and then slowly bowed. The Sentinels followed his homage.

Nuelle surveyed his palms. So now he could heal others too? What was this growing power inside? He'd only just turned seventeen a month before leaving to the academy. Could he really grow to be as mighty as Father someday?

Ave and the others straightened. "I shouldn't have disrespected you."

"Me either." Riff wiped a tear from his eye as he pouted like a giant toddler. "From now on, no more challenging you."

Nuelle hesitated before answering. "I forgive you both."

"Victory!" Riff strode to him and Ave and scooped them into his arms. He lifted them off the ground, his tight squeeze crushing.

"All right, mountain." Nuelle managed to utter. "Put us down before we break."

As he released, Surta shook her head. "I imagine we all can agree it feels safer being around you now."

The others nodded or voiced agreement. Nuelle put the canister of tears in his satchel. "We should continue the search." He led his Sentinels onward into the steamy woods. They were still alive, but they were close, real close to not making it. Especially Elisena. *These naive souls are for you now, but what happens when their loved ones begin to turn on you, prince? How will their loyalty fare then?* Raysha's voice taunted. Nuelle's response followed... *They're willing to die for me, just like Zagan was willing to die for Antikai.* But how many times would they escape death? Sure, his tears managed to rescue them today, but what about the other dangers they'd face? The Acumen hadn't promised any of their lives—nor his. What if Elisena had died? Would Javin and Surta still be willing to die for "the Hope of the Faithful"? And Sophana; her loyalty was already frail, she had even confessed that the only reason she became his Sentinel was because she didn't want to be a slave to her father's will. And with all the times she'd shown defiance, or had an outburst, she'd been the least trustworthy of them all. Nuelle looked at the princess, striding a few paces away from the group.

"I told you I wanted answers," Nuelle said. "Why are you so angry at everyone?"

She glanced at the others, her stare lingering on Elisena who peered at her and nodded, as if to say the time was now. Sophana stroked one of the leaf-blades on her arm. "I'm sure you heard the rumors that Ludwig and myself were courting."

He nodded.

"Well, they were true. After King Vyden was dethroned, my parents and I stayed at his palace for his and Ludwig's last night there." Her eyes moistened. "While everyone was asleep, I snuck out of my guest chamber to see how Ludwig was doing." She lowered her hand, her leaves rippling. "We were alone in his bedchamber, sitting on his bed."

Ave stared at her, his brow furrowed. Heat filled Nuelle's palms as Sophana continued, a tear now rolling down her cheek. "It was foolish of me to be alone with him, but I just wanted to see if he was okay. He started telling me how much he loved me, how much he…Anyway, he tried to take advantage of me, and he almost succeeded, but"—she looked at the sharp leaves on her arms—"because of these, I got away. I fled the same night."

Ave gawped and blinked at her as Javin shook his head, and Riff clenched his fists. Elisena and Surta looked at each other. Nuelle's wind stirred. Those few encounters with Ludwig while at Ideya were enough to show he certainly had issues with pride and entitlement. And after experiencing that kind of betrayal from someone you love and trust enough to devote and unite yourself with in marriage? No wonder Sophana had been so guarded and hostile. That wound left bitter pain and a lack of trust in others. But with that albeit reasonable fear, she'd also unintentionally made herself untrustworthy.

Nuelle spoke. "That is why Ichabod is after you, because you rightfully wounded Ludwig in self-defense?"

Sophana huffed. "Probably. I'm sure that blow scarred his once flawlessly-kept skin."

Surta spoke gently. "Do you think Ludwig will hunt for you again?"

"He's not the type to give up easily…"

Ave gazed at Sophana, his face resolute, though his eyebrow twitched. "I—I mean we—will never let anyone harm you."

A small smiled curled the ends of her lips. Riff slapped Ave's back. "Spoken like a Gavrailian groom."

Elisena jumped suddenly, her eyes bulging. "I sense someone."

"Where?" Nuelle stepped in front of her.

"Over there." She pointed to a turquoise tree ten yards directly across from them. The others formed a circle as Nuelle crept toward it. Wind leaked from his palms, ready to defend him and his companions. They followed at his side. His arm hairs rose. He quickened his pace, closing the distance by a few yards. The hot sweat on his back turned cold, and his heart hammered in his chest. Nuelle fixed his eyes on the large turquoise trunk before him. He extended his palms, the wind now wrapping around them. Leaves rustled from behind. Nuelle spun around. The yellow tree they'd stood by trembled. Javin inched toward it.

Surta reached for him. "What are you doing?"

Nuelle's pounding heart eased, and his skin no longer crawled. He looked back at the turquoise trunk before trotting to Javin's side, the others trailing. The danger that threatened them before had fled. They should be safe now. The rustling stopped. Elisena looked up at Nuelle, her umbrella tilted. "It's okay now. The threat is—"

A green foecry burst from the leaves. It soared to Ave. He ducked as it flew over him. The winged-creature's ebony talons just barely shaved his head. The foecry swooped around and flew to Javin, its wings flapping frantically. As he concentrated on the terrified creature, its agitated flailing calmed, and slowly, it rested on his shoulder. He stroked its shiny beak, a buttery-sweet tree-bark scent emanating from him, a pleasant aroma for once. "She thought we were someone else."

"Someone else?" Nuelle approached them. "Who?"

Javin's brow furrowed. "A bad man in a dark covering."

Nuelle looked at Elisena. Her fair skin turned paler.

"She said he had been stalking a man in a green robe," Javin continued.

"Have you seen the man with the robe recently?" Nuelle asked the foecry.

She chirped at Javin. "A few hours ago," he answered for her, "by the blue trees."

Nuelle's heart leapt. "Can you lead us there?"

The foecry fluttered off Javin's shoulder. She sailed ahead of them at a slow, steady pace.

Ave peered behind as he walked next to Nuelle. "But what if this is a trap?"

Nuelle opened his palm and released a gentle airstream. "Just stay alert."

Ave scanned the surroundings while drawing closer to Sophana who plucked her leaf-blades for a ready arsenal. Nuelle focused on their feathery guide as she glided forward. There lurked a malicious visitor in the forest—probably a Savage Shifter, and the hair-raising and accelerated heartbeat he experienced when nearing the turquoise tree indicated that this shifter was stronger than the others. He glanced at Ave as he walked alongside Sophana. Ave usually feared the worst, but there had been times when he was right. Hopefully, this wasn't one of them.

Javin pointed ahead. "There they are."

A circle of blue trees towered before them, their large bright leaves resembling fire. A giant tree stood in the center of the gathering. Its long, hanging vines reached to the ground, creating a curtain that concealed its trunk and anything else stretching beyond it. The foecry flew away.

Nuelle walked toward the tree, his Sentinels following beside him. He extended his hand to the hanging vines. Gently, he pulled them back. A hole in the trunk big enough to walk through revealed a passageway leading to an all-green forest. He motioned for his friends to follow before stepping inside. As they traversed into the emerald region, the temperature dropped. Nuelle looked up, beyond the massive jade leaves to the darkening sky. The daystar hid behind the clouds.

"What's that?" Surta gestured to Nuelle's foot.

Something lay in the grass by his boot—a piece of emerald velvet. Part of the robe King Bertil wore in the dream! If the dream was right about the blue trees and the king's garbs, maybe he really did have vital information to share.

A sudden ripping noise sounded behind Nuelle. He whirled around with his arms outstretched and wind flowing.

"For Zephoris' sake!" Ave shook his head at Riff.

"What?" Riff dug his hand into a bag of Dragon Spice. "I can't eat?"

"Do you have any self-control?"

"It's fine, Riff." Nuelle stopped his wind. "Just eat quickly." He picked up the piece of emerald velvet. "I think we're close." As he led them onward, the grass no longer crunched, as if it attempted to mask their steps. He exchanged looks with the others as they slinked through a patch of thorny bushes. Though they broke through the thin branches, not one of them made a sound, as if they also sought to hide him and his Sentinels' presence.

"Over there!" Elisena pointed to a small blue light. It flickered as it moved forty yards ahead. "I sense great fear."

"That must be him." Nuelle hastened his stride and fixed his eyes on the light while he and his friends crossed over a stream. After several minutes of tracking the blue glow through denser and denser patches of undergrowth and thorn bushes, it finally stopped moving.

"What should we do?" Javin whispered.

Nuelle sprinted through the shrubbery and leapt over bushes. He landed in a vast clearing. Fifteen yards ahead, a lone green tree stood with a curtain of leaves identical to the blue one that led them to this part of the forest.

"Not again," Surta panted as she and the others approached.

"Wait here." Nuelle walked to the tree.

Elisena hurried to his side. "We're not supposed to leave each other alone."

He smiled as he took her hand and gave it a gentle squeeze. "I'm never alone."

She stared at him, her soft lavender eyes warming his heart.

"I'll be back soon." Nuelle released her hand and turned away. He stepped through the curtain. A dense green trunk without a large hole greeted him. Nuelle circled behind the tree—only grass and more veil-vines. He walked to the front again and pressed his palm against the rough bark. There had to be something here. The person carrying the blue light couldn't have just vanished. He stiffened. Unless it was the Savage Shifter … The veil-vines behind him moved. He spun around.

Ave lifted his spongey blue palms. "I just wanted to make sure you were all right."

Nuelle exhaled. "There has to be another way." He continued poking and prodding at different places on the trunk. As he pushed against the lower middle, the bark's light around his hand brightened. With a crack, it caved in an inch, and a green circle lit up the grass beneath his feet.

"That's interesting," Ave said.

"This has to be—" The outlined pasture suddenly collapsed.

"Nuelle!" Ave shouted.

As the grassy chunk carried Nuelle underground, he gripped his satchel. He plunged deeper inside a black tunnel, Ave's shouts growing fainter and fainter. Finally, the shaft opened into a cave sparsely illuminated by blue light. The platform stopped, and Nuelle ventured into the darkness. "Hello?" His voice echoed off the stony walls and traveled down a small opening to the right. He walked toward it. As he neared, a mumbling grew louder, and the blue light illuminating the cave brightened. He released a warm airstream from his hands. In seconds, he would be facing whoever it was hiding here—the King, or the Savage Shifter.

"I'm ready to die." A mess of purplish-black hair concealed the face of a skinny, emerald-robed man huddled at the back of the cave, his head against his knees. A trembling hand marked with scratches and stained with dirt gripped a glowing blue twig. "All I ask is that you kill me speedily."

Nuelle knelt down beside the man with the voice from his dream. "King Bertil?"

He slowly lifted his head, his vivid blue eyes wide with shock and gleaming with joy. "Prince Nuelle, you found me!" He wobbled to his feet. Green leaves and twigs entangled his beard, and the bottom-half of his emerald robe had been torn off. Like his hands, scabs and scrapes covered his legs.

"Nuelle!" Ave's voice echoed through the cave. He darted toward him and King Bertil before halting.

The king jumped in front of Nuelle and pointed the twig at Ave. "Who are you?"

Ave's hands expanded as he rolled them into large blue fists.

Nuelle slowly pushed the twig down. "He's my best friend."

"Oh." King Bertil held the stick at his side.

"What happened to you?" Ave asked him.

"He sent someone to come for me." King Bertil's gaze darted around the cave. "He thinks I have the sword."

Nuelle squeezed his satchel. "What sword?"

The king of Kaimana's wild stare focused on him. "Your father has yet to tell you"—he bent forward.

"Watch out, Nuelle." Ave's arms outstretched, pushing the king back into the wall. "He may be dangerous."

The king swatted at the stretchy limbs. "Apparently you're the dangerous one!"

Nuelle touched Ave's shoulder. "I…believe he is trying to help us."

King Bertil nodded like an anxious child. Ave frowned before releasing him.

The king continued. "Your father has yet to tell you about the crystal sword?"

"He mentioned it, but I've only seen it in a portrait of him and …" Nuelle's brow furrowed as he glanced at Ave. "In the beginning of the dream I got of you in the forest."

King Bertil scratched the top of his head. "In the message I sent you through the dream I did not say anything of the sword."

"You didn't, but before you came into the dream I saw someone who looked like me, and he used the crystal sword to slay my father."

King Bertil craned his head toward the ceiling. After a long moment, he peered at him again. "He must have sent you a nightmare before I sent you the dream."

"You mean your son, Antikai?" Ave asked.

The king slapped his hands to his ears. "Do not say his name!"

Nuelle eyed Ave as King Bertil observed the glowing stick in his hand and sank to the floor. Nuelle knelt beside him. "He can send nightmares?"

King Bertil surveyed the stick and slowly twirled it. "A warped version of what the gift should be used for, one I discovered too late that he had." He jolted as if shocked by lightning and then scrambled to his feet. "The man He sent for me asked if I knew where the sword was hidden. They want the sword, Prince Nuelle!"

"Why?"

"It holds the power of life and death."

Nuelle's heartbeat quickened. He peered at Ave. His stunned expression mirrored the look he had as they traveled home that tragic night his father perished.

King Bertil traced an index-finger down his twig. "The crystal sword is double-edged. The golden-trimmed side can resurrect a worthy life. The black-trimmed side can destroy any life."

Nuelle drew out his next words. "Then it could destroy the Acumen?"

Bertil nodded frantically.

"Do you know where the sword is hidden?" Ave asked.

King Bertil drew close to Nuelle, his rotten breath warm. "At one point, your father entrusted me to hide the sword."

Ave's eyes shimmered with tears, as did Nuelle's. He addressed Bertil. "That's what was in the rucksack Amador gave you."

"Correct. I hurriedly pursued my mission, and then returned home where I discovered the news of His high treason. After what my own son did, and then with all the nightmares I was receiving, I did not trust myself with the information about the sword. So I fled here to live in seclusion and ensure that I would never tell another soul of the sword's whereabouts." He lowered his voice to a whisper and brought his face a hairsbreadth from Nuelle's. "After I realized I was being tracked and would surely be killed, I sent the location of the sword to someone through a dream and asked him to hide it again."

"Who did you ask?" Nuelle and Ave said.

The twig's blue light bounced off King Bertil's eyes, making them appear to glow. "Vyden."

Ave's neck veins protruded. "Vyden, as in, the once king of Ideya?"

King Bertil withdrew his face and nodded, staring at the ceiling again.

Nuelle pressed his satchel against his side. But did this man tell the truth? He had fled his palace, and thus, forsook his kingdom, and he left Amador to die at the hands of Antikai's—his son's—savages. And obviously, Bertil wrote the emerald-sealed letter found at the Academy. In it, he confessed to not being able to trust himself, so how could they be expected to trust him now?

"How can we know you're telling the truth about the sword?" Nuelle asked.

Ave gawped at him as Bertil's gaze left the ceiling. "Well...I..."

"You don't even trust yourself, and you abandoned Amador at Onipur where he died at the hands of your son's henchmen."

Bertil's head bowed. "All of that is true. I am a coward, but I am not a liar." He reached into his torn robe's pocket and removed a battered scroll with a round daystar seal—Father's insignia! Bertil held it out.

Nuelle took the yellowish parchment and unravelled it. Father's scarlet writing lined the page.

My dear friend,

I know the times are especially dark for you; what black seas engulf and attempt to drown you. Fear is nothing new to you, beginning with your early concerns of Antikai's behavior toward your palace servants and then his growing confrontations and rebellion against you. And now you've received word of his attempt to slay me.

You have only desired to help your son, but though your concern for him always stemmed from love, it is controlled by fear. Somewhere along your journey, you've placed your peace in Antikai's well-being. If he succeeded, if he practiced good, you were content and at ease. But when he chose evil, you grew anxious, and as his evil magnified, so your circumstantial, and thus, feeble peace became eclipsed by fear.

Your own fear plagues you more than the evil within Antikai. For you see, dear friend, his wicked rebellion is in him, it is not in you. But fear is within you because it comes from your own thoughts about Antikai and it is warping your discernment of the truth, which is that you are not your son. You are your own soul, separate from that of Antikai's. And thus, your life is not dictated by his actions, and nor should your peace be.

I ask you to remember my laws, to fix your eyes on whatever good is in front of you, even if you must strain past the fog and darkness to see it. When you focus on these things, the truth will begin to once again cast its light on you, and your vision will clear. Then, you will be free of the fears you've allowed to imprison you.

Nonetheless, I commend you for still seeking to do what is right by handing over the sword to another. I pray you can see how even though your fear and the nightmares have caused you to believe a lie about yourself, the truth of who you are—a faithful citizen of mine—is apparent by your actions when you're awake. I hope to see you again soon, my friend. Your Supreme King and beloved companion,

Nifal

Nuelle gripped the parchment. His heart ached as he rolled it and peered up at the king, at this friend of Father's. Father was somehow able to see the best in this man, despite his fear and failures. And he had to flee Onipur to hide the weapon. That was his mission, and he fulfilled it.

Nuelle handed Bertil the scroll. "Do you know where Vyden is hiding?"

"That, I do not know."

Nuelle nodded. "Thank you for sending for me and giving us this information." He removed a mangeen from his satchel. "Take this. I'm sorry I don't have more to offer."

King Bertil lowered his head. "For all that has befallen the both of you—" he looked at Ave—"and your families because of my son's evil, I am unworthy of such grace."

Ave frowned at him with watery eyes.

Nuelle put his free hand on the king's bony shoulder and placed the fruit in his palm. "You are not your son."

King Bertil wiped a tear away. "I pray there will someday be an end to his wickedness."

Peering into the face that Antikai's once so resembled, Nuelle spoke with new confidence. "I will make sure of it." He released King Bertil's shoulder. "Stay safe." With a subtle nod, Nuelle motioned Ave to follow him out of the cave.

As they exited, Ave whispered, "How do you know he can be trusted? What did your father's letter say?"

Nuelle stopped before they reached the grassy platform and faced his best friend. "He confirmed that Bertil gave the sword to another, and if my father trusts him then so do I."

Ave kept Nuelle's stare for a moment, as if unsure of his answer. Ave's glassy blue eyes still carried doubt, which was understandable. After all, his father died when the fearful king fled, and now he hid thousands of miles away from his kingdom while his son continued to influence rebellion even from the Obsidian's shadows.

Nuelle shunned the silence. "You don't have to believe in Bertil, Ave, just trust my father—and me." His own words challenged him, but he quenched his self-doubt—for now.

Ave smiled. "I think I can do that."

Nuelle returned the gesture and then stepped onto the grass-platform.

"Of all the people in Zephoris," Ave said as the platform ascended, "lewd Ludwig's father has to be the one who knows where the sword is."

"I wish it was someone else too," Nuelle replied. And Ideya was the first to dispose of their king. If the people of Jazerland were unwelcoming when Nuelle and his Sentinels arrived, how would those in Ideya react if they discovered the Supreme Prince visited their unruly land?

The platform stopped, and they stepped through the curtain of vines and into the emerald forest.

Elisena and the others scurried toward them. "Did you speak to King Bertil?"

"Yes," Nuelle answered as Ave glanced at Sophana.

Riff stepped forward. "What did he tell you?"

Ave quickly shook his head.

"It's not safe to say here," Nuelle said and then addressed Javin. "Send for vanaphs. We're going back to the academy."

Fifteen: Taken

Carrying the copy of the Acumen, Preceptor Sage faced his dormitory's narrow entryway. He peered at the sapphire stone shining in its center. The large gem reflected his silhouette. How thin he had become since the Savage Shifter's attack, how frail. Too long had he wasted away in the Medic, unable to eat because of the hole in his side. He touched the spot, now a massive scar, and winced. Though Miss Alesia's diligent and skillful hands had done an excellent job, it appeared more time was needed until he reached complete health.

Gripping the copied Acumen, he spoke to the sapphire. "Nathanael Sage." At his voice, the door creaked open and he walked into his lodging. It had been two lengthy weeks since he'd seen the inside of this place. A layer of dust coated the dark-wood bookshelf behind his dining table, where a lantern sat unlit beside his open journal. He trudged past the table and into his kitchen. The odor of rotten food assaulted his senses. Black critters feasted on a moldy, half-eaten loaf of iris-fruit bread atop the counter.

Nathanael turned away from the grotesque sight. Though his stomach ached for food, he'd have to wait until morning to have a decent meal in the banquet hall. He reentered his living area and sat at the table. Setting the copied Acumen down, he blew into the lantern beside his journal. A blue-flame ignited and he read his last entry.

The younger son of the great King Nifal was in my class today. He looks just like his father; his amber eyes even flicker like his, though not as fiercely. It is now seven years gone-by today that the King visited me in my lesson room on that first day of the year with his special, remarkable golden book. The image burns in my mind as bright as the daystar just after dawn. King Nifal had glided into my room so soundlessly, when I noticed him I was startled. He removed the Acumen from a satchel and strode to the corkscrew table my uncle made me for my first year teaching at the academy. The great King placed it atop the table, and with a voice as deep as the waters of Kaimana he said, "I need you to hold onto this." He lifted his palm and as he muttered, it glowed bright orange, and a matching ray of light encircled the Book.

I approached, slowly and with much trembling. "Until when, my lord?"

"Until my younger son arrives," he answered. And without another word, he left me alone with the original Acumen, the one specifically made for Prince Nuelle. And now he has come, and I have given him the Book. The little he read before my eyes drained the very color from his face. I know only of the prophecies in the copied versions of the Acumen, and some have already come to pass. Who knows what pens the pages of that original, sacred work? I fear the days that seemed so far away have now come upon us, and like a dragon disturbed from its rest, the flames of rebellion have already begun to consume.

Is this Young Prince truly prepared for all that awaits him?

The fire inside his lantern flickered. He rose, scanning the commons. His palms tingled with magnetic energy. An icy gust blew his journal off the table. Nathanael turned. A shadow-man lunged at him. He moved aside and magnetized the lantern into his grasp. He threw it at the shifter. It crashed into his arm and it ignited in flames. As the shadow-man wailed and frantically patted out the fire, Nathanael ran to the entryway, his side aching. He grasped the rusty knob. A cold hand gripped his shoulder and spun him around.

"You are coming with us, preceptor." A familiar green-haired girl smiled before they vanished.

Nuelle and the others rode their vanaphs over the orange forest surrounding Knight's Elect Academy. "Get ready to land," he called over his shoulder as he tugged the reins. His vanaph slowed its pace and descended onto the magenta grass. He clenched his satchel as his Sentinels dismounted.

Sophana swiftly hopped off of her vanaph and strode toward him. "What did King Bertil tell you?" She glanced at Ave as he approached.

Nuelle held in a sigh while everyone encircled. Hopefully she'd handle the news better now that she'd at least been able to speak about what happened with her ex-suitor…"You know the crystal sword my father is holding in that portrait from Sir Dangian's lesson room?"

"What about it?"

He looked at the others. "It has the power to destroy the Acumen."

Elisena and Surta gasped while Javin's eyes lightened, and Riff gawped.

"There's more." Ave's face turned taut as he looked at Sophana. "King Bertil was entrusted with the task of hiding the sword. When he found out one of Antikai's followers was tracking him, he delivered the information about the sword's whereabouts to Vyden and had him hide it again."

Every leaf on Sophana's arms trembled. "Ideya?"

Surta rested a hand over Sophana's. "Remember what Ave said. We won't let anyone harm you."

Elisena grasped Sophana's other hand. "You're not alone anymore. You have us now."

Riff slapped his bulging chest. "And this bulwark." He jabbed a thumb at Ave and Javin. "And these little ramparts."

Nuelle stepped beside him. "And me."

As Sophana's eyes passed over each of them, she smiled. "Thank you, but—"

A gut-wrenching scream coming from inside the Servants' Lodge stabbed the air like a sword. Nuelle and his Sentinels raced to the entryway, their vanaphs departing. Javin faced the worn door and stated his name. It slowly creaked open. Nuelle blew a hot gust against it and hurried inside with the others. A horde of prodigies crammed the Master Hall. Some scattered, while others held their mouths or cried, creating a circle around something—or someone.

"Move aside!" Lady Bridie shouted through a silver amplifying tube as she bustled through the hallway from the opposite end, two knights with her.

Nuelle and his Sentinels weaved through the gathering. A blue-haired girl sprawled on the floor, gasping. Blood soaked her neck from a gaping bite wound. Surta and Elisena covered their mouths as Lady Bridie and the Knights broke through the crowd.

"Quickly!" Lady Bridie said to one of them. "To the Medic!"

He scooped the girl into his arms and trotted off.

"Everyone, to your dormitories," Lady Bridie cried into the amplifying tube. "And lock the doors behind you. Do not leave your abode until further instructed."

"What's happened?" Nuelle strode toward her as the prodigies dispersed.

She set her palm on her disheveled braided hair. "O, Supreme Prince, it's awful. The Savage Shifters have been appearing at random and attacking prodigies. We've already lost a few."

Heat consumed Nuelle's head, and his blood boiled within. Antikai and his heartless savages needed to be stopped.

Lady Bridie looked at Sophana. "We've sent a messenger to your father to send healing fruit. We ran out last night, but they'll take at least two weeks to get here."

Nuelle rushed through the hall to the Medic's office and hurried inside, Lady Bridie and his Sentinels trailing. Groaning prodigies lay on bloody sheets across the floor. Preceptors and other Medics stooped on their knees, tending to the wounded, leaving minimal walking space. Nuelle swiftly knelt beside the blue-haired girl. A torn tunic soaked in blood wrapped around her neck. Her glazed yellow eyes stared lifelessly at the ceiling. He quickly slipped his satchel over his shoulder and handed it to Ave. Nuelle grasped the dying girl's ice-cold palm. A faint pulse tapped against his thumb. Taking a deep breath, he released her hand and gently laid both of his around her neck. The warm blood seeped through the tunic's linen and onto his skin. Nuelle closed his eyes. *I don't know how to do this, but please, whatever healing power is in me, extend your grace to this poor girl and save her life.* His forehead scrunched as he concentrated on the heat in his palms.

The agonizing groans and frantic scuffling of Medics faded. A searing pain stabbed his neck, and heavy silence plugged his ears. Violent shudders wracked his bones. As his neck burned in agony, an inpouring of coldness pervaded his body. He opened his eyes to fog and a gradually consuming darkness. The oxygen left his lungs, and his heartbeat slowed to a painful throb. *So this is what dying feels like.* The blackness receded. A surge of warmth penetrated his cold limbs and flowed to his chest. His heart pounded faster. Nuelle's hands still clasped her neck, but now they glowed orange. The blue-haired girl's eyes shined with awe and life. She inhaled, her chest rising, and then exhaled steadily. Nuelle slowly removed his palms and gently lifted her head. He carefully unraveled the tunic around her neck, his Sentinels and Lady Bridie watching with wide eyes.

"Don't." An older Medic with blood spotting her face and gray hair scuttled toward him.

He dropped the ripped-tunic, revealing the girl's neck. Dried blood smeared her skin, but the gaping wound was gone. The Medic and Lady Bridie gasped. Nuelle smiled as he swiftly turned to another prodigy lying behind him. The boy lay with his eyes closed and a sheet covering him up to his neck.

Nuelle peered at the gray-haired Medic. "What's wrong with him?"

The Medic stooped beside the boy and pulled back the covers. One of his muscular arms was missing. A bloody cloth enveloped the stub. Nuelle looked at his Sentinels. Tears fell from all of their eyes. With gaze fixed, Ave nodded as if to say, 'I believe in you.' Turning away from him, Nuelle breathed in and reached for the boy's stub, his hand already glowing orange. His palm met the cloth enclosing the boy's severed limb. An excruciating tearing sensation sliced through Nuelle's left arm. He grasped it and wailed.

"Prince Nuelle!" Elisena dropped to her knees and touched his back.

Tears spilled from his eyes as shooting pains raced up his shoulder and down his spine. He leaned over, panting as he clung tightly to the boy's stub. Something firm pushed his palm downward. His Sentinels applauded and cheered as the boy's muscular arm elongated. Nuelle blinked while the boy's wrist, hand, and fingers grew back. As the comforting warmth returned, the pain in Nuelle's upper body receded, but he still held onto the boy's hand.

With tired red eyes, the boy awakened. "Prince Nuelle?" His gaze traveled to his renewed arm. He jolted upright, and Nuelle released his hand. As he studied his once-missing limb, he shook his head and smiled. "You did this?"

"He certainly did," Lady Bridie answered.

The boy beamed. "Thank you!"

Nuelle looked around at the many wounded others. Most of them lay with bloody bandages around their heads or side, coughing, groaning, or just still—barely breathing. And who knew how many more filled the Medic rooms. The comforting warmth saturated his heart. This had to have been what Father meant when he said they needed him.

He stood to his feet, his head somewhat light, and began tending to the others; a girl with burns all over her back, another with burns on her face; a boy missing an eye and a good chunk of his right cheek. With every prodigy he healed, he felt their pain, their agony, the stabs and the blows that brought them to such a helpless condition. The wounds were so real, so violent and merciless. These savages had thrown their hearts away and operated like pure, blood-thirsty beasts. This was the evil Antikai desired to rain upon the people of Zephoris. This is what he wanted; no mercy, friendship, compassion, or love; just darkness, rage, and hatred.

As Nuelle laid hands upon the final victim cramped in the last room of the Medic, an Ideyan girl who suffered a dagger-strike through her shoulder, he focused on what the Acumen said. Though darkness would begin to reign, the Faithful had a refuge, a safe-place from the dangers, pain, and death of this world: the Incandescia, and he would make sure each one of them got there…eventually. Until the Acumen disclosed the location and timing of their exodus, he needed to stay alive.

His hands glowed orange, and the now familiar searing pang of a stab thrust itself into his shoulder. He pursed his lips, tears blurring his vision, while the girl's deep wound closed. The last of her skin grew in place, and Nuelle released her shoulder. Still lightheaded, his body swayed to the right and left, his muscles weak and legs wobbly. Ave and Riff clasped each of his arms, and Miss Alesia entered the room.

Surta's eyes shined with pity. "He looks terrible."

"Lay him down," Miss Alesia said.

The Ideyan girl he'd just healed quickly rose from her bloodied sheets on the floor, and Ave and Riff laid Nuelle on his back. His Sentinels knelt around him, all the healed prodigies also encircling.

"You did amazing, Supreme Prince." Elisena's soft voice coaxed Nuelle's muscles and they relaxed.

Sweat slid down his temples and into his already wet hairline. More sweat soaked his tunic, making it stick to his stomach and chest. His limbs ached and sagged into the floor, too heavy to lift, like how it felt sparring Tane that last time in the courtyard, just much more severe. Miss Alesia scuttled away as his friends surveyed him with worried eyes. Nuelle stared at a splintered patch of wood on the ceiling. Where was the soothing warmth? It never took this long to come and heal his body. His heart jumped. Had he spent all the healing power he had on the others? Could he stay in this condition for the rest of his life?

The Medic returned with a small, damp towel. She placed the cloth upon his forehead, cool to the touch.

"You're going to be okay, Prince Nuelle." Elisena gently squeezed his hand.

He focused on the warmth emanating from her palm and closed his eyes. Fear would not rule his heart. The people of Zephoris needed him. His destiny was far from being fulfilled so it couldn't—it wouldn't—end here. For Father's sake, for the Faithful's sake, for love's sake, he would see his mission through no matter what it cost—even unto death.

A slow-rising warmth trickled into his chest, easing the heaviness weighing it down. As the healing warmth gradually spread to his arms, he opened his eyes. Elisena smiled at him, the others still with taut, stressed faces. He smiled back and pressed his palms against the floor. He pushed himself up with all the force he could muster, Ave, Javin, and Riff quickly grabbing his arms.

"Can you stand?" Sophana asked, now holding his satchel.

Nuelle's right leg twitched, but resisted moving. The warmness had just begun to make its way down his abdomen.

He sighed. Although not as swift as before, at least his healing power had returned. After another few, long minutes, the warmth finally reached his knees. He grasped Ave and Riff's biceps, while Javin clasped his waist, and wobbled to his feet.

All the surrounding prodigies and Medics broke out into cheers again, many touching his back or shoulders. He reached his palm out to Sophana. "May I please have my satchel?"

She extended it to him. As he gripped the leather, warmth from the Acumen graced his hands. The pulsing remained steady, but had dwindled in force, mirroring his own weakness. Hopefully, he'd return to complete strength soon.

"You are truly a gift, Prince Nuelle." Miss Alesia bowed before him, the others doing the same.

He slipped his satchel over his shoulder and smiled at them all as they straightened. He looked past the crowded gathering. The bed Preceptor Sage once laid in sat empty. Nuelle stopped smiling. "Where is the preceptor?"

Lady Bridie's brow wrinkled. "He offered to return to his dormitory earlier to make room in the Medic for the others."

"Has anyone checked on him since?"

"Not with all the chaos."

Nuelle turned to his Sentinels. "I want to bring the preceptor to my lodging. We'll all dwell there together for now until we figure out what to do about the Savage Shifters." He faced Lady Bridie. "Send for me immediately if the savages return."

"Yes, my lord."

The prodigies moved aside and made a narrow path to the doorway. Nuelle marched to the exit, his Sentinels behind him.

As they entered the Medic hallway, Ave brushed his bangs back with a shaky hand. "Those beasts need to be stopped before they can kill anyone else."

Nuelle squeezed his satchel, the Acumen pulsing slightly stronger. "We can check the Acumen for instructions when we get to Preceptor Sage's dormitory." He hurried from the Medic and led his Sentinels out the Servant Lodge's entryway. He veered to the left where the six-story Staff Tower stood fifty yards away. Swiftly, he closed the distance and darted up the steps to the door. He pushed it open and scampered inside. Nuelle hurried to the platform at the end of the short corridor, the others trailing closely. He and his friends mounted the device and ascended to the fifth floor. When it stopped, Elisena's eyes lightened.

"What's wrong?" Nuelle asked as they dismounted.

"I can't sense Preceptor Sage's heart."

Nuelle raised his palms and ran to the preceptor's dormitory door. Wind poured from his hands as he banged on the wood beneath the sapphire stone. "Preceptor, are you in there? It's Prince Nuelle." After a moment, he stepped back and blew a gust at the entryway. The door burst open. A journal lay on the floor near the table beside a fallen, smoking lantern and a black jar. Nuelle dashed to the journal. Lifting it, he skimmed over the neat writing. He read the last sentence. *Is this Young Prince truly prepared for all that awaits him?* His stomach churned, and the back of his neck moistened.

"What is that?" Surta pointed at the jar. It shook. Sophana readied a leaf-blade and aimed. Nuelle set the journal down and reached his hands toward the jar, wind flowing.

"Nuelle, just wait," Ave whispered.

The container burst, and shards of glass showered them. Green ashes scattered as a swarm of buzzing black creatures with eyes glowing red flitted around. The creatures whizzed above and beside one another, forming curves and lines in the air with their bodies as if they were … spelling something. They suddenly ceased moving.

Surta's spectacles reflected the creature's blood-colored eyes. "It appears to be a message."

The black buzzers exploded into bright green light. The emerald glow formed a sentence.

If you want to spare the lives of the preceptor and the prodigies, bring me the book and come alone.

As the light faded until it disappeared, Nuelle's stomach hollowed. The preceptor was taken because of him. Yet again, this faithful man had been endangered to the fault of the 'Young Prince' and supposed 'Hope of the Faithful.' How, how could Father call him this when right and left, his life continued to cause hurt rather than hope? Just living, just breathing, just existing in this darkening world seemed only to add to that pain and darkness. And yet somehow, he was destined to lead people to everlasting light?

"Go to the Obsidian by yourself," Javin said loudly, arresting Nuelle's self-loathing thoughts, "where Prince Antikai and the Savage Shifters are?" His eyes lightened. "Is it just me, or does that sound like a terrible plan?"

"I agree." Riff rubbed his fists. "I say we wait for another Savage Shifter to show up, and just kill them off one-by-one."

"We don't know when and where they'll attack next." Nuelle gazed at them. "Something has to be done, soon."

Ave's eyes shined. "Tane was killed by Antikai. I don't think you should follow in his steps, Nuelle."

He winced at the thought of his older brother, the painful ache in his heart returning with vengeance. Of course he couldn't go alone—even though that would be best and safer for everyone else.

Sophana lowered her leaf-blade. "I don't think you should either. If you die, what is going to happen to Zephoris?"

Surta shrieked, looking toward the doorway where a boyish man stood, wearing a gas-mask and night-robe, clenching a duster. "Oh my gastro-acid of a swamp-leaper!"

He skittered toward them. "Thank sovereignty you all returned safely!"

"Yeah ..." Riff sized him up as he approached. "Why are you holding a duster?"

"This is no ordinary cleaning article. With one jab it will release a cloud of dust that will leave you sneezing for a week!" He lifted his gas-mask—Preceptor Wit, the knowledge instructor. His glasses magnified his eyes by at least three-times, and his tousled black-and-white hair didn't match his youthful face. "Where is Preceptor Sage?"

Nuelle's Sentinels turned to him. Heat poured into his palms along with that sting of guilt as he answered. "He has been captured and taken to the Obsidian."

Preceptor Wit gasped, his eyes instantly watering and widening with fear.

Nuelle glanced over his friends. "Maybe my father knew this would happen and has instructions for us." He quickly removed the Acumen from his satchel. As he opened it, everyone gathered around. Silence seized them while he skimmed the pages. *The Perilous Eve ... rebellion will infect the land ... the Fallen Prince shall take lives and breathe threats.*

He stopped skimming and read Father's words aloud. "The Fallen Prince will kill many in an attempt to acquire the book, and the Young Prince shall bring it to him." Nuelle gripped the Acumen, its warmth growing stronger. "But do not fear, my son. Antikai will obtain the Acumen, but he does not yet have the crystal sword." He slowly closed the book. Don't fear, don't be concerned even when your mortal enemy has part of what's keeping you alive in his murderous hands?

"Antikai doesn't have the crystal sword *yet*," Ave said. "But what happens when he does have it?"

Surta sat in one of the chairs at the table. "I am uncertain as to why King Nifal would have you do such a thing—walk into enemy territory without we who have been assigned to protect you."

"Yeah." Riff stood beside her. "I thought you needed us to survive."

Nuelle stared at the Acumen's golden cover, at Father's protruding center insignia, resembling the daystar, but with a twirl blossom intertwining in its midst. Everything they were saying was true. The Acumen declared that if he should remain alive, he needed Six Sentinels, he needed those who had become family to continually sacrifice their lives…but maybe, before the week finished, that would end. "We can split up." He put the Acumen back into his satchel. "Surta, Riff, and Javin can come with me, and Surta, you can create the illusion that I'm alone."

"But then what about the rest of us?" Sophana asked.

Elisena spoke before Nuelle could. "We'll search for the crystal sword in Ideya while you four journey to the Obsidian, then we can hide it and come for you."

"Ideya?" Preceptor Wit squeezed the duster and a cloud of gray particles burst from it. Ave stretched his coral arms and absorbed the dust.

"Sorry." Preceptor Wit carefully laid the duster down.

Nuelle released a subtle sigh. "I know this journey isn't getting any safer. And it's probably only going to get worse." He balled a fist. "But that's why I need to survive long enough to fulfill my purpose—and hopefully, that'll be no more than a week."

Javin put his arm around Elisena. "But how can you be sure?"

Uncertainty clawed at Nuelle's heart again. "I'm not."

As his Sentinels and the preceptor exchanged looks, Javin spoke once more. "Well, I'm sure that I don't want my sister traveling to Ideya without me."

"But I can really use your gift if we encounter any beasts in the Obsidian," Nuelle said.

"But she—"

"Javin." Elisena slipped out of his grasp. "I will be fine. Prince Nuelle needs you."

A frown twisted Javin's mouth as he focused on Nuelle. "If anything happens to my sister…"

Elisena rolled her eyes as Nuelle questioned him. "You'll what? Forsake your calling and abandon your mission?"

Javin's shoulders squared with tension. "I'm still here."

"Because Elisena is."

Javin glanced at her as Nuelle continued. "But I wonder if you'd still be standing here if she wasn't. You were against me at first, then you read my father's words and suddenly have a change of heart. But are you really changed?" He focused on Elisena. "You would know better than any of us. Is your brother truly for me?"

Now every eye shifted to her—including Javin's. His twin stood beneath her open umbrella, looking more uncertain than she ever had.

"Go on," Nuelle said, "take a look."

She pressed a button on her umbrella and it closed. Slowly, she lowered it to her side and concentrated on Javin. Their similar purple eyes analyzed one another. Unlike usual, as the moments passed, Elisena's irises remained their normal, deep hue. A swelling hollow filled Nuelle's gut. Did she even read him? Or did she pretend for his sake, to hide his disloyalty in order to protect him? After a seemingly everlasting minute, Elisena turned to Nuelle. "He is for you."

"How do I know you aren't lying?"

Her jaw dropped and her irises finally lightened to lavender. "I'm…I'm not lying."

"Nuelle, what's wrong with you?" Ave said. "You're not acting like yourself."

"You mean I'm not being naive?"

"Oh, I see." Ave stepped toward him. "You're acting like Tane."

Heat billowed in Nuelle. "And what's wrong with that?"

"Well for one, it's causing us to waste time."

"And causing you not to think efficiently," Surta said to Nuelle.

He glared at her. "Have you been reading my mind?"

She averted her spectacled gaze and twirled a strand of her blue hair with an index finger. "Mostly on accident."

Nuelle snorted. "I guess none of us trust each other."

"No." Elisena stepped his way. "I've read every one of our hearts. We all trust you. And there was a time when you trusted us." She peered at him with the same intensely sincere gaze that captured his confidence the first time they met on the day of the challenge.

Javin opened his mouth and spoke slower than usual, as if careful of his words. "Prince Nuelle, me and my sister know about abandonment. The one person who should never leave you left us as if we were nothing but mistakes." His irises faded to lavender. "I admit, I've had some trust issues ever since—"

"Some?" Elisena said.

He glimpsed at her before focusing on Nuelle again. "That's why most of my friends are creatures—"

"Most?"

He looked at his sister again and she shrugged apologetically. He continued. "They tend to be more faithful than humans, and I don't have to worry about them betraying me because no one can understand them anyway." He inhaled. "I know I say dumb things sometimes, maybe spending so much time with animals made me lose a few manners. But when I do trust someone, I'll be there for you no matter what."

Nuelle kept his gaze on Javin. His lavender irises didn't look away. They mirrored Elisena's and really seemed… genuine. Nuelle's burning anger cooled. "I'm sorry. Let's just stay focused on our mission." He addressed Ave. "After you find the sword, bring it to me immediately."

"Do you really think we should bring it to the Obsidian?" He replied. "If Antikai manages to get a hold of it, he'll destroy you."

"True. But if I have it, I can destroy him—and his followers."

Ave held his stare, his eyes glossy and uncertain. They once looked much like Lady Purine's, but now they appeared more firm and hard, like a smooth stone turned jagged by storms. They mimicked his father's. After another long moment, he finally averted his gaze.

"Well." Surta fidgeted with her spectacles and then cleared her throat. "This will be a voyage for future history books."

Preceptor Wit adjusted his own round spectacles. "If you are journeying to the forbidden darkness, you must be able to see. Wait here." He scuttled out the room. In less than a minute he returned, carrying a wooden crate. He scampered before them and held it out to Nuelle. Inside the crate lay a pile of thick glowing-blue goggles.

"What are these?" Nuelle asked as he and the Six grabbed a pair.

"Dark-O-Specs," Preceptor Wit said. "I was planning on using them with the prodigies for an escapade of the rare querapas' burrows."

"What is causing them to glow?" Surta asked.

He smiled at a pair held by Javin. "A small amount of fire and life orbs."

Surta grinned. "Astoundingly whimsical!"

Preceptor Wit put the crate down and reached into one of his night-robe pockets. He removed a small leather bag and a vile of sparkling gold liquid. "Unfortunately, I couldn't find more of this to help the wounded prodigies, but maybe it can aide you on your journey. It is a bag of healing fruit seeds and this is a vile of querapa saliva. If injured, just dig a seed in the ground and with a drop of this saliva, a healing fruit will immediately sprout. There's only one seed for each so use them wisely. And"—he dug into another pocket and pulled out a round flame-holder. "Just blow on it, and the flame will brighten."

"Thank you, Preceptor," Nuelle said as he took the gifts.

Preceptor Wit held his thin shoulders back. "I offer myself as a guide for those of you voyaging to my homeland."

Nuelle smiled at the kind preceptor and then handed him the bag and vial. "Then you should take these."

"But—"

"I can heal," Nuelle said as he put the flame-holder in his satchel.

The preceptor frowned at the declaration. The others nodded as Nuelle continued. "And Surta is going to hide herself and the others by an illusion. You can't harm what you don't know is there."

"Very well." He placed the items in his pocket and turned to Elisena and the others. "Ideya is exceedingly dangerous." He looked at Elisena's umbrella. "Forgive me, but the more we blend in, the better."

"I need my umbrella. Especially in a place like that."

"Is it a weapon?"

"No, it emits a force-field that helps me control my gift."

He rapidly circled her, poking and fanning his hand underneath the umbrella. "Fascinating. Do you mind if I add a few upgrades?"

"I suppose not." She hesitantly closed the umbrella and handed it to him.

"And might I ask why you are journeying specifically to Ideya?"

"We need to find Vyden," Sophana said. "He knows the crystal sword's whereabouts."

Preceptor Wit slapped the umbrella. "All right then, let us not delay any longer. We need to find an old king." He faced Nuelle and bowed low. Elisena and the others followed his homage. When Ave straightened, his doubtful stare again landed on Nuelle.

"We'll make this work." Nuelle tightened his grip on the satchel where the Acumen—his very life—lay. King Eliah's words haunted him. *Young Prince, you must stay alive until the prophecies come to pass. You are our only hope.*

Sixteen: Separate Journeys

Stone and wood towers wore the mauve evening sky like a hat. Side-by-side, the lofty structures stood in ranks that encircled the town square as if barricading and lording over the citizens below. Angry eyes followed Elisena as she, Ave, Sophana, and Preceptor Wit walked through the bustling Ideyan square. Elisena gripped her satchel and open umbrella. She huddled closer to the Preceptor as he led them past floating stands with quick-talking merchants.

"This tawter-catcher is not worth three coins of silver, let alone twenty," a man with wooden gloves shouted at a lengthy-bearded man standing on a hovering shop.

The bearded man shooed him. "Then take your business elsewhere, piker!"

"What did you call me?" Wooden-gloves jumped and grabbed the seller's beard. With a thrust, he yanked the merchant from his stand, punched him with his wood-covered fist, and strode on as the seller stumbled to the ground unconscious.

Preceptor Wit scurried ahead. "My, how rapid things have changed since my last visit."

"When was that?" Elisena asked.

"Four months ago, before they petitioned for King Redmond to step down."

"What happened to these people?" Ave whispered.

"Remember what Colden told Lady Bridie?" Sophana looked over her shoulder. "Antikai caused the uprising here. His corruption inspired theirs."

Elisena addressed the Preceptor. "Where are we going?"

"To visit my sister." He hastened his gait. "My niece used to be one of Ludwig's seamstresses."

Sophana stiffened as he continued.

"She might know where Vyden is staying now."

"Vyden?" The wooden-gloved man walked alongside them. His open shirt revealed a long scar on his chest. He stepped in front of Preceptor Wit. As five other men—two being Gavrailian—stood alongside the scarred man, he smirked. "Did I just hear you mention that tyrant's name?"

"I, I, um," the preceptor stuttered.

Ave strode to his side, blocking Sophana. "We don't want any trouble."

A crowd swiftly gathered and surrounded. The scarred man surveyed Ave from head-to-toe, and then turned to his gang. "Apart from the old man, they don't look like they're from around here, do they gentlemen?"

They mumbled agreements. The man squinted at Elisena's umbrella. "An umbrella in the Days of Warmth? What are you really shielding yourself from?" He reached for the umbrella.

As Sophana tore off a leaf-blade, she stepped around Ave and stood in front of Elisena. "Keep your hands to yourself."

The man craned his neck to the side. As he gazed upon Sophana, a smirk curled his pale lips. "And who are you, lovely lady? I like the leaves, they're quite exotic."

"These are a lot more than exotic."

His eyebrows raised. He chuckled as a shopping stand carrying barrels floated above. "Lovely and feisty." He looked at his men. "I think she'll be good for the coliseum."

One of the Gavrailian thugs removed a whip from his waist. Ave's arm shot toward the stand overhead and swiped the barrels off. They collapsed in front of the men. Elisena and the others shoved through the crowd and ran into a dark alley.

"Get them!" the leader shouted. His mob threw and kicked aside the barrels and sprinted after them. Elisena and the others raced over broken glass and dashed out of the alley.

"This way!" Preceptor Wit veered to the left onto a gravel road. Citizens rode past on giant stone-wheeled carriages. Elisena screamed as she evaded the colossal contraptions. The preceptor weaved through the riders, remarkably fast for his age. Ave and Sophana kept pace with him, but Elisena lagged behind.

"Wait!" Sophana halted and looked back.

Elisena pushed onward. Why was her stupid body so slow! She had certainly lost weight from all the training, and had begun to eat better after her talk with Nuelle while in the Medic. But no, her legs just had to be stubby and move like a feeble elderly wom—her ankle twisted. Searing pain shot up her calf as she stumbled onto the rough terrain, dropping her umbrella. Her head prickled. Feelings of anger and frustration flooded her heart. Bitter, perverse, greedy, hateful thoughts pounced her mind. She curled into a ball and froze, paralyzed.

A cold hand clasped her shoulder tightly. The Gavrailian carrying the whip towered above, smiling. All kinds of perversions and lust rained from his heart and drowned hers into deeper darkness. A small voice whispered through the wicked, suffocating thoughts. *King Nifal, help me!*

A brief moment of immense calm washed over. She snatched her umbrella and pressed the handle's button. Green acid spurted from its tip into the Gavrailian's face. He recoiled, boils sprouting on his smoking nose and cheeks.

Ave and Sophana grabbed Elisena's arms. They pulled her to her feet and ran after the preceptor. Elisena limped as she leaned upon her friends. More pangs stabbed her foot and lower leg. Preceptor Wit led them off the dangerous road and into another part of town. Narrow four-story homes with round terraces stretched for a mile. Many balconies housed drinking men and women, their legs dangling carelessly over the edge. As Elisena and the others hurried by, the drinkers pointed and mocked. Preceptor Wit bustled to the side of a house and leaned against its dark stone wall. Elisena, Ave, and Sophana joined him. Wincing as she pressed against the smooth rock, Elisena's ankle pounded and swelled in her boot.

"My sister lives about seven miles down," the Preceptor panted.

Ave gawped. "Seven miles?"

"Do you have any ideas for transportation?" Sophana asked.

Preceptor Wit removed a handkerchief and wiped his forehead with a trembling hand. "Well, as you can see, the citizens here aren't very hospitable, so I presume we will have to remain on foot."

"On foot?" Elisena sucked in a breath, tears blurring her vision as she removed her boot, revealing a swollen, black-and-blue ankle. The preceptor grimaced.

"I sprained it back on the road," Elisena said. "I don't think I can walk that far."

Ave looked at the preceptor. "The healing fruit seeds and querapa saliva!"

"Right!" Preceptor Wit dug his hands into his pocket.

The two Gavrailian men from the gang appeared behind Ave. Preceptor Wit jumped. One of them punched Ave in the back, knocking him unconscious. Elisena screamed as Sophana thrust a leaf-blade, but the other Gavrailian slapped it from her grasp and wrapped his whip around her wrists. The first Gavrailian struck Preceptor Wit's face. He dropped motionless to the ground like Ave had.

The scar-chested man appeared from around the corner, two men with him, one holding a sack. "You all really have some fight in you."

Sophana kicked at the Gavrailian restraining her. He yanked the whip and she fell on the dirt, busting her chin.

"With the four of you fighting together in the coliseum, my partners and I may very well land ourselves a hefty bounty." The leader grinned, greed and amusement saturating his wicked heart. "If you last of course."

The man holding a sack shoved it over Elisena's head. A piercing shock stabbed her spine and jarred her body. Malicious laughter filled her ears. Her eyes slowly closed and she exhaled before falling limp.

Beyond the Aurora Forest, a void of blackness consumed from ground to sky. It cut off the daystar's golden light like a flame blown out by a forceful wind.

"Get ready," Nuelle called to Surta, Javin, and Riff as their vanaphs neared the end of the trees' colorful expanse below. Nuelle raised his Dark-O-Specs to his eyes and gripped the shoulder-strap of his satchel, the wall of darkness closing in. "Remember, Surta, I'm alone."

She gave a nod and then she and the others disappeared. Nuelle stared ahead. Cold blackness swallowed him as if he'd lost too much blood and gone unconscious. The icy air bit into his face and arms, stabbing at them like needles. He winced while tugging the reins of his vanaph upward. His fingers swiftly turned numb. The vanaph grumbled, defiantly staying its straight course.

Nuelle pulled the reins again. "Come on, boy, down."

Its wings flapped wildly. The vanaph halted and groaned. Nuelle tightened his hold as his bottom slid down the creature's back. "Peace, boy, peace!"

It jerked forward. Nuelle flung off. As his stomach lurched, he swiped at the air and grabbed hold of the reins with one hand. His vanaph fluttered madly as he squeezed his satchel. Two of the creature's six wings slammed into him. Dizziness wracked his brain as ice formed on the reins. He clenched them, the watery surface causing his fingers to lose grip. He had to be at least five-hundred feet above ground. Who knew if anything below would break his fall? To let go could mean plummeting to his death.

Two of his fingers slipped off the reins. His back and face ached from the vanaph's pounding wings. Surta and the others must have feared if they helped him, they'd be exposed. His thumb released, only two fingers clasping the reins now. The vanaph jerked backwards with jarring force. Nuelle lost grip and plunged through the freezing sky. The air penetrated his clothes and numbed his body. He couldn't die. The preceptor and the prodigies needed him!

He collapsed onto something hard, stopping him midair. Back now aching worse, Nuelle peered below. He hovered over what appeared to be nothing. Carefully turning himself over, he grasped the invisible vanaph. "Nice catch," he whispered to whoever rode it, and it descended to the ground. His muscles locked in the harsh, dry cold. He slipped off the creature. Warmth slowly coursed through his body, easing the back pain and loosening his muscles. Hopefully his friends were okay in this brutal and unnatural chill. He quickly removed the flame-holder from his satchel and blew in it until a medium-sized fire grew. With Surta's illusion still in place, there was no telling how they held up. Subtly, he nudged his elbow to the side. It touched a thick yet firm bicep—Javin. Good; they all must have been right beside him.

Tightening his hold on the flame-holder, Nuelle trekked forward. The Dark-O-Specs and flames shed their cerulean light on the nothingness before him. Dense silence made it seem as though he'd lost his hearing and truly walked alone in this accursed land. Although the quiet surroundings promised solitude, somewhere in the darkness, enemies waited.

A cool wind blew past. "Nuelle," whispered several voices. He looked around. The thick blackness made it impossible to see beyond six paces. If anyone was out there, he'd have to rely on a different sense. The wind stirred again, agitating the holder's flame. "We know you are here."

Nuelle's arm-hairs rose. Someone or something lurked, cloaked by the darkness, watching from the shadows. A slimy sound dragging swiftly across the floor grew louder with each second. He blew on the flame and extended the holder as the fire brightened. Hot wind poured into his free palm. The slime-sound intensified. A rancid, fishy smell engulfed the area.

"What is it, Javin?" Nuelle whispered.

"I don't know," his invisible Sentinel replied in a hushed voice. "But it's not kind."

A giant creature emerged from the darkness, gliding toward them on eight furry tentacles. Closed eyelids covered half of its hairy face. Nuelle slowly set the flame-holder down and raised his palms. Two tentacles launched toward him. He rolled out of the way. The tentacles wrenched back and then swung around. Nuelle ducked. The grayish limbs swiped over his head. A dozen images of himself appeared, all running in different directions. He joined the mirages and raced ahead, the beast slapping its massive limbs through the illusions. A tentacle whipped at his leg and wrapped around it. The creature jerked him toward itself. Three of its other tentacles coiled around what seemed to be nothing but air.

Nuelle writhed in the slimy hold, heat rising within. This beast had somehow seen through Surta's illusion, though she still miraculously maintained it. The creature's eyelids snapped open. In the center of each eye, a tiny black pupil watched. As the beast peered into Nuelle's eyes, its pupils grew. Weakness crept into Nuelle's body. Energy left his struggling limbs, and his temperature cooled.

The beast leaned its face closer. Nuelle's heartbeat slowed, and his head lightened. This beast was draining the life out of him. He squeezed his eyes shut and focused on breathing. As if fighting against a magnet, his heart-rate rose and fell, striving to normalize. *Come on. I can do this.* The memory of the warmth that surged through him while battling against Tane's power flooded his mind. *Don't give up, Nu,* his brother's strong voice returned as if he stood before him. Warmness quickly swelled inside his chest. It rushed to the rest of his body.

The tentacles binding him tightened their grip, crushing his sides and coercing the breath from his lungs. The Acumen's heat emanated from his satchel and pressed against his rib. Its warmth seeped through his tunic and into his skin. Sweltering hotness overtook him. The beast released Nuelle and recoiled. He opened his eyes. Fire torched the tentacles that had just tried to crush him. The other sticky limbs constricting his friends uncoiled, and the beast slithered back into the darkness. Nuelle looked at his palms. Rather than normal blue flames, a bright orange fire danced along his hands and fingers. *This is new.*

"Stab my leg with a spear," Riff said from somewhere in front of him.

"Shh." Nuelle closed his fists, and the fire evaporated. It was great that his power was apparently growing stronger, but his Sentinels had to remain hidden. A surprise attack on Antikai and the Savage Shifters could save their and the preceptor's lives. Nuelle retrieved the flame-holder and led his unseen Sentinels onward into the Obsidian's menacing unknown.

Time dragged by, or sped by; maybe an hour or two, or possibly even three had passed. One couldn't be sure in this land wrenched by darkness. It seemed as though the surroundings hardly changed, and that death cursed the ground and air. A while ago, a black lake had appeared on Nuelle's left. But did it really stretch that long? Or had he been leading himself and his friends in circles? With no clear roads or paths, how would they even find their way out of this hollow land?

After maybe another hour of trekking through nothingness, the area around Nuelle lightened. He breathed in the icy air. *Finally.* A metallic bridge with only black depths beneath stretched ahead. Forceful gusts blew past, thrusting Nuelle's hair back. The wind strengthened. A subtle whirring hissed in the air. He planted his feet, the orange fire igniting on his palms. With each second, a rushing noise in the distance behind intensified.

Nuelle peered over his shoulder. Fifty yards away, seven whirlwinds bounded toward him. The massive cyclones neared at a rapid pace. He raced ahead and bolted across the bridge, hoping his friends kept up. As he approached the end of the crossing, he looked back. The whirlwinds evaporated just before reaching the bridge's entrance. Nuelle finished crossing over and then paused. A crooked path with metallic trees that bent and sagged led to somewhere ahead. Antikai had to be close.

He strode forward. The whirlwinds reappeared in front of him. He stretched his arms at his sides and released a gust of wind in hopes that his Sentinels would be thrust aside. The cyclones merged together into one colossal whirlwind. It closed in, sweeping Nuelle off his feet. His body spun rapidly as it lifted higher and higher. His stomach reeled. Everything morphed to a gray blur.

The wind crushed his abdomen and choked out the air in his lungs. He revolved for what felt like the hundredth time. His satchel ripped off his shoulder and disappeared in the torrent. *The Acumen!* A heavy force slammed against his back like the hand of a giant, throwing him down in the middle of the whirlwind. The cyclone evaporated.

Nuelle's head pounded and his vision rotated as he heaved in breaths from his aching lungs. Where had his satchel flown to? Would his Sentinels find it? Had they even made it out safe? Warmth trickled into his upper body, and his lungs relaxed. He drew in a long breath and staggered to his feet. A swirl of colors replaced the darkness, and his spinning vision steadied. He lowered his Dark-O-Specs.

The daystar beamed on a throne with a little chair beside it in the midst of a garden imbued with pink and purple blossoms. Thick vines draped the smaller chair's armrests. One of Sophana's leaf-blades swiped past his cheek. It slammed into the little chair. As more leaf-blades pierced it, the vines tore off. With sudden speed, they thickened and expanded. Two of them shot toward Nuelle. They wrapped around his wrists and dragged him to the small chair. The vines forced him to sit, binding his arms to the chair's armrests. More vines sprouted from the ground beneath his feet. The plants twined his legs and progressed to his upper body. They enfolded his abdomen and tied his neck to the chair's back. The vicious vines squeezed. Searing heat filled his arms. The temperature rose, but the vines tightened their grasp, unaffected.

Nuelle closed his eyes. There had to be something to get him out of this. The pressure on his body released. He reopened his eyes. An orange forest surrounded—similar to the one bordering Knights' Elect Academy. A pink river flowed nearby. Nuelle crept toward it, continuing to scan the surroundings. Was this some sort of mind game? Where had the cyclone carried him, or did he lie unconscious somewhere in the middle of the Obsidian while his friends wandered alone?

"Nuelle." Elisena stood in the river a few yards down. She smiled as she swayed, tracing her fingers on the soft ripples.

"Elisena?" He walked along the water's edge as she continued to play in the river. The waters churned. A rushing torrent resounded. Nuelle turned toward the sound. Tumbling waves surged in Elisena's direction. She paddled away, but they tossed over her and dragged her downstream. Nuelle jumped into the river. His body shuddered at the cold as he thrashed against pounding waves. Elisena drifted farther and farther. Nuelle gulped air and dove under water. He stroked forward several times before swimming to the surface again. He scanned the river. *Where is she?*

A wave crashed over, thrusting him down. He fought the current that tried to keep him under, and pushed onward. He had to get to Elisena before it was too late! Nuelle swam up to the surface. His Sentinel floated a few paces in front of him, completely limp. "Elisena!" He reached for her. A heavy torrent shoved him to the side and his head collided into a rock. Blackness prevailed...

Nuelle's eyelids fluttered open. He lay face-down on dry ground. Feeling his head for an open wound, he rose to his feet. Where was Elisena? He peered at his hand—free of blood. A full-length mirror appeared across from him. His clothes had dried entirely, and after everything he'd been through, he remained unscathed. This must have been a vision, or a dream. Either way, it was time to wake up already. His friends and the preceptor needed him.

A blue-green pigment emerged on his arms and quickly spread. His heart pounded as spots opened on his skin. Blue warts sprouted in their place. He stepped back. His head and ears enlarged, patches of russet fur growing on his face and neck. He turned away from the mirror. Another one appeared. He veered to the left. A third mirror blocked him. He spun to the right as yet a fourth prevented him from escaping. Nuelle lifted his hands. Yellow claws protruded from his fingertips, his amber eyes the only feature that remained. He blinked. His irises shifted to green. He slowly backed away from the mirror. These weren't visions. They were nightmares.

The mirrors disappeared. Nuelle gazed down at his body —instead of blue warts and russet fur, he now wore white-and-gold garments. An aisle adorned with fuchsia petals extended in front of him. Tiny pink creatures flitted around fancy-garbed guests seated in benches on either side of the aisle in an auditorium. Lady Purine sat in a gallery on the right, wiping tears from her eyes as she waved. King Redmond and Queen Elva sat in a gallery on the left. The king traced his index finger across his throat and glared at Nuelle while Queen Elva wept into a handkerchief.

Sophana approached from the foot of the aisle. Diamond barrettes pinned up half of her pink hair, the other half flowing down her shoulder. Her white gown fluffed so wide it engulfed the walkway as she took slow, small, steps toward Nuelle. He looked to his left, his heart hammering in his chest. He stared at himself in a gold button-down and bottoms. Riff and Javin stood behind him in the same attire. *Wait, if I'm standing over there, then that must mean I'm*—Sophana stopped before him, a smile lighting up her face.

Nuelle's body automatically leaned in. "No, wait! I'm not Av—"

Her soft lips pressed against his mouth. He tried to pull away from her, but couldn't. Sophana suddenly recoiled. Tears filled her eyes as her cheeks turned pale green. She clasped her mouth and ran down the aisle. The auditorium vanished. Nuelle's body loosened as a red-wood forest and log cabin with a large door emerged in front of him. That little throne in what appeared to be a royal Athdonian garden—

Sophana's homeland; Elisena dying, his appearance becoming hideous and intimidating, Sophana not wanting to marry him—these nightmares, they weren't *his* greatest fears. They were his Sentinels'.

The cabin door opened. Nuelle approached. A foul, rotting carcass odor invaded his senses. He hesitated before stepping inside. Light flooded in from two open windows, illuminating a large commons table and couch that occupied most of the room. A framed portrait of Riff and a beautiful older Gavrailian woman sat on the table. The rancid smell intensified, pouring in from a door standing ajar on the right. Nuelle covered his nose and walked to the doorway. The Gavrailian woman from the portrait lay on a bed, her long, bony body molding. His stomach churned. He ran to the open entryway. The door slammed.

"It's the crazed girl!" a child with an Ideyan accent shouted from outside. Banging pounded the door and walls of the cabin, causing it to shake. "Watch out!" another child yelled. "Her mind is leaking!"

Laughter boomed and children chanted, "Run, hide from the crazed girl's mind!" Ideyan girls and boys stood outside the windows, blocking the light. They trampled over one another and climbed inside. The door collapsed, and a stampede rushed at Nuelle. He raised his palms and wind poured forth. The children surrounded, unfazed by the gust. Nuelle clasped his head. This needed to end already. Antikai may have discovered Surta and the others by now!

The children and cabin vanished. Nuelle scanned the area. Agapon's immense marketplace materialized around him. The daystar blazed in the sky, showering golden light on the empty stands. Beside the Main Tunnel leading to the Supreme Palace, the ruby center-fountain sat waterless.

Nuelle walked toward it. Dirt and mold layered the inside as if it hadn't spouted in years. He trotted through the Main Tunnel, his footsteps echoing off the marble walls. Soon, he entered a village bordering the fortress. Wall-vines smothered the gem-homes, and withered blossoms lined pathways to doors, all of which stood open. He strode through a rocky pathway and peered into a dwelling. Dust covered the commons, and black critters scurried along the couches and walls. He walked inside.

A doorway to the left revealed a bedchamber. Cobwebs layered the corners, and green crawlers stalked a crib. Nuelle ran out of the dwelling and raced to the palace. He hiked up the steep hill leading home. A chilly breeze blew past. Instead of the airy music usually sung by the wind, an ensemble of wails and groans encompassed the breeze.

His thumping heart decelerated to a slow throb. Near the palace's entrance, thousands of men, women, and children shoveled white dirt splotched with crimson. Each citizen bore a chain on their ankles, and a pile of corpses lay in heaps beside them. Nuelle barreled to the palace entrance. He rapidly ascended the steps and threw open the crystal doors. Racing up the staircase to Father's Throne Room, fire ignited on his palms. He shoved one of the gold doors. Tane lay sprawled across the floor in a pool of blood at the bottom of the throne steps.

Nuelle's heart sank to his stomach. "Brother!"

Antikai beamed from the throne, Father's crown on his head. His scaly hands clutched the crystal sword. The Acumen lay on the floor before him.

"No!" Nuelle dashed to the steps.

Antikai turned the blade to its black-trimmed side and drove it down. It sliced Father's golden insignia. As a blinding orange light exploded in the room, a rush of coldness drowned Nuelle's heart, and weakness coursed through his limbs. He dropped to his knees. His vision blurred, the cold overcoming him. The orange light gradually faded. The Acumen was gone.

Antikai approached, dragging the sword's tip across the marble floor. Nuelle's body quivered with feebleness as he peered up at the betrayer.

"Goodbye, Nu." Antikai raised the sword overhead and thrust it downward.

Everything blackened.

This place reeks of looming death. Elisena covered her nose and mouth. Numbness itched her bottom from sitting so long on the stone floor. Fumes from bitter spirits, manly urine, and underarm sweat wafted through the hot air, making breathing unbearable.

Drunken laughter from guards outside the dungeons mingled with clanging iron from slaves down the tunnel, sharpening prisoners' weapons. Many of the surrounding captives/coliseum-contenders slept, a few snoring, apparently used to the noisy atmosphere. Others trained by punching the air and dodging invisible foes. Their scars and blood-stained garbs proved they'd engaged in many a battle, experience etched in their chiseled arms and sturdy legs. With cold, enraged hearts, darkened by slaughter and bleeding passionate hatred, these men had trained themselves to survive. They were ready to kill without mercy anyone condemned to the coliseum.

If only I had my umbrella. Elisena's gaze shifted from her and the others' future opponents and onto her bluish foot, now two times bigger than normal. It still throbbed with pain, though a tad more tolerable. Elisena touched her swollen ankle. A pang shot through her foot and up her leg. She winced, biting her lip as tears welled. Preceptor Wit sat in a corner, holding his hanging head, and Sophana leaned against the vault's wall, stroking one of the tiny stems dotting her arms. Dried blood circled the slowly growing stalks that'd been forcefully torn off by their captors.

Ave clasped the iron bars. "Nuelle sends us here to find Vyden, and we get captured within minutes of arriving. What great Sentinels!"

The shaggy, silver-haired man seated on the chamber floor to their right turned his head. His cloak's hood hid half of his face.

"We have to get out of here somehow," Ave continued.

"Not to worry, twig." A bald Gavrailian man grasped the vault bars across from theirs. "Me will rip your whiney soul out of your bony body soon enough."

Sophana strode to Ave's side and glared at the Gavrailian. "He may not be as abnormally bulky as you, but he can stretch his arm right across this vault and strangle your oversized neck!"

"Strangle me with those puny hands?" The man released a bellowing guffaw from his scarred lips. As he cackled, Elisena focused on her friends.

Ave raised his bluing arms to the sides. They stretched and morphed to coral, expanding five times their original size, his right arm reaching into the cloaked man's cellar.

The Gavrailian stopped laughing. Ave grinned as his limbs shrank to normal. The cloaked man watched. As Ave gazed at Sophana, his grin disintegrated. From the moment they all woke in the dungeon, he'd felt immense shame and disappointment. "I didn't strangle the scum who dragged us here." His stare lowered to her arms. "I broke my promise. I let those brutes hurt you."

Sophana smiled. "It doesn't hurt as much as they hoped it would."

Ave rubbed his chest and glanced at Elisena. She averted her gaze. His feelings of unworthiness were far too relatable. Elisena shifted her attention to Sophana, whose heart held the same angry disappointment, but a lot of courage and confidence, too. Yet, underneath all the bravery and strength, fear's hollow hum stalked, with a thick layer of sadness.

Elisena's ankle throbbing, she sucked in a breath. "Do you ever miss the palace?"

Sophana slowly circled the cell. "The place itself, no. I never cared for all the pampering and nosy gazes watching my every move, as though since I'm a princess I need to behave extra proper twenty-four-seven." Her stiff shoulders sagged slightly. "But I do miss my family."

Elisena lifted an eyebrow.

Ave did the same. "You and your father didn't seem very…buttery together."

She sighed. "He can be really hard on me, but he wasn't always as rigid. Though he was"—she winced—"wrong about Ludwig, after our engagement fell through and trouble began brewing in the kingdoms, my father became overprotective and it was like all of his old lightheartedness and ease crumbled under the circumstances."

"I can't imagine what all of this rebellion in the kingdoms can do to a king's heart…" Elisena said.

Ave neared. "Neither can I. Being a royal cook is the best work. You're in a kitchen all day, breathing, creating, and eating the choicest foods, and your only concern is that everything tastes delightful." He frowned. "And that Old Lady Flemm won't accidentally burn the kitchen down."

Sophana grinned. "I like her."

Another pang rattled Elisena's leg and she grunted. Sophana frowned as she approached. The warm, gentle caress of…compassion emanated from her. "We need to figure out a way to escape. You can't go into a coliseum with a horde of crazed warriors in this condition."

"We're going to be killed!" Preceptor Wit blew his nose into his handkerchief. "And it is entirely my fault!"

Elisena peered into his magnified eyes, wet from crying. Guilt weighed heavy upon his heart, drowning it in despair. He felt like a fool, a failure with not even a glimmer of hope left.

"Ave, Sophana," Elisena said, "can you please help me stand?"

They hesitantly extended an arm. Elisena grasped their hands and pulled herself up. As she leaned upon her friends, they brought her before the preceptor. "Thank you." She stared at the poor, broken man, and spoke softly. "We all make mistakes. We all feel like a failure at one point or another, but you are still alive, and that means there remains hope for you, for all of us."

He sniffled, his nose red from blowing out snot. Though he must have been in his late sixties given his black-and-white hair, his youthful face pouting and stained with tears almost made him look like a wounded child not sure if he would ever get better again.

Elisena smiled. "A good man falls seven times, but gets up again." Releasing her hold from Sophana, she reached her arm out to the preceptor.

His mouth quivered, and a small smile grew on his face. He clasped her palm and rose to his feet. "Well then." Preceptor Wit lifted his spectacles, hurriedly wiped his eyes with his handkerchief, and then shoved it back into his pocket. "Let us form a plan."

"I have a plan." The aged man from the dungeon on their right slowly stood. As he turned toward them, Sophana gasped.

Vyden walked to the bars dividing his vault from theirs. His teal eyes concentrated on Sophana and glistened. "What terrible circumstances we find ourselves meeting in again." He lowered his voice as she and the others approached. "We do not have much time before the games, maybe minutes."

He addressed Ave. "I'll get the guards to come to my vault. One of them has a key that hangs on his hip. While I distract them, stretch your arm out and take the key."

"But then what?"

"Follow me." Vyden scurried to the entryway of his chamber. "Hey, you drunken nitwits," he called to the guards down the hall, "squelch your reeking mouths before I tie your tongues around your hollow heads!"

"Swhat did syou say to us, old man?" one of them slurred.

Vyden chuckled. "My sovereignty, there really isn't anything in those thick noggins."

"That's it!" The screech of chairs scraping the floors sounded, followed by hot-tempered stomps. Four guards marched to his chamber, their eyes glassy and red from drunkenness.

"I don't think the King is sgoing to survive sthe coliseum again once we're dones with him, right boys?" A lanky man unsheathed a glass stick with a wooden handle from his belt. A key-ring with one large key dangled from it. He pressed a button on the handle of his weapon, and the glass glowed orange.

"Wait, you fools." One of the guards grabbed his arm. "You can't use a—"

Ave's arm stretched through the vault. He clasped the key on the lanky man's belt and yanked it off. As Ave drew his arm back in, Vyden reached through the bars of his vault and clasped the orange glass stick. Vyden's eyes glowed orange, and the glass's light faded. Vyden raised his palms and an orange force-wave burst from them, past the iron bars and into the guards. They flew backwards against the Gavrailian's vault.

Ave unlocked their cellar and hurried out while Preceptor Wit and Sophana helped Elisena. "I've got you, warrior," Sophana said.

Elisena smiled. "Thank you."

"What do you pebbles think you're doing?" the Gavrailian growled from his dungeon.

"Escaping." Ave unlocked Vyden's vault.

"I guess you won't be ripping his soul out of his bony body after all," Sophana said as Ave freed Vyden.

The once-king grabbed the guard's stick weapon. "Stay close." He ran toward the slaves sharpening weapons at the end of the tunnel, Elisena and the others trailing.

"Guards, guards!" the Gavrailian shouted from behind. "They're getting away, hurry!"

Their satchels lay in a heap beside an emaciated and shorn elderly man, woman, and little girl. Manacles chained the slaves' feet. The little girl handed Elisena her acid-spitting umbrella while Vyden grabbed two metal-gloved arm-braces. He frowned as he turned to leave. "There is nothing we can do for them now."

"Wait." Elisena pointed her umbrella at the slaves' chains and launched the acid. The metal quickly melted. As the slaves jerked their chains free, another group of guards rushed into the tunnel, wielding strange wide-barreled weapons hoisted over their shoulders.

"Time to go!" Vyden darted to the right and rushed out of a wooden door.

Elisena and the others followed him up a stairwell. A golden ray poured in from a door's window at the top of the landing. Elisena clung to Preceptor Wit and Sophana as Vyden led them outside into blistering heat. A massive coliseum encircled. Thousands filled the stands, and hundreds more flooded in through an open gate leading into the town. Vyden sprinted across the dirt terrain—darkened with blood—to the gate. Guards darted from the dungeon behind, their wide-barreled contraptions aimed. A ball launched from the devices and spread into large nets.

"Ave!" Elisena cried.

He stretched his arm and caught the nets. He tossed them aside as they reached the gate. Halting, Vyden turned on the orange stick as the freed-slaves ran past. He grasped the weapon with his metal-gloved hands and absorbed its light. The metal glowed orange, and he released a small force-wave from his palm. It slammed into the guards. His gloves still glowing, he lifted the hood of his cloak and gestured Elisena and the others to follow him through the crowd entering the gate. After squeezing and nudging their way beyond the horde, Vyden led them past a brothel and toward a row of large fish-shaped platforms with steering-sticks. He hopped onto one and clutched the sticks. Orange light flowed down them, and the platform ignited with energy and hovered from the ground. Vyden smiled. "All aboard."

"Brilliant!" Preceptor Wit and Sophana helped Elisena onto the riding-device as Ave jumped on. Railings sprouted from the platform and it swiftly rose ten feet above ground. Three more guards shoved past the mob of coliseum attendees and bounded their way.

"Hold tight!" Vyden tapped one of three pedals with his bare foot and pushed a stick forward. The device lurched into motion, zooming over the citizens below. The guards hopped onto the devices and pursued. One of them fired a net. Vyden jerked the steering sticks to the left. The riding device jolted to the side, avoiding a floating stand. Elisena staggered, and a pang stabbed her leg. She grunted as she grasped a railing.

Ave frowned at Preceptor Wit. "Do you still have the querapa saliva and healing fruit seeds?"

"I do!"

Ave addressed Vyden. "Get us somewhere safe with fertile ground."

"Certainly." He pressed on a pedal, and the platform rose higher.

A few of Sophana's arm leaves grew back. She plucked one and chucked it at a guard. It pierced his shoulder, knocking him off the riding device and tumbling into two women.

"Nice aim." Ave stretched his leg toward another flying-device and kicked the hands of the guard navigating it. The steering-stick broke in half, and the riding-device flipped backwards into the guard's behind him. Both spiraled out of control and crashed into a floating stand.

Sophana smiled at Ave. "Nice kick."

"What worthy Sentinels." Preceptor Wit beamed.

"I wouldn't say we're worthy," Ave replied. "Just chosen."

Despite her worsening foot pain, joy overflowed Elisena's heart. Here she was, someone who had been teased and despised all her life; even by her own mother. No one had ever believed she'd be anything more than the strange daughter of Ronen—until she met Prince Nuelle. He saw more in her, and chose her and the others from all those who came to show off their skills before him. Minus the constant reminder of very real danger, it was surreal that she'd become one of the Seven Sentinels. No longer an outcast, she was now a chosen guardian and friend of Zephoris' Supreme Prince, destined for the greatest task of all: protecting Hope Himself for those who remained faithful to him and his father, and whoever would eventually choose to be.

As the town's outskirts neared, Preceptor Wit inched closer to Vyden. "My lord, how did you end up in the coliseum?"

Squeezing the railing, Elisena locked her gaze onto the once-king. A deep sorrow and heavy disappointment weighed on his heart. But the sadness also carried a hollow pain, as if something that formerly resided in his chest had died. Elisena reached for her umbrella. But then let her hand fall. She'd felt and known so many terrible emotions and desires today, but it wasn't often she had the chance to see into the heart of a king.

Breathing in the hot breeze blowing against him, as if he needed much of it to speak his next words, Vyden briefly closed his eyes. He exhaled, and then opened his mouth. "Ludwig sold me to a wealthy slave-trader."

"He what!" Sophana yelled.

Ave glanced at her. "How could your own son do something so vile?"

"He was not pleased at having been ousted from the palace," Vyden spoke quietly as they flew out of town and over vast magenta hills. "He desired I order my army to destroy all who opposed my kingship, but I refused. He'd become embittered toward me. So one day, while visiting the marketplace for food, he used one of his inventions to bind me, and right in the middle of the square he began bargaining with the crowd."

Sophana scratched at one of the open wounds on her arm. Ave curled his fingers around hers. After a long moment, she spoke in a miraculously leveled tone. "Where is he now?"

"I do not know." Vyden kept his stare ahead, a tear trickling from his eye.

Elisena shifted her own stare. Clearly, not everyone born into royalty was like Prince Nuelle. Antikai and Ludwig used their position for entitlement and lordship, rather than to sacrifice and serve.

Vyden wiped his tear away. "So why did Prince Nuelle send you all to search for me?"

"We need to find the crystal sword," Elisena answered.

He glanced over his shoulder, his eyes wide. A grave fear meshed with disbelief now washed over his heart.

Elisena loosened her grip on the railing, though her ankle still seared. "The prophecies are coming true, and Prince Nuelle is probably in the Obsidian as we speak—days away from here—bringing the Acumen to Antikai."

Vyden stepped on the third pedal, and the platform descended. As it landed on a hill, he released the sticks and faced her. "The sword cannot go anywhere near Prince Antikai."

Ave released Sophana's hand. "But that's how Nuelle plans to defeat him—with the sword."

Vyden shook his head. "You do not understand. If Prince Antikai is able to destroy that book, Prince Nuelle will die, and this land will become a kingdom where darkness reigns." His voice quaked with the fear plaguing his heart. "The daystar will no longer shed its light, for the evil that consumes the ground will be so repugnant, the very elements will turn against it, and all hope will be utterly vanquished from this world."

Preceptor Wit trembled like Vyden's speech. Now fear and doubt swathed their vicious grip on his heart as well.

Elisena walked away from the railing, ignoring the agony screaming through her leg, and stopped before Ideya's old king. "Prince Nuelle is the Hope of the Faithful. Either you trust him, or you do not." She gestured to Ave and Sophana. "But we have seen his power and know his character, and both only grow stronger."

As Vyden stared back at her, he rubbed his chest. The disbelief had vanished like the morning mist, but fear still reigned on the throne of his heart.

Ave strode to Elisena's side. "Nuelle is my best friend, and we were chosen by him to be his Sentinels because he believed in us."

Sophana bustled forward and joined them. "And just as he is faithful, we will be faithful to complete the task he has entrusted us with."

Vyden gazed at all of them, continuing to rub his chest. The fear remained, but a spark of hope ignited in the midst of it, like the flames of a torch illuminating a dungeon. He looked at Elisena's ankle. "It shouldn't take too long for the healing fruit to get that leg functioning normally." His stare drifted far beyond the hills. "You will need it where we're going."

Please don't tell me I died.

Rushing wind filled Nuelle's eardrums. The air pushed forcefully against his face, causing his cheeks to ripple. A powerful gust consumed and swept him upward. Swirls of dark gray engulfed as the crushing wind pressed against his body from every angle. His insides churned, giving way to nausea. He pursed his lips together to refrain from releasing bile. *I guess I'm not dead.* After several more spins, the cyclone spat him out. He crashed onto the black ground of the Obsidian at one end of the bridge, and the cyclone whirled off. The flame-holder sat nearby, burning bright.

"Prince Nuelle!" an invisible Surta whispered. "Supreme Prince, are you all right?" She patted his back rather forcefully.

He coughed. "Can you. Please not. Do that."

Riff chuckled. "Good to see you're still alive."

"Likewise. Sort of." His heart jumped. "Where's my satchel?"

"Right here." Javin spoke from the left. Large strong hands helped Nuelle to his feet—Riff. Someone placed the satchel in Nuelle's hand. He quickly opened it. The Acumen gleamed safely inside. Warmth flooded his sore and queasy body as he sighed. So it was all just a nightmare. Father's book remained intact, and that traitor still hadn't acquired the crystal sword or he would have shown up by now. Nuelle slid the strap onto his shoulder and carried the satchel close.

Surta spoke again, her voice trembling. "I thought you were…"

"I'm okay." Nuelle scanned the surroundings for any sign of movement. Icy air pierced through the flame-holder's feeble warmth. He breathed in the familiar cold. Despite Antikai's threats and whatever power he'd come to attain, Tane's slayer would be avenged. Avenged for him, avenged for the Overseer, for Darcy's little sister, and everyone else who had been unjustly killed because of the fallen prince's corruption. Flames ignited on Nuelle's fingertips. *Tonight, Antikai's evil will finally come to its end.*

He picked up the flame-holder and stepped forward. Something gleamed in the ground near the path of leafless trees. The dirt around the shimmering item separated and circled, revealing metallic suits of armor. The soil reversed toward the suits and seeped inside them as though sucked in by an invisible force. Something else metallic rose from the ground beside the suits—swords. The possessed armor grasped the weapons and stood at attention like soldiers ready for battle.

The flames flickering on Nuelle's fingertips spread to the rest of his hands. He dropped the flame-holder. Raising their swords, the ground-soldiers marched in his direction. One of their heads suddenly toppled from its mount. Riff. Or maybe Javin. A dirt-knight launched its sword at Nuelle. He caught the blade before it could pierce his forehead. His flaming hands set the sword on fire and he grasped the hilt as the mob of ground-soldiers attacked. Swinging the blade, he decapitated two of them before impaling another in the chest and setting it ablaze. He thrust a blast of flaming wind at three others. Their armor blew off, and dirt scattered as he slashed at limbs and took down more ground-soldiers.

One grabbed him in a headlock from behind. The cold metal squeezed his throat, blocking his airway. He jumped and kicked the chest of a ground-soldier in front of him. Thrusting himself off the accursed suit of armor, he shoved the one choking him backwards. They collapsed, the dirt scattering from the armor. Nuelle rolled to his feet.

The three remaining ground-soldiers each fell back as if struck by invisible blows. His friends finished the last of them, and he ceased his fire and wind. It seemed Antikai wanted to kill him before he reached wherever the traitor dwelled. Maybe he had lost hope in finding the crystal sword. Maybe Ave and the others had already attained it, and were in route to the Obsidian now.

He clenched his satchel and turned to the path of leafless trees. He'd give it more time; taking a rest and waiting for another attack would be best before moving forward. His Sentinels needed to bring him the sword so he could defeat Antikai once for all, and who knew if even a single day had passed yet. He frowned as he stared at the crooked path ahead. Father did banish Antikai eternally to the Obsidian. And clearly no daystar shined in this territory. Maybe time didn't exist here. How else could that vile man be sentenced to live here forever?

Nuelle's stomach knotted. But if that was true, did that mean Antikai was immortal? A giant, armored calf three times Nuelle's size rose from the dirt across from him. Dust rapidly gathered to a metal suit bigger than all of the others combined. Nuelle's palms ignited into crackling flames, heat coursing through his limbs. The colossal ground-soldier straightened and stood as if being hoisted by invisible ropes. It towered at least a hundred feet high.

"You might be a little harder to take down," Nuelle said.

It swung its gigantic sword. He sprinted through its legs. His enormous adversary spun around and faced him, raising its boot. Nuelle rolled aside as it stomped, and then leapt to his feet. Its other foot bore down. He dodged it. In swift motions, the ground-soldier brought its sword downward. Nuelle clung to his satchel as he evaded the blade, just barely missing the steel. The ground-soldier's sword came spearing from above.

Nuelle raised his flaming palms. Wind burst from them. The fiery gust blew against the blade. Nuelle's body trembled, the searing heat coursing through his arms as the giant pressed downward, fighting the wind. The flames devoured the blade and hilt, setting ablaze the ground-soldier's enormous hand. Nuelle moved aside as the soldier dropped the sword and shook its arm to douse the fire. Nuelle released a burning gust at its chest.

The ground-soldier stumbled onto the bridge and fell backwards. Its giant suit of armor smashed into the wood, planks bursting, and plummeted aflame into the black depths. Sweat slid down Nuelle's forehead and dripped into his eyes as his fire diminished. Since there was no longer a bridge to cross, hopefully his Sentinels' vanaphs would be more obedient when they arrived with the crystal sword. A biting gust blew past, stinging his cheeks and raising the hairs on his arms. Antikai was close.

He reached into his satchel and removed a canister of his tears, ones he had recently shed. Taking a tiny sip, he sat against the trunk of a drooping tree along the path. Where was Father now? Did he subdue his foes and stay at the palace, or had he forsaken it? And where were Ave and the others? Did they find the sword, or had something terrible happened to them?

Closing the canister, Nuelle pressed the back of his head against the cold wood. What would be the end of all this? Amador died. The Overseer died. Tane died. Antikai's blood-stained hands and savage heart were spreading like a plague throughout the land and had even infected home—the central kingdom, right on through the doors of the Supreme Palace.

He slowly breathed in the dry, bitter air. *Please, Ave, come soon.*

Seventeen: The Polarian Canyons

A few stars hung in the evening skies—distant from the night star and one another, their cold light dim and hesitant on the frozen canyons below. The massive glaciers cast shadows on the valley of frosted ground, like alert giants guarding their territory. Mountains lifted their peaks high, even grander in size than the mounds of ice.

Choosing careful steps along the slippery surface, Ave clenched his satchel as Vyden led him and the others onward into the abandoned territory. Ideya's old king blew into his flame-holder, making the fire bigger. Sophana, Elisena, and Preceptor Wit shivered behind the hoods of the cloaks they obtained from the settlers in Innovian's outskirts. Even in sparse lighting, Sophana's yellow irises shined like the stars. Pink highlighted the smooth skin on her cheeks and perfect nose. Her similar, pink-gold leaf-blades also shimmered, appearing slightly less lethal, and almost...gentle.

Ave huffed, his breath a white mist.

Sophana's eyes narrowed. "What?"

"I was just thinking about how this darkness is somewhat disguising how deadly and scary you are."

"Darkness is funny like that. The less you see, the better things look."

Ave groaned. "You drive me crazy."

Sophana balked. "Ugh, I've heard that one before."

"No, no, I don't mean in a...that kind of way. I mean, don't get me wrong, you're beautiful, but there's just so much more to you that I'm finding difficult to figure out."

She held her shoulders back and stared at Elisena and the others, treading ahead. "Maybe I like having you blind."

"Whoa, whoa, I didn't say I was completely in the dark about you."

"Oh really? Amuse me."

"You asked for it." Ave cracked his knuckles and then rolled his shoulders. "King Nifal gave you your gift for a reason. He had to have known you'd be brave and tough, and different, and independent."

She smiled. "I like this list."

"But, he also knew it would protect you because he made you beautiful, and selfish cowards would try to take advantage of your beauty rather than honor it."

Sophana turned her face toward his. "Interesting assumptions. I never really…thought of it that way."

Ave continued. "And maybe he knew you'd need someone who would treat you with caution. Someone who would respect your strength and be gentle with your weaknesses."

She looked away again. "Or maybe he knew no one would be that way toward me and so I'd never marry and that's why I'm so independent."

Ave shrugged. "Maybe. Maybe not."

As she watched him once more, he instantly regretted his big mouth. His best friend was still in the Obsidian, waiting for them to bring him the sword. He could have been captured by now, or lost. And Nuelle wanted them—wanted Ave—to focus, not to fall for a fellow Sentinel. He tore his attention from Sophana.

Elisena chattered. "My-my lord, where exactly is the sword?"

Vyden gestured ahead with his flame-holder. "It's at the heart of the canyons, about ten miles onward."

"Ten miles?" Sophana asked. "Why didn't we take one of those riding devices?"

"This place is too cold. The engines would freeze within seconds."

Preceptor Wit huddled closer to the flame's warmth. "I imagine without cloaks and a fire, we too would freeze within seconds."

Vyden shook his head. "Not seconds, minutes."

Ave shivered. No wonder none of the citizens lived here. If this place had been so terribly brutal, who knew what the Obsidian was like? His chest tightened. Nuelle knew.

Vyden pointed up at one of the mountains with his metal-gloved hand. "We're going to need to take cover in the highlands. At dawn's first light, frost hounds hunt for food, and they only eat meat."

Preceptor Wit quaked all the more beneath his cloak. "Vile creatures they are. I've read that though smaller, they have an appetite greater than a Massadon due to their hyper-sped metabolisms."

Ave quickened his pace. "We better reach the mountains in a hurry. Nuelle needs us to survive long enough to bring him the sword." Something cracked beneath his foot. He lifted his cloak, dusted at the bottom from the frosted ground. Around his boot, a sheer layer of ice revealed blue water seeping through cracks. Sophana and the others stopped walking. Vyden slowly moved his flame-holder from side-to-side, revealing a large span of frozen water that encircled at least fifteen yards in every direction.

"This isn't good," Elisena whispered.

Vyden turned a knob on the flame-holder, and the fire extinguished.

"What are you doing?" Ave said.

"The flames will melt the ice quicker." He slipped the holder into his pocket and slid his foot forward. "We must move swiftly, but cautiously."

They all began gliding ahead. The icy wind assaulted Ave's body. His teeth chattered, and his heart-rate hastened in angry disagreement with the flames' missing warmth. Freezing air cut through his garbs and pricked his skin. A few more strides and his face turned numb. His glassy eyes fogged his vision.

"It's cracking around me." Elisena grimaced as she watched the ground.

"Keep moving," Vyden replied. "We're almost there."

Only a few yards of the icy layer remained.

"Oh no." Sophana looked at the sky. A golden glow crawled along the outline of the night star.

Ave and the others hurried their glides. Just a couple of paces now. As he breathed in quick inhales, his lungs and chest seared from the cold. He was almost there. Finally, his stiff legs stepped into frost. Vyden, Sophana, and the preceptor crossed over next. As Vyden swiftly removed the flame-holder and relighted it, Ave's stomach flopped. Elisena trembled three yards back. She stood frozen in fear, thick cracks surrounding her.

Ave extended his arms, the fire's warmth blessing his hands. "You're almost here, Elisena. Just keep moving quickly and gently."

"I c-cant," she stuttered in the cold, her lips purple. The light around the night star grew brighter.

Ave beckoned her. "Yes you can. You must!"

"It's g-going to b-break."

"We have to get to the mountain, or we're all going to die!"

She clasped her cloak at the hips and raised it. Closing her eyes, she bustled forward. The ice shattered. She collapsed into the water.

"Elisena!" Sophana screamed.

Ave threw off his cloak and dove in after her. The icy water soaked through his tunic and jarred his bones. His heart thrashed in a futile effort to fight the deadly cold. He opened his eyes, though it stung to do so. Elisena sunk, her arms raised and mouth open. He swam toward her and grabbed hold of her waist. He pushed through the water and broke through the surface. Numbness attacked his limbs and they grew heavy.

"Come on, Ave!" Sophana called. "Hurry!" A golden ray shined on her face, illuminating the fear in her glossy eyes.

Ave forced himself to swim onward, but Elisena slowed his pace. His body quaked and his lips trembled. As he neared the end, a chorus of shrill wails echoed off the mountains.

"Hurry, boy!" Vyden said.

Ave paddled onward, his arms like wood. He finally reached the end. The others grasped his and Elisena's drenched arms and pulled them out of the water. Preceptor Wit pumped Elisena's chest while Sophana covered Ave in his cloak. The wailing drew closer.

"Come on, girl!" Preceptor Wit thrust his palms against her heart, and her eyes fluttered open. She coughed as he and Vyden helped her up, water spilling from her mouth.

An assembly of growls rumbled from behind. Ave braced himself as he peered over his shoulder. Eight blue-furred beasts with white chests and eyes hunched nearby. Their slobbering snouts exposed fangs.

Vyden dashed ahead, clasping the flame-holder. Ave and the others followed. The combination of icy breeze and soaking garbs battered his body. They neared the foot of a mountain. A pathway curved up its frozen sides. The frost hounds barreled after them, the beasts' swift paws slapping the ground as if moving too fast to sink in its thick frost. Sophana grunted. Ave looked to the right. She had fallen on all fours! One of the beasts leapt in her direction, its snout opening wide, and blue tongue hanging. Ave extended his arm and grabbed hold of the hound's tongue. He tugged hard, and the beast slammed into the ground. The others gained. Ave grabbed Sophana's hand and yanked her to her feet. They sprinted onward.

The mountain loomed a few yards away. The beasts' pounding paws loudened. Sophana plucked a handful of leaf-blades. She looked back and began throwing. A blade pierced a frost hound in its white chest. It yelped and collapsed onto the ground. Six more pounced. Ave grabbed Sophana's arm and pulled her in. His legs extended and he towered twenty feet over the beasts. They gazed up at Ave as he clasped Sophana close. Growls eased from their throats. One of them snapped its snout at Ave's leg while the others circled.

"Now what?" Sophana asked.

The morning daystar burned in the skies. Its vibrant light shined off the hungry and hollow white eyes of the beasts. With no pupil, it almost seemed like their eyes had been made from frost.

"Climb onto my back," Ave whispered.

Sophana complied. The hounds snarled and bit the air again at Ave's calves. He shot his arms out and yelled at the top of his lungs. His cry echoed through the mountains behind. The beasts peered up at the highlands and backed away. Ave hollered again and stepped forward. The frost hounds spun around and dashed away. When they disappeared beyond the glaciers, Ave shrank back to size. Applause sounded from behind. Vyden and the others stood at the foot of a pathway lining the mountain.

Sophana pecked Ave's cheek. "Thank you." She scuttled to their friends and hugged Elisena. Ave blinked away the daze from her kiss and bustled onward. The warmth from Vyden's flame-holder embraced him, soothing his shivers.

"Brilliant spectacle, young fellows!" Preceptor Wit pulled him and Sophana in for a hug. His skinny arms squeezed, and he beamed as he released.

Elisena hugged him, too. "And thank you for coming after me, Ave."

He shuddered at her freezing and soggy embrace, but warmth filled his heart. He was glad she made it. Glad they all had made it this far.

"My lord," Preceptor Wit said to Vyden as he peered up at the curved path, "why are the frost hounds afraid of the mountains?"

The flame-holder's fire shined off Vyden's teal irises, making them glow. "They fear the lazawards."

"Lazawards?" Sophana slid her remaining leaf-blade into her cloak. "What are those?"

"You shall see." He trekked up the mountain path. "Let's find a place to rest and get our clothing dry. We'll continue our voyage at high noon."

The scrape of a sword leaving its sheath sounded from within the Throne Room. "The start of restoring peace will begin with Antikai's death." Tane spoke with a certainty as hard as the blows he could inflict with his weapon.

"Your words speak of victory," Father said, "but your heart has already been defeated."

Tane? Nuelle's eyes opened to the wilted tree branches he rested under. Light from the flame-holder's fire highlighted the dead wood—cold and dark, like the rest of this condemned land. He sat up, grasping his satchel. The ache in his chest reserved for Tane unleashed itself from the depths of his pain. He lost his brother not once, but twice. If only Tane listened to Father instead of stubbornly going against his will. Brother let the wrath in his heart lead him, rather than the peaceful words of their Father, and look at where it brought him—slain by the one he sought to destroy!

Nuelle pulled his satchel over his shoulder and pushed off the black ground. The orange flames kindled in his palms. He would finish what his brother started. This time, Antikai had to be the one to fall. A cry in the distance locked Nuelle's knees in place. "Preceptor Sage." His fire extinguished as he looked around at the encompassing nothingness. Did his friends also sleep? Or had they kept watch? Were they even around?

A small hand clasped his and squeezed gently. Surta! He held in a sigh of relief. His Sentinels were still here, faithfully protecting him. But what about the others? He was close to Antikai, and still didn't have the sword. Tane had fallen to the traitor so it was best to wait, to have the weapon that harbored Father's power. Tane was one of the mightiest warriors in Zephoris, but Antikai would not be able to overcome the Supreme King's strength.

Another gut-wrenching cry from the preceptor impaled the air. Nuelle gripped Surta's hand, smoke rising from his arms. But then again, he had gotten stronger, and he was the Hope of the Faithful. If anything, Antikai needed the sword to vanquish his power—like the nightmare showed—and to let Preceptor Sage die would be just as heartless as the traitorous prince and his savages.

"Wait here," Nuelle whispered through the side of his mouth. "When the others arrive with the sword, come bring it to me." He released Surta's hand and jogged down the pathway. Soon, it narrowed, and the temperature dropped. His palms filled with fire, shunning the cold.

Metallic thorn bushes replaced the leafless trees. About twenty yards away, an open wrought-iron gate with a barbed top materialized. He slowed to a steady stride, his satchel bouncing against his ribs, firm and warm from the Acumen within. As he walked through the gate, an ebony-stone castle emerged from the void. Though easily four-stories high, the palace's walls offered no windows for those dwelling inside. A black pond sat still beside it, and heads of strange creatures adorned the ends of wide steps leading to the doors. The castle blended with the darkness, as if they were one. Preceptor Sage wailed from within the ebony walls.

Nuelle's fire disintegrated and he removed the Acumen from his satchel. "I brought what you wanted!" He lifted the golden book that contained his life in both scarlet words and powerful energy; the book that had led him every step of the way and still had more light to shed on his destiny. "Now release the preceptor!" The doors swung open, and Preceptor Sage tumbled down the steps. Nuelle raced to his side. Frozen mucus bordered his nostrils as he chattered, and frost particles coated his hair and garbs. Heat flooded Nuelle's palms as he placed them on the preceptor's shoulders.

The icy mucus melted, and Preceptor Sage ceased chattering. "Thank you, my lord."

"Let's go." Nuelle helped him to his feet and turned toward the gate.

Raysha stood at its entrance with Jilt, Brone, and Emmer alongside her. "Saying farewell before you've said hello?" the evil woman crooned.

"Let the preceptor go, and I'll hand myself and the Acumen over to Antikai."

Her blood-red lips twisted into a smile. "One moment." She disappeared.

Preceptor Sage coughed, covering his mouth with a trembling hand. Nuelle grasped his thin bicep. "You're going to be okay." He winced, recalling how he'd repeated the same words to the preceptor the first day at the academy as he bled from a hole in his side delivered by one of these revolting savages.

Raysha reappeared. "Master Antikai will take your offer." She glided away from the gate, her lifeless blue eyes never leaving Nuelle. "Make way, friends." Jilt, Brone, and Emmer followed her lead.

Preceptor Sage gazed at Nuelle with tired yellow eyes lined by dark circles. "But my lord, what about you?"

"You don't need to be concerned for me." He released the preceptor's arm.

Forehead wrinkled with confusion and doubt, Preceptor Sage slowly walked forward. Like Raysha, Jilt and Brone stared at Nuelle, ignoring the preceptor as he limped by. He stepped through the gate and then halted. Peering over his shoulder, his watering eyes penetrated Nuelle's heart. It was as if he cried a silent plea for Nuelle to leave with him.

The painful ache designated for Tane emerged in Nuelle's chest again. Similar to how he had begged Tane not to leave without him that night he left to defeat Antikai. Nuelle tried to keep his face taut, to signal to the preceptor that he had a plan and that he needed to stay in order to fulfill it. Words would have gotten the message across so much easier, but he couldn't voice them. Just like he had to do many times with Father, Preceptor Sage simply needed to trust him.

As if hearing Nuelle's thoughts, the preceptor lowered his gaze and continued into the darkness ahead. Nuelle's eyes watered. *Protection surround him and hope lead him out of this wretched land.*

Raysha reached her palm out. "The book, please."

Giving it one last squeeze, drawing its life-throbbing warmth into his skin, Nuelle handed it to her. She smirked and then fired a green orb at the preceptor's back.

"No!" Nuelle's hands erupted in flames as Preceptor Sage collapsed. Jilt released a thick line of green energy and it wrapped around Nuelle like a rope, restraining him.

Raysha beamed as she strolled to the preceptor. His back bled and smoked from the blast. She pressed her boot into his scalding skin, her grin widening. He hollered and dug his thin fingers into the dirt.

Nuelle's body blazed. "I gave you the book, now release him!"

She knelt down, leaning her weight onto her leg, causing her foot to lodge deeper into Preceptor Sage's back. Her cold, blue eyes studied Nuelle's. "Do you care for him, Prince? Do you love him?"

He squirmed in the dark power binding his limbs. "Yes, I do."

"Like I loved my brother?"

"Raysha, please. You have what you want. Just let him go."

"I do not have what I want." Her hollow gaze wandered to Preceptor Sage. "Yet." She grabbed his shoulder and spun him face-upward. Her hand clasped the back of his neck and she pulled him toward her as green cheek-fangs elongated.

Fire engulfed Nuelle's arms. "He isn't the threat. I am."

"Enjoy the show, Prince." Raysha sank her fangs into Preceptor Sage's neck.

"Preceptor!" Nuelle cried.

Preceptor Sage's mouth hung open. Tears filled his eyes as the veins in his neck and cheeks rapidly turned green. Nuelle yelled, his chest ripping apart and bleeding with agony. He strained to free himself from Jilt's bondage. His arms and legs ached at the effort, but his heart screamed at him to keep trying. The preceptor lay just a few paces away, and there was still time to heal him.

Raysha released, and Preceptor Sage fell back. He exhaled and inhaled, slowly, painfully. The tears seeped from his eyes as they concentrated on Nuelle.

"Preceptor Sage." Nuelle balled his blazing fists.

"My lord"—he coughed and choked before gasping for air. His eyelids grew heavy.

Tears flooded Nuelle's vision. As he fought against the pressure wrapped around him, his body quaked. He just needed to rest his hands on the Preceptor, to draw the poison from his blood and take it upon himself until it vanished completely.

Preceptor Sage stopped panting, and his eyes closed.

"No!" Nuelle's cry resounded through the surrounding void, echoing off the black castle.

Raysha rose and passed the Acumen to Emmer. "Bring this to the Master."

"This was fun"—Emmer gave it to Jilt—"but I have plans of my own that need tending to." She disappeared.

Raysha focused on Jilt. "Master was going to kill her anyway. Go."

He vanished. A smirk lifted Raysha's mouth, and her eyes glinted. "Shall we, Prince?" She fired a green orb at Nuelle. It speared into his stomach and launched him onto the castle steps. His back collided with the stone as his abdomen burned. He toppled down the stairs and landed face-up in the black dust. Brone stood over him as blood seeped from the bubbling red burns on his stomach.

Raysha glided toward them. With twisted joy, she smiled at Nuelle and dug her boot against his searing wounds. "Bring him to Master Antikai."

Tears stung Nuelle's eyes as he stared at Preceptor Sage, at his friend, one last time before everything went black.

Glowing green shackles clamped around Nuelle's wrists and ankles illuminated a cold chamber. The bitter atmosphere reeked of carcass, similar to the Massadon cave in the forest surrounding the Servants' Lodge.

Nuelle's knees bore into a moist floor coated with black dust. The shackles' chains kept him close to a metallic wall. His stomach grumbled. How many hours had passed since he'd gotten captured? And where were his Sentinels? Had they found the crystal sword? He tugged on the chains and they jangled loudly, rattling his mind. Preceptor Sage! That heartless woman had seized his life. Another faithful soul ripped from this world without mercy. A cry twisted in Nuelle's gut before piercing through his throat and filling the chamber. Another life sacrificed because of him, another victim to those consumed with darkness. How many had to suffer because of him? When would it stop? A tiny flame on a mantel to his right flickered, shedding light on the Acumen atop it and casting shadows on the wall behind.

"My, how you've grown." Antikai's green eyes floated in the darkness a stone's throw away.

The mantel's flame grew, exposing him. Thorns protruded from the top of his onyx throne, and a foecry head mounted the end of one armrest. A black pond with a frozen strip across its center led to Antikai's scaly feet. His greasy purplish-black hair covered only half of his scalp, the green scales on his face presenting him as no longer just a man, but a beast. Nuelle jerked the chains again.

Antikai's scales lifted and fell as he smiled, his gums black. "I presume there are many things you believe about me, many things that are not true."

"You tried to slay my father, and you killed my brother! And one of your soulless followers just murdered Preceptor Sage! And you said you would release him. There isn't an ounce of truth in you."

Antikai's gaze wandered to the Acumen on the mantel. "I did not try to slay the Supreme King. I merely desired to help him."

"Help him?" Nuelle's hands smoked. "You're a liar, and many have been slaughtered because of your thirst for power." Ice formed on Nuelle's palms, dousing the heat flaring inside.

"Slaughtered because of me, or because of you?"

Nuelle closed his mouth, his heart sinking. Yes...blood stained his hands.

"How many more lives are you willing to sacrifice for yourself?" Antikai slid to his feet and glided toward him. "Who else's blood will be spilled for you? What makes your life more important than theirs?"

Nuelle held his tongue. It was true. Why did he have to live while others died for his sake? How much more guilt could he carry? Maybe if he offered his life, if he just stopped thinking he was somehow needed, souls could be spared.

"I pity you. All this weight your father has placed upon you for the sake of false hope. To protect your fragile, young mind from the truth, as if a lie would somehow prevent the inevitable."

His words gnawed at Nuelle's heart. He had to put his guard up. But what did Antikai mean?

As if reading Nuelle's thoughts, Antikai flicked his hand toward the Acumen. It zoomed off the mantel and crashed into Nuelle's chest before dropping to the floor. As he coughed, it opened to a page midway through. A green glow highlighted a sentence at the bottom.

All peace shall be removed, and chaos and destruction will rule the land until it is no more.

Nuelle's heart raced. How could the great land of Zephoris be destroyed? What about the Faithful? Warmth burned in his chest. The Incandescia, their safe place from the destruction of this world. That must have been why he needed to lead them there.

Antikai gestured to the Acumen and it slammed shut. "Your father has been lying to you, causing you to believe in fables like the Incandescia. But Tane knew the truth."

Nuelle's eardrums buzzed as he peered up at him. "What are you talking about?"

"I urged Tane to tell you the truth, but he kept saying you were too young to handle it." Antikai motioned to the Acumen. It rose from the ground and floated back to the mantel.

Nuelle clawed at the black dust, every inch of him trembling. *Is that what Tane meant before he left for the Obsidian? He always told me I was too young to understand, and he never mentioned the Incandescia. He believed the only way to restore peace was to kill Antikai. For some reason, Brother didn't trust Father. Did he know something I don't?*

"Tane was a dear friend, but when your father understood his weakness was being exposed, he turned your brother against me. He came here to slay me, but I hid myself from him. When he could not find me, he departed, and I have not seen him since."

Sweat seeped from Nuelle's palms. Did Antikai tell the truth? Could Brother still be alive?

Nuelle looked at the Acumen as it shined on the black mantel. No, Antikai was a deceiver. He killed Tane, just like he attempted to kill Father, and that's why Tane never returned to Agapon.

"Do you not wonder why your father never came to the Obsidian in search of Tane?" Antikai knelt down. His freezing breath stung Nuelle's face. "It is because he knew Tane was better fit to serve as Supreme King, and your father is clearly not yet willing to release the power. Your brother could still be out there, lost in the darkness or destroyed by the beasts that lurk in this shadow land, and King Nifal has left him to his fate, just like he will leave you to yours!"

Tears blurred Nuelle's vision. Yes, Father never journeyed to the Obsidian to find Tane, but he must have had some good reason for it. Maybe he knew that Tane had already died. But if that was the case, why didn't Father bring Antikai out of the Obsidian and have him slain for bloodshed?

"What is hidden in darkness shall come to light eventually." Antikai slowly stood and then glided back to his throne.

The morning daystar now spread its golden light upon the mountain and every inch of surrounding canyons. Its rays glistened off the frost, wrapping warmth around Ave and soothing his frigid-stiff limbs. Warm brightness that embraced—what a contrast to where Nuelle was—icy gloom, lodging enemies who desired him dead. Never mind the fact that he never sought to make enemies of them. Never stole their property or killed their families. No, his crime, his evil lay in his identity: the second son of Supreme King Nifal, destined to be their end. What fools. That prophecy wouldn't even exist if they hadn't hated him and his father without cause.

"Do you think Prince Nuelle and the others are okay?" Sophana said while they trekked up the mountain, as if pulling a Surta mind-reading trick on Ave. Her silky pink hair, falling at the sides of her lovely face, shimmered in the light as if made of sugar crystals.

Ave dug his hands into his wet cloak pockets and then quickly removed them. "I hope so." Their boots crunched in the frost, joining Vyden and the others' steady steps.

Walking behind the old king and Preceptor Wit, Elisena looked back, a frown on her face. "I'm still finding it troublesome to reconcile all of this in my mind. I never would have imagined Zephoris becoming what it is now."

The stomach churning hole in Ave's chest throbbed with pain. None of them did. He kicked the frost. Why? Why did the citizens have to rebel? None of the kings abused their authority. In fact, they were all quite sacrificial and servant-hearted. They didn't deserve to be overthrown, but the people disposed of them anyway. In their puffed up minds, the citizens believed they could rule themselves. But as soon as Law had been thrust from the land, they rose up and practiced all kinds of evil. Because of them, Papo was dead, and the number of slaughtered only grew with each passing day.

He balled his fingers into fists. They would find that crystal sword, and Nuelle would finish Antikai, ending his twisted and vile influence on the people once for all. And when Nuelle reached his fullness of power, he could be crowned Supreme King along with his father and eradicate evil from the land forever. And like he said, hopefully that would come true by the week's end.

Vyden led Ave and the others around a corner. Elisena and Preceptor Wit—in front of Ave and Sophana—halted. Just paces from Vyden, stood three nine-foot beasts with indigo and purple streaked fur. Their azure eyes glowed like water and fire. The center one surveyed Vyden from head-to-toe as the others observed Ave and his friends. Ave stretched his arms. The two beasts alongside the middle one growled and raised clawed-hands.

Vyden turned to Ave. "No need to defend ourselves, my boy." He faced the center beast. "These are friends."

"They don't seem so friendly to me," Ave replied.

The middle one smiled, revealing frosty-white fangs. His grin almost made him look … human. "Welcome back, Vyden," he said with a deep, rumbling voice somewhat like King Nifal's.

Ave hesitantly drew in his arms.

"Everyone," Vyden said, "meet Folkvar, the lazaward."

As Folkvar extended his burly arm, Vyden did the same, and the two scratched each other's stomachs. They chuckled—Folkvar's laughter thundering over Vyden's—and then the lazaward gestured everyone to follow him.

"Fascinating creatures," Preceptor Wit whispered.

Vyden grinned. "If only you could see the polaragon."

He gawped. "I thought it was a myth!"

Elisena looked at Ave and Sophana. "I read the leader's heart. He's dangerous, but very kind."

"Interesting …" Ave looked at the umbrella clipped to Elisena's back. She'd been using it less and less, which was good, but still uncomfortable. Thankfully, he hadn't felt her peering into his heart for a while. Which was really good, because his desire for Sophana kept growing—something Nuelle would be very unpleased about. Ave stared at the lazaward pack-leader as he marched to the left, his guards at his side. The trio stood before a layer of ice-covered mountain-rock. Folkvar banged on the rock with three powerful knocks that seemed able to cause an avalanche. The ice shattered, and the stone opened, revealing a hidden door.

A thin lazaward stood in the doorway. "I see we have guests," it spoke with a husky yet feminine voice.

"They're just in time for lunch." Folkvar stamped inside and whiffed deeply with his cobalt nose. "Is there enough for us all?"

Four smaller lazawards the size of a tall adult man sat at an ice table. Another stood to the side, carrying an armful of frost hound heads.

"I believe there is," the female lazaward who greeted them said, her bright eyes on the one holding the heads. The others grumbled as the lazaward with the frost hound remains served them a head each. Folkvar scratched behind the ear of a smaller lazaward as he joined them at the table.

It giggled like a child, and its foot tapped the floor. "Stop it, Papa! That tickles!"

Ave's chest ached as he and the others found an empty block of ice, or a space on the moist floor to sit. He too had called his father papa when he was young. Holding back tears, he and the others set their satchels down.

Vyden placed the flame-holder on the table, a small fire still kindled. "Do you mind, old friend?"

Folkvar snatched a head and bit into its snout. "Not at all."

Bile rose in Ave's throat. With forced effort, he swallowed it back down. As the two lazawards who were with Folkvar sat beside him, the serving lazaward came around and dropped a frost hound head before Ave and the others. The strong fumes from the deceased creature wafted into his nose. He pursed his lips as the other lazawards devoured their portion, tearing off ears with their sharp fangs. A furry chunk landed on Ave's cheek, just beneath his eye.

The lazaward beside him snickered, apparently a girl. "Sorry, mortal."

Sophana and Elisena laughed as the husky-voiced female lazaward sat at the table's end, alongside the one who served.

Folkvar smirked at the motherly creature. "For our new friends, this is my lovely mate, Gebira."

She smiled, her shining teeth even more flawlessly white than his. "It's not often that we have guests, so I am thankful for the extra company."

"I am too." He reached over and clawed out an eye from one of the smaller lazaward's frost hound head.

"Papa!" the boy whined as Folkvar licked the eye from his finger.

"These baby-kin need to learn more about those from other parts of our world." He scratched his belly. "So Vyden, what brings you back to the canyons after such a short time?"

The once-king set his unappetizing lunch down. With face taut, he peered at the head lazaward. "The prophecies concerning the Young Prince have been rapidly unfolding."

Folkvar's gaze landed on Gebira. She nodded as if answering a telepathic command, and quickly rose from the table. "Camina," she said to the lazaward that had served them, "let's take the children hunting for tonight's dinner."

"Yay, hunting!" the boy lazawards cheered and hurried from their seats.

The family trailed Folkvar's mate out of the icy home. When the door closed, his stare slowly scanned the others. "And who are these young mortals?"

"We are three of Nuelle's Sentinels," Ave answered.

Elisena concentrated on Folkvar. "We have come to retrieve the crystal sword."

The two lazawards beside him stiffened.

"Prince Nuelle is a half-day away in the Obsidian as we speak," Sophana said.

Folkvar's glowing azure eyes flashed. "Then why are you all sitting at my table?"

Vyden shivered. "We were going to wait until the frost hounds departed at high noon."

"There is no time to wait." He rose from the table, his shoulders squared. His guards and everyone else did the same, grabbing their satchels. Vyden snatched the flame-holder and scuttled to the door. Ave and the others hurried after him. The once-king jogged down the frosty mountain path. Piercing howls from the frost hounds resounded in the distance.

Ave and the rest trailed Vyden to the bottom. The ravenous hounds seemed a good way off, but staying alert in this frozen land was crucial. There could be worse beasts here. Veering to his left, Vyden blew on the flames in the holder. The fire grew large enough to emanate its warmth through Ave's cloak. He let out a long sigh. Freezing to death was one less thing they had to worry about—for now.

Sophana extended her palms before the flames. "How far are we from the sword?"

"Seven miles give or take," Vyden replied.

Elisena tightened her cloak around her. "But my ankle hasn't completely healed yet."

Folkvar walked to her side. "You can mount my back."

She glanced at Ave and Sophana before responding. "That is very kind of you. I suppose I can for some of the way."

The giant lazaward dropped to his knees. Elisena slowly climbed onto Folkvar's back, clasping her arms around his neck. He chuckled as he rose. "Light as a feather."

She blushed while he suddenly stiffened. His fur stood.

Vyden raised the flame-holder. "What is it, friend?"

"Stay alert everyone," the lazaward said in a low voice. "We might have company." He strode onward.

Sophana's cloak trembled near her shoulders.

Ave stepped close and raised his arm some. "Just to make it a littler warmer—for both of us."

"I...guess it's okay."

He gently wrapped his arm around her, careful not to get pricked by her leaves. Their body warmth combined, and she stopped shivering. "Thanks, fish sticks."

"No problem, nettle cakes."

"Sweet and prickly. I like it."

"I think there's a food to describe everyone."

She nodded toward Elisena. "What about her?"

Ave watched as the kind, heart-reading girl clung to the lazaward's back. "Sweet-stem and vigor root stew."

"Really sweet, but strong." Sophana smiled. "Accurate enough. How about her twin?"

"Hmm. Grumbo melt."

"Yes! That stuff is putrid."

"Has just about every kind of creature from land to sky in it, and you never know how it'll turn out."

Sophana's voice softened. "What about Prince Nuelle?"

Ave skimmed through the whiteness. Giant icy mounds jutted in the distance, trimmed with gold under the daystar's glow. "Supreme Bunyon Lacquer."

"Never heard of it."

"It's an ancient recipe King Nifal made. He said it was the first meal he shared with the elders of the five tribes. It has really rare ingredients, some you can't even find anymore. And it's such a complex process that literally takes days to finish. Every time I try and make it, it doesn't come out right, because I'm missing something and can't find the right replacement."

She peered up at the golden skies. "Prince Nuelle is quite the mystery. Sometimes, I'm not even sure he's human."

Ave chuckled, though something deep within him trembled. "He is destined to become greater than all. And his father is the creator of essentially everyone. But growing up with him at the palace, always eating at the table with him, King Nifal, Tane, my parents…going on adventures with him. He's been like a brother to me. I tend to forget who he really is…"

"The Hope of the Faithful."

"Right."

"I guess he really is something special." Sophana's shimmering eyes met Ave's. "Like you."

Tingles ran up and down his back as her soul-searching gaze penetrated his heart and made it race. She was acting… different. Not so threatening. As if she'd…lowered her defenses.

"What makes me so special?" Ave asked.

"For one, the way you look at me. So many men undress me with their eyes, but you, you look as if you're trying to—"

"Figure you out."

"Exactly." She continued to watch him and then pressed her plump lips together and released them, as if preparing her mouth for something; as if…inviting something…

Oh mangeen pie. Ave's tingling worsened. *Should I just do it? Out here while the others are concentrated on the path ahead? While no one's watching…Should I kiss her?* His pounding heart yelled at him to take the golden opportunity—to kiss this beautifully complex girl. All the servant girls at the palace were like an open book, and their friendships were enjoyable. They were easy to read, like a simple recipe. Which was fine. But Sophana…she was more like a delicacy that you needed to be very careful with, one-third of a teaspoon off and you'd mess up everything. But, if you worked hard enough, took your time, and cooked with love, it'd come out amazing.

A small curl at the ends of Sophana's lips reeled Ave in like a hook. His face drew close to hers. She closed her eyes. He kept his wide open, his heart practically jumping out of his skin. His mouth neared hers. Warm breath from her nostrils teased his upper lip, just a hairsbreadth from hers. So close…

Courtship is a noble thing, but do you really believe now is the best time for it? Nuelle's voice cut through Ave like a knife. He stopped.

Sophana's gaze once again studied him, and she frowned. "What's wrong?"

He pulled away from her and stuffed his hands into his cloak pockets. "I'm sorry. I shouldn't have done that."

"You shouldn't have done what? Lead me on?"

"I don't want us to become distracted from our mission."

"I see…" She looked ahead. "Yet another man's opinion ruling my life."

Ave peered at her. "I'm just trying to honor Nuelle's wishes."

"Oh, so he's the man ruling our lives."

"Nuelle isn't just another man. You said it, he's the Hope of the Faithful, and we've been tasked with keeping him alive. And what if I'm out there in battle one day and Nuelle needs me, but you do, too? If I let you mean more to me, I'll risk choosing you over him, and then everyone would be lost."

Her striking eyes struck his. "I don't need you to rescue me, Ave."

"Oh really? How many times have I saved you now? What was it, oh yes, three!"

"And who saved me from Ludwig? Was it you? Was it my father? It was me. I saved myself. Prince Nuelle chose me because I'm able to hold my own." She glared at him. "You know what, you're right. Let's just focus on our mission."

His temperature managed to rise. "It's just now's not the right time."

"Don't worry. Maybe you can kiss me at my funeral." She marched off toward Elisena and the group.

He exhaled, his breath a visible puff. *A royal delicacy.*

Time dragged. Miles and miles they trekked through the relentless frost. The two lazawards marched at the sides while Elisena still clung to Folkvar who never slowed his stride. The frost hounds' wailing had grown faint, and then silent. Only the crackling fire in Vyden's flame-holder and the group's footsteps tramping in the ground remained.

"We are close." Vyden stopped at the edge of a cliff that descended into an icy slope. The curved drop led to the mouth of a cave a hundred yards away. Icicles as sharp and large as full-grown massadon fangs bordered the cave's circular entryway. "It is in there." He pointed at the cavern.

Ave peered at the slippery slope. Blue water sat underneath the ice, as if a river had somehow been cut-off midstream.

"We're going to have to slide down and aim for the cave," Vyden said.

"Then let's hurry." Elisena released Folkvar and stepped toward the edge.

Preceptor Wit leaned over and peered at the frozen cut-off river. "Is there no other way?"

"I am afraid not." Vyden turned the knob on his flame-holder and the fire extinguished. The three lazawards looked back.

Folkvar stretched his clawed fingers and growled. "It is time to move, friends."

Ave turned. A large lump of frost thirty yards behind glided toward them at a rapid pace. "Right." He clenched his satchel and inclined forward. As he slid down the ice-slope, Sophana and the others trailed. Freezing air pierced through Ave's cloak. He increased speed, and the breeze hastened against him, worsening the cold.

Something shattered from behind. Shards of ice rained down, followed by a torrent of water. It surged over Ave and the others. The cold waves jarred his body. He broke through the surface, chattering as he glanced back. A white, curved-fin the size of Riff cut through the waves and gained on them. *Glacierdon. Delicious when dead, deadly when alive.* Ave faced forward and thrashed through the water. The circular mouth of the cave loomed, its spiked-entrance threatening to slice off their limbs.

"Form a single line!" Vyden called.

Preceptor Wit grabbed Vyden's hand before reaching back and clasping Elisena's. Ave looked over his shoulder to grab Sophana's palm as she held onto Folkvar, the two other lazawards last in line. The glacierdon followed only ten yards away. Ave faced ahead. The cave's entrance closed in and they all slipped through, just barely missing the blade-like icicles. Everyone released their hold. The rushing water smashed into more icicles that protruded from the walls. Jagged chunks and thick sheets ripped off and fell into the water. Ave glimpsed behind. The beast trailed.

"Split up!" he yelled.

As everyone obeyed, the glacierdon rose from the water. Its gray eyes sparkled with hunger, and its humongous mouth flashed giant fangs. It veered toward Elisena. Ave stretched his arm as its mouth neared. He beat its head with his fist. It turned toward him. Folkvar and the other lazawards kicked it repeatedly. Its mouth closed and then jerked in their direction.

"Hungry, beast?" Folkvar raised his clawed hand.

The glacierdon's mouth opened, tons of water pouring in. Ave expanded his fingers and poked the beast's eye. It winced and sank underwater. Sophana hopped onto a chunk of ice and balanced as she tore off a handful of leaf-blades. She maneuvered the icy slab around fallen icicles, maintaining her poise.

"Where'd it go?" Preceptor Wit asked as the torrent led them onward.

The glacierdon burst from the water in front of them, mouth agape. Sophana aimed and fired. The barbed leaf pierced one of the beast's eyes. It wailed, its cry echoing through the cave. The glacierdon closed its mouth and descended into the water. Its fin glided out of the cavern.

"N-nice aim, m-my g-girl!" Vyden's teeth chattered.

Sophana smiled, but then her lips swiftly pursed. Straight ahead, the water receded into a gaping hole. Ave held his breath for the dive. The waters that dragged him and the others onward lowered to his calves. His heels dug into moist frost. As the hole drew close, the freezing liquid sank to his ankles. At least if they fell, the waters would weaken the impact, though at any moment they could die from the cold.

Ave closed his eyes and awaited the plummet into freezing depths. He slowed to a halt, his feet buried in the frost. He opened his eyes. They all had stopped at the edge of the drop. Lowering his shivering arms, Ave smiled. "Well. That was fortunate." The ground quaked. He peeked back. A frost-ball bounded toward them, increasing in size and speed with each second. "Never mind."

The frosty sphere plowed into them. They toppled down the hole and plunged into the water. Ave broke through the surface, his limbs stiff. Darkness doused all traces of light. His heart raced in a futile effort to increase blood-flow and muster warmth. They had to get out of the water immediately! He paddled forward. "Feel around for a way out."

Someone's freezing palm touched his face. "Sorry," Sophana said.

A different kind of shiver tickled his back.

"There is solid ground over here!" Vyden called from somewhere not too far ahead.

Ave swam toward the once-king's voice, and his hands met frost. As he pressed his palms down, his arms quivered, and with forced effort he pushed himself out of the water. He dropped onto his bottom and swiftly shed his drenched cloak.

A flame ignited, exposing Vyden holding the flame-holder. Folkvar and the other lazawards helped Preceptor Wit, Elisena, and Sophana out of the water. They still carried their satchels. As a lazaward brought Sophana to the edge,

Ave reached for her and pulled her out with whatever energy he had left.

"Thanks," she said without looking at him. As she crawled to the fire, Elisena and Preceptor Wit followed, and the lazawards shook out their furry coats. Vyden blew on the flame and it enlarged. The fire penetrated Ave's soaked clothing, warming his skin and calming his shivers. Elisena gasped and pointed across a cave with icicles protruding from its ceiling. Burrowed in a block of ice near the cave's center lay a rectangular case of gold.

"Folkvar," Vyden said as he approached the ice. "Would you be so kind?"

The giant lazaward marched toward the frozen block. He drew his huge fist back and launched it in the ice. It shattered into a thousand pieces.

"We must hurry!" Elisena shuffled to his side, the others trailing. She lifted the golden case's lid and pushed it aside. She grabbed the sword's hilt and tugged, but to no avail. She tried again. The sword remained immovable.

"Uh, my dear lady," Vyden said, "only—"

"I'll get it, Elisena." Ave clutched the hilt and yanked. It didn't budge. As he released the hilt, Vyden shuffled forward and closed the lid.

"We cannot wield this sword, so stop wasting your energy trying." He grasped the case and carried it with his metal-gloved hands. "Time for you all to deliver this to Prince Nuelle."

A cloaked man dropped down the large hole they had fallen through. Ice emitted from his palms and smothered the water's surface before he landed on top of it. Only half of the man's colorless face showed, his eyes hidden beneath his hood. The uninvited guest stepped forward. "How kind of you to find the sword." His raspy voice sent chills up Ave's spine. Sophana launched a leaf-blade.

The man's hands aimed at the ground. A wall of ice rapidly rose in front of him. The leaf crashed into the icy barrier and it shattered. Folkvar and the lazawards leapt into the air and bore down on him. Raspy-voice unsheathed a sword from his belt and slammed the blade into the frosty ground. It rapidly cracked, and a wave of energy burst from the frost, propelling the trio backwards into a wall.

The man strolled toward Vyden. Ave thrust out his arm, aiming a punch at the man's gut. He grasped Ave's wrist with a green-nailed hand. An onyx-stone metallic signet-ring wrapped his ring-finger. A Savage Shifter. He pushed Ave's arm away and aimed his palm at the ceiling above Ave and the others. Icicles collapsed on top of them. They toppled into the frost. The cold smothered Ave's body as he struggled to push himself up.

A loud crash resounded from behind as the ice bore down on Ave's back, too heavy for him to lift. He quaked in the engulfing cold. His heartbeat slowed and his chest tightened. Gradually, darkness shrouded his vision. *This is it. I'm so sorry, Nuelle. Forgive me for failing you.* Ave closed his eyes. The weight of the ice atop him lessened. A huge bulk of it thrust off his back. Furry hands grabbed him by the waist and hoisted him onto his feet. Folkvar and the other lazawards cast the large icicles off the others and helped Elisena and Sophana stand. Vyden lay limp, a gash on his forehead.

"Vyden!" Sophana rushed to his side as Folkvar swept him into his arms.

"He is breathing," the lazaward said. "He is just unconscious for now, but my daughter, Camina, can tend to his wound."

"Oh no." Elisena looked down. The golden case lay open, with no sword inside.

One of the lazawards pointed to the cave's back where a huge hole provided access to the outside. "The man thrust the crystal sword into that wall and then escaped on a winged-beast."

Ave and the others sprinted from the cavern. Why wouldn't the Savage Shifter just teleport out of the cave?

"How did that man know we were here?" Preceptor Wit asked.

"I read his heart," Elisena said. "He followed us."

Eighteen: The Chase

As the daystar melted behind the rushing wall of water in the distance, beyond the gem homes of Agapon, Nuelle approached Tane. He stood on his bedchamber terrace, both hands on his hilt, his sword's tip touching the marble floor. "What do you want, Nu?" he said without looking back.

Nuelle stood beside him as a warm breeze hummed a soft melody. "To talk."

"I'm tired of talking when no one's listening."

"Maybe you're not talking loud enough."

Tane smirked as he released a hand from his hilt and rustled Nuelle's hair. "Who's the elder brother here? Only I can give you advice."

Nuelle pushed brother's hand away. "I'm almost a man."

"There's no such thing as almost."

"Then I am a man."

Tane raised his sword and swiped it. Nuelle ducked as it whizzed overhead. "Hey!"

"Sorry, am I not playing fair?"

"You can call it that."

Brother sheathed his weapon. "The world isn't fair, Nu, so don't expect it to be."

Nuelle jabbed at Tane's stomach. He blocked as Nuelle smiled. "But you aren't the world, you're family."

"Ah, but even family can be unfair sometimes."

"What do you mean?"

"You're too young to understand now."

"Is that your answer for everything?" Nuelle asked as darkness descended and the silver night star seeped into the skies.

Brother smiled as he tousled Nuelle's hair again. "Concerning you, yes."

"Then when will I no longer be 'too young' in your eyes?"

"Hmm...the day you beat me in battle. Though"—he turned, his bronze eyes shining with all the strength and love he owned—"I think you'll always be too young in my eyes."

"That's...encouraging."

"What I mean is, a part of me will always believe I have to protect you."

Nuelle stared up at Brother, standing just a head taller. "From what?"

Nuelle opened his eyes. Blackness gradually faded as coldness intensified. *Where am I?* Glowing green shackles chained him, and carcass stench assaulted his senses. Weakness weighed on his bones, his muscles, his mind. The green light brightened and faded, then blurred and doubled. He blinked the obscurity away, but it kept returning.

Green eyes materialized in the midst of the darkness ahead. "Yes, your father still hasn't come for you. But then again, I hear his palace was overtaken. Maybe he, too, was finally overcome."

Antikai? Nuelle shivered in the cold and coughed.

The green eyes glided forward, and more of Antikai's scaly, warped frame emerged. "If there is anything I have learned in my twenty-nine years of existing it is this: you will reap what you sow."

Nuelle stared at the black dust layering the floor. Yes. He was still in the Obsidian. His Sentinels must have kept searching for the crystal sword. Or maybe they found it and were coming for him? Or did they...

"Let's see…" Antikai said. "Overseer Enri, poor little Adira, a number of innocent prodigies, and now Preceptor Sage have all perished because you exist. Isn't that ironic? Your life has taken theirs." His flaking feet appeared in the dust Nuelle focused on. Antikai kneeled, his frigid presence prickling. "Who will die next because of you? Surta? Princess Sophana? Riff? Javin, or maybe his precious sister, Elisena? Or how about your best friend, Ave? Maybe he will be with his father soon."

Nuelle breathed in the icy air and shuddered. Yes, one of them could die, all of them could, just like the others who fell because of him. It was his fault they were taken from this world. He sank lower into the misty black floor. *Why did Father give me this destiny? Why did he create me if all I bring is pain and death? And what if I fail? How many more would be lost?* Tears dropped from his eyes, as if pushed out from the pressure, the weight of everything Father had placed on his shoulders. It was so…crushing. And was it even true?

Antikai sat. "Tell me, Young Prince, if your father is so good, why does he allow such innocent souls to die? Think of your Sentry, Amador. Wasn't he a faithful servant to King Nifal? Didn't he obey every supreme law, every command, even unto death? Why did he die, and a coward like my father gets to live? Does that seem fair to you?" He vanished, and the ebony fog stirred where he'd sat.

Nuelle's trembling worsened. Tane's voice swelled in his thoughts: *even family can be unfair sometimes.* It was a notion he never contemplated. Why did so many innocent lives perish at the hands of evil ones? Where was the justice in that?

Preceptor Sage's voice now probed his mind: *Angered and hurt by their perpetual, selfish betrayals, King Nifal cursed their lands.*

So death was a curse brought about by the rebellions of the first tribes? But why did everyone have to suffer for the actions and choices of some?

What he told Elisena after she'd confessed to not eating crept in: *Unless they're perfect, their opinions shouldn't rule your life.* Yes, no one was perfect. Some purposefully hurt others, while some harmed themselves and unintentionally hurt others in the process. In either case, both chose their actions, and both were wrong. So no one was perfect…everyone betrayed themselves and each other, and ultimately, Father. Where was the good in that? Where was the hope?

Father's written words whispered in his heart: *An age shall return when voices rage and fists strike against all authority. Restless souls shall stir unrest, and quivering kingdoms will collapse. Only in One does Zephoris' hope reside … you shall lead the Faithful to the land of the Incandescia.*

Warmth trickled into his chest. *I want to believe you, Father, but I'm losing hope.* Nuelle took a deep breath. *Think, Nuelle. Why do you trust Father?* He looked up at the Acumen, still lying on the mantel. *The Acumen said we were one. Antikai's Savages kept trying to destroy it. If I wasn't such a threat, why did they keep coming after me and the Acumen?* "Enemies shall come for you, for they know you can become greater than all…" *Father's words proved true in that area, and in the sixth Sentinel being added to me. In fact, everything I've read in the Acumen so far has come to pass. So why shouldn't I believe the rest of his words?* "…And that you shall lead the Faithful to the land of the Incandescia." The warmness strengthened, spreading to his shoulders and easing down his abdomen and arms. *Yes, this world was cursed, but Father made a way for the remorseful tribes to overcome their enemies by sending them help—the Sentries. And now, the Incandescia is the new way of escape from this cursed world, and I'm the help, the one destined to become greater than all, greater than even the first Sentries of old. And as long as I'm alive, I'm the Hope of the Faithful.*

Antikai reappeared a few paces across from him. "Have you come up with any answers?"

Nuelle's dry throat burned. "I'm the answer."

The traitor's green eyes glowed brighter. "Come on, Nu, don't be so naive. You're just a youth. You really believe you can save all of Zephoris?"

"Not all, but some."

Antikai grinned, his grayish gums and jagged teeth wet with metallic blood. "The Faithful?" He waved his hand. The Acumen zoomed toward Nuelle and crashed into his chest, knocking him backwards. It dropped onto the floor and opened. A green glow highlighted a sentence in the middle of a page.

In Zephoris' last hour, will anyone be found faithful? All have fallen and who remains?

The Acumen slammed shut. "Your brother was right," Antikai said as the Acumen slid back into the shadows. "You still have much to learn." He drifted closer then slowly bent down and clasped Nuelle's neck. His freezing hand squeezed, and his sharp nails pierced Nuelle's skin. "But I will make sure you see."

Ave dropped to his knees, tears filling his eyes. What would happen to Nuelle now? An enemy who worked for Antikai had the crystal sword and it was only a matter of time before the traitorous prince retrieved it. Ave slammed his fists against the frost. The hope of Zephoris—his best friend—was in more peril than ever, and half of his Sentinels were hundreds of miles away.

He repeatedly slapped his fists against the frost, ignoring the increasing numbness attacking his skin. They had finally retrieved the sword, only to have it seized! Now Nuelle might die, and the only chance for the Faithful would perish with him! This was it, they lost the war. Darkness would have its reign, and hope would never again shine in the hearts of the people.

The frost beneath Ave moved. He stopped punching it.

"Uh, Ave …" Sophana called, standing outside of the cave with the others. "I think you should step back."

As he scrambled to his feet, a huge lump of frost emerged from the ground. He staggered to keep his balance as it ascended. A four-legged, furry beast flew upwards with two pairs of immense wings. Blue coated its paws and the tips of its floppy ears.

Ave fell on his bottom and gripped the beast's fur. It opened its mouth and roared. Frost surged from its throat. Sophana and the others ran out of the way as the frost landed in a large heap.

Folkvar, still carrying Vyden, yelled at the creature. "Don't fear, they are friends!"

The beast turned its head. Its royal blue eyes squinted at Ave as if wary of him. He smiled as far as his mouth would stretch and stroked its fur. "Friends …"

Its four wings flapped. Ave gripped the fur as the beast descended.

Preceptor Wit jumped. "A real-life polaragon! Magnificent."

Folkvar approached as it landed. "They need to fly out of here immediately. They are traveling to the Obsidian."

A rumble reverberated from the polaragon's throat, sending strong vibrations through Ave's body.

Elisena rested her palm atop the creature's snout. "Please. Prince Nuelle is in danger."

The polaragon nudged her gently with the tip of its nose.

"That means yes." A lazaward grasped Elisena by the waist and aided her up the beast's back. The other grabbed Sophana and helped her on.

Elisena smiled as she patted the polaragon. "Thank you."

Hope burned in Ave's heart and melted away the unmerciful cold of despair. They had a chance now. They might be able to get the sword back! He peered down at unconscious Vyden, then at Preceptor Wit. "You should stay with him and journey back to the mainland."

"I agree." Preceptor Wit quickly dug into his pocket and removed the vial of querapa saliva and bag of healing seeds. He thrust them into Ave's hand. "I pray you all succeed."

"I am sure they will." Folkvar scratched Ave's belly. "Farewell, Sentinels."

As Elisena waved, Sophana scooted behind Ave and gripped his shoulders. His stomach fluttered as he stared ahead. "To the Obsidian, friend!"

The polaragon kicked off the ground and zoomed into the air. Ave gripped its ivory fur as fierce wind threatened to blow him away. The mountains and frost below meshed into a white blur. The racing wind stung his eyes. He released a hand and removed his Dark-O-Specs from his satchel. He slipped the goggles on and blinked away tears. The glass shielded from the freezing air, and his sight quickly cleared. In mere hours, the frosty canyons disappeared, and he and his friends flew over the Aurora Forest.

"We're almost there!" Ave shouted. "Get your Dark-O-Specs ready."

"He's not too far ahead of us," Elisena said as she put on her goggles.

Ave tightened his grip on the polaragon's thick fur. "Faster, friend!" It darted onward, and the Obsidian's darkness appeared.

"We're coming, Nuelle," Ave said. Blackness closed in. His heart punched the walls of his chest. Directly in front of them, a tan winged-beast glided, ridden by the cloaked man.

The polaragon flapped fervently and swiftly gained on him. Raspy-voice reeled his creature around. Green liquid sprayed from a hole on the tan beast's forehead, forcing the polaragon to veer left. The man pulled on the reins, and his beast faced forward again.

"Come on!" Ave shouted. "We need that sword!"

The polaragon zoomed after them. In seconds, it flew beside the man. Raspy-voice wrenched the reins. His creature slammed into the polaragon's side. It swerved to the right then realigned itself as the man yanked the reins again. His creature head-butted the polaragon. It growled and spewed a stream of frost at the tan beast. The white slosh surged into its face. It veered left and right in blind confusion as it descended. The cloaked man wiped the frost from its eyes and booted its side. It sped forward.

"Get lower!" Ave said to the polaragon. It hurriedly obeyed, still on their tail.

"We're close!" Elisena called.

Raspy-voice released his beast's reins and stretched his palm back toward Ave and the others. A ball of ice formed over the man's hand. The frost grew into a small boulder. With his other hand, he drew his sword and impaled the icy sphere. It shattered into hundreds of shards.

Sophana squeezed Ave's waist. "Stretch!"

He expanded his palm ten times its size. The ice smashed into it, stinging his coral-like flesh. Down below, metallic thorn bushes appeared, and a black castle materialized from the darkness. The polaragon descended as the cloaked man landed. His tan creature soared away.

Ave leapt off the polaragon before its paws hit the ground and he tackled Raspy-voice. The crystal sword skidded on the black dirt and landed several yards away. The man struck Ave's temple. A shock-wave of pain rattled his brain. He shook his head and raised a fist, his vision doubling. Raspy-voice grabbed Ave's elevated arm. Ice immediately formed, freezing his forearm and hand.

A leaf-blade bore down on Raspy-voice. He launched a stream of ice at it. It froze, and dropped to the ground. The ice on Ave's arm rapidly spread to the rest of his body, the piercing cold more painful than the man's punch. His throat dried and begged for a drink as the ice covered his water flasks. Riff appeared behind the man and struck the back of his head. He reeled forward and onto his stomach. Riff swung another punch into the ice on Ave's chest. It shattered every inch of it off his body. He breathed in and chattered. He tried to stretch his limbs, but they wouldn't budge. Javin and Surta appeared and ran toward the polaragon just as the cloaked man rose.

"We can't let him get the sword!" Ave pointed at the Savage.

Javin scrambled up the polaragon's neck. "I'll guard the sword, you all get Prince Nuelle!"

"Where is he?" Ave asked as he opened a water flask.

Surta gestured to the castle. "Shackled inside. Jilt has the key, but he's always disappearing."

Ave raced with the others to the black doors as Raspy-voice engaged Javin and the polaragon. Ave brought the flask to his mouth, but nothing came out. The water was frozen!

Sophana shoved the entry open. "Elisena, search for Nuelle's heart!"

"Down the hall to the right!" she replied. They dashed through the long, dark corridor. When they reached the end, they veered to the right.

"Up the stairs," Elisena said.

They sprinted toward a spiral staircase. Brone appeared at the foot of the stairs. Ave raised his arm, but it wouldn't stretch. *Not a good time to be parched and without water.* The Savage Shifter strode toward him.

Riff reached in his bag of rocks. He removed an empty fist. Apparently out of stones, he stood in front of Ave anyway. "Why don't we finish what we started back in Jazerland?"

Brone grinned and beckoned him forward. Riff front-kicked the brute. He hardly budged.

"I'll handle him while you get Prince Nuelle." Riff charged Brone and the two grappled while Ave and the girls scurried up the steps.

When they reached the top and entered another hall, Elisena pointed to the left. "Down there!" She led the way through a wide corridor and then halted at a pair of double-doors. Ave thrust one open and bustled inside with the others. A small flame flickered on a mantel, shedding its faint light upon an onyx throne in the center of an icy room. Nuelle sat shackled in a corner by glowing green chains. With head hung low and shoulders sagged, his face had paled and thinned.

Ave approached. "Nuelle!"

With what little energy he had left, Nuelle peered up. His best friends darted to his side.

"Dragon," Ave said, "we have to get you out of here."

"Antikai has the Acumen." Nuelle coughed. "Did you get the—"

Jilt materialized beside Ave, fist swinging. Ave ducked, and threw a kick, but Jilt disappeared. As Nuelle and the others looked around, Jilt reappeared behind Ave and punched the back of his head. Nuelle tugged on the shackles as his best friend dropped to his knees. Elisena pointed at multiple places a second before the Savage Shifter appeared, giggling as he rapidly teleported to different parts of the room. He reappeared in front of Surta, his palm glowing green. "The poor Sentinels are too slow."

Ave rammed into the savage and shoved him across the chamber and into a wall. Jilt hopped onto his feet as Ave straightened. Sophana threw a leaf-blade. It pierced Jilt's shoulder and pinned him to the wall. He lifted his opposite hand to remove the barb. She fired another, piercing his right shoulder. Jilt gritted his teeth as she marched to him and aimed a barb at his chest. "Where's the key?" she asked.

"I'll never tell you, princess."

"It's in his pocket," Surta said.

His eyes bulged and he shifted into a shadow. Sophana jammed the blade into his rib. He grunted and his body re-materialized. She dug her hand in his pocket and removed a glowing green key. She tossed it to Ave and he unlocked the shackles. The green light faded, and the manacles snapped open.

"Did you get the sword?" Nuelle asked as Ave helped him stand.

"We found it," Elisena replied, "but a Savage Shifter followed us who was able to wield it. Javin is on a polaragon guarding it from him now."

Warmth pumped into Nuelle's heart, and he dashed out of the makeshift throne room. It was only a matter of time before Antikai got hold of the sword and used it to destroy the Acumen! A bloody-faced Riff staggered before Brone at the end of the hall near a staircase. The savage uppercutted Riff, and he toppled down the stairs. Nuelle sent a flaming wind Brone's way. It seared his skin, and he rolled against a wall to stop the fire. Weakness attacked Nuelle's limbs, and his heart raced. Whiteness entered his vision. Sophana chucked a leaf-blade at Brone's back. It lodged in between his protruding shoulder blades. He wailed and fell onto the floor as the flames consumed.

As Ave aided Riff to his feet, Elisena grasped Nuelle's bicep. "Your heart is weak."

"We have to get that sword." He pulled away from her, and descended the steps, his heart hammering in protest. His Sentinels followed him into the corridor leading to the entryway. Raysha—in gigantic green crawler form—fell from above, blocking the doors. Surta disappeared as Sophana launched a leaf-blade. The beast dodged it, jumping onto the wall. It scurried toward them, a line of web shooting from its rear at Ave. It fell on top of him and Riff, entangling them.

Sophana hurled another blade at one of the crawler's eight eyes, but the beast leapt across the hall to the opposite wall. Sophana fired three more. The beast's rapid steps eluded each one. As she prepped another, the crawler spewed green liquid. Nuelle blew a gust at Sophana that shoved her out of the way, and the poisonous acid landed on the floor, sizzling and smoking. The crawler hissed as it pounced in front of him and Elisena. Its mouth opened in almost a smile, the green fangs that ended Preceptor Sage's life pulsing hungrily.

"Hey, you hopping abomination!" Surta stood near the entryway, carrying the crystal sword. She raised it. "Looking for this?"

The beast's head twisted in her direction. Nuelle released a fiery gust at the crawler. It propelled backwards, screeching as flames engulfed it. Sophana yanked off a leaf-blade and sliced the web binding Ave and Riff. Nuelle's mind spun. He stumbled, but Ave caught him.

"His heart is very weak," Elisena said. "He should stay here while we get the sword."

Riff pointed at Surta as she approached with the crystal sword. "But Surta has it!"

The sword dematerialized. "I wish I did."

Ave frowned. "Nuelle needs to come. We can't wield it."

"Maybe we can lure the cloaked man to bring it inside," Sophana said.

"We can't waste another minute." Nuelle leaned on Ave and walked to the door. He and the others hurried outside. Javin rode an enormous white polaragon, its mouth spewing frost at a cloaked man launching an ice-stream from his palms. The ice clashed with the frost. With one hand, the man reached for the crystal sword on the ground in front of him.

Mustering what inkling of strength remained within, Nuelle bounded forward, releasing a flaming gust in the savage's direction. He grabbed the sword and raised it. The crystal blade absorbed Nuelle's fiery wind. The man spun the sword toward the polaragon. Fire exploded from the blade, dissolving the frost and then smashing into the creature's face. It wailed and recanted, Javin sliding down its back.

They both collapsed while the cloaked man aimed the sword at Nuelle as he drew near. More of his flaming wind burst from the blade. Nuelle rolled out of the way, but some of the flames scorched his calves. The fire seared his skin as he landed on the ground. He groaned as he smothered his legs in the dirt and quickly doused the flames. Pink boils covered his calves, now charred and bleeding. The man hurled ice at Ave and the others, freezing them before doing the same to Javin.

Nuelle staggered to his feet, his heart laboring beats. Healing warmth crept into his legs at too slow a pace. He launched a stream of fire at the ground near his Sentinels before lunging at the man and tackling him. They crashed into the dirt, and the crystal sword slipped from the man's grasp. It landed a few paces away. He punched Nuelle's temple. His vision blackened briefly as the man rushed forward on hands and knees. Nuelle crawled after him, his mind spinning and every part of him throbbing. The savage reached for the sword. Nuelle grabbed his leathery boot and pulled him back. Growling like a beast, the man kicked Nuelle's forehead with a clad-heel. Another brief blackness clouded his sight and jarred his brain. Head pounding and bloody, he yanked on the man's ankle again before scuttling over him to the sword. They both reached for it. Their hands grabbed the hilt.

The man tugged, lurching Nuelle forward. He squeezed the hilt. The sides of the man's freezing, green-nailed hand touched his. A metallic and onyx signet-ring wrapped around his ring-finger. As Nuelle clutched tighter, blood rushed to his head, and his eyesight tripled. The blood on his forehead seeped down his nose. His healing warmth entered steadily. Wind coursed through him. It rose to a blazing temperature, making his body sweat. His adversary growled again, the hilt gradually slipping from Nuelle's grasp. The sizzling airstream inside of him seeped out of his arms, causing the man's hand to smoke. Nuelle's body quaked. His healing power strengthened. A hot gust burst from his chest, blowing the man's hood down.

Nuelle's heartbeat slowed. His wind evaporated. Brother's eyes stared into his, glowing as green as Antikai's.

The sword loosened from Nuelle's grip. "Tane?"

Brother smiled as he grabbed the hilt and stood. His once tan skin was now pale. "Call me Diabon, Nu." His voice had changed, now raspy and dark; saturated with corruption.

Tears welled in Nuelle's eyes. "What's happened to you?"

"If you understood what Antikai and I desire for Zephoris, you would not be asking that question."

Nuelle's stomach churned. Who stood before him? Because this wasn't Tane. Tane was dead. Nuelle pressed his palm against his pants' pocket where the Supreme Prince's signet-ring had been all this time. "Antikai said my brother came to the Obsidian to kill him, but he hid and never saw Tane again."

Diabon sheathed the sword. "He told you that so if you escaped you would not be able to inform Nifal that I still live."

The throbbing in Nuelle's temples grew painful, his thoughts screaming the daunting truth. "You didn't come here to kill Antikai." A wave of dizziness crashed over his mind. "You came here to join him."

Diabon's eyes brightened. "And to protect you."

"Protect me?"

"Antikai is passionate about saving our world, even if that means eliminating any and all who threaten my reign. But if I possess this sword, no one will be able to destroy the Acumen..." His voice softened, "...to destroy you."

Nuelle trembled in the chill binding him. "I want to trust you, but you lied to me, Tane."

He stepped closer. "Had I not lied to you and Nifal about my reasoning for journeying to the Obsidian, I would have been banished."

"For joining a traitor!" Nuelle's voice raised. "He attempted to kill Father!"

"Nifal is weak, Nu. I tried to convince him to take control, to fight for his sovereignty, but he refused to listen. And look at all the rebellion now! By the time I ruled in his place, the kingdom would be diminished to ashes with none to rule, and I could not take that risk."

Warmth seeped into Nuelle's throbbing head. "Is it only about ruling? Where is your love?"

Diabon chuckled. "You sound as weak as your father."

"Our father!"

"Not anymore!"

The wind left Nuelle's lungs as tears rose. Tane was certainly dead. A different man stood before him, one he could never again call brother. As Nuelle stood, Antikai walked out of the black castle, carrying the Acumen. Nuelle glanced at his Sentinels. The ice binding them had melted half-way. He raised his palms, the flaming wind stirring.

Diabon released a stream of ice and froze them, then aimed the stream at Nuelle's legs, locking him in place. Antikai stopped beside Diabon and ran his flaking hand across the Acumen's cover, over Father's noble insignia, as if it were a woman he sought to seduce. "Did you not read what the fate of Zephoris will be if your father remains Supreme King? We now hold the power to put an end to Nifal's weakness and seat your brother on his rightful throne."

"With this sword, no one will be able to rise against my rule," Diabon said. "You can help save Zephoris, Nu. There is no other way." His green eyes shined as brazenly as Antikai's.

"What about the Incandescia?" Nuelle asked.

He slowly stepped forward. "Nu…"

"Go on." Antikai still gripped the Acumen. "You've seen what he can do. Your brother is no longer too young for the truth."

Diabon's raspy voice softened. "All this time I've been searching for this incredible land of light. I've scoured the four corners of Zephoris and it's not here, Nu. It doesn't exist."

Nuelle lowered his gaze to the gleaming Acumen. "But Father said—"

"Father lied to you, Nu! To all of us!"

The ice around Nuelle's chest cracked at Diabon's outburst. As he stood there panting, another rumbling voice entered Nuelle's thoughts. *Your words speak of victory, but your heart has already been defeated.*

"Trust me, Nu." Diabon's panting steadied. "We can restore peace together."

Warmth coursed through Nuelle's arms and legs as he remembered how Father spoke the same words to Tane before he left. Nuelle envisioned the Supreme Prince signet-ring in his pocket, the one his brother once wore. And then Nuelle spoke to the fallen man standing just paces away. "My allegiance is with my father."

Diabon's green eyes brightened as Antikai turned to him. "You have now witnessed it yourself. Nuelle is currently Supreme Prince of Zephoris, being next in line to occupy the Supreme Throne, and he stands here in defiance toward you." The heartless beast gestured to his castle. "You have seen his power, Diabon. He has subdued all of our followers, and he is only going to get stronger. Then he will banish you and rule with the same weakness as his father while Zephoris tears itself apart!" Antikai extended the Acumen to Diabon. "You must destroy him if you are to restore order to this land."

Diabon slowly took Father's book, continuing to hold Nuelle's gaze. The healing heat in his body intensified, and the ice on his arms and legs began to melt.

"You must kill him, Diabon," Antikai said, "for the sake of Zephoris."

Diabon dropped the Acumen. He lowered his stare and fixed it onto the gold cover, on Father's protruding insignia, shimmering in spite of the surrounding darkness. With trembling hands, Diabon slowly raised the crystal sword and turned it so the black side faced downward. "I am sorry, Nu."

Nuelle broke out of the ice and hurled a fiery gust at Antikai as Diabon brought down the sword. Nuelle redirected the wind to the crystal blade, stopping it an inch from Father's insignia. His body quaked as Diabon roared like a wild beast. Now he quivered, his green eyes ablaze. Nuelle's head pounded and spun. This battle of strength drained every ounce of power coursing through his blood. Too many times had he warred against his once older brother's might, and so many times he failed. But not the last time they sparred. The last time he broke free. But just as he'd grown in power, Diabon had too. The darkness pumping through his veins boasted through his morphed eyes and flaunted itself in metallic and onyx on his ring-finger.

A growl emerged from Diabon's throat, and his muscular shoulders leaned forward, his face inches away. Nuelle dug his heels deeper into the dirt ground. His temples banged like a beating drum, fast and painful. *Do not give up, son.* Father's voice filled his mind, just as it did the last time he sparred Tane in the courtyard. Warmth surged from Nuelle's heart. The pounding in his temples eased its rapid pace. Diabon trembled violently, thick green veins bulging on his neck and forehead. Nuelle stepped forward, and his airstream strengthened. He stared into Diabon's glowing jade eyes, full of fury and corruption. The cruel coldness of one without love inside emanated from the skin on Diabon's face and his panting breath. Nuelle's wind blew stronger, but his mind whirled. Diabon's panting morphed to heaves. His knees buckled. Slowly, his fingers uncurled from the crystal hilt. He dropped the sword and collapsed.

"No!" Antikai thundered as he rose to his feet, parts of his black garbs torn and smoking from the flaming wind.

Nuelle snatched the sword and Acumen. "Free my friends and destroy this land!" He lifted the sword over his head. Antikai ran to Nuelle while he drove the blade into the ground. The wicked prince halted a foot from the sword as tremors rippled across the black land. They shoved him back and broke the remaining ice off Nuelle's Sentinels. The walls of the castle cracked.

"Let's go!" Nuelle slid the sword in his belt and raced to the white polaragon. He stopped before it and looked around. Where was the preceptor's body? By the black pond, Preceptor Sage's corpse lay—the ground around it crumbling rapidly. Nuelle handed Ave the Acumen and dashed to the body. A giant hole opened alongside his thin frame, and his body rolled towards it. Nuelle dove onto his stomach as the preceptor's corpse sank into the pit. He grabbed Preceptor Sage's arm and tugged with all the strength he had left, pulling the body out. The polaragon hovered overhead—his Sentinels mounted upon its back, with Javin at its neck. Riff extended his large hands and lifted Nuelle from his underarms and hoisted him and the preceptor's body onto the polaragon.

A shrill shout encompassed the imploding land. Antikai staggered around before his collapsing castle. A forceful current grew stronger with each second, pulling the polaragon toward it. It flapped its wings against the powerful pull.

"You can do it, Rasmus!" Javin gripped the polaragon's fur. "We're almost out of here!"

Rasmus slowly ascended out of the darkness as Antikai's castle and everything around it imploded. Diabon raised himself off the ground. His glowing green eyes stared up, into Nuelle's. Tears welled in his as he clenched the sword and Preceptor Sage's limp body. "Goodbye, Tane."

Rasmus pushed forward and soared away from the disappearing blackness, Antikai's screams growing fainter and fainter.

Nineteen: Gone

Light shined.

As Nuelle and his Sentinels coasted the sky on Rasmus, Nuelle closed his eyes. Being surrounded by cold darkness for so long had almost snuffed out the memory of what it felt like to walk in the day, to bask in the light. Comfort embodied the daystar's warm rays. They kissed his skin while the breeze above the Aurora Forest embraced him like Father had so many times before. A lump rose in his throat as he opened his eyes and peered into Preceptor Sage's pale face. His brown hair had also faded, drained by death. Like the blowing wind and fading light, life in Zephoris didn't last. Safety fled the land as its honor had, and yet another precious soul had been vanquished in this dying world. Nuelle's heart ached as he looked away from the preceptor. *Who else will die for me?* The question plagued him. Would it ever relent? He forced it from his mind.

"Where should we bury him?" Elisena's irises shimmered like the lavender grass below.

"He was from my homeland," Sophana said. "I would be honored to have him rest in one of my palace gardens."

Nuelle smiled despite the growing weight in his chest. "That would be a worthy place."

Still carrying the Acumen, Ave frowned. Nuelle peered into his best friend's face. His cheeks had thinned, making his jawbones more prominent.

Nuelle turned away. "Let's gather food for the journey."

"Down, Rasmus," Javin said, his body emitting a frosty and minty smell. He stroked the polaragon's neck and it descended. After landing near lavender trees, Nuelle slowly lay Preceptor Sage's body on the creature's back, and then slid off with the others. His hand brushed against the crystal sword at his hip. It pulsated warm energy that seemed to have grown stronger since they left the Obsidian. Riff ripped a clump of diamond-shaped fruits from a tree and handed some to Surta. Javin plucked one for Elisena, and Ave picked a few for Sophana. She reluctantly took them.

"Here, Prince Nuelle." Elisena held out a fruit.

"Thank you." He took it and bit into the soft skin. Sugary juices poured into his mouth as he breathed in the equally sweet scent. He swallowed, and his stomach grumbled as if asking for more. When was the last time he'd eaten, the last time he simply enjoyed being alive?

"Supreme Prince?" King Bertil emerged from behind a red tree and walked toward him.

Nuelle wiped his mouth and lowered the fruit. As King Bertil approached, he took slow steps. Dark circles shrouded his eyes as if he hadn't slept in days, but the scratches on his bony arms and legs had almost disappeared. He stopped before Nuelle and peered at his feet, all the way up to his face. Tears engulfed the King's blue irises, and he threw his arms around Nuelle and sobbed. Dropping the fruit, Nuelle returned the broken embrace. The shudders of King Bertil's sorrow knocked against Nuelle's chest, and pain pressed on his heart. Though Antikai had been a traitor, a vile man without a shred of good in his heart, he was also a son.

King Bertil pulled away. This man, this father, had lost his only child, just like Father had lost one of his.

Nuelle gestured to the polaragon. "You can come with us. We are headed to Athdonia."

"Thank you, my lord, but I will stay here. This place has become much like home for me. And besides"—King Bertil wiped the tears from his face—"I have nothing to return to."

Elisena and the others bowed their heads or lowered their eyes. Even they could sympathize with the king who felt as though he'd lost everything, and in some ways, he had.

"If you'd ever like to visit," he said, "you know where to find me."

Ave and the other Sentinels slowly bowed before mounting the polaragon.

"You proved yourself trustworthy." Nuelle smiled at King Bertil. "When I see my father again, I will tell him you accomplished your mission, and with your help, I now wield this sword."

His lips quivered, a hint of a smile upon them. "Thank you, Young Prince." He bowed. Nuelle did the same.

When King Bertil straightened, he peered over Nuelle's shoulder at Rasmus, where Preceptor Sage's corpse lay. He frowned and then spoke with a quivering voice. "Maybe his life was worthy…" He turned and trudged back into the vibrant woods.

Nuelle frowned before climbing back onto the polaragon, beside Preceptor Sage's body.

"All right, big boy." Javin patted the creature's neck, his fishy odor returning with ferocity. "I'll tell you where to go."

The polaragon moaned and pushed off the ground. Nuelle pressed his palm on the preceptor's chest and grabbed a handful of the polaragon's fur with the other. He peered down at the distancing forest to the place King Bertil last stood. Maybe someday they'd all meet again.

Sweet aromas floated to the skies from the royal garden below Nuelle, his Sentinels, and Rasmus, masking some of Javin's minty polaragon scent. The light above dimmed, but the miniature hills of bright blues, purples, reds, and yellows still paraded their vibrancy. The banner of proud colors flared behind the Athdonian castle like an army of rainbows. Its commander—a giant gate carved of gloss-wood—guarded the perimeter. Fuchsia blossoms the size of full-grown trees stood like pillars near the entryway, similar to Father's lindia garden back at the palace.

Nuelle grasped the crystal sword's hilt. It burned in his palm, pulsing with even more energy. The Obsidian's blackness imploding replayed in his mind. How powerful this weapon that an entire land could be consumed by it from one blow. And yet he was able to wield it like he had his old training sword—the one he had used against Tane.

Sophana pointed at the gate. "That is where we will be landing."

"You got it." Javin scratched the polaragon's head and it descended onto the colorful hills. The mounds jumped, and small winged creatures fluttered away revealing trim magenta grass. Sophana slid off the polaragon first, then Riff, clasping Preceptor Sage. Nuelle and the others followed Sophana to a patch of red dust flowers. As Riff gently laid the Preceptor down, Nuelle's heart ached. This was the third person they had to give over to the ground. Tears trickled slowly down Nuelle's cheeks as Javin's words in the Aurora Forest invaded his mind: *Being around you is like a death sentence just waiting to happen!* A breeze swept past and the crimson dust flowers dispersed like blood in the wind, exposing golden stems. *The crystal sword is double-edged. The golden-trimmed side can resurrect a worthy life. The black-trimmed side can destroy any life.* King Bertil's words rushed through Nuelle like his powerful tempests.

"Wait." He squeezed the crystal sword's hilt and approached Preceptor Sage's body. Heat waves washed over Nuelle's chest and head. He stopped and raised the sword, turning it to the gold-trimmed side. His Sentinels inched back.

"Whoa, whoa." Javin put his hands up. "You don't have to slice him in two so he's easier to bury."

"Shhh," Ave said.

Nuelle closed his eyes. *Father, I believe this man was worthy. He risked his life for me and eventually lost it. He's served at the academy as Wisdom Preceptor of the Servants for decades and believes your words. If you agree, may he rise again.* Nuelle brought down the sword.

The blade glowed with luminescent amber. A hot, orange wave of glistening orbs burst from the crystal sword, blowing through Nuelle and his Sentinels. They all staggered. Nuelle's trembling eased. He slowly lowered the sword to his side. He knelt down. Preceptor Sage lay as dead as before. Nuelle's head bowed. Maybe it was just his time.

"My lord?"

The girls gasped. Ave and Javin jumped. Riff bit his fist.

Nuelle locked eyes with Preceptor Sage's shining yellow ones. His tan complexion had returned, and his previously, faded-brown hair again obtained its darker hue. As Nuelle clasped the Preceptor and helped him sit up, the Sentinels stood frozen, mouths agape. Nuelle smiled. "I knew you were worthy."

Preceptor Sage gave a weak smile in return. "I'll never be worthy of your father's grace, my lord, but I try to live my life in thankfulness for all he has done."

Nuelle peered over his shoulder at the Sentinels. Their stiff bodies and blank expressions made themselves look lifeless. "Riff, can you help me carry him?"

The Gavrailian slapped his face and blinked rapidly. He slipped his muscular arm beneath the Preceptor and raised him. "I've never been that scared before in my life."

Nuelle laughed as he sheathed the crystal sword. "Me either."

Elisena touched her heart. "And I've never felt a heart come back to life." Her eyes shifted to lavender. "It was this burst of joy, love, peace, gratitude, resolve."

Preceptor Sage nodded weakly. "Now I really plan on living like every day is my last."

Ave stared at the sword, his brow furrowed.

Surta poked Preceptor Sage's cheek. "Remarkable."

"Can you not do that please," the Preceptor said.

She recoiled. "What was the other side like? I would be thrilled to imagine it and show all of you—"

"I think I need to eat first."

Sophana looked the Preceptor up and down. "And probably get some rest."

"I agree." Nuelle held Preceptor Sage by the waist and carried the Acumen in his free hand. "Lead the way."

"I'd prefer sneaking in," Sophana said. "We can stay in one of the guest chambers and face my father tomorrow." As she led them out of the garden and into one of the palace's rear doors, a spark of hope reignited in Nuelle's heart. Not all was lost…

Darkness and quiet consumed the guest chamber. Laying sideways on the floor, Nuelle breathed in the sweet, flowery fragrances lathering the air. A ray snuck in through the circular dome window. Vines smothered the ceiling as if they'd long ago invaded this palace and made it their home.

He stroked the hilt of the crystal sword, resting beside him and the Acumen. Riff and Javin had a snoring contest nearby, and Ave lay a few paces behind them, while Sophana and the girls slept nearest to the king-sized bed Preceptor Sage slept in. Antikai had strutted about the Supreme Palace just like these dome-vines and paraded his evil when he tried to kill Father. But the Obsidian swallowed up Antikai and his pride perished with him—and Tane.

Nuelle's eyes welled with tears, but he denied freedom from their place. He slipped his hand into his pocket and removed the gold sword-engraved Supreme Prince ring. Nuelle slid it onto his ring-finger. He had already mourned for his brother when he believed him dead. But Tane was truly gone now, and he had forfeited his right to be supreme heir to Father, taking on a new identity; a vile name he wielded like a sword.

If any more tears would be shed, they'd fall for the ones betrayed, for Father. *Your words speak of victory,* Father's last words to Tane leaked into Nuelle's thoughts, *but your heart has already been defeated.* Nuelle clenched the Acumen. Father must have known of Tane's plans, but he still allowed him to leave. Did he believe his first-born would change, or did he let him go for other reasons?

"Sophana," Ave whispered.

"Yes," she whispered back.

"Are you awake?"

"Obviously."

"Sorry. I just, I've been, you know, thinking. And since Nuelle is safe now, I can't stop thinking about…"

Nuelle resisted the urge to interrupt his best friend before he'd say something regretful.

"Yes…?" Sophana said slowly.

"Cooking you nettle cakes."

She laughed softly. "What have you really been thinking about?"

Ave hesitated. "My father."

Awkward silence ensued. Nuelle subtly turned his head just enough to see Sophana laying on her side with her head propped on her hand, and Ave in the same pose, peering at her.

"Okay..." Sophana said.

"I've been thinking about all the time I lost with him now that he's gone, about all the things I wanted to do with him... and it makes me think about how I don't want to lose any more time with you."

"What are you saying, Ave?"

"That I don't want to kiss you at your funeral."

Sophana dropped her hand. "Are you suggesting we——"

"Yes, I mean no. Not now."

"Pardon me?"

Ave slowly sat up. "What I mean is, I'd want to kiss you when I sort of deserve to, when I've earned it...you know, if we ever got..."

Sophana froze. "Married?"

"Yeah." Ave messed with his bangs. "I'd feel somewhat worthy then. At least, the timing would be right."

Nuelle held in a laugh. Of course Ave wouldn't give up completely on pursuing Sophana. When he wanted something passionately enough, he'd wait for it. Maybe all that time in the Grand Kitchen preparing and cooking meals helped make him patient—especially having to deal with old Lady Flemm every day. And perhaps it was fine for him and Sophana to court now since their enemies had been vanquished. And Ave never let his pursuits of servant girls overshadow his cooking duties. As long as he and Sophana both prioritized their roles as Sentinels and didn't let youthful love consume them, causing neglect of the Faithful, then it could work...

Sophana snickered. "That was gutsy, fish sticks."

Ave sounded like he did after making a perfect meal. "You're rubbing off on me, nettle cakes."

"Nah. You're just a good, home-cooked Agaponian boy."

Nuelle closed his eyes and smiled as dreamless sleep finally overcame.

Reasonably overprotective and overbearing King Redmond, here we come with your daughter, bruised and battered like a Gavrailian punching bag. Nuelle and his friends followed Sophana through the Main Hall, filled with the daystar's golden light. Preceptor Sage stayed back in the guest chamber, still asleep. Nuelle and his Sentinels, his family, stepped into a grand foyer where twin staircases twined with purple flowers curved up to the second floor. Rather out of place, a massive ball of thorns obstructed the foyer's pillared main-entrance. Several silver knights with gold, floral-patterned armor, posted on either side of the rebellious undergrowth.

"Extra security." Sophana's leaf-blades rippled. "Thorkkis."

While Nuelle and the others approached, the knights bowed.

"Sophana!" Queen Elva bustled down one of the staircases, her pink hair like the flowers she passed. Though more lovely than they, she wore a plain gown, humble like her soul. Tears adorned her pale cheeks like sad crystals as she reached the bottom and embraced Sophana. As she pulled away, she grasped Sophana's hands and frowned at her dirty cloak. "What has happened?"

"Elva, my love?" King Redmond's voice traveled down a hall on the left. "Why have you left your resting?" He turned from around a corner and stepped into the foyer, wearing a velvet cloak. A young man closely resembling Queen Elva, and a silver knight stood with him. The King halted, his yellow eyes wide. "Sophana."

"Father." She bowed.

"Sophie!" The young man on King Redmond's right rushed to Sophana and squeezed her. "The academy is making you even more of a warrior, sister."

She smiled, but it quickly vanished.

"Alden," the King said, "have the servants prepare a meal."

"But they just arrived." The young man released Sophana. "Can't I just spend a moment with my—"

"Go now." King Redmond kept his eyes on Sophana.

Alden frowned before scurrying out of the hall, the silver knight striding after him.

The King approached Nuelle. "What brings you all to my palace?"

"Much has happened at the academy," Nuelle replied. "Prince Antikai's Savage Shifters were attacking prodigies."

Queen Elva gasped and staggered as if his words delivered an invisible blow.

King Redmond grasped her waist. "Silvanus!"

A round-bellied man scuttled in from another hall.

"See the Queen to her chamber at once and call her medic."

"Yes, my lord." The man cupped his arm in Queen Elva's and escorted her up the stairs at a much slower pace than he'd entered with.

King Redmond's gaze lowered to the crystal sword at Nuelle's hip before concentrating on him. "You journeyed here directly from the academy?"

Nuelle glanced at Sophana. "We went to the Obsidian where I confiscated this from our enemies. That land of eternal darkness is now destroyed, along with Antikai and all of his followers."

The King paled as he surveyed Sophana, her garbs worn, bearing the many battles she had survived. With glassy eyes he embraced her. A single tear slid down his cheek and disappeared into his beard. As he released Sophana, he focused on Nuelle. "I assume you are here then because your father has fled from his kingdom."

Nuelle's gut churned. Father left Agapon? Where did he go? What happened to the Supreme Palace?

"I guess you are unaware of his departure," King Redmond answered as if reading Nuelle's mind. "His palace has been besieged by Elite Knights. He fled last evening."

"And no one's doing anything about it?" Riff nearly yelled.

King Redmond glowered at him. "What do you suggest we do? Bertil is gone, Vyden has been removed from his throne, and now the very Supreme King has been ousted from his dwelling and who knows where he has run to." He motioned to the hall his wife and Silvanus exited through. "My queen is ill, and my kingdom is threatened by accursed enemies. I need every knight in my command in order to protect my own land and family." He gazed at Sophana. "Which has led me to make a necessary decision regarding your future."

She glanced at Ave, staring at her with fear-seized eyes.

"I must take every measure to keep our citizens and our family safe. So I am meeting with King Lothar to arrange for you to be married to his son."

"What!" Sophana's voice filled the foyer.

King Redmond raised his cloak's hood over his head. "I was on my way out, but since you are here, I will wait for you in the chariot. Pyra!" A short woman with fuscia curls entered the hallway. "Gather Sophana's maidservants and pack her loveliest gowns and sufficient necessities for four days."

Tears cut through the dirt on Sophana's cheeks. "Father, you can't do this, I love someone else!" She glanced at Ave as he beamed. Smiling back, Sophana clasped his hand and spoke quickly. "Besides, he's already proposed."

Javin crossed his arms and whispered to Riff, "When did Ave find time to do that?"

The color fled from Ave's cheeks and he spoke low. "I wouldn't exactly call it a proposal…"

Surta jumped and clapped. "What a joyous announcement! One of my favorite imaginations is serving as a ceremony planner. I can handle everything! The invitations, color schemes, arrangements, and other decorations."

Riff crossed his arms. "I thought you said you never imagined anything romantic."

She adjusted her spectacles. "Who said covenant union ceremonies had to be romantic? Why can't they be adventurously themed with dragons and fire and—"

"Not now you two." Elisena scrutinized King Redmond.

He surveyed Sophana and Ave. His stare dropped to their twining fingers, then ascended to Sophana's resolute face. A shadowy gloom darkened Redmond's countenance, and the light in his eyes dimmed as he concentrated on Ave. "You will not marry this peasant."

Nuelle's body seared as Ave bowed his head.

"He is not a peasant, he's a Sentinel!" Sophana said.

"If you want your friends to have a place to stay until they decide what to do, you will stop arguing with me at once!"

Sophana's lips pressed together as more tears spilled from her eyes.

"You have one hour to make yourself presentable." King Redmond veered around and marched toward the thorns. They unraveled before him and he strode out of the entryway's massive door.

Sophana faced Ave and cupped his cheek with her free palm. "I won't let him seize this from me."

He lifted his chin, his eyes carrying the same heavy sadness they did after discovering his father died in battle. "But...he's your father."

Her hand fell. "I thought you were gutsy."

He shook his head. "But I will never be royalty."

She blinked, the tears smudging the dirt on her face. Her leaf-blades drooped. "I guess you won't." She ran through a corridor.

Surta raised a hand. "Maybe I can—"

"She wants to be alone," Elisena said quietly.

"So do I." Ave turned.

Nuelle stepped in front of him and grasped his shoulders. Ave's gaze riveted to the floor.

"Look at me."

Ave hesitantly complied.

"Your social class, birth place, ancestry, not even your upbringing can determine whether or not you are worthy of anything. Only what's in your heart, and He who made it dictates what good you receive in this life. King Redmond has yet to understand he has no place in dismissing you when he doesn't truly know what is in your heart."

Ave's chest lifted as Nuelle continued.

"I can say with confidence that you are full of honor. Despite all you've been through because of me, you've remained a faithful friend who only continues to grow into a better man." Nuelle's voice quaked with passion. "You are Ave Purine, Sentinel of the Supreme Prince of Zephoris. You are a loyal companion, a brave warrior, and a loving beacon that pierces through the darkness in our world; someone who is offering his life to ensure there is still a hope for any faithful soul that remains." He released Ave's shoulders. "You would be an amazing husband to Princess Sophana, and I know she agrees."

Ave half-smiled and bowed. "I'll never be worthy of your friendship, Nuelle, but nonetheless, I'll always be grateful for it."

"We all are grateful." Surta walked toward Nuelle with quick, desperate steps. "But what is going to happen now that the Supreme King has departed?"

Nuelle gestured for Javin to hand him the Acumen. He grasped the living book. Both it and the crystal sword throbbed with warmth and power. "All I know is we have to gather the Faithful and bring them to the Incandescia, and now that Antikai is gone, there's no better time to start."

"But what about Sophana?" Javin asked.

Nuelle looked down the hall she had departed through. "Clearly, if she gets married to Gavrail's prince, we would lose her as a Sentinel." He peered at Ave. "We don't want to dishonor King Redmond, so our only option at keeping Sophana would be for you to convince her father that you are indeed worthy of her hand."

Riff laid his massive arm around Ave who bent beneath the weight. "Can't we just tell King Redmond all the great things that this little mountain has done, and how he's even saved Sophana's life?"

"We can," Nuelle replied, "but with all his current fear, and the love he has for his family, it will take much more than words to win his approval."

"I can relate." Javin pulled Elisena in. "Whoever wants to marry my little sister better be the best man Zephoris can offer."

Her cheeks flushed and she touched her forehead before continuing. "Kind Redmond's heart has grown much harder since the last time we saw him at the academy. Prince Nuelle is certainly right about his grave fear of losing his family and failing his kingdom. His love is fiercely devoted, yet tainted by fear. Sadly, the latter is what currently drives him."

Nuelle gestured his chin toward the hall where Queen Elva retreated with Silvanus. "If the medic is that way, there's probably a drawing room or someplace we can rest from standing, and plan further." He followed the hallway to a foyer furnished with floral-designed couches and tables. A few knights guarded either wall. Nuelle and his friends took a seat at the table nearest to a terrace that overlooked a white-petal garden. He spoke low. "I know none of us"—he glanced at Ave—"want to lose Sophana, but with how rapidly things in our land are declining, we have to be very intentional in discovering where the Incandescia is, and then start gathering the Faithful and journeying there. We also need to determine how to begin rallying the people and the safest way to transport them."

Surta raised a finger as if in a lesson. "To save time, I can finish the entire Acumen in approximately three days or so if I do nothing, but sip tea and read."

"You haven't read it before?" Nuelle said.

"The copied versions multiple times, but not the one specifically written for *you*. It may disclose the location of the Incandescia."

"I appreciate your offer, but I think it's best if I read it first since my father dedicated it to me and gave me the role of leading the people there. And now that Antikai"—he swallowed a lump down—"and his allies are dead, I can focus more on reading."

"Understood." She folded her hands. "Should we set a time-frame for when we begin our journey with the Faithful?"

Nuelle concentrated on Ave. "I know this may sound difficult, but I want us to begin our mission in a week. And I want to start in—"

"Agapon." Ave smiled.

"Yes. If the sword was able to resurrect Preceptor Sage, it might be able to bring back Amador."

Ave's smile turned into a scowl. "But how are we going to retrieve Papo's body from the Supreme Palace Burial Grounds now that Prototis and the fallen Elites have taken over?"

Nuelle squeezed the crystal sword's hilt at the reminder of the traitors who chased Father out of his home, the one he'd graciously allowed them and their families to live in; where he provided their every need. Nuelle drew in a slow breath before answering. "We have a week to figure it out."

Ave slowly nodded and then tapped his chin. "And King Redmond said it'd be a four-day trip so that gives me three days to win him over."

Nuelle shrugged. "It also gives you four days to prepare."

His tapping slowed. "Right."

Javin spoke. "Maybe we can ask around as to what impresses her father most in a man."

"We can ask her brother, too," Riff said.

"Great idea." Nuelle smiled at his friends' wisdom. "They seemed close."

"They are," Elisena replied. "I read Prince Alden's heart when his father dismissed him. He was disappointed, but very understanding. He fought a seemingly engrained urge to further resist, and thus empathy overcame."

"But you're forgetting something, sis." Javin pointed at his chest. "Like me, Alden is a big brother, too. Chances are he's also going to have to be won over."

Elisena rolled her eyes. "You're only older than me by three minutes."

Ave straightened. "I'll do whatever it takes to earn Sophana."

Nuelle glimpsed at the knights posted along the nearest wall and spoke in a whisper. "Wait a second. King Redmond chose Gavrail's prince as a potential husband. Their army is undeniably the strongest now that most of my father's knights have turned against him. King Redmond may be using a covenant union in order to ensure having King Lothar as an ally."

Elisena gave a nod. "That's exactly what he's doing."

"That means his resolve will be even stronger, since he believes the union will garner greater protection for his family and kingdom." Nuelle looked at Ave. "Together, we defeated the savages. We have to show King Redmond that Sophana will be just as protected—if not more—if she remains a Sentinel."

"And how are we going to do that?" Ave asked.

Nuelle peered over his Sentinels and squeezed the crystal sword's hilt, a rush of fiery power surging up his arm and into his heart. "We're going to defeat the Thorkkis."

CREATURE GUIDE

Eebon: Stout forest-dweller with ebony fur and eyes, and extra-long arms. After the Great Terrestrial Curse in first-century Zephoris (100Z), to aid against new threats, Gavrailians enslaved many eebons and taught them to use the bow and arrow, utilizing their lengthy limbs to shoot over long distances.

Foecry: Small, beaked and winged forest-dweller. It feeds on critters. With their highly keen sight, foecries are excellent trackers.

Frost hound: Native to the Polarian Canyons, blue-furred with white chest and eyes. Due to their hyper-sped metabolisms, frost hounds have voracious appetites. They hunt in packs at dawn and are carnivorous, using their strong snouts and fangs to tear through prey. They are blind, but have incredible scent and speed. Their only predators are lazawards.

Furscrabber: Brawny, medium-sized, heavy-furred forest-dweller. Its shoulders are nearly as large as its head and it walks on two legs. Furscrabbers are known for their tender and savory meat when cooked.

Glacierdon: Native to the Polarian Canyons, a giant, aquatic, white-finned beast dwelling in freezing depths. Its leathery skin keeps its warm, and its gray eyes see clearly through even the murkiest waters. Its unmatched size make it the top sea predator in its territory.

Glowfish: Native to Sunezia, an aquatic creature that is typically purple with translucent, light-emitting scales. They are often used decoratively in aquariums.

Glowflitter: Native to the Aurora Forest, tiny flying creature that feeds on the forest's glowing leaves. It emits the light of the last leaf consumed. This also enables the glowflitter to camouflage with whatever plant it feeds on, disguising itself from predators.

Graether: Burly, silver-furred and fanged beasts. They dwell in forests and roam in packs. These vicious carnivores prefer to be elevated in trees, using height and shade to surprise-attack their prey. Their large fangs and knife-like claws make for quick kills.

Kastora: A swamp-dwelling creature covered with purple, needle-like spikes. It lives in lakes, has webbed feet, and long top and bottom teeth. Kastoras build their water-homes from stones, branches and other swamp-materials. Their skin secretes a moldy-odored moisture that contains numbing properties; their needle-spikes absorb the secretions and inflict temporary paralyzation to predators. After the Great Terrestrial Curse, Ideyans desired querapas' creative craftsmanship to build weapons and to have querapas as allies for their ability to paralyze. Ideyans incorporated riddles to engage the creatures and teach them to speak, and used trade and bribery to win their alliance.

Lazaward: Native to the Polarian Canyons, this mountain-dweller is nine-feet tall and has indigo and purple streaked fur. Its azure eyes glow, aiding in intimidating adversaries. It is carnivorous and the only predator of frost hounds. Lazawards are highly intelligent and were created with human-like qualities such as the ability to speak, a protective nature and a close bond with kin.

Lightsquirm: Tiny cave-dweller. It comes in a variety of hues. All day, lightsquirms' bodies absorb and feed off of the daystar's light. To cool down and rest, lightsquirms squirm into caves and cling to the walls until dawn. The daystar's bright energy is displayed through lightsquirms' translucent skin, and they are a desirable food source to many creatures. At dawn, lightsquirms leave the cave and return to basking in the light with one midday break and then continue basking until nightfall.

Massadon: Massive, gray-furred cave-dweller, with a flat nose and an immense omnivorous appetite. Its three-pupil eyes help it see in darkness and its black fangs are used to consume large tree branches and prey. Once satisfied, it returns to its cave to rest until roused again by hunger.

Polaragon: Native to the Polarian Canyons, this giant beast has thick, ivory fur, four legs, and two pairs of wings. Blue colors its paws and the tips of its floppy ears. Its main food source is frost. It has two stomachs; the first gathers energy from the frost's nutrients, and then the frost passes through to the second stomach where it is stored. The polaragon can later regurgitate the frost for defensive and offensive means.

Querapa: A medium-sized bronze, short-furred creature with a slim snout. It dwells in burrows in both warm and cooler climates and uses its golden-colored saliva to hasten the process of plant growth. In effect, querapas can provide themselves with food without having to wander far from their burrows. They move slowly and sleep most of the day. Due to their capabilities, querapas were frequently captured and forced to work restlessly in farms. Without their needed rest, many died, and have now become nearly extinct.

Roto: Native to Sunezia, large red-feathered, winged creatures used by Sunezians for speedy transport. Rotos can enclose themselves in their wings, roll into a ball, and ram into attackers, also making them effective protectors.

Swamp-leaper: Small swamp-dweller with stretchy limbs used to climb trees and other plants. It has four eyes, two in front of its head, and two on the back, making it a difficult prey. Swamp-leapers also produce an acidic slime that can cause temporary burns to predators, keeping many at bay.

Tawter: A round, white, and fluffy forest-dweller. Its compact size, soft fur, and friendly, affectionate nature make it a desirable pet. Tawters are also obsessed with keeping themselves clean and for this reason they are easily domesticated.

Thorkkis: After the Great Terrestrial Curse, thorny vines sprang up from the gardens of Athdonia and formed into bodies of up to fifteen feet in height, becoming vicious attackers. With poisonous thorns that wither human bodies, and expanding vine-limbs, they are highly dangerous foes.

Vanaph: Mountain dwelling creatures with a white, long-neck, six wings, and golden hooves. They feed only on pasture, and are utilized across kingdoms for speedy travel.

Weemut: Native to Gavrail, medium-sized, four-legged creature with many sharp teeth. Its large nostrils make for excellent tracking. Gavrailians train weemuts and utilize them for hunting game. stored. The polaragon can later regurgitate the frost for defensive and offensive means.

ABOUT THE AUTHOR

I'm a Cuban-American, born and raised in Miami, FL, who's unfortunately had fifty-three boyfriends. (My first heartbreak in Kindergarten counts, too.) By God's grace, He helped me off that vicious dating-then-breaking-up cycle, and I met my dream prince at age nineteen and got married by twenty. We have two awesome sons, Arrow and Braven, and are in pre-production for an urban-fantasy style web-series for teens and young adults.

Want more Seven Covenant tales through the eyes of the Sentinels? Visit:

NATASHASAPIENZABLOG.WORDPRESS.COM

Made in the USA
Coppell, TX
10 October 2022

84341222R00204